TRACI E. HALL

Love's Magic

Medallion Press, Inc.
Printed in the USA

DEDICATION:

To my husband, thanks for the magic

Published 2008 by Medallion Press, Inc.

The MEDALLION PRESS LOGO
is a registered tradmark of Medallion Press, Inc.

Cover Illustration by James Tampa and Adam Mock

Printed in the United States of America
Typeset in Adobe Garamond Pro

ISBN# 9781933836270
10 9 8 7 6 5 4 3 2 1
First Edition

ACKNOWLEDGEMENTS:
Heartfelt appreciation to everybody who believed —
and kept on believing

Chapter One

Montehue Manor
England, 1192

"I don't feel well," Celestia Montehue said the instant before the bailiff threw open the twin wooden doors to the large main room.

"Visitors approach!"

Celestia looked up from the long dining table on the raised dais. The family was just finishing their midday meal of sliced duck breast in almond sauce and wedges of eel pie. *Eel pie*, she thought with dismay, pushing at her trencher.

Taking a sip of watered wine in an effort to calm her belly, she wondered who might be coming, as no company had been expected. A troupe of entertainers, mayhap. Preferably acrobats and jugglers instead of minstrels, who sang their silly songs of court gossip and love. A chill started at the base of her spine and raced upward, settling at the nape of her neck.

Briefly touching her temples, she tried to ascertain

from whence the chill came. It could be a draft that had followed the bailiff in like a wayward pup.

It could be a premonition.

Celestia shivered, then pulled her thin woolen shawl tight around her shoulders. She wished she were better at discerning these strange feelings that warned of desperate trouble, or a spring rain.

"Is something amiss, 'Tia?"

She startled when her sister Galiana tossed a bread crumb at her nose. "Hmm?"

"You have that odd look on your face, the one you get before you sneeze," Galiana laughed.

"But then you do not," her youngest sister, Ela, held a finger below her cute, upturned nose. "Sneeze. You say something strange instead."

"I can't help it," Celestia defended.

"So? What did you see in that head of yours?" Galiana, who at sixteen was a renowned beauty, crossed her bright green eyes and stuck out her tongue. "The man you will marry?"

Ela snickered, a most unladylike sound. "I liked it when you predicted wild geese flying through the stables. I won a halfpence off of Abner the stable boy because of that."

Bemused, Celestia blinked. "You must not gamble. And you both know I'll not marry." Squeezing her eyes shut, she focused on the foggy vision in her mind. "It makes no sense. A monk riding a sway-backed nag? Wearing only one sandal?" She rubbed her forehead as her stomach rolled. "Ridiculous."

The bailiff blew his horn, and a group of men, all

dressed in blue and gold, stepped into the large hall.

Celestia immediately noticed the large blond man with handsome sideburns and a trimmed beard. He wore his colors proudly, and the scabbard at his side shone with obvious care.

The other knights stood behind him, as if shielding something. Blue and gold were the Baron Peregrine's colors. Why had he sent his men? Her dislike of the baron didn't matter; he was her family's liege lord and they owed him fealty.

Leaning forward, her stomach fluttering with nerves, Celestia braced her hands against the table.

"Announcing Sir Petyr Montgomery with a missive from Baron Peregrine."

Her father got to his feet, his features deceptively calm. "Welcome, Sir Petyr. Come forward."

Her family had to be remembering that the last time the baron sent men, they'd raised the rents—on behalf of King Richard and his religious quest, of course. Celestia could not turn her eyes away from the comely knight, who looked exactly the way her dream man would look, if she cared about those things. She sensed that he was not her destiny, more the pity.

He came to the front of the dais and held out a scroll still sealed with the baron's insignia. "I apologize for interrupting your meal, Lord Robert," Sir Petyr said, including all of the family with a quick glance, but pausing for a second longer on Galiana. Her sister had that effect on men.

"Would you join us for a bite?" Whipping his eating

knife from the loaf of bread, her father used it to break the seal on the letter.

"Nay, my thanks." The knight's posture remained formal, and Celestia surmised that the missive didn't contain happy news. The baron went through wives and babes like melting snow in the sun. Mayhap he'd lost another? Or was this about her younger twin brothers, fostered at the baron's castle?

Her father's ruddy cheeks grew even more mottled as he read.

"Aloud—will you read it so that we all may hear?" Her mother tugged at Lord Robert's green sleeve, her lack of manners a sign of agitation.

"What is the meaning of this?" Lord Robert demanded.

Sir Petyr did not pretend to misunderstand. "It is the Baron Peregrine's most urgent desire."

Leaning down so that his face was in Sir Petyr's, her father ground out, "Is it an order?"

The knight swallowed audibly. "Aye."

Lord Robert slammed the scroll down to the table, knocking over a goblet of red wine. Like spilled blood, it dripped to the rushes below.

Celestia pressed her fingers against her lips, understanding without being told that her brothers were fine, and this somehow concerned her.

"Why? I received special compensation when I swore allegiance to him nigh on twenty years ago. My daughters are not to be pawns in the marriage mart."

The talk of marriage chilled Celestia inside and out. Had the baron decided to marry one of his vassal's daughters? Perhaps he thought, wrongly, that by marrying a healer he could keep a babe. Her grandmother had mentioned once that the baron's seed was cursed.

Her mother grabbed the scroll and read it for herself. Lady Deirdre stood, her red hair bright against the paleness of her skin. "Nay. I forbid it."

"My lady," Sir Petyr said in a low voice. "There are consequences if you do not obey."

"Aye, and you ask that we pay them all, and why? My mother is a healer, my daughter is a healer, what need of a *wife* has this broken man?" Her mother shook the scroll.

Celestia exchanged frightened looks with her sisters, but they dared not breathe a word. Her mother, by calling the baron "broken," was saying too much already. Sir Petyr's hand dropped to his sword hilt at the insult, and Celestia felt the press of Ela's fingers in hers. She would not be surprised to see her father turn Viking on the baron's knight, killing the man with his own sword, if he did not take a step back from the dais.

"Your eldest daughter is to marry. Not the baron," Sir Petyr said, dropping his hand away from the sword, excusing the slur.

Gasping, Celestia's knees went weak. Marrying the baron would have been a death sentence. But to wed a stranger? Even worse. She could not be a wife. If she married without love, her healing magic would wither and die. No matter the obvious differences she bore when compared to her family, her healing gifts marked her as a true descendant of Boadicea. Her eyes strayed to the group of men left standing by the bailiff.

If she wasn't to marry the baron, then who?

Sir Petyr bowed his head, as if acknowledging the Montehue's angry disbelief. "Baron Peregrine has his reasons for breaking the oath he made. His son."

"Son? Baron Peregrine has no living son." Her father's eyes narrowed, then he tossed the knife in the air, catching it by the handle before slamming it back in the bread.

"Aye, he does have one. A brave man, Sir Nicholas is in need of both healing and a wife. Your daughter, Lady Celestia, is of marriageable age and, Sir Petyr nodded in her direction, seems healthy. The baron demands that the wedding take place immediately.

"Healthy? Wedding?" Unable to keep silent for even a heartbeat longer, Celestia shot to her feet. "There can be no wedding. I have an infirmary to operate. Who will take care of the people? They need me!"

The full force of Sir Petyr's gaze leveled her, stopping her chatter. The man was deadly serious, and she had a sinking feeling there was nothing anybody could do about it. "I am sorry to be the bearer of such news," he said.

"Sorry!" She knew that she should act the docile female, but she could no more hold her wayward tongue than a butterfly could walk. "You do not understand at all, sir. I am a descendant of Queen Boadicea,"

"The Warrior Queen?" He eyed her up and down, which, thanks be to her short stature, did not take long.

She flushed, but continued. "Aye, and I am a healer. We cannot marry without lo—"

He dismissed her, turning to her father instead. "Your twin sons are being fostered with the baron, is that not correct?"

Lord Robert was so furious the air around him crackled. "Aye."

"They would be elevated in status, no doubt, once there is a babe of this union."

"Babe? Are you crazed?" Celestia grabbed the closest weapon she had, which was a dish of watercress. "I will not marry," she looked to her parents and beseeched of them, "I cannot, as well you know."

Galiana quickly took the bowl from her hand. "Hush, 'Tia, let us listen to everything the knight has to say."

Sir Petyr had treated her with scorn, as if she did not matter, damn him. To him, she was no more than a helpless twit. Her hand fisted at her hip.

Ela slipped an arm around Celestia's waist. "Keep your temper, 'Tia," her youngest sister whispered. "It will go worse if you shame Father."

Swallowing hard, Celestia peered at the huddled group of knights left near the bailiff. "Do any of them have the look of Baron Peregrine?"

Galiana, her eyesight as perfect as her skin, said, "Nay. Not a hooked nose among them. Although I wonder what they are hiding."

With a mounting sense of dread, Celestia pushed her sisters aside and walked down the three stairs that elevated the dais from the rest of the hall. Chin tilted, she deliberately relaxed her fingers and folded her hands together primly at her waist. Her slippers had tiny bells that rang with each step she took, announcing her arrival as if she were a collared cat instead of the charging lioness she wanted to be.

She curtsied before the group of men, her mouth suddenly dry. Good day to you. Her mother said that a lady should always be polite. Even if she wanted to scream.

"Good day," they chorused nervously.

"What have you, behind your backs?"

They flushed various shades and stammered incoherently.

She picked one knight out from the rest. "You, sir, what is your name?" He was young for a knight, mayhap twenty, barely older than she, no doubt.

"Forrester, my lady." He was so nervous that his eye twitched.

Filled with sympathy, she put her hand on his bare forearm, sending soothing and calming thoughts despite her own upset. "What have you, Sir Forrester?"

He swallowed, his throat moving visibly. "Sir Nicholas, my lady."

She stilled, nerves knotting her entire body like a leg cramp. Inhaling through her nose, she dipped her head in a regal motion, and the knights parted.

Revealing one very unkempt man, dressed in a monk's brown, rough wool robe, with a rope belted around his slender waist. He looked almost emaciated, and she glanced at the knights with questions she could not possibly ask in polite company.

Sir Forrester, taking pity on her, whispered, "He is the baron's son."

She slowly looked down, and yes, the man was only wearing one sandal.

His other foot had none.

This was her destiny.

More the pity.

Tears burned at the back of her eyes, but she would not shed a single drop in front of anyone. She'd longed for a blond man, a kind man, a generous man.

The stench of sour ale floated beneath her nose, and she added, a *sober* man.

Two of the knights had been propping him up between them, and now that the secret was out, they let her get a good look at the man she was expected to marry and waste her ancestors' gifts upon.

There it was, she noticed, the hooked nose that pronounced him a Peregrine.

His skin, waxen and damp. His hair, ebony and curled with wet—wet?

"Why is he wet?" she asked.

Sir Forrester answered, "We dumped him in the trough, my lady, in an effort to wake him. He's ill. Your bailiff saw us and demanded that we be announced immediately–his duty, I know, but it was not our intent to cause you embarrassment." His skin flushed and he hastily looked away.

Why couldn't this boy be the one, she railed against Fate. She locked her gaze on Sir Nicholas's bare foot. "And his shoe?"

"Lost, my lady. It was a long ride from Crispin Monastery."

She nodded, not comprehending at all. "Baron Peregrine wants me to marry a monk. Is that not against the rules?"

"He is no monk; he is a hero, a returned Crusader, my lady," Sir Petyr's slick voice whispered in her ear.

Her head could not make sense of what was happening. "A drunk, crusading monk." Tapping her toe, and setting the tiny bells to jangling, she raised her brow in question.

Sir Petyr sighed heavily. "I can explain. He is very sick, and the only way we could get him his herbs was in his ale. Lots of ale. He did not want to come, you see. We had to tell him that he was going to . . . Bertram, where did he want to go?"

"Spain, sir."

"Yes, Spain, my lady."

The chill spread through her veins. "You deliberately drugged his drink and told him he was going to Spain."

"On pilgrimage," Sir Bertram added helpfully.

"For his soul?" Celestia peered at the man's thin, gaunt face. He certainly looked as if he needed divine intervention.

A thought occurred, along with a stomach cramp so strong she almost bent over. But, no, it could not be. Who could force a grown man to do something against his will? "Does he know *why* he has been brought to Montehue Manor?"

The knights grew quiet. The silence within the manor was so total that if Celestia dropped but a needle it would have echoed throughout the hall, and still not one of the men dared to answer her question.

Sir Nicholas chose that moment to rouse from his stupor, and he struggled against the knights who were holding him. "Where are we?" he demanded huskily. "Petyr!"

"I am here."

Celestia grew alarmed at the green tinge Sir Nicholas's skin was taking on.

"I . . . I don't feel well," he said, opening his eyes and echoing her own sentiments exactly.

She was stunned by the depth of black despair he'd hidden behind those blue-veined lids. Her heart flickered like a candle's flame, and somehow she was drawn to this man with one sandal. His pain was hers. She reached out, her fingers trembling. She had to touch him, she had to . . .

"My lady!" Forrester shouted before grabbing her by the waist and lifting her up.

And out of the way, as her betrothed vomited all over her family's hall.

Nicholas Le Blanc felt the pounding of his head in rhythm with the stabbing pain of his heartbeat. His chest thudded with an irregular tempo, and he wondered, briefly, if he were dying just when he'd made the decision to live.

And to kill the bastard who had sent him on crusade, betraying King Richard and Saint James for coin. He gritted his teeth, which sent a slicing jolt up his jaw.

The pain meant that he was alive.

Gnawing fire in his gut made him wary of how long he might continue to draw breath. By all the saints, he'd not give in until he ripped Baron Peregrine's innards to shreds with a dull blade.

The unexpected touch of a cool hand against his forehead startled him into stillness. Feminine. Soft. He had no illusions that those hands could be equally cruel and dangerous.

His time as a prisoner in the Saracen desert, kept for a ransom that never came, and then kept . . . his mind shied away from memories more awful than he could stand. Baron Peregrine would pay dearly.

Fingers trailed down his jawline, prying his mouth open. A lukewarm liquid slid down his abused esophagus, soothing and slick. It didn't make him want to puke, which was the most important thing.

Nicholas used his considerable willpower to separate lids that felt as if they'd been sewn shut. Two girls wearing wimples and five chins, five chins? He blinked, bringing the girls, no, one girl, into focus.

A heart-shaped face stared down at him, pink lips pouting together without a hint of a smile. Brows so fair it was no wonder she didn't follow the custom of shaving them. They arched over eyes that tipped up at their oval ends. Odd eyes. One green, one blue, framed by golden lashes. This was not a girl, but a woman.

"Are you a witch?" he croaked, not caring one way or the other. "Save me," he ordered.

The question, or demand, brought an annoyed

frown. "No. And I am not in the habit of letting my patients die."

Nicholas felt drawn to her warm voice, despite the bite in her tone.

"For you, however, I might make an exception." She pointed her chin in the air, challenging him to ask why.

"We have never met before, I am certain of it. You have the advantage over me." His voice sounded hoarse, yet he attempted a smile. It felt like a grimace. At least the fire in his stomach no longer burned as hot.

She held his gaze, but her expressions changed so fast that Nicholas wasn't sure what she was thinking. He saw curiosity and disappointment—but not a hint of fear.

With women, one had to tread carefully and read their eyes, rather than listen to the words that fell from their soft, lying lips.

Attempting to sit up, Nicholas's stomach protested with a sharp stab. "What did you give me?"

"Honey, lemon balm, and peppermint. Have you had this stomach ailment long?"

Nicholas crossed his arms over his gut. "It is nothing. A few chills."

She stared down at him. "And fever. How long?"

He leaned back, closing his eyes. How long had he been ill? How long had he been poisoned? How long had Leah, deadly Leah, been feeding him the opium he'd grown addicted to? "Do not bother me." Suddenly he was so tired he couldn't move, yet there could be no rest until the Reaper's debt was paid. Before he slid into sleep he instructed, "And don't kill me, either."

She sniffed. “Oh, I promise, you’ll live. For my brothers’ sake, if naught else.”

Her brothers? At sleep’s door, he heard another voice coming from the opposite side of the room. It was older, huskier. Laced with amusement.

“Celestia, are you badgering your patient?”

Celestia. An angel, not a witch.

“No, Gram. Are you worried I might kill him and be done with it?”

Nicholas should have been worried. Leah had tried to kill him, although she hadn’t succeeded, treacherous woman. But for some reason, mayhap the laughter he detected in the angel’s voice, he was not afraid that she would harm him on purpose.

Her bare hand dropped to his naked shoulder. Warmth, like a banked fire, spread throughout his body, almost reaching his frozen heart before he dismissed the feeling. He was a warrior, damn it all. A knight on a mission to murder his liege.

Nicholas deliberately brought out the painful memory of dark-haired Leah. The betrayal he’d known when she’d whispered that no ransom would be coming. Why would the man who had paid for the attack on the caravan carrying the sacred relic of Saint James *pay* to have the only witness returned to England? Besides, she’d whispered seductively, her husband grew suspicious of her interest in his prisoner.

He’d begged for his freedom. In his semi-sleep, Nicholas squirmed with shame. He’d lost his pride after a few months of captivity. Pride did not feed him, or clean him or give him opium. Pride was a cold bedmate.

Leah was not.

"Shh."

Roused fully by the whisper in his ear, Nicholas sat straight up, his heart drumming so loudly he was surprised his chest didn't explode.

"You were having a nightmare," the angel-witch said softly, her breath sweet. She smelled of oranges and cinnamon. "Now you are awake."

The spiciness spiked his racing adrenaline, and Nicholas spun around, panicked like a wild thing. Stone walls, flickering candles, and oil lamps. Not a cell? He was in a dungeon. He jumped off the table he'd been lying on, searching frantically for a weapon. Any weapon. "Where am I?" His voice hardly shook as he lunged to the left and snuffed a tapered candle, fisting the solid candlestick like a dagger. "I'll not be held captive." *Never again.*

The pale young woman looked ethereal in the dimly lit underground. She should have been afraid of him, so why were her lips twitching? *Celestia.* That was her name.

"You are in my infirmary. At Montehue Manor? You came here with friends."

"I have no friends," he said, denying even Abbot Crispin. He was alone, which was the only way he could survive.

A brief glimpse of sympathy passed over her face before she reached for the linen cloth wadded up on the table where he'd lain. He didn't like that look, but if he could use her pity to escape, he would.

She held out the cloth. "You have no clothes," she

said, cheeks bright.

The realization that he'd been standing before her, naked, caused him discomfort. His manhood, something he hadn't given any thought to since his escape, chose that moment to stir and lengthen. *Just another one of life's betrayals.* Grabbing the cloth, he quickly wrapped it around his hips. "Thank you," he managed in a tight voice. "Where are my clothes?"

She tilted her chin. "Burned."

"What?"

"They were filthy."

He bristled. "They could have been washed."

This time, both fists went on her hips. "I am a healer, not a laundress. Your rosary is there, by the table. Where is your pack? Mayhap you will have another robe inside."

Nicholas pushed a thumb against his temple, feeling the return of a headache. Dreams and nightmares collided together. What was real, and what was not? "My pack? I don't even know how *I* got to be *here*."

She clapped her hands together so that it looked like she was praying for patience. "You were sick. You came from Crispin Monastery. For certes, you don't remember?"

He watched as she struggled for words. Intrigued, he noted when she gave up the idea of telling him the truth and chose to placate him.

"My talent for healing is well known around here. You were so ill they brought you to me. You will be safe."

He lowered the raised candlestick, setting it back on the table. "I have never heard of you."

"You have been away. On crusade?"

Choking back a bitter laugh, he snarled, "You make it sound like a pleasure voyage. It was no pleasure." Without questioning why he wanted to ruffle her smooth feathers, he said, "I was captured and all of my men were murdered."

Her eyes widened.

"I was tortured. Here." He pointed to the ragged scar on his side, and the rope burns on his wrists. Then he touched the puckered scar at the base of his throat, a constant reminder of how close Leah had gotten to killing him.

Instead of weakening, the stubborn wench let her hands fall to her sides. "I assumed as much. I saw the lash marks across your back. You did not give in easily, I imagine. You are indeed a hero."

The remembered sting of the lash made him wince, but he straightened his shoulders. He was far from heroic, and her empathy was catching him off guard. "I need to leave."

"You do?"

"Aye." He bit his tongue before he told her why. She had to be a witch, for he felt compelled to tell her things he would rather keep hidden. Suspicion laced his voice as he asked, "Where are the 'friends' you said I came with?"

He'd escaped the barren desert alone, trusting no other. It made no sense that he'd join a group.

Turning slightly, calculating a way to escape, Nicholas recognized the worn wooden cross dangling off the table's edge. A flitting memory of a soothing voice and the light fragrance of warm apples gave him chills, and Nicholas rubbed his neck.

In the naïve rush of excitement to be a good knight for God and the baron, he'd forgotten the rosary at the monastery. It was the one thing he had left of a mother he couldn't remember. It comforted Nicholas to warm the smooth wood beads between his fingers, and wonder if his mother had done the same during her prayers. He'd missed it most during during his captivity–mayhap it could have given him the courage he'd needed to be strong.

He'd failed. Unease weighted his shoulders as dark memories filtered through the murkiness in his head. "*Who* are they?"

"I'll get them," she said softly, and Nicholas wondered how she stayed so calm in the face of his madness. She walked toward a stone staircase, tiny bells singing from her shoes, and pulled on a dangling rope. A sound blasted, then a door opened and a husky voice called down, "Yes, 'Tia?"

"Gram, Sir Nicholas is awake. And," she cleared her throat, "he needs a tunic or robe, if you please."

Turning back to him, she splayed her hands, palms up. "Although I do not think you are well enough to leave the manor just yet."

Light footsteps clattered down the stairs, and a woman with bright red hair shot through with silver leaned over the wooden rail until her green eyes landed on him. Nicholas shivered beneath the gaze.

"How do you feel, sir? Surely, you are not ready for travel."

He drew himself up to his full height, ignoring the

line of perspiration cooling his back. "I appreciate your kindness," he said pointedly. "But I am my own man."

"Well, that may be," the red-haired grandmother said with a chuckle. "But for certes, ye've the look of—"

"Gram!"

His breath caught in his chest with a painful squeeze. "Who? I am a bastard born."

"Being born out of wedlock doesn't stop you from being the very image of your father." Celestia smiled gently.

Nicholas eyed the candlestick. Mayhap it was not he who was crazy. He was on the verge of demanding answers, but the noise of several pairs of boots clomping on the wooden ceiling above kept him silent. The door crashed open.

"Sir Nicholas! Ye're awake?" A blond giant of a man took the stairs at a fast clip until he stood at attention before him.

Nicholas held on to a vague memory teasing the edges of his mind. He tensed, remembering. "Sir Petyr?" The knowledge came back to him with the all of the ease of a raging sandstorm.

Fevered and ill, he'd crawled like a dog back to the monastery where he'd grown up. A bastard. Dead mother, no father, just God and the abbot. And then, later, his liege lord. Nicholas ground his back teeth together in impotent anger.

Nightmares had twisted with feverish ravings, and Nicholas told the abbot, in great semi-lucid detail, that Baron Peregrine would die by his hand. Abbot Crispin suggested that Nicholas pray for divine insight, but all he wanted was vengeance for the loyal men who'd followed him into a trap.

"The abbot hired you," Nicholas said while taking Petyr's measure; the steady eyes, the well-fitted blue tunic with gold edging. "To escort me to Spain."

Petyr nodded once, his expression closed.

"In hopes that the saint would forgive me for losing the sacred relic to the enemy." *Lies.* Yes, it was coming back in bits and pieces. The concerned abbot, afraid for Nicholas's soul, begging him to pray the stain of his sins away. Aye, he thought with regret, he must have, in his delirium, told his mentor everything. But surely Abbot Crispin would keep his secrets?

Tightening the cloth around his hips, Nicholas considered his new plan, and decided it was more to his liking. God had abandoned him for failing to protect the relic, and what better way to regain favor than to go after earthly justice? He would beg forgiveness once he delivered Baron Peregrine's head to Saint James. A relic for a relic—it would be fair.

"Abbot Crispin may have hired you to ride with me to Spain, but we'll do one thing before we go," he told Petyr.

Sweat dotted his forehead and his belly cramped. To think, sweet mercy, that this sickness was an improvement over how ill he'd been.

"Nicholas, we must talk," but Petyr was interrupted when another man came down the stairs. Tall and angry, this man's blue eyes were grim promises of dire retribution.

For what? Nicholas braced himself for an attack.

"Sir, have we met?"

"No."

The man stopped in front of Nicholas so that they were eye to eye. But the man had clothes and a stubborn chin, which put the balance in his favor. Intense dislike blazed from him. *That chin.* "You must be the healer's father." *What cause had this family to hate him*?

"Aye," he said. "I am Lord Robert Montehue."

Nicholas didn't flinch, even though his head was cleaving in two. "I am—"

"I know damn well who you are. Ye're the spittin' image of your sire."

Thoroughly confused, Nicholas said, "I have no idea who you think I am, but this is an obvious instance of mistaken identity."

Lord Robert barked a laugh. "With that nose? I don't think so. I promise ye that if I can find a way out of this noose around my neck, I will."

The agony between his eyes clouded his vision. "Noose?" *They knew his father? Who was he?*

A woman's light gasp sounded and Nicholas turned, seeing three, or he thought there were three, red-haired females all staring at him from over the rickety railing.

The youngest one, a girl on the verge of becoming a great beauty, pronounced, "He looks exactly like Baron Peregrine!"

Dizzy, he swayed on his feet.

He looked like his sworn mortal enemy?

Sweet Jesu, Nicholas thought as the pain burst inside his head like an overripe melon.

Chapter TWO

His fever is gone, 'Tia, and he is resting. Won't you come to bed? It has been three days." Her grandmother finished the last stitch on an altered tunic for Nicholas, tearing off the thread with her sharp teeth.

Celestia put a cork in the jar of rosemary oil, glad to have had her grandmother's company. It kept her from thinking too hard. "I was worried that he might not live to see this morning. None of my herbal recipes were taking effect. Did you notice that the little bit of poppy tea I was able to feed him only made his ramblings worse, instead of helping him rest? It was as if the medicine was causing *more* pain instead of easing it. I have never seen a reaction like that before."

"Nor I," her grandmother agreed, setting the garment aside. "You could not have worked any harder, and now your diligence is rewarded. How are your hands?"

She held them out toward her grandmother, noticing the slight tremor. "There was a point when I thought they would burn off, battling the heat around his liver." Celestia tried to laugh, but it came out as a sigh. She lowered one hand on the tunic. "Thank you for doing that."

"His nakedness bothered you?" her grandmother teased.

"No," Celestia lied. It had torn at her heart to see how his fine limbs had been scarred. Long legs, muscled thighs, and a wound that even in his deepest delirium he would not let her touch. "If I had to be the one to sew, the hem would be uneven."

"'Tis truly a skill that you struggle with," Lady Evianne laughed softly as she stood, her hand to her lower back. "My age is catching up to me."

"Who are you fooling? You will never get old." Celestia did not want to think about how empty her life would be without her grandmother in it. If the baron had his way, the separation would come sooner than later.

"You could have let him die."

"'Tis not possible, and you well know it. If I can heal," she lifted her left hand, "then I will. Same as you, no matter what you say."

"Will you marry this man?"

"No." The answer came swift, though she knew it for the untruth it was. Her family's well-being was at stake, and she would die for any of them. Worse, she would give up her identity. "I don't want to. Galiana longs for a husband, let her have him."

Lady Evianne clucked her tongue. "Shame on you. Besides, the baron specifically said that his son was to marry the eldest Montehue daughter, the healer—which is you."

Feeling a smidgeon of guilt for tossing her sister to the wolves, Celestia said, "I could run away."

"Hmmm. Well, I suppose we could hide you with your Aunt Nan in Wales. But I don't know what would happen to your brothers, then. Your parents could steal away to France in the dark of night, and mayhap your sisters won't mind being paupers."

"Gram," Celestia sighed.

Lady Evianne held up a slightly bent hand. "If I were you, I would want to learn everything I could about this man. Mayhap ye might find something to love."

"He's no bargain." Celestia glanced over at the table where Nicholas was fighting sleep. He'd passed out cold at hearing that he was the Baron Peregrine's son, desperately sick. A moan sounded, and Celestia sniffed, not appreciating the pull of sympathy at her heart. "Nor does he rest easy. A guilty conscience, mayhap?"

"Men go to war."

"Battle is either kill or be killed," Celestia said dismissively. "Why would that cause nightmares?"

"You could ask him," her grandmother said with a wink. "Get to know him. His will is strong."

"He didn't know that he is the baron's son, and look at what happened. He does not know that he has been ordered to marry me." Celestia knotted her hands together. The last time she'd been betrothed had ended in disaster, with her fiancé rejecting her in a humiliating fashion. Considering Sir Nicholas's temperament, she could not imagine him taking the news with a smile. "Tomorrow will be a rotten day."

"Sir Petyr is most closemouthed about what is going on. I even sent Galiana in as company to flirt and get what information she could, but that man can keep a secret."

Celestia smiled fondly. "Impervious to Gali? The man is dead."

Her grandmother laughed but then sobered abruptly. "Do you think you could love Sir Nicholas?"

"How can you ask me that?" Celestia's stomach fluttered and she held out her life-healing hands. "The risk is too great. All of my abilities will disappear," she snapped her fingers, "and I will be as nothing."

"Nothing? Even without your powers you know more about herbal remedies than most wise women. But if you can love him, and earn his love in return, the rewards are tenfold."

Celestia looked around the dungeon space that she'd turned into an infirmary. It had taken hard work, but she had earned the trust of the serfs. Her jars and pots were neatly labeled, her cloths folded and clean, her instruments sterile. "I am safe here."

"Safe?" Her grandmother slapped her knee as if she'd heard a joke. "Nobody is safe, 'Tia. And you cannot hide in this manor for all of your life. You are beautiful."

"I am not." Suddenly the unfairness of it all came to a boil, and she had to bite her lip to keep from crying. "I am not like the rest of you! I am a dwarf in a family of giants. I am a ghost in the presence of vibrant color. I, oh, Saint Brigid, my hands and my healing gifts are the only thing that tie me to the rest of you. By marrying, I lose *everything.*"

Her chest ached with tears she wouldn't shed.

Instead of empathizing, her grandmother scoffed, "Is this about Lord Riddleton? For certes, that man was odious. I do not understand what your father was thinking, letting that toad court you."

That odious toad was the only man who had chosen plain Celestia over breathtakingly beautiful Galiana. Hence the appeal, she thought with a shameful pang.

Since her mother, Galiana, and Ela all looked like younger versions of her grandmother, she didn't expect for the Grand Lady Evianne to understand.

Head lowered, she murmured, "I will go to bed, as soon as I finish crushing this last bit of lavender."

"You don't want to discuss this anymore?"

Celestia gave her grandmother a hug. "What else is there to say?"

Nicholas heard the thrum of soft, feminine, *English* voices and struggled toward awareness. Inky black clouds of despair threatened him as he escaped the binding ties of sleep. Leah's voice taunted him, teased him, and made him feel like the scum of the earth. His bones ached, ach, he hated sleeping, yet he was so damnably tired. He heard the sound of feet climbing stairs, the rustle of a kirtle, the closing of the door at the top of the stairway.

Yet Nicholas sensed that he was not alone.

The light jingle of bells told him that Celestia was

still with him in the room. A sharp floral smell permeated the air, and he detected the scrape of a mortar and pestle. Turning on his side, he opened his eyes and watched her work.

She'd removed the headdress she'd worn earlier. Her hair was the exact shade of dried wheat. Hanging down her back in a long sloppy braid, the tail danced at hip level as she worked the pestle round and round. He sniffed, wondering what she was grinding. Nicholas noticed, how could he not, how her simple dress hugged her curves. For all her petite stature, her figure was shapely.

Uncomfortable, he shifted, making certain that all his body parts were covered.

She whirled, tipping the mortar over. "You are awake!"

He sat up, swinging his legs over the side of the table and pausing until he knew if he had the strength to stand. "Aye. Did you not expect me to?"

Her lips twitched as she fought a smile. "Oh, aye, but not until the morn. How do you feel?" She wiped her fingers on the apron she wore around her waist and came toward him, one hand outstretched.

Drawing back, he avoided her touch and stood. He would not accept any more kindness than need be. "Better."

She had a tiny vee of wrinkles in her brow when she frowned as she was doing now. Nicholas had the ridiculous urge to smooth the lines away with his thumb. "I was only seeing if you had a fever," she explained, dropping her hand.

"I'm fine." He remembered more of the circumstances of why he was here and swallowed, his throat sore. "I owe you about a hundred apologies."

Tilting her head to the side, she did smile, just a little. "So many?"

His stomach tightened, but it wasn't with nausea. "I vaguely remember being ill, violently ill, in your presence. And then, correct me if I am mistaken, I was again sick."

She cleared her face of all laughter, though he imagined it was difficult. "Tis true, you were not well. But you have been resting for three days. The fact that you are awake is apology enough for me."

"Did you heal me with magic?" He felt incredible, cleaner and more clearheaded than he had in years.

"Not magic. I told you once already that I am not a witch. Please, won't you sit down?"

"Before I fall down."

"Aye," she stepped forward to wrap her arm around his waist, easing him back onto the table. "Let me get you a cool cloth." She turned and pierced him with a look. "Stay?"

Clutching the edge of the wooden table, his legs dangling over the side like a child in his father's chair, he nodded.

Her braid swung out behind her as she turned. A bundle of energy, he finally placed the scent coming from her work area.

"Lavender?"

"Yes," she said with surprise. "Do you like it? It soothes headaches and allows for a calm sleep. I tried an opiate for you, but it didn't work as well."

She'd given him opium? Lord Jesus. His skin heated from the inside out, and sweat dotted his upper lip. Had he yelled aloud in his night terrors? Some secrets needed to stay buried. He could not trust himself to sleep too deeply, not unless he was alone.

"I hope I didn't scare you," he attempted a jest.

"Oh, no, you were simply restless. From the fever, no doubt."

Let her think that, he thought. The truth would send her running for her father. And being as her sire was a big man, that was not a good idea.

Sire. *Hellfire.* He gasped, unable to take in air as he remembered the last thing he'd heard before crashing. It felt as if someone was squeezing him hard enough to break his ribs. He was choking, strangling, and then suddenly, he could breathe again. Celestia had one hand on the back of his neck, and a cool cloth pressed against his forehead. "Is it true?" he croaked.

Her touch was light, yet warm, and her tone compassionate when she answered simply, "Aye."

Sitting there together for a few minutes, absorbing a truth so large it was suffocating, he finally asked, "Did you always know about me?"

She dipped the cloth in a dish of water, wrung it out, and placed it against his wrists. They both ignored the thick ropy scars that marred his skin. "No. We thought that the baron was childless. All his bairns seem to die as infants."

"I had heard that, as well. Not that I gave it much attention," he laughed dryly. "Why should I have?" Celestia's silence prodded him to speak, even as he longed to find a safe place to rest and think. Did this knowledge change his vow to kill the baron? So what if the man was his father? He was still an arse-wipe. "Men do not care about such things."

Celestia lifted one brow, the right one, over the blue eye. "Like family?"

He stiffened. "I was brought up an orphan at Crispin Monastery. My entire life I worked outdoors and said prayers, and when I was offered to serve allegiance to Baron Peregrine and train to become a Crusader for God and King Richard—I thought that I was the luckiest bastard ever born."

"Hmm." She walked, jingled actually, to the black pot over the fire. She took two bowls from the side cupboard, and dished something fragrant and meaty from the pot into the dishes.

Nicholas's stomach growled, and his mouth watered.

She came back and handed him a bowl with a chunk of bread. "'Tis beef soup," she said. "Eat slowly. You look like you have not been well for some time." Sitting on a stool opposite him, she lifted the bowl to her lips and blew into it before taking a small sip.

"You must think me the lowliest man you've ever met," he said, staring at her smooth face. Why should it matter what she thought?

"That's not true. I know some worse than you."

"Lord Riddleton?"

She looked up. "You heard the conversation between my grandmother and me?" Her pale cheeks turned scarlet.

"Some of it. I was not eavesdropping on purpose. It's

not often that a man is referred to as an odious toad."

Celestia smiled and Nicholas noticed the flash of a dimple in her left cheek. "Well. Did you hear anything else?"

"No. I probably missed some very interesting gossip, too." How could he banter like this, when not long ago he'd been pounding on death's door? He shook off the feelings of camaraderie.

"You have no idea," she agreed, soaking a bread crust in the warm liquid before popping the piece in her mouth.

He held her gaze, thinking that a man would never get bored looking at such a beautiful woman. "Does it bother you, having one green eye and one blue?" Nicholas finished his soup, hoping that he hadn't just offended her. "Never mind."

"Besides having to overcome the fact that people want to know if I am a witch, you mean?"

"You are mocking me."

"Of course." She stood and collected their bowls, setting them on the counter next to a bunch of dried herbs, and sending him a shy smile over her shoulder.

Lord Riddleton must have been a dunce. "I have been too long from polite company."

"'Tis no matter. It is time for another tisane, lavender and—"

"I don't want to sleep."

She put a hand on her hip. He was learning she did that when she wanted her way. "I do. 'Tis late."

God's bones, he was an inconsiderate oaf. She had been playing nurse to him, his chest tightened, *for three days.*

She looked at the covers on the table. "Let me shake

them out. Oh! My grandmother took in one of my father's tunics for you." She quickly grabbed a folded garment and handed it to him.

"You did not do it?"

"I can mend bones, but clothing is beyond me. Unless you want a ragged hem?" Celestia piled the dishes into a bucket of water, quickly cleaning them and then setting them to dry. Next, she mixed the tisane.

Raised in a monastery, he was hardly a judge on womanly character. He knew nuns, and he knew whores. Celestia was neither. Was that why she fascinated him?

Nicholas slipped the fine fabric over his head, noting the way she deliberately kept her back turned, granting him privacy, despite the fact that she had seen him naked already. His heart warmed. She made him *feel* . . . a dangerous thing for a man with revenge on his mind.

"Before you go to bed, my lady, could you tell me what you know about the baron?"

She paused before nodding. "But I do not know much."

It was important that he know his enemy, Nicholas thought. "Please."

"He is our liege lord."

"I also swore fealty to him," Nicholas interrupted gruffly.

"How is it you never met him?"

"I promised a blood oath through his head knight. Not Petyr, but another Montgomery. He was killed." In Tripoli. "Enough about that—do I really have his looks?" Nicholas rubbed the scars on his wrists bitterly.

"Very much in the face. Your body," she blushed,

"is slimmer."

While he'd been starving and nauseous, the baron most likely dined on creamed trout and fruit pies. Nicholas tightened his jaw.

"I have twin brothers. They are being fostered at his estate on the Scottish border. Peregrine Castle. It is a fine opportunity for them." She folded her hands in her lap, and he sensed that she was being overly careful with her words.

Why? she wondered.

"Is he a cruel man?"

She sucked her lower lip between her teeth, and Nicholas's belly clenched with a sensual hunger.

"My brothers do not complain, not much. But they are not the best of writers. They're only twelve, and they've been with the baron for less than a year."

"How many siblings do you have?"

"I am the oldest, then next is Galiana, and then the twins, and then Ela."

He remembered the youngest girl on the stairs. "They all have red hair? Except you."

Sighing, she twiddled her thumbs. She wondered if he would find Galiana more to his taste; most men did, especially when comparing the two. "Aye, 'tis the truth. Well, except the boys, they have blond hair, like our father. And they are tall—everybody is, except for me."

He realized that this bothered her. "There is nothing wrong with being short."

Her lower lip trembled.

"Is there? Something I do not know about. Can

you not ride a horse? Or climb a tree—well, you are a young lady and probably don't climb trees, so are you upset because," he looked around the room and noticed all of the footstools, "you have to use a footstool to reach the highest shelves?"

Covering her mouth with her hand, she teased back, "I challenge you to a horse race, sir. And as for climbing trees? How else do you get the choicest apples? I am not afraid of heights, as Gali is. It simply would be *nice* to be tall."

"You must admit it, though," he pressured. "There is nothing wrong with being short."

She rolled her eyes. "I will admit to nothing, except that we have gotten quite off topic." Feigning a yawn, she stood and said, "I have to sleep. May I trust that you will not try to sneak off before morn? We have guards around the perimeter, and you might accidentally get shot by an archer." Smiling, she added, "You've no breeches, and your legs are as white as milk. They'd think you a ghost."

"You were looking at my legs?" Nicholas pretended to be shocked. She'd seen all of him, including his scars, and hadn't run away. Lady Celestia was made of stern stuff. "You would protect me?" His body tensed with an unidentifiable emotion.

"Sleep, Sir Nicholas," she said with a giggle and a wave as she went up the stairs. "No one will harm you here."

Setting the cup on the counter, he knew it was time to leave.

He got as far as the stables before getting caught.

It was her youngest sister's snoring that woke her, and Celestia did not even mind. The three days of nursing Nicholas back to health had taken all her energies, but the solution to her problem had come to her in a dream.

She had to protect her family and marry Sir Nicholas so that her brothers would not come to harm. Running away would only cause her family worry, not to mention that if she was to directly disobey her liege lord, her family could lose their lands and be outcast. The needs of the many most definitely outweighed her own need to be happy.

Except . . .

What if she spoke to Sir Nicholas before he found out that they were to wed, and what if she assured him that they could get an annulment once they pleaded their case to the baron in person? The baron could not refuse his own son, not face to face. Could he?

For certes, she'd not stand in the way.

And if she could speak to Nicholas privately, he would not have the chance to reject her in public. Celestia shoved the covers back, setting her bare feet on the wooden floor.

"'Tia? What ails ye? You look green."

Shoving her arms through her robe, Celestia realized that green must be the color of remembered humiliation. "Go back to sleep, Ela. You can't have slept well, since you kept me awake most of the night."

Her sister sat up, her bright red hair exploding from

her long braids in wispy curls. She rubbed her eyes. "Sir Nicholas has a gray aura, something I have not seen before. It is too dangerous for you to wed him. Tell Father you cannot do it, please, 'Tia?"

Unsettled by her sister's announcement, Celestia expelled a loud breath. "You know that I have no choice." She crossed her arms defensively. "Why are you in my bed, anyway? What is the matter with yours?"

"I am afraid for you," Ela said, her lower lip trembling and her green eyes brimming with tears.

"Oh, shhh, now, don't cry." Celestia sat back on the edge of her bed, pulling her sister into a hug. "I am a powerful healer," she said in a storyteller's voice, "what is a gray aura to one such as me, eh?" She laughed, tickling Ela until the tears dried.

"I will miss you," Ela said, climbing from the mussed covers.

"Miss me?" Celestia repeated, a shard of ice lodging in her chest.

Galiana threw open the door to Celestia's room and marched inside, followed by a line of five serfs. One carried a bathing tub, one carried two pails of hot water, another carried two pails of cool water, one carried breakfast, and the last carried a huge basket of oils and lotions that Galiana had made.

"Quick, 'Tia. Ye must bathe and dress, sleepyhead. We've all been up since dawn, except you two. Were you crying, Ela? No matter. Go to Gram, she has your dress laid out, you'll carry the flowers."

"Flowers?" Celestia asked, the cold traveling through

her blood.

Galiana would not meet her eyes. "You're getting married."

Celestia's knees gave out. "Now?" she squeaked, sinking to the floor in a puddle of boneless nerves. "But I . . . Nicholas doesn't even know, and I was going . . ."

Clapping her hands, Gali dismissed everyone and shut the door behind them, Ela included.

Taking a seat on the floor next to her sister, Galiana said softly, "Nicholas knows."

Heart beating rapidly, Celestia burned to ask how. "If I am to be married right now, he must have agreed to it."

Gali covered Celestia's hand with hers. "Aye."

Apprehension was thick in the air, and Celestia bowed her head. "Tell me. The truth, please."

"Nicholas tried to escape the manor last eve, but Sir Petyr caught him at the stables."

"He is not well enough to travel!"

Galiana, her brow smoothly plucked, said with exasperation, "Well or no, Sir Petyr told him of your betrothal."

Celestia whispered, "He can't have been pleased." Remembering the way Lord Riddleton had renounced their betrothal over breakfast in the hall, she cringed at what Sir Nicholas might have said.

The moment of silence stretched into two and finally Gali spoke, "He was not happy. And when he found out that Sir Petyr was the baron's man and not hired by Abbot Crispin, well . . ."

"Just say it!" Her stomach was a giant knot of tension. "He hates me for keeping him from Spain."

"He punched Sir Petyr in the nose," Galiana said with admiration.

"No!"

"It didn't even bleed, but Nicholas promised him it would be worse once he regained his strength."

Groaning, Celestia asked, "So how did Sir Petyr coerce Nicholas to agree to the wedding?"

"Your life."

She put her hand to her throat. "What?"

"Sir Petyr reminded Sir Nicholas that you had saved his life, and that he owed you a personal boon."

"I never thought of that, why, then I can simply say that I do not wish to wed. 'Tis perfect!" Celestia started to rise.

Pulling her sister back down, Galiana shook her head. "Sir Petyr said that the boon to be granted was wedding you, to save you from being stoned as a witch."

Celestia felt the blood drain from her face and the cold expanded to every inch of her body. "What?"

"The baron says if you two are not wed by sundown on this date, he will have you accused by the bishop, and put to death."

Celestia raced out of her bedchamber, as if chased by the hounds of hell, to the one place that always gave her solace. Her herb garden. How dare the baron threaten her with witchcraft? She had never treated the man in her life. So far as she was aware, nobody in their family had.

And, of course, Sir Nicholas, told that he owed her his

life, would comply. Despite the first impression he'd given, she surmised that he was a decent, if haunted, man.

She'd easily evaded her mother in the chaos of the family upheaval and slipped out through the rear kitchen into her private garden, hoping to find the strength she knew she would need to continue this farce.

Celestia wiped bitter, angry tears from her eyes and made her way to the wooden bench her father had made. Her gifts were blessed by God, and had nothing to do with the devil. She was able to destroy a black tumor with the focused energy in her fingertips. She could turn a breech babe, saving both mother and child in the process, with little to no pain. Never accepting coin, she helped whomever, serf or peasant or lord, because it was her duty to heal.

Damn the baron.

She plucked a wild rose blossom from the bush and crushed its fragrant petals between her fingers. What was she to do? She tossed the broken bloom to the ground and choked back a sob.

Gali had told her that Sir Petyr had produced a special marriage license, and when her parents had argued that food and drink would need to be prepared, Sir Petyr had said they'd hunt, then they'd produced casks of burgundy as a gift from the baron. Lord Robert had stabbed at his breakfast meat, intent on killing something, by God.

And as for Sir Nicholas?

Galiana said that he'd been pale. Stunned by circumstances, yet steady. It seemed they were both trapped in a snare, not of their own making, she thought with a twist of her mouth. But why? If she knew the answer, mayhap she could find a way around it. *Married.* She'd never thought that marriage would be hers to embrace. She rather thought she'd be similar to her Aunt Nan in Wales and live a single life. An old crone in a waddle hut filled with drying herbs and cats.

She was startled from her reverie by a loud thrashing behind her in the bushes. She reached for her eating dagger and jumped to her feet. A lost deer? A wild boar? Panic loomed.

Her garden was rectangular in shape and walled in by fragrant bushes and manicured hedges. The entrance to the kitchen was too far away to run to for safety, and running would only attract the deadly beast's attention. She planted her feet as she had been taught and held her knife out in preparation.

A dark shape came crashing through the rosebushes and tripped over the bench.

Celestia relaxed at once. Wild boars didn't curse fluently in what sounded like Arabic. "Sir Nicholas." Her tone was dry as she stared down at him. His face was covered in scratches from the rosebushes, and his sleeve was torn. She watched his cheeks color as he stood and brushed away the dirt and leaves from his tunic.

"Lady Celestia." He bowed his head, glancing at her drawn dagger. "I was walking, lost in thought, and . . . you can lower your weapon, my lady. The next thing I knew, I was attacked by thorns."

Celestia kept her expression neutral, a difficult task,

as he was wearing a rose above his left brow—completely at odds with his masculine features. Ebony hair dipped down over his broad forehead. The nose that pronounced him a Peregrine was strong and noble, and his dark gray eyes, clear of pain and fever, pierced her through. He made her belly swirl with excitement, and the feelings unexpectedly rose like bubbles in water.

She reached over and plucked the rose from his hair. It had to go. Her lips twitched, and she gestured toward the bench that he had knocked over. He immediately set it to rights and they sat, side by side.

"We should go in," she said. "I will clean your cuts."

He lifted a shoulder. "Nay, they are nothing." He glanced around the garden, anything but look at her. "It seems that once again I have made an ass of myself, my lady."

"I would forgive you trampling my garden, Sir Nicholas." She looked at the rose in her palm. "Just as I forgive you trying to steal away into the night. I know that the baron threatened to claim me a witch and that you agreed to wed, and save me."

He started to speak, but she shook her head. "Please, let me finish. Under normal circumstances, I would refuse your kind gesture. But these are not normal circumstances. My family has too much at stake, and I am unable to free you from your noble gesture."

She paused, waiting for . . . what? Words of comfort that would never come—he did not love her, and she did not love him.

Her muscles tensed and she continued, "But I have a plan." Careful not to touch him, bare skin to bare skin, she placed her hand on his covered arm.

Nicholas looked at her, unflinching, and nodded. "Tell me."

"What say you to an annulment?" Her words came out on a rush of breath, and she hardly believed her own daring.

His eyes turned stormy and unreadable. Then he bowed his head and clasped his hands over his knees.

"The baron will not release your brothers from service until you and I have a babe."

Getting to his feet, he laughed without a trace of humor. "Preferably a boy."

Chapter THREE

"A boy?"

Nicholas understood the shock on Celestia's pale face, as he'd been reeling from it, as well. "Aye. The bastard's trapped us. But why? Why you and why me, eh?" The man was evil and cunning enough to know that Nicholas would not abandon an innocent woman to a falsified charge. The fact that he owed his life to Celestia made it impossible for Nicholas to refuse her. His respect for her grew as he watched her swallow tears that would not change anything.

"I see." She stood as well, swaying slightly. "I don't suppose we could kill the baron, then feed his body to the wild fox, thereby freeing us both of his ridiculous command?"

If she only knew, he wanted to tell her. But while she joked, he was deadly serious. He'd learned his lesson from Leah well. No matter how sweet or innocent women might look, they were not to be trusted. He'd not tell her that while she'd been planning a possible annulment, he'd been planning the baron's quick, yet painful, demise. "Murder is a sin, my lady, as well as a criminal offense."

She brought her hand to her lips, her odd eyes widening. "It is my turn to apologize, Sir Nicholas. I had forgotten that you were raised at the monastery. My words were a poor jest, meant to be taken lightly."

Now he felt guilty for making her feel bad. He gave a clipped nod. Writing for the abbot had been a solitary task with plenty of time to think. Being a knight was a strength-building honor that was oftentimes opposed to the teachings of the Church. Surviving captivity had left him weak. Focusing on the death of the baron was crucial to his peace of mind, not to mention his soul. *Forget about Celestia's feelings.*

"How old were you, when you came to Abbot Crispin?" She placed her fingers on his sleeve, staring up at him with bright interest.

Nicholas had not even started to think about why he'd been raised as an orphan when he had a father who obviously liked to meddle in his life. "Six?"

"Hmm. I wonder . . ."

He could see she had another question forming, an indelicate one, by the way she was frowning. "Go ahead," he said. "Ask. I doubt I have any more answers than you do."

She blushed. "Were your mother and father truly wed?"

"Ah." He pulled out a piece of paper. "Petyr just gave me this. 'Tis the deed to Falcon Keep, my mother's ancestral home. King Henry arranged the marriage between my mother and father, so that Falcon Keep would stay in English hands. The property is rural, close to the border. It is now mine," he swallowed at the awkwardness of it all, "and soon to be yours."

Celestia's chin trembled.

"It is wild country, but safe enough." He felt the onslaught of new guilt, since he knew he was going to leave her there, mayhap for good. "Don't cry."

"I am sorry." She sniffed once, then tilted that stubborn Montehue chin. "I know that you didn't want this, or mayhap you did, but with a wife of your own choosing."

He ground his back teeth together, burying any emotion that dared to surface. "I had thought to be a scribe. It was a happy enough time, copying divine works for the abbot." He paced the small garden, his borrowed boots crushing basil and rosemary, sending sharp scents into the spring air. "I was twelve when the baron's men came, one of them called me a 'strapping lad,' and the next thing I knew, I was training as a squire. I did not understand why I had been picked for such a great honor, as I had never met the baron."

Picking a sprig of mint, he squished the leaf between his finger and thumb. "What an idiot I was, to never even think he could be my father. I thought . . ." He turned to Celestia, who hadn't run away while his back was turned, even though she could have, and he wouldn't have blamed her. "I thought that one of the other men was my sire, and that he was not able to claim me as his own, so he did what he could. It was a game. Pick out which man looked the most like me."

"Nicholas," Celestia said, a wealth of compassion in her voice as she patted the bench. "Won't you sit?"

Why did he tell her these things? Instantly angry at himself for letting his guard down, he kicked the bench leg instead. "Nay. Do not think of me as some kind of hero, with you the damsel in distress. I will marry you, and tup you until you quicken," his heart raced as he imagined Celestia beneath him, "but then I am gone."

She flinched at his harsh tone. "You want to go to Spain, for your soul. I know."

Nicholas did not clarify the misunderstanding. He did not need to care what she thought, he was doing what he had to do to save her brothers, and to save her from burning as a witch. Then they'd be even. He said, "It is settled. There will not be love between us, but we will marry this afternoon."

Unable to read the expression that flew across her face, he nevertheless understood that she was hurting, with a pain that he'd deliberately caused. He pressed further, not trusting her to hold a promise. "Do we have a bargain?"

"Yes." She bowed her head.

He turned his back on her and walked away.

It was a beautiful afternoon for a wedding, Celestia thought absently. It was too bad that the wedding had to be for her. Father Jonas was to perform the ceremony outside in Galiana's flower garden, with the entire manor in attendance.

"Ela! Stop fussing, please. My hair is fine."

"Just this last sprig of honeysuckle . . . there. Oh, you are beautiful."

Celestia gave her image a cursory look in the polished silver. She supposed she would do, not that it mattered. The baron had ensured that she marry his son, but why her? With his title, he could have forced a much better match for money and land, and perhaps beauty, too. She lifted her chin. Her sacrifice would be for the good of her family, and she would live with her choice without whining. All right, she told her conscience, mayhap a few private tears, but she would put on a good face.

Numb, Celestia followed her sisters down the stairs. Galiana looked ravishing in a pale yellow silk dress with flowing sleeves. Her headdress made her seem even taller and more regal. Ela, her head covered in a light green silk kerchief, walked as if she were leading her sister to the gallows. The bouquet of spring daffodils shook in her hands.

Celestia lifted the hem of her ivory gown, careful not to trip on her grandmother's gold chains. They looped from the braided gold girdle, adding a heaviness to her clothes that matched what was in her heart. Silver heeled slippers peeped out as she descended, and the gold and silver bells in her curled hair made muffled protests with each step. She'd cried in her bath, cried as her sisters and mother and grandmother all patted her and assured her that Destiny would prevail. She'd sobbed as they'd curled her hair, and was only sniffling by the time Galiana placed sliced cucumbers on her eyes.

If she'd really been a witch, there would have been hell to pay.

Falcon Keep was north, on the Scottish border. A rough and untamed land, much like Nicholas, she supposed. Celestia had never met anyone so nobly broken.

Her mother and father waited at the bottom of the staircase, her grandmother, as well. The sound of the lute player out in the enclosed garden carried through the windows, and Celestia hurriedly lowered her eyes, determined to hide her pain from her family.

"I have changed my mind. We can send you to my sister, Nan. Abner has a horse saddled for you," her mother whispered in her ear.

"Or you can go to the church. Surely Baron Peregrine can't have you labeled a witch from within the nunnery's walls."

"Father!" Celestia gasped. The consequences to a Montehue rebellion had been made clear.

Her parents flanked her on either side. "Just say the word," her mother said, gripping Celestia's elbow so hard, she knew there would be a mark. "We will help you escape. But it has to be now."

Clearing her throat, she stopped walking and demanded quietly, "And what of you if I were to be so selfish? Hmm? Your reputations would be tainted. Gali and Ela still need bridal portions, and what about the twins? Nay." Celestia lifted her chin and put her fist on her hip. "I will marry Sir Nicholas."

"But . . ." her mother said, letting the word fall from her lips.

Taking a deep breath, Celestia accepted her father's arm. She smiled brightly, yet falsely, as they walked out of the manor and into the colorful garden. He said in a low voice, "An accident can be arranged, if need be, daughter."

Saying nothing to that, she focused on the beautiful arbor, which had been entwined with flowers and ferns, and decorated with ribbons of gold. The sun shone its blessing down upon them, and butterflies added color and beauty wherever they landed. She nodded to everyone, right and left, coming to a halt before the priest.

Sensing Nicholas, and his gaze upon her, she knew that he was the one person she couldn't look at without crying. *He would never love her*.

Nicholas stared down at the petite blond whose head barely reached the middle of his chest and felt a stirring of protectiveness. It didn't matter that he didn't want this; she was as much of a victim as he. The hard shell around his emotions cracked as he saw the damp lashes, but no tears. She was strong and brave, yet so small and fragile in appearance. His fingers itched to touch her flaxen hair, but he knew that he would not give in to such a foolish gesture. It would be pure folly to care for her, even a tiny bit. His soul was already dark, and he planned on blackening it further.

Bowing his head as he listened to the droning of the

priest's prayers, Nicholas wondered at how he had come to be in this garden, next to this woman, when he'd been on his way to mete out death's justice without thought of what would happen if he didn't die himself in the process.

He did not care about tomorrow.

Father Jonas discreetly elbowed him, loudly clearing his throat. Nicholas snapped to attention, realizing the priest had given him an instruction and he had no idea what it was.

"Join hands, please," Father Jonas said kindly for the second time.

Celestia brought her hand forward slowly, and he could see the uncertainty as plainly as if she had written it down. She was afraid. He would never hurt her, he thought with surprise. He just could never love her.

A cloud passed over the sun, darkening the sky.

Nicholas reluctantly clasped her slender outstretched hand.

Panic clawed at her breast as he took her hand. Tempted to jerk it away, Celestia knew she could not. She'd been wary of touching him unguarded after she'd merely brushed the wounds at his wrists with her fingers and she'd been inundated with his pain. As an experienced healer, she was trained to look at injured body parts and see what she could mend, but his scars were too tender, as if he was protecting himself even deep in delirium.

The same had been true when she'd skimmed his unmarred flesh. His deepest injury lay buried within his spirit. Unprepared for the shock of it, she'd almost fallen into his despair. After that, she'd avoided touching him because it had felt like an intrusion on his privacy. As an innocent woman, she was terrified of the feelings he brought out in her. She could not afford to give him her affections, because lust without love would ruin her. As a healer, she was mystified by his hidden wounds.

The heat from their joined hands was not unpleasant, as she'd feared. In fact, it was more like a low-energy version of how her hands tingled when she healed. The warmth traveled from her fingertips to her wrist, to her elbow, then her shoulders and her breasts, and finally landed in the pit of her belly, robbing her of breath. Surprised, she glanced up and met his dark, dark gaze.

Innocent, yes. Naïve? No. Celestia knew this was desire.

Father Jonas announced heartily and loudly, "You may now join in the kiss of peace, and may God bless this union with love."

The sound of cheers and clapping could be heard, but Celestia froze in place. Kiss him? Nay!

He must have read the look of bewilderment on her face, because she watched as he tried to think of a way around it.

There wasn't one. He gave her a shrug.

Swallowing hard, Celestia leaned forward, her chin tilted up in defiance. Nicholas bent down, his lips parted slightly. Celestia didn't dare breathe as his firm mouth covered hers. She kept her lips still beneath his, her eyes wide. Would the flesh-to-flesh contact send images through her head? Celestia felt scared and exhilarated at the same time.

They touched.

Nicholas's eyes darkened, and she didn't trust the way her heart was fluttering in her chest. His lips captured hers, softly, as if he had planned on making the kiss a light melding to satisfy the people who watched, and yet he lingered. His breath tasted of mint and wine, and she carefully pressed back. Her stomach was on fire, and her legs trembled. She felt faint, and tension hummed through her veins.

He was nothing like Lord Riddleton.

With a great effort, they broke apart like naughty children, much to the enjoyment of their audience.

Celestia brushed away Nicholas's steadying hand and stood on her own two feet. Nobody needed to know that her knees were shaking like a newborn lamb's.

She was Lady Celestia Montehue . . . er, she swallowed sickly and straightened her shoulders . . . Le Blanc? Peregrine. It didn't matter, as she hadn't chosen the title. She sent the spectators, along with her family, a wobbly smile. A lady did not collapse like a melted beeswax candle on her wedding day, and that was that.

"Ye'll be packed and ready to leave first thing in the morning," Lady Deirdre cried. "I hate the baron, I hate him, and I do not care who tells him I said so," she ranted, looking more beautiful and warrior-like than any painting of Queen Boadicea. The outdoor setting, the dusky night, and the bonfire all added to the pagan allure.

Sighing with all of her might, Celestia knew her family needed her to be strong, even stronger than before. "It was wonderful of him to give us the keep in which Nicholas was born." Sending a pleading look toward her sister, who was playing the flirt with Sir Petyr, Celestia said, "I just do not understand why we have to go immediately. What is the rush?"

"Something to do with protecting the keep, I think. Your father questioned Sir Petyr about the knights already there. You will be fine." Her mother blinked quickly. "Very well protected. Petyr claimed his toast this evening will be good news, for once." Lady Deirdre glared at the knight, who buried his face in a mug of ale.

Gali appeared at her side, handing her a goblet of honeyed mead. "Drink, sister dearest, for tonight is your wedding night."

Nicholas coughed, and Petyr slapped his back, laughing like a boy.

Galiana slid a glance to where Sir Petyr and Nicholas were talking, dark head bent toward blond head. "He is certainly handsome."

Surprised, Celestia giggled softly and whispered, "Aye, he is handsome. And with good food and no more bouts of fever, he shall only get more so. I especially like that he has on a *pair* of shoes this eve." She watched to see if Nicholas returned her sister's admiration, but Nicholas seemed oblivious to everything around them. It warmed her spirit to see that he hadn't fallen to Galiana's charms.

"Hmm? Oh," Galiana laughed and lightly smacked Celestia's arm. "I was talking about Sir Petyr."

Celestia closed her eyes briefly in relief. Not that her sister would take a man from her side on purpose, but men seemed to gravitate toward Galiana like a horse to water. Her sister's beauty was as legendary in their county as her own healing powers.

Their mother pulled them back into the men's conversation. "It will be Galiana's turn next, and I vow we shall find someone suitable. With land of their own," she added pointedly to Sir Petyr.

Celestia felt a stab of guilt. Galiana had turned down more offers of marriage than there were eligible men in the county. She said that she did not have any desire to wed, but Celestia knew that her sister had waited, longing for a man to sweep her off her feet like a minstrel's romance. "I will keep my eye out for any stray gentry in the woods of Scotland," she promised, a touch tipsy.

"Nothing less than an earl, if ye please," Galiana laughed and curtsied.

Celestia sometimes envied her sister's lack of healing ability. Gali could be beautiful and witty and fun without worrying over the world. Her creams and lotions were much-wanted gifts, and her perfumes were nothing short of heavenly. Men wrote sonnets and laid them at her feet, and she didn't have to fret over sickness and health, life or death.

Nicholas chuckled at a jest she couldn't hear, but Celestia sensed his underlying unease. Was it caused by being with crowds of people? People he did not know? Or being with a family he'd been forced to marry into? Truly, he looked the knight gallant in the loose-fitting tunic, leggings, and calf boots. His hair was as dark as a raven's wing, and his mouth . . . she licked her lips and turned away.

Being married, sharing that magical kiss as the priest blessed them, had caused a yearning within her breast for something more. It gave her hope to try for more.

She shouldn't want to feel his mouth pressed to hers. Nor should she wonder what it would be like to share a bed with someone other than her sisters. A man. Her husband. Celestia's stomach knotted, and she blamed the warmth in her blood on the wine.

He captured her gaze, and slipped his hand beneath her elbow. "Shall we walk?" he asked easily, taking her from the others.

"Aye," she blushed, grateful that the night was dimming so he would not see her face. He would think her new interest in him foolish, especially after he'd told her that he was not staying. She planned to show him that she had a heart that could be his, if he would but use it gently. They were each honorable people, attracted to one another—surely love could grow from that?

If Gram was right, it might be a start. Heart pounding with anticipation, she leaned into his warmth, wanting him to want her, too.

"We'll get an annulment."

She tripped. "What?"

"I have been thinking on your earlier suggestion and

I believe it sound. It would be a wise choice for us to abstain from our marital rights until we arrive at Falcon Keep, and then I'll go on to Peregrine Castle."

Celestia didn't know whether to laugh or cry. Nicholas was going to ruin her with his honor. At least his rejection of her wasn't public, she thought, although it was hard to be grateful. It was difficult, but she kept walking. "So you think we should try for the annulment after all?"

"I do not trust the baron. Aye, I know everybody says I am his, by nose alone they would know it," he sighed tiredly. "I have been trying to puzzle out why he would go to such great lengths to see the two of us, specifically in all of England, wed. It is suspect."

Remembering Nicholas's dark, hidden pain, Celestia tamped down her own hurt at his easy dismissal of her. "'Tis obvious that he wants me to heal you, but I would have done that without marriage. My family already swears fealty to him, so he didn't need a political ally. You have no family."

He stopped in the night, and she heard him grinding his teeth in frustration. She would not be surprised if he had worn them down to nubs.

"That is all true. So if my," he stumbled over the word *father*, "suddenly wants me healthy, I need to know why. He does not seem the sort to do a deed out of kindness."

She empathized with the ache she heard in his voice, and cautiously reached out to put her hand on his sleeve. If she touched his skin now, his pain would overwhelm her. "Does Petyr not know?"

"He could be a spy for the king, he is so close-lipped. All I know is that he has promised a gift during the bridal toast. Considering what else he's given on behalf of my . . . er, the baron, I admit to fearing this 'gift.'"

She laughed before realizing it, and he smiled in return. Celestia had thought to spark the beginnings of a relationship on her wedding night, but he'd push her away if she got too close. Her husband, she shivered though there was no wind, was not one for emotional ties.

"Are you cold?" he asked.

"No," Celestia answered, taken back by his concern. God help her, but she had accidentally married the most noble man in all of England. "Simply a chill." Now was not the time for one of her hunches. "Let us go make Petyr tell his gift, eh?"

Jaw tight, he nodded. "Aye, and Celestia, we are agreed that we will have to fake our joining tonight, are we not? I know that there should be," he stammered, which only made him more endearing to her, "blood. I will cut my thumb, so that you won't be shamed."

Not sure what to say to that, she pulled away before she grabbed his hand and begged him to reconsider their future together. He was honorable, kind, handsome and wounded. If only his pain wasn't somehow magnified, if only she didn't care. But the chinks in his noble armor were killing her.

Nicholas felt as if he'd been running forever. His

chest was tight, his body tense and his muscles sore. He'd been married for half a day, and he was beat.

When would she realize that he was a fraud? When would she look at him like the bastard he'd always thought he was? But she gazed at him with those angel-witch eyes like he was a damn hero instead of a murdering, gutless sod. Celestia had more courage in her petite frame than he would ever know.

She was warm, and God's bones, he was so tired of being cold. She was light and he was filled with darkness. He could not touch her, for fear of dousing her goodness. He had never been around a family like the Montehues. Close-knit, they argued as loud as they yelled their adoration for one another.

He'd been threatened by each of them, from Lord Robert down to ten-year-old Ela. Even a waddling peasant woman gave him the evil eye, warning him to treat their lady right. What would it be like to be, no—he shied away from finishing that thought. Love was not for the likes of him.

"There you two are!" Petyr said loudly, clapping a heavy hand on Nicholas's shoulder. "It is time for the toast, before I get tossed into the fire."

Nicholas would have liked to offer comfort to Celestia, but did not dare. He had let her get too close already, which was dangerous.

Lord Robert bellowed, "Get on with it, eh? What gift was so grand that you had to wait until everyone was drunk?" He laughed loudly, as did everybody else, even Celestia.

"He has a good point," she whispered up at him with

a wink.

Nicholas saw her heart-shaped face in shadow, and the refracted brightness of her eyes. He had to stop being such an infant. He grunted for an answer, as if that would put up a barrier between them. At least, once he had exacted his revenge from his "father," Celestia would be left with property. The thought eased his guilt over knowing he would leave her—by death, or pilgrimage, either way.

"Here, here," Sir Petyr shouted, getting everybody's attention. "I have a gift for Sir Nicholas and the Lady Celestia, from the baron himself. For years I have been the baron's man, but starting tonight, I am, along with the five men with me, swearing my loyalty to *Lord* Nicholas of Falcon Keep!"

The crowd cheered, and Nicholas realized that his value had just risen. He had a beautiful wife, a keep with land, and now he had his own men.

For a fellow who only wanted revenge and the honor of dying with his soul intact, he was doomed.

"We leave at first light," Sir Petyr said, grinning proudly. "Your new home awaits ye."

"Aye, dawn it shall be," Nicholas agreed. Maybe sometime during the four-day journey he could get Petyr drunk and finally get some answers.

Celestia was the only one not cheering. Their eyes met, and it seemed as if she completely understood what he was feeling. They were being drawn tighter into a web they hadn't spun, so strong that they couldn't break free.

Forrester, Bertram, Willy, Stephan, and Henry all gathered round. "Hip hip, hooray! Three cheers for our new lord!"

Nicholas smiled, as he was expected to do. Sweet Jesu, he even gave a speech as gallant as any he'd ever heard before. And while he thought to argue with Petyr's announcement, he realized that it mattered not. The sooner they left, the sooner he could force Baron Peregrine to atone for all he'd done.

He placed another brick of blame at his *father's* absent feet.

Celestia watched her husband make his way through the throng of people. He did not push, or shove, and yet a path cleared for him as he stalked toward her. The scowl etched onto his face did not scare her, as she assumed was his intent. Saint Blessed Mary's virtue, but the fierce expression made her blood race and her thighs tremble.

She'd not felt the like before, and the feelings were as exhilarating as riding bareback into a rainstorm.

Mulberry wine had soothed her nerves, leaving her languid and giggly. Most assuredly, she was not in the mood to be a lady. Born to run a house, she'd learned the basics, as her interest had lain in medicine and not accounts. She was the most gifted healer of her generation, and so allowances were made. She hadn't had a chance to explain her abilities yet to Nicholas. Mayhap this evening.

Her lips tingled as she remembered the pressure of his mouth against hers. It was only the second amorous kiss she'd ever received, and it hadn't been the sloppy wet mess Lord Riddleton had bestowed on her, when he'd unwittingly caught her in the stables alone. The chance meeting had changed her mind about marriage entirely.

Shaking off the humiliating memories, she tilted her chin as Nicholas approached. She thought she saw a touch of panic in his gaze, but when she blinked, it was gone. The look had been replaced by a studious coldness that stopped her mouth from wanting.

"We must talk."

"Yes." She bowed her head.

"Is it true that you have two wagons packed for the journey?"

That was the problem? "Aye."

"It will slow us down, and make us a bigger target for thieves. I've not the men to defend a caravan. I will not have it!"

His anger surprised her, and she looked up. His gray eyes were black with emotion, and she backed up a step.

"I know you said to bring only the essentials, but I need two wagons."

He said nothing, just winged a dark brow upward. Celestia caught a glimpse of desperation in his stance as he crossed his arms. "Those things such as linen sheets do not just make themselves, my *lord*," she emphasized. "Nor do the pots and pans simply appear, or food stuffs—my infirmary alone will take an entire wagon, and I won't leave without it. What if the herbs I need don't grow where we are going?" Hoping she sounded reasonable, she reached to put her fingers on his arm, still avoiding his bare skin.

His eyes narrowed dangerously, and a thrill settled over her as he stared down. She squealed when he grasped her by the waist and set her up on a stone half wall, so that they were nose to nose.

"We are married, aye?" His deep voice rumbled through her body, and she found herself barely able to nod an affirmative. His fingers stayed at her waist, and Celestia imagined them so hot they might burn through her dress.

Her breath quickened.

His eyes dilated in the moonlight.

Would he change his mind about abstaining? Yes, she thought, parting her lips the merest bit. Then she shook her head, clearing it of all carnal thoughts. Pushing his arms away from her body, she jumped to the grass below. "We are married, 'tis true, but we desire an annulment, remember?"

Nicholas tightened his jaw. "I remember well. The sooner we leave here, the sooner we get to the border."

Celestia was grateful for the dark evening, hoping it hid her embarrassment. Of course he'd only wanted to hurry their journey along so that he could get on with his real life's goal. Spain. A life where she'd be left in ruin because he refused to even try to love her.

"I've studied a map of the area, and it looks as if once we arrive at Falcon's Keep, Peregrine Castle is but a day or two away. I'll go."

He was going to leave her there, at the keep? Alone?

"My brothers are at the castle. I shall ride with you, then," she stated, not wanting to admit her fear of being abandoned with strangers. People did not always judge her kindly at first.

"My journey requires but me, besides the servants will need to get to know their new mistress. It will not take me long. I promise to look after your brothers." His dark eyes were hiding something, but Celestia had no idea what. The man had more secrets than the forest had trees.

"The servants will not need to know me, not if you get the annulment granted. Then I can return home."

"Then you will not need to pack over-much. Why must you argue?"

"Why must you boss me? I know my own mind! And Nicholas, you are not well enough to travel a week on the rainy roads." Without thinking, she reached out to grab his wrist. "It could be dangerous, and you could relapse, then you'll be sorry I didn't have my herb—"

As her hand clasped his scarred skin, her fingers received a chill so cold her teeth immediately started to chatter.

She saw the concern on Nicholas's face, but she was unable to speak. An odd sense of disembodiment caused her to sway first to the left and then the right. She'd had some wine, but she wasn't drunk. No, no, she thought with a groan. Another vision so soon? Why had she touched his bare scars, knowing that his pain affected her so strongly?

It seemed as if Nicholas's voice came from far away as she sank to the grassy ground in a swoon. Fog and ghostly murmurs swirled through her consciousness, and it was as if she was being warned away from Nicholas.

Warned away from Falcon Keep.

Or was she being drawn toward it?

"Celestia, what's wrong?" The sound of Nicholas's worry made her struggle toward awareness, but it was impossible to shrug off the icy touch of the otherworld.

It was rare to be visited by spirits—it hadn't happened since her grandfather had passed on a few years ago. She had not been afraid, not of him, and when she'd told her family the next morning that Grandfather had died but sent a message of love for them all, her odd announcement had been accepted as fact.

Her grandmother had bowed her head in prayer, asking God to let the old badger into His heavenly home, then cried buckets of tears. The message confirming his death came a sennight later.

This was not the warm spiritual embrace of her grandfather. This was frightening and strange, and she felt as if she should be listening for some sort of message. Which was made more difficult with everybody around her talking so loudly.

She blocked them while opening her mind to accept a glimpse of her future, whatever it might be. With Mary Magdalene's courage bolstering her own, Celestia reached for the clouded image, searching for answers. The journey ahead would be difficult, but she couldn't get a clear vision of why. Damn fog, she thought irritably. It was not natural.

The tantalizing scent of apples calmed her, but then suddenly, out of the murky edges of her subconscious, she visualized an arrow shooting forth from the woods. It whistled as it catapulted through the thick air, setting Celestia's nerves on alert. Oh, no, she thought, turning in slow movements, realizing that she could be too late as the white feathered arrow flew straight for Nicholas's heart.

The shaft was already covered in blood.

Terrorized by the vision from which she could not run, Celestia opened her mouth and screamed with all her might.

When she came to, she found herself bundled in Nicholas's arms and he was rocking her to and fro, whispering soothing nonsense into her uncovered hair.

Leaning her cheek against his fast-beating heart, she realized that his tunic was soaked with her tears. What must he think of her?

"Perhaps you could tell the baron that I am mad? 'Tis a good reason to grant an annulment," she whispered against his muscled chest.

"This is no time for jesting," he answered hoarsely. "What happened to you? You sounded so afraid, and you were calling my name."

Her sister Ela piped up, "I told ye she was having a vision. Ye should not have touched her."

"Vision?" Nicholas released her as if she had a contagious disease, and Celestia tumbled to the grass. She felt his instant fear of her, and her heart broke. The connection between them was gone; he most likely thought her possessed or some such nonsense.

Sir Petyr quipped, "Tame her fast, my lord, afore she faints again!"

The crowd laughed good-naturedly, whispering excuses for her behavior, such as too much to drink or a bride's nerves. Celestia drew herself up and brushed the pieces of grass off of her gown with impatient strokes, not daring to look at Nicholas. She'd worked so hard to gain the respect of her people. 'Twas always difficult to let strangers get to know her and understand that she was not such a freak after all.

She scrubbed her cheeks with her palms, feeling her grandmother's hand at her back.

"Not to worry," Nicholas said in such a stone-cold tone that Celestia's stomach knotted and she knew what he was going to say before the words ever left his lips.

"My lady will have plenty of time to rest, as I am leaving her here when we journey in the morn."

Heart cracking into tiny shards, Celestia admired him for his misplaced sense of honor. So what if he thought her crazy?

Mayhap she was.

She only knew that she could not let Nicholas travel without her. Even if it meant giving up her healing gifts, she could not let him go alone.

Summoning the last of her bravery, she put her hand on her hip and accused like a seasoned fish-wife, "You don't get your way, my lord, and already you think to leave me behind?" She clucked her tongue loudly and turned to face her parents and the rest of the spellbound group. "He expects me to leave without my herbs and, and . . ." the tears that came were not so forced after all, but greatly gained her the sympathy she needed to play this off. "And he says I cannot take my own horse!"

The expression on Nicholas's face would have been worth remembering, if only she hadn't been so damnably worried that he would die before learning to love her.

Chapter Four

The last servant finally left the chamber, and Nicholas's shoulders eased. "I was afraid your father was going to gut me before he took his leave," he said, staring at the closed door.

Celestia, dressed in a silk gown so sheer he could see the outline of her skin, laughed nervously. Candles cast a warm and cozy light; mulled wine spiced the air and shadows from the small flames in the fireplace chased one another on the tapestry-covered stone walls. Nicholas had the sense he was dreaming; the sort of dream that exuded goodwill, just before the jerk of the hangman's noose.

"Would you care for some wine?" Celestia offered him a silver goblet; she was as tempting as Eve must have been with the apple.

"Nay. We leave early in the morn, and I would be clearheaded." He wanted to know what had happened out there, if she'd really seen something, or if he'd just been duped into marriage with a crazy woman. The entire manor could be laughing at him. Was she really a—?

"I am not a witch," she said firmly.

"Do you often have these," he scratched the back of his neck, "visions?"

Celestia sipped before answering, as if weighing her words. "No. And Saint Paul knows that I am not good at receiving them. Sometimes they are clear, and sometimes," she paused to take another drink, "they are not."

"You invoke the Saint of Truth," he huffed. Nicholas had seen enough of the world to understand there were things that were not understandable. His Truth was that he'd lived in hell, and had not once heard from God or Satan, or any of the damn saints. "The vision tonight, it involved me?" He would know if she was playing him for a fool.

"Aye." She shifted uncomfortably, perched at the edge of the bed. "But it was not right."

"You called my name." He paced forward, challenging her words. He would believe, if there was but proof. "What did you see?"

She bit her lower lip, and he could tell that she lied. "Nothing, it was mostly just a sense of danger, a warning, mayhap?"

Disgusted, he folded his arms across his chest. "Why play this game? Do you want people to think you a witch? That you have magic in your fingertips . . . for fame? Coin? Why?"

"You are shouting," she said as she put her goblet on the

small side table, and he swore he heard hurt in her voice.

He slowly lowered his arms. "Fine. Explain to me what happened this evening."

"I cannot." She pulled at the neck of her gown. Was she too warm?

"Stubborn wench, how can I trust you when you lie?" *It was definitely hot in the chamber.*

"Baring my soul to you, sir, will gain me nothing but misery." She stood, and Nicholas took an involuntary step back. There was something about her that made his mouth dry and his palms damp.

"What does that mean?" *What made women lie as if it were naught?*

"Only that you will not like, nor believe, what you hear. I have worked very hard to make a place for myself here, in my own home."

"'Tis your parent's home, my lady, and your place in it is different now." He narrowed his eyes, wondering at the heightened tension between them. She stirred him. It was as if someone was fanning the flames of desire for the sole purpose of it burning wild, and out of control.

God's bones, but the sight of her standing up to him ignited his blood more thoroughly than any drug ever had. Heat coiled through his lower belly.

Her eyes widened and she swallowed, her breaths coming faster beneath his stare. "We agreed to an annulment," she said on a ragged whisper.

"I know." But he couldn't think of all the reasons they should *not* be together; instead he stared pointedly, envisioning the kiss they'd shared that afternoon. The pull of lust alluring for the first time in a long while, he thought of all the ways he could teach her to kiss him, to hold him. She flicked her pink tongue over her full lower lip, her eyelids heavy. He was aware that she had no idea how heavenly she looked. The heat between them ratcheted another notch until he could stand it no more.

"*Angel.*" Nicholas reached out and grabbed her by the wrist, pulling her to him until her mouth was beneath his. He kissed her as if his life depended on it, and if she did not return his passion he would fall into a spineless puddle at her tiny feet.

His surprise was great when he felt the push of her warm tongue against his lips. Her hands rubbed the sleeves of his tunic, as if she would strip him of it. Up, down, the fabric slid against his flesh until the heat of her fingers bumped against the ropy scars on his wrists.

A zing so hot it felt cold made him pull back, and she cried out, as if in agony.

"What?" Nicholas panted. "What was that? What is the matter with you? You've seen my scars, I thought that you didn't mind them, I . . ."

"It hurt," she said, her face pale, her eyes without the familiar sparkle.

"It didn't." The realization of what she'd said came slow.

"It was hot, dark, you were hurting terribly."

Nicholas's desire ebbed, but the intense feeling was replaced by fear. "What do you mean?"

Her eyes filled with tears that sparkled like gems upon her lashes. "You were hurting. You were being made to feel the highest level of pain, on purpose. I'm sorry, I am so sorry, Nicholas." Tears tracked down her cheeks.

Horrified, Nicholas lashed out, "You know nothing about my life, pain or otherwise." His basic instinct was to protect himself, and his secrets. He put his hands out, symbolically pushing her away. "Close the neck of your gown. If you want to act the whore, I am happy to oblige, my lady. But if you wish to return to this house as pure as when you left it, then I suggest you keep your hands to yourself."

The blood drained from her face as he insulted her over again. "Or we can consummate this farce of a wedding, and I can leave you at Falcon Keep. God knows, I'll not stay there! You can take as many lovers as you like after I'm gone."

"What? Why are you saying these things?"

His energy depleted as fast as it had spiked, and he raked his hand through his hair. "Stop crying, your tears will get you nothing. I will sleep in front of the door. No one will come in."

She dried her eyes, but refused to adjust her gown. Her shoulders were proudly set. "My heart is breaking for you. Can you not trust me?"

"You've already lied to me once!"

"I didn't lie, exactly. I saved your life."

Cold spread through his body. "And I've saved yours. We shall see who made the better bargain."

One small gasp escaped before she covered her mouth with her fingertips. "You can be cruel. Is that where the darkness comes from?"

"I'll not talk more about it. Sleep, and in the morning

we will pretend this never happened."

"I am not tired," she said stubbornly.

Nicholas exhaled, then picked a pastry from the platter. The idea of taking a bite made his stomach turn. He didn't want to hurt her, and he would, if she stayed with him. "I don't want you to come with me." She would ruin everything. She made him want to live, and he had to be prepared to die. It was not his first choice, but a man needed to look at all the options.

"You are not leaving me behind, Nicholas."

He saw that she was serious, and he remembered that she had a stake in this game, too. He'd saved her from being burned as a witch, but the baron still held the lives of her brothers. "No wagons, then. I am in a hurry."

"No wagons?" She bit her lip. "One wagon. I will take my book of recipes, and my kitchen plate. And my clothing, simple as it is."

"We will have no cause for anything fancy," he yielded.

"And here I thought you would take me to see the king," she retorted in a voice dripping with sarcasm.

His temper faded a little more at her show of spirit.

"Lucky for you, sir, that I've never desired to go to court. My plain gowns serve me well."

Nicholas had noticed that she wore little in the way of adornment, other than the bells on her shoes. Since the wedding had been the only occasion needed for something more stylish, and since he was wearing her father's tunics because he had no clothes of his own, he hadn't felt in a position to judge. "One wagon."

She smiled. "Thank you. Nicholas, about that kiss . . ."

Closing his eyes, Nicholas knew he would remember both kisses for the rest of his life. They'd been so good he dare not have another. "We are getting an annulment." He opened his eyes, walked in front of her, and made certain she was listening. "We will follow through on the plan, and we will each get what we want."

"My brothers will not be freed until I have a baby." She looked up at him with trust. How could she? She was blindly placing faith in him, and he didn't deserve it.

"Don't worry."

"That is easy for you to say, you are hiding something. You can trust me, Nicholas."

He heard the plea for an olive branch in her tone, but he couldn't give it. If she betrayed him, it would mean his death. His death had a purpose if his soul was ever to be his again.

"Can we try to be friends, at the very least?"

Sighing, Nicholas shook his head. "Caring for you is dangerous to me."

He was surprised when she laughed out loud. "Really? You are not the only one who is risking everything."

"I want to believe," Nicholas cleared his throat but the lump remained. "But there is nothing. Get some sleep, Celestia."

"I will keep your secrets."

His stomach tightened at her breathy promise. Another woman had made lying promises, and he couldn't take the chance. Celestia solemnly pulled back the coverlet on the bed. "There is no need to sleep on the floor. I understand that you do not want me."

Not want her? Christ, Jesu. His eyes dropped to the pink buds of her breasts beneath her gown and the way her loose golden hair curled over the curves of her hips. She was the epitome of womanhood, and so beautiful he ached. He gulped and looked away before he did something stupid. Like lunge across the bed and truly claim her.

His voice was raspy as he changed the subject entirely. "Petyr said that the Scottish rebels are creating havoc along the borders. The baron probably thinks a show of colors will suffice to make them stay clear of the keep."

She didn't appear to hold a grudge as she stood by the bed. "Ah! That does make sense. By sending you he sends a warrior as well as his son, who has a rightful claim on the property." Celestia faced him, unaware that a long tendril of silky hair cupped around a full breast. The sheer gown teased the senses. The heat rose in the room as they gazed at one another until Nicholas ground his back teeth and paced the floor. *Witch.* If there was anything magical, it had to be the instant desire between them. Ancient chemistry, male calling to female.

Keeping his eyes on anything but his bride, Nicholas talked as a distraction. "The baron probably thinks I'll be grateful for his interference in my life. He doesn't know me." He pushed up the sleeves of his tunic, which were scratching at the irritated skin on his wrists. "The bastard has much to answer for."

"And Petyr, will you give him a chance to prove his loyalty to you?"

Nicholas stopped before the fire, his eyes on the dancing flames. Putting together a story when one had only torn pages was difficult, but he'd finally gotten Petyr to admit that he'd never worked for Abbot Crispin, and that he'd always been Baron Peregrine's man, until now. The betrayal of his mentor burned, and he absently rubbed the scar at the base of his throat. "I trust no one."

A waft of oranges and cinnamon warned him that Celestia was at his back. He remained unyielding as he felt her hand at his shoulder. She slid around so that she could see his face, and he made sure to keep his expression neutral. "Try me," she said in earnest. "I'll not betray you."

"You would be the very last person I would ever trust." He held her gaze until her smile faded. It hurt him to see the wounded look in her eyes. *She is innocent,* his heart cried. But in his head, he knew there was no such thing, and he had to protect himself. "Go to sleep."

Celestia dipped her head before returning to the raised bed. Climbing in, she sat against the headboard, making a commotion, smoothing the blankets around her waist. Nicholas felt the pulse beat at the base of his neck as he waited to see what she would do.

Opening her mouth as if she might argue, again, she paused and then shrugged. "You must do what you think is right. Will you sleep? I could make you a—"

"I want nothing, my lady." His chest tightened at the lie, and he placed a chair in front of the slowly dying fire. "Our secret will be safe, until we are ready to make our move." He sat, compelled to listen to the soft rustlings

Celestia made as she got comfortable. It felt like he was spying, since he'd never slept in the same room with a lady before. Leah, though female, was definitely not a lady, and what they'd done together didn't involve sleep.

His stomach churned, and he banished the dark memories to the back of his head. Thinking of that evil woman in the same breath as Celestia was sacrilege.

He waited until he heard her even breathing before taking a fur rug and stretching out, as he'd promised, in front of the door. Dozing fitfully, controlling his wayward thoughts, he passed the night through.

At the first hint of dawn coming from the tiny slats of the window shutters, Nicholas got up. He couldn't help peeking at Celestia as she slept. Her delicate beauty drew him like a moth to flame, and he stared at her pink lips, lightly turned down at the corners. What might it be like to have the love of an angel?

He was turning into a sop, he thought angrily. Nicholas gave the bedpost a shake. "Get up," he ordered gruffly. "And don't forget to play along."

Celestia's eyes flew open, and he saw the bewilderment there. While they were different colors, and they certainly beguiled, he didn't think them evil. His sense of righteousness nagged him for his display of foul temper.

None of this was her fault. The baron thought nothing of ruining people's lives, and the attitude ran through to his men. Petyr had been dismissive of the baron's refusal to honor the Montehue's marriage dispensation, laughing that when Lord Robert had made the request twenty years ago, he hadn't had daughters that the baron needed.

"Pull back the covers."

She did, and Nicholas took a knife from the pastry platter, sliced the base of his palm, and smeared the bottom sheet. "It's done."

Celestia watched his actions in silence, saying nothing at all when he walked out the door. Feeling like a giant ass, he added the latest sin to the others, wondering if Saint James even *had* the power to be so forgiving.

He thought the manor deserted, but then the loud snores of warriors sounded from the main hall. In the monastery he'd had his own small cell, a place where he could be alone with his thoughts. To read, or copy works. Until he'd sworn fealty to the baron and agreed to lead the caravan with the sacred relic of Saint James to King Richard in the Holy Land, he'd thought to live a simple life.

Perhaps to marry a woman of the land, who could be his helpmate. She would bear his children, plant and weed his garden, cook and sew and plow, if need be. He'd tell stories aloud after their evening meal. They'd be content. And if, in his very secret heart, he'd ever envisioned this woman who might stand by his side, for certes she had not looked like Celestia.

Petite to the point of daintiness, regal in her bearing. Nicholas couldn't see her ankle-deep in oxen muck, following him as he plowed a spring garden. A chuckle broke free and he dropped his hand to his side. His life had changed much since he'd been that naïve young man. Now he knew the identity of his father. He had a keep of his own, men he couldn't trust, and a wife he hadn't chosen.

"What's so merry this morning?"

"Lord Robert!" Nicholas looked up into the suspicious face of Celestia's father.

"Where's my daughter?"

"Upstairs, sir." Uncomfortable with the man's stare, Nicholas adjusted the tight sleeves of his tunic, keeping the scars covered. It wouldn't do to make Lord Robert more of an enemy, and he owed the man much—even though pride was hard to swallow. "I don't know how to thank you, Lord Montehue, for all of your kind gifts." Nicholas set his jaw and continued, "I had but robes at the monastery, and just one left of those. I will repay you as soon as I am able."

Lord Robert puffed out his barrel chest. "'Tis nothing but a few tunics. I can't have my Celestia marry a man with no clothes. Verily, the greatest gift I gave you was my daughter, and you'd best take care of her with your life's last breath." Lord Robert's bushy blond brows came together as he scowled. "You and your father have given me no reason to trust nor like you, and would be to God that I knew why the baron insisted upon a hasty wedding. But know this—if my daughter comes to any harm under your watch, I will hunt you down and kill you myself, baron or no."

Well said, Nicholas thought. He held the man's gaze without flinching. "I will keep her best interests at heart, sir."

Lord Robert exhaled and gave Nicholas a slap on the back with enough manly camaraderie to knock Nicholas forward a step. "Good. I agree that it would be safer traveling with one wagon, instead of two. It's already done, and loaded with fresh provisions. Women. They can't move into a new household without half of the old." Robert pulled on his mustache, leading the way out a side door, which took them to the front of the manor. "The baron's letter mentioned an injury?"

"Yes. How did you know I only wanted one wagon?"

"Deirdre told me, and you don't question the women in this family. Crusader, eh?"

Nicholas kept going, confused. He'd been sleeping in front of the door; for certes he'd have noticed if Celestia had left the chamber. It was impossible.

"Did you see the king before you were brought down?"

The man was like a starving dog after a ham hock, but Nicholas refused to speak of his time as a prisoner. That was his shame alone, and one he could not share with another. He stepped faster.

"Petyr says that you were a hero! Escaping prison and making your way home from Tripoli. Where was that injury?"

Nicholas decided that he'd spent enough time alone with his father-in-law. "I never met King Richard. Neither the baron, nor Petyr, were there to judge if I was a hero." His vision blurred with hot anger, but he tamped the beast down. "The wagon's packed, you say? I'll go hurry Celestia along so we can be off." Nicholas walked away from Lord Robert's probing with as much dignity, and speed, as he could.

He interrupted a flurry of activity. The bedsheet, with its telltale stain, was off the bed. Deirdre was crying and patting Celestia's shoulder, while the grandmother, Lady Evianne, quirked a red brow in his direction before turning back to the maid. "Bess, do not forget Celestia's embroidery hoop."

"But, Gram," the youngest girl said, "she doesn't—"

"A lady has to keep her hands busy, Ela child. Do not argue. Oh, and Bess, tell Viola to get the spices from Cook. I had her prepare a few blends, just until . . ."

Ela snickered, and Nicholas wondered at the joke. "Until what?" he asked.

"Nicholas!" Deirdre cried at the sound of his voice, "my son, come and sit by me."

Sitting down next to his sobbing mother-in-law didn't seem wise, but he couldn't ignore her order. He leaned over to give her the kiss of greeting, and she smacked his cheek. "There," she said with a brilliant smile, "for causing my darling pain. But now! Welcome to the family." With that, she burst into fresh tears.

Nicholas backed away, glancing at Celestia, who was biting her bottom lip. Galiana was outright laughing, her pretty eyes glittering with mirth. "Mother is very upset, this is all so sudden. And who but Celestia can soothe Mother's migraines before they begin?"

He'd feared going insane, and God help him, there had been times when being crazy would have been easier than living with reality another day. Now that he was witnessing insanity with his own eyes, he had even more reason to fear it.

"Nicholas?"

He turned away from the mayhem as he heard Petyr call his name.

"Pardon me," Nicholas said quickly as he walked to the hall and peered out. "Petyr!" He lowered his voice, hoping that nobody had heard the momentary panic. "Petyr. Lord Robert says the wagon is already packed. Are the men ready?" He could not survive another round of tears and laughter and keep his wits.

"Yes. Cook has laid out bread and meat; we can eat and go over the map. I'm concerned with the stretch of woods between—"

"Hold." Nicholas looked back into the room, where five pairs of feminine eyes stared expectantly at him. "Ladies? I must go." Nicholas, unsure of what to do next, sent them a half bow and quickly urged Petyr away.

"Coward!" Lady Evianne called after Nicholas's retreating figure. "Not that I blame him. Deirdre, your emotions go willy-nilly. I think you terrified the young man."

Celestia finally released the laughter that she'd been holding in. "His expression when you welcomed him into the family was most amusing. But you need be kind to him, Mother."

Deirdre wiped her eyes. "Aye, I've gained a son."

"Mayhap." Celestia jumped off the bed. Dressed for riding, she just needed her lightweight cloak and hood and she was ready to leave. True, she hadn't wanted to wed, but since the marriage was to be annulled, it shouldn't count against her when it came to losing her powers.

She'd have to ask Gram. Rather, she was embarking on a grand adventure before coming back home to Montehue Manor, possibly disgraced. *Thrilling.*

Besides, how could she let Nicholas sacrifice himself on her behalf, and then let him walk into danger, unaware? The man trusted nobody. It was up to her to save him.

She would prove that her gifts were God-sent, and then he could stop looking at her like she was the village idiot. Her stomach tightened. She much preferred when he looked at her like she was marzipan and chocolate and he had a sweet tooth.

Nicholas. She'd woken once, and found him stretched out on the floor, just as he'd said he would. It had been comforting to fall back asleep knowing she had her own gallant knight to protect her.

Celestia glanced around the corners of her room for any last small thing she might have missed.

"Mayhap?" Her grandmother tapped her on the shoulder. "That sounds mysterious."

"I simply meant that one does not know what the future will bring." Celestia peered beneath the bed one last time.

"Did you have another vision, 'Tia?" Ela asked, her braids wound around her head like a crown.

"You've never had so many in a row. I was worried, but Mother said being married can bring on all kinds of maladies." Galiana handed Celestia a corked bottle with a bow around it. "Did you remember any of it?"

"What's this?" Celestia untied the bow. "You know

how the visions can be, unclear or nonsensical. I am sure it was nerves, and nothing more," she fibbed. If she told her family that Falcon Keep was swathed in danger, they would lock her in the dungeon infirmary and never let her go, despite what the baron could do.

She took the cork out and the trapped scent of orange and cinnamon, her very own fragrance designed by her talented sister, was released into the room. Her heavy heart lifted. "Gali, thank you! No one can make perfume like you. I thought you said there were no more oranges?"

"Cook found some at market three weeks ago and I've been hiding them ever since. I thought to give this to you at Christmas, but . . ." Galiana sniffed and blinked back tears.

Celestia reached up to hug her sister. "This will remind me of you and home whenever I open it."

"No tears!" Deirdre pronounced, her arm slung around Ela's waist. "'Tis time for our last meal together as a family." She started to cry again. "My oldest daughter, a woman, and leaving me. How can I stand it?"

"You will live, Deirdre," Lady Evianne advised sagely. "I smell ham and toast, and I'm famished. Let us go before the men eat every last crumb."

Celestia's stomach rumbled, and she assured herself that it was from hunger and not apprehension over plunging into the unknown.

"Well before midday," Forrester said with a straight

face. "And we are on the road. Not quite the first blush of morning like ye'd hoped, eh?"

Petyr grunted, while Nicholas ignored the impertinent young knight. Trying to get these women done with their good-byes and out of the manor was enough to make him want to run back to the monastery, and forget all about revenge. Who needed a soul?

He tucked the canvas down over the back of the single wagon, his shoulders tight. Lord Robert had been more than generous with the household stuffs, and Nicholas added more guilt to the burden he already carried. Jesu, leading another caravan, with knights wearing the baron's colors of blue and gold, was not something he'd ever thought to do again.

The toast and ham rumbled in his belly.

Nicholas continued down the line, checking the packhorses along the way. Horses. He didn't recall having a horse, but he must have ridden something to get here—not that he remembered any of that. He turned back to Petyr. "Which horse is mine?"

Forrester, who had been standing next to Petyr, suddenly found the clouds of great interest. Petyr's cheeks reddened beneath his beard as he gestured toward the sway-backed nag that Nicholas had passed by. "There."

"That is my mount?" The toothless horse looked well used, and ready for pasture. A far cry from the stallion he'd ridden off to war on. What had he been thinking? "I had better walk, lest I kill her."

Forrester pursed his lips and refused to meet Nicholas's gaze. Petyr said defensively, "You were drunk, though you don't remember, and wanted a poor beast that could carry you on your way to Spain in the most humble manner. You chose her."

Nicholas coughed behind his hand. "I was drugged, Sir Petyr, and out of my mind, as well you know." He was getting tired of looking the fool, but Fate was not finished with him yet. "If I thought she was good enough for Spain, then for certes, she should be good enough for Falcon Keep."

The mare neighed obligingly before lifting her tail to piss. Forrester could hold his merriment no longer and burst out laughing until tears ran down his cheeks.

Nicholas stole a quick look at Celestia, who was leaning down from her glorious white mount and whispering in her father's ear. Lord Robert looked over toward the nag and laughed as he waved to one of his squires. He whispered something to the man, who walked around to the Montehue stables.

The squire came back, leading a large brown stallion with a glossy chestnut mane. Lord Robert took the reins and said loudly, enjoying the moment, "Lord Nicholas! My daughter has asked that she be allowed to give you a wedding present. If it were up to me, I'd say to let that old nag carry you as far as she will before she falls over dead, but 'Tia, she has a softer heart."

Lord Robert handed the twin strips of leather to Nicholas. "Here's your gift!" he said so all could hear. "Remember I will kill you if you hurt her in any way," he whispered for Nicholas's ears alone.

Nicholas tried to return the horse, but Lord Robert

would not take it. "Celestia raised the stallion from a foal, when we all thought he'd die. Beasts or people, she heals them all. He is hers to give to whom she chooses."

Embarrassed, Nicholas turned and sucked in his breath. The sun broke from behind a cloud, shining upon Celestia, who sat atop her mare as if she were one with it. She could be the mythical goddess Diana astride her white horse; all she lacked was a golden bow and arrow. Why, dear God, couldn't she have been fat or plain? He didn't want to think about his wife as if she was a desirable woman. He shouldn't care that he preferred her hair long and flowing, as she had worn it last eve, to the tight braids she had now, coiled about her head.

"I thank you, Lady Celestia. The stallion is generous, indeed." He paused, then reached beneath his shirt and pulled out his rosary. It was the only thing he, Nicholas Le Blanc, personally owned, and he'd once considered it a talisman against evil. If he'd had it on crusade, mayhap his men wouldn't have died.

"Take this. It was my mother's." A shadowy memory pulled at him of a woman with dark hair, and apples for Saint Vitus's sake, but no more.

Celestia reached down with a slim, gloved hand to accept the polished wood cross on its worn beads. "Your mother's? Nicholas, I cannot accept such a beautiful gift."

He narrowed his eyes, daring her to give it back and add to his public shame.

She straightened abruptly and slipped the chain over her head. "You are certain?"

"Aye," he said curtly, his heart unaccountably tight.

"I will cherish it. Thank you."

She sounded sincere, but how could she care for him, even the smallest bit? He'd done nothing but make a fool of himself in her presence. He'd hardly shown her the side of him that was strong and worthy; instead she'd seen him ill and angry and confused. It seemed his destiny was to be his lady's jester. But only for a short while more, and in the end, she would have Falcon Keep.

Patting the white mare on the neck, he walked back to the magnificent stallion. "Does he have a name?"

She sent a look of approval toward him that went directly to the place his heart was supposed to be.

"Aye, I call him Brenin, which is Welsh for 'king.'"

"'Tis perfect." Nicholas spoke a soft greeting to the animal before mounting. Being of Welsh descent would explain all of the red hair amongst them, he thought, noting that Lady Deirdre was knotting a linen handkerchief between her hands as she cried

He accepted the blame for the family's upset, on his father's behalf, simply because it strengthened his own need for revenge. Nicholas could hardly tell the Montehues that their darling daughter would possibly be a widow soon, and returning before summer's heat. Brenin shifted beneath him and he cantered over to Celestia. "We must leave if we are to reach Middon before dark."

"I am ready," she said, holding her body stiff. "I have said my good-byes."

It was difficult, but Nicholas denied the spark of pride he felt toward her. Worried he might say something he'd regret, he turned his back on her and rode to the front of the line.

The wagon rolled into place, driven by Sir Geoffrey, a graying Montehue knight whom Lord Robert had insisted go with the wagon. Viola and Bess, Celestia's two maids, sat next to the man on the bench seat.

He whistled, and the men he couldn't accept as his own flanked the wagon. Stephan guarded the rear, while he and Petyr took the point. Celestia trotted in behind them. Nicholas's gut ached with tension and memories that wouldn't die, even though the men in them were nothing but bones in the desert.

The fast clip-clopping of another horse came around the wall and Nicholas reached for his sword—only to find he didn't have one. Oh, aye, he thought bitterly, I am certainly ready to protect this caravan and all of the people with it.

Bertram, noticing the impotent gesture, tossed his own sword over. Nicholas had not held a weapon in years, yet he caught the heavy weight of the hilt as he'd been trained. "My thanks," he nodded with a frown.

"You'd slay me?" Lady Evianne, clad in riding clothes and astride a black mare, laughingly joined Celestia at the rear. She looked strong and stubborn, and Nicholas noted the similarity in the grandmother and granddaughter's daring, oval eyes.

Lady Deirdre moaned, while Ela grinned from her perch atop the stone half-wall surrounding the manor. Lord Robert muttered something, but it was Petyr whose composure visibly crumbled. "Nicholas, Baron

Peregrine specifically said he wanted you to make haste. I have overlooked the wagon and the servants, but the old dame? This is too much!"

Sighing, Nicholas patted his stallion's neck. Petyr grossly overstepped his authority, and Nicholas quickly weighed the consequences of a public reprimand against the need for Petyr to take over once they reached Falcon Keep. He had to have Petyr and the men to help guard the little caravan, and later to care for Celestia whilst he brought justice to Peregrine Castle. He did not expect them to fight the baron. This was his quest alone.

"Nicholas?" Celestia questioned.

She would be forced to follow whatever order he gave. He understood too well what it was like to do something against one's own will. Choosing between Petyr or his temporary wife, it made more sense to allow Petyr his way. Yet he said, "I see nothing amiss for a member of the family to join our party." Nicholas met the green-eyed glare of Lady Evianne. "You will keep up, won't you? Or you will ride in the wagon."

"I will be no hindrance, sir knight."

"I thought not, my lady."

Petyr grunted and Nicholas let his hand hover near the hilt of his borrowed sword. It would not do to call the knight out in front of every man here, but Nicholas knew that a reckoning would come. Petyr clamped his lips tight, then, snapping the reins of his mount, he led the way onto the road leading through town, and beyond.

Chapter FIVE

Celestia waved until she couldn't see her family anymore. She was surprised at how many of the peasants had come to see her off, as well. Wee Timmy had even brought her a bouquet of dandelions and a plum tart from his mother.

She longed to tell them all that she would be back, but she'd promised Nicholas she'd hold her tongue.

Her tears were gone, and she was empty of all but stubborn determination to keep Nicholas alive until they got the annulment from Baron Peregrine. Nicholas would not be allowed to sacrifice his life for hers.

She reached for her grandmother's hand. "I should do the mature thing and tell you to turn back, but I will not. What made you come? Did Mother know? For certes, this will not be an easy journey, and who knows what we will find at the end of it. With my luck of late it will be naught but a broken pile of stones."

"You forget that I was born and raised in Wales, my dear, this is nothing to me. For over sixty years I have lived and never did I shy at an adventure." She chuckled and pointed to Petyr's stiff back. "He may not approve that I joined the party, but I do not mind. It is you that your sister and I worry over, so I decided to come along. Ela put my pack in the wagon, and she'll smooth things with your mother."

"Ela knew?" Celestia remembered what her youngest sister had said about Nicholas and his gray aura, but kept the information to herself. The last thing she needed on the journey was another evil portent.

"Aye, that child has something of my great granny to her. Eerie, almost."

"I thought that there was but one healer in each generation." *If I lose my healing gifts, Ela will be there to continue the line*, Celestia thought with a bit of self-pity. They don't need me.

"Ela is no healer. I do not understand all that she can do; it is hard to tell with her mischievous ways. She could be a saint or end up in the stocks," Evianne laughingly shrugged one shoulder as they cantered down the hard dirt road. "'Tis good that your husband finally put Sir Petyr in his place." At the sound of his name, the knight turned back and scowled. "Although I doubt he will stay there."

Celestia felt a thrill at the word *husband,* but didn't examine why. "I don't think Nicholas fears anything, including Petyr, or any of the knights the baron sent."

Evianne clucked her tongue as she always did when

teaching a lesson. "Look closer, Celestia. I would say that he lives and breathes fear."

"Hmm?" Celestia stared at the proud set of Nicholas's shoulders as he and Petyr led their little band of travelers. He turned his head to the left, then the right, his eyes taking in every rustling tree branch or falling leaf. He didn't look the least bit afraid. Nicholas was the epitome of knighthood, his borrowed sword resting at his hip but within quick reach of his fingers. The tunic Evianne had sewed fit across the breadth of his shoulders and tapered down to his thigh. The brown hose hugged his legs, and she remembered the muscles in his calves and . . .

Her skin warmed and she blamed it on the spring sunshine. The mindless travel as they followed the road allowed for plenty of time to consider Nicholas's past. What was it that drove him to be so very honorable? Celestia quickly tapped the wooden cross around her neck and promised to keep him safe. Whom she made the promise to, she didn't know.

"Celestia!"

Startled, she tightened her hands on Ceffyl's reins, and her mare neighed in complaint. "Aye?" she said on an expelled breath.

"I said that tonight we will sleep at Middon, are you ready?"

She hadn't given where they would sleep much thought at all. "Four days of travel, Godspeed, with two nights in beds, and two under the stars, unless we can find a barn or some such thing. Why would I need to be ready? Think you that we'll need our own sheets?"

She bit her lip, wondering if she could easily access the marigold powder to keep away fleas.

"I was not referring to unpacking the wagon. I was referring more to the wedding night?"

Celestia turned red. "Gram!" She'd never had reason to lie to her grandmother, but should she tell her of the plan to get an annulment? Mayhap Gram would help. She had the distinct idea that Nicholas might not approve, and since he had issues with trust, Celestia kept quiet.

Her grandmother gave her a knowing look. "I know full well that the marriage was not consummated last night. It was I who checked the sheet, and then I noticed the cut on Nicholas's hand."

Humiliation burned deep. "And you kept our secret because?"

"I would know why the two of you schemed together. An old lady's curiosity? You behaved as if you would be returning to the manor, instead of creating your own home."

Well. "Your eyes are sharp, but you are mistaken." She dropped her voice to a whisper and brought her mare closer to her grandmother's. "I but begged him to wait until we get to know one another better. I would not risk losing my powers over a love that might not happen. If I do not give my heart, then how can it be broken?"

Whatever else she'd been expecting, it was not the laughter that bubbled from her grandmother's lips with all the force of a spring flood.

"Hush! This is no jest, but a sound plan." Nicholas glanced back, his brow arched in question. Celestia waved her hand and waited until he turned around again before hissing, "What is the matter with you?"

"You think that you can fool with your fate so easily? You are married, Celestia. You must make your husband love you. And not just physically, although there is naught to fear, if the man is kind. The pleasures of the body are one of God's great gifts."

Heat rushed to her cheeks. "Married, yes. But in name only. We've agreed," Celestia said without looking at her worldly grandmother. She found it much more to her liking to focus on Nicholas's strong back. "Although the baron has vowed to hold Ed and Ned until Nicholas and I have a child," her belly warmed at what that act might entail, "Nicholas seems to think he can change the baron's mind."

"The baron is up to his arse in something," Evianne spat. "That old codger can't be trusted."

"I keep thinking it has something to do with our family history."

"Boadicea?"

"What else might it be? Nicholas has no family. His mother is dead, and he was raised by the abbot." She smiled suddenly and patted Ceffyl's mane. "What if this is something as simple as the baron realizing how much he's missed and he wants Nicholas as a father wants a son?"

"That old man just wants a babe who won't die. An heir to pass on his name to," Evianne said darkly.

Celestia heard the underlying anger in her grandmother's tone. "Have you met Baron Peregrine before?"

Her grandmother paused before nodding. "Aye.

There's never been a reason to tell the tale afore now, and I am not a spreader of gossip."

Goose bumps raced down Celestia's spine. "Yes?"

"Fifteen years or so ago, he called me to heal one of his wives. The third one, mayhap, although it doesn't matter. She and her babe died before I got there." She glanced toward Nicholas, then back to Celestia. "He told me that he'd been cursed. He wanted me to lift it."

"What? We don't know how to do that," Celestia's hands chilled even though the sun was warm.

"So I told him, so I told him, but he was torn with grief. Over the child, more so than the wife, but that is between him and God. Still, I'd never seen a man, then or since, so angry. I explained that we are healers. I told him," the Lady Evianne blushed, "that I was the last of my line."

"*What?*"

"What if he wanted to marry you? To stop the curse he believed he was under? Marry a healer, and perchance . . ."

The cold spread from her fingertips to her toes as she realized what her grandmother was saying. "It is possible, then, that he didn't know I was a healer, not until recently."

Her grandmother nodded. "We do our duty, pay our tax, and stay out of the baron's way. Your father trains many knights who serve the baron, which makes him more valuable than some of the other of the baron's lords. Mayhap one of those he trained talked of you."

"Heaven help us," Celestia slowly blew out an exhale. "Would he have married me off to ensure that the curse visited on him was not handed down to Nicholas?"

She frowned, shaking her head. "A child—he wants to know that his blood will not die out."

"'Tia, I am sorry. I wish I had the answers," Lady Evianne said, her voice wobbling.

"Do you believe in the curse?" Celestia caught the scent of apples, but just for a second and no more.

"I do not know the details of it, I was so frightened of him that night that I didn't want to stay and ask. But," she lowered her voice, "what else could kill so many women and bairns?"

Celestia straightened and scoffed, "Poor health, not enough meat or fruit—there are all sorts of things that can go wrong." Her shoulders slumped. "What are the chances of a babe bringing peace between Nicholas and the baron? Perhaps if he could learn to forgive whatever grudge he holds against his father, he might be happy."

"Do not meddle, Celestia. Instead put your mind on making your husband love you. You are married in the eyes of the Church and God, and if you would keep your healing powers, Nicholas needs to fall head over heels for you."

Only that? "I am doomed, then." Celestia flexed her gloved fingers around the reins. "For he keeps his heart under strictest guard. He has been sorely injured."

"Pah—you are thrice as strong as I, so doesn't that make you the finest healer in all of England?" Lady Evianne's brows rose so high they disappeared underneath her headdress.

Laughing, Celestia rolled her eyes at her grandmother's boast. "Mayhap."

"Then heal your man. Forget the baron, and take the happiness that is yours if you are brave enough to reach for it."

Courage was not the problem, Celestia thought as she gazed toward her husband. The white arrow she'd seen in her vision could have been a real weapon, or it could be symbolic of something else. She sensed that Nicholas was struggling within his own psyche for a balance of good and evil. Blood on the shaft of a white arrow could mean that, couldn't it? Chills raced beneath her skin, and she vowed to never let Nicholas out of her sight.

Petyr looked back at the women, then said to Nicholas, "Your bride and her granny seem to be having a lively conversation."

"Aye, I can hear." Celestia's sweet voice called to him, but he plugged his ears.

"Shouldn't you be using this journey to get to know your wife?"

Nicholas stared straight ahead, for his eyes wanted to do nothing more than gaze at the petite blond who, according to the law, belonged to him.

"She seems nice enough," Petyr said.

If Petyr was truly supposed to be "his" man, he had an odd way of showing it. Nicholas tightened his jaw. "I suppose. I don't want to know her."

"You married her—you can't just exchange vows with her and then leave her at Falcon Keep."

The man would not leave him be, so Nicholas cantered forward, thinking it to be a broad enough hint. He didn't wish to discuss the situation.

"God's blood! Is that what ye've planned? Is that why she's got more baggage than the king's court? Her servants, her gold plate—her grandmother, for pity's sake. You plan on dumping her there, alone."

Flinching at the accusations, which were exactly true and so were a direct hit, Nicholas's temper rose until he was close to exploding. The last thing he needed was to lose control. Knights did not lose control, or else they put the caravan at risk.

"Not alone. She'll have you."

Petyr grabbed the reins of Nicholas's horse, jerking them around so that Nicholas swayed on Brenin's back. "You can't do it. The baron wanted you to have a true marriage."

Nicholas snatched them back, damned tired of being told what his "father" wanted. Grinding his teeth, he leaned forward so that Petyr would hear every last whispered syllable. "Ever since I met you, you tell me what I can and cannot do. If you are to be loyal to me, then remember your place. I don't need a nursemaid."

Petyr's lips turned white with anger. "Your father never spoke of you until a few years ago, and then you went off on crusade. I'd like to think you were a real man, instead of the weak, disinterested fool you are now."

"Enough!" Nicholas punched Petyr square in the nose, his fist landing in the center of the knight's face with a satisfying crunch. "Mind your business, or be gone."

Petyr fell from his horse with a loud crash into the brush, blood streaming between his fingers as he covered his face with his hands. "That's twice now, damn you."

Satisfied that he'd made his point, Nicholas was surprised to hear a feminine shriek of anger.

"What?" he asked as Celestia quickly halted her mare and dismounted in a fluid jump. She seemed more concerned over the blood pouring from Petyr's face than any insults the knight might have been spouting.

"'Tis nothing," Nicholas said. "I warned him."

She glared at him, her light eyes flashing as she shouted, "Why did you do such a thing? And to your own man?"

Nicholas started to tell her the truth, that she was the cause of the fight, but halted his tongue. Celestia had turned her back on him anyway, and he watched with fascination as she ripped a swatch of cloth from her hem and bathed as much blood as she could from Petyr's face.

Then she stripped her hands of her gloves and tossed them aside, rubbing her palms together, as if creating a spark to tinder. She was humming something beneath her breath, and he swore he could feel a lick of heat from where she knelt in the dirt. When she put her hands on each side of Petyr's nose, the knight groaned, but not like it hurt—more as if the pain had eased.

Uneasy, Nicholas heard the snap as she set the bone. The bleeding stopped, as did her chant.

Petyr, his blue eyes wide with fear, scooted backward so fast that Celestia was knocked to her rear. Nicholas knew that the knightly thing to do would be to jump down from his horse's back and hold out his hand to help her up from the ground. Yet he was frozen.

"Are ye really a witch?" Petyr asked, his voice squeaking like a lad's.

"Nay!" Celestia reached toward him, but Petyr crawled backward on his elbows. "I am a healer."

Nicholas could see the hurt Petyr's question caused in the rejected slump of Celestia's shoulders. Still, he could not move to soothe her when he had more questions of his own. The hot desire between them, was it magic—not real? Had she attempted to bind him to her through lust? Nicholas straightened, his belly sick.

"Sir Petyr, please, do not be afraid. I am no witch that casts spells or lures demons to do my bidding." She got to her feet and brushed her reddened palms against her legs.

"She was born with the gift, blessed by God, you stupid oaf."

Petyr glanced at Nicholas, then to Evianne, then back to Celestia.

"One woman in each generation is blessed; however, Celestia is the most gifted, to my knowledge." Evianne sent Petyr a sassy wink, and Nicholas was amazed at the old dame's audacity. Her quick defense of Celestia broke the line of accusation he'd been following. Stunned, Nicholas realized that he may have witnessed his first miracle.

Or, Nicholas snorted, his wife was in league with the devil. They'd be the perfect match if such were the case—although if she ever thought to rule him with sexual power, there would be hell to pay.

Celestia was saying, "I have some water; we have but to wash your face, and you are good as new."

Then she turned her gaze to him, and Nicholas shuttered his thoughts so that she could not see into his head.

"So long as someone keeps their hands to themselves, you should stay that way," she challenged.

He dipped his head to her. Witch? Angel? It didn't matter. He looked down at Petyr and said gruffly, "Hurry, man, you lay about like you've never been tapped on the nose before. We must make haste if we are to reach Middon before dark."

Celestia was grateful when Nicholas broke eye contact. She'd been powerless to pull away from his dark, judgmental gaze. It was this very thing she'd thought to avoid last night when he'd asked about her vision. His jaw looked to be carved from hard marble; his posture was just as cold. Had she frightened him, as she had Petyr, with her gift? Her heart beat painfully against her chest, but she wouldn't show him that she was affected. She could be just as outwardly cold as he.

He hid his pain well, but she could detect it. And thanks to Gram's revelation, she searched for vulnerable fear, which she couldn't find in the set of his brow.

Could she live with her husband's hate? She lifted her chin defiantly. She was a healer, by all that was holy, and she would continue to use her gifts until they disappeared under Nicholas's disdain.

She made a running jump onto her horse, grabbing the saddle horn and pulling herself up. Not being tall, she'd had to develop upper arm strength that held her in good stead while she practiced with her bow and arrow.

She was both a woman and a renowned healer, descended of a Warrior Queen. If she couldn't cure her husband, then who could?

Petyr rose and mounted his horse, glaring at any who dared to stare. "My apologies, Lord Nicholas," he growled. "But liege or no, if ye think to tap me again without a fight, ye'll be sorry."

Nicholas said nothing.

Celestia refused to cower as Petyr turned his ire to her. "You may be a healer, or you may be a witch," he raised his hand to stop anyone from coming forward to defend her name, "but if I need healing again, I will thank you to let me suffer instead."

Lady Evianne snorted. "Fool. Let him know the meaning of pain, then. Are ye all right, 'Tia?"

The burn of rejection stung, and knowing that Nicholas witnessed it made the sting twice as painful. "I am."

"Liar," her grandmother teased.

Sir Geoffrey, Bess, and Viola all sent her an encouraging smile as the wagon lumbered forward. These were the people who understood her.

Maybe she was making a mistake, venturing so far from home. What skills did she have in running a manor? She did not make new friends easily. She should turn around now and—her family was relying on her to save her brothers. Catching sight of Nicholas as he checked the line, Celestia wondered if he realized they both were equally trapped by family and honor.

They rode in silence for a while, and Celestia's anger stewed. He could not possibly believe that she was a witch! Finally she could take no more, and she cantered forward. "Nicholas, wait, I would have a word with you."

"Not now," he said, turning his back on her.

"How dare you dismiss me?" she blurted in disbelief, her bare hands tightening around the leather strips in anger. "Do you think to treat me poorly, without giving me a chance to explain?"

His gray eyes were akin to chips of ice as he looked at her. "What makes you think that I would believe what you say?"

Ceffyl pulled short as Celestia yanked up. "You don't know what you are talking about."

"I will tell you what I know." He leaned forward so that his words were for her alone. "This caravan needs to find shelter before nightfall. The roads are not friendly after dark, and I would hate to put everyone at risk. I believe we are being followed, and until I know whether it is by friend or foe, we ride on a little faster. This is precisely why I didn't want any wagons."

Celestia fought the urge to turn around and look behind them. "That is your strategy? To ride a little faster?" Ceffyl, picking up Celestia's panic, sidestepped on the road.

He clenched his jaw and she saw him count to ten before he explained, "Stephan has circled 'round the back with Forrester to protect us from the rear. It could be nothing."

Or it could be the danger she'd envisioned.

"Get near the wagon," he instructed.

"Nay, I will be with you." She stared to reach for the pack slung over her horse's rear, but Nicholas took her hand and squeezed tight.

"Must you argue, now? I need to concentrate, and you are distracting me. Stay calm and do not alarm the others. We have but an hour's ride until we reach Middon." He gave her hand another warning squeeze before releasing it.

Chastised but not beaten, Celestia allowed Nicholas to ride ahead of her. He could think he was in charge all he wanted, but she wasn't going to let him out of sword's reach.

Nicholas could feel Celestia's eyes boring into his back like sharpened stakes. After his time in captivity, he no longer feared the unknown. It was the human element that had his healthy respect. Never once had he seen a spiritual entity, and heaven knew he had prayed for intervention with all of his might. The men who had held him imprisoned had done more harm than any ghost or demon could have, and when the men were finished, Leah was there with a different kind of torture.

He was none too proud to admit there had been times when he would have gladly traded his soul to the devil in exchange for death. In the end, he'd lost his soul anyway.

He glanced down at his wrists. The tight manacles

hadn't been the worst that had been done to him, although the scars served as a reminder to be on his guard. Against everyone, man or woman. Nobody could be trusted.

Nicholas had been allowing Celestia, with her fey beauty and her brave spirit, to affect him. It had been a blessing that she'd revealed her uncanny nature before it was too late and he found himself caring for her despite his vows.

Refusing to look behind him, even though his wife's anger was a tangible thing, he let his gaze drift over the green of the trees. There had been a time when he had not been vigilant enough, and Lord knew, he was still paying the price for his folly.

He did not believe in witchery, despite what he had just witnessed with his own two eyes. There were people trained in herbal medicine who could perform near miracles. One of the Saracen priests in Tripoli had been so talented that he'd kept Nicholas alive long after he'd been beaten in both body and spirit. Watching Celestia heal Petyr had thrown him back in time.

As if the thought conjured him from thin air, Petyr was suddenly visible in the distance. He'd gone ahead to find possible shelter. What was Nicholas going to do about his head knight? Sighing, he continued to peruse the area. He was going to put Celestia in Petyr's care, and go on with his plans for vengeance. That was all.

Nicholas lifted a hand as Petyr trotted toward him, already talking. "There's a smaller village, halfway to Middon. We can stop there, if need be. Set the tents in the fields."

Nicholas returned Petyr's curt message with a nod. He probably shouldn't have punched him in the nose, but the man would have to stop badgering. The pressure of being in charge rode heavily on Nicholas's shoulders.

He turned Brenin and rode to the back of the caravan, taking the glares from Celestia's servants as his due. They could be angry; they just couldn't *die.*

He heard the sound of pounding hooves and tensed his hand over the hilt of his sword. Relieved, he saw it was Forrester and Stephan racing around a curve in the road, with a boy thrown facedown over the rear of Stephan's horse. Nicholas stayed near the wagon and waited until the riders got closer. The boy was scruffy but dressed in the Montehue green.

Celestia, who had stayed right on his heels, kicked her mount and rode by him.

"Abner?"

The boy looked up, a grin splitting his dirty face. "Lady Celestia!"

Again, Nicholas was speechless as Celestia fearlessly halted Ceffyl near Forrester's large warhorse. Had she no idea how dangerous that was? "What is wrong? Release him at once, he's our stable boy."

Abner had already dropped to the ground, as agile as a monkey, Nicholas noticed with a pang. The boy glanced around, excitement in his voice. "Lord Nicholas, Lord Nicholas!"

"What have you?" Nicholas said, a reluctant smile tugging at his mouth even though he worried over the news. The lad could not contain his joy at being a messenger, yet he doubted Abner had run all day just to return a forgotten brooch or a glove.

Sprinting across the road, Abner said, "The Lord Robert, he sent me with a message—the baron's men, they came right after you left this morn! Hundreds of them, well, not so many as that, but there were a lot—"

"You've been following us all day?" Celestia led Ceffyl away from the large stallions before dismounting, and Nicholas was able to breathe a little easier, seeing her out of harm's way. "Here, drink," she said, handing over her leather waterskin without thought to her rank, or the boy's.

Abner stared up, hesitant to take it.

Nicholas was about to intervene, when Celestia clucked her tongue and put the skin in Abner's hand. "Drink, all of it, or you will be sick. Was I to save you over the winter only to have you ill now? I think not," she tapped her foot expectantly and Abner drained the last of the water before handing the skin back.

"Excellent. What news have you, now?"

Calmer, Abner took a deep breath and recited from memory, "I'm to tell Lord Nicholas that Crispin Monastery has been burned to ashes."

"What? The abbot?" Nicholas curved his hand to a fist.

Abner stammered, "He lives, my lord, but barely so. With Lady Evianne and Lady Celestia both away from the manor . . ."

"I'll go back," Celestia said, already turning for her horse.

"Wait!" Nicholas dismounted and knelt before Abner so that they would be face to face. "The monastery is gone? Why?" Dread filled him from the top of his head to the pit of his stomach. "They were good men.

Godly men." Better than he, for certes.

"Were there other survivors?"

Abner shrugged, then chewed his lip, as if trying to pull the exact words from memory. "The abbot says to tell ye that he thinks the baron is looking for something." The boy shivered and Nicholas noticed the cooling spring air, and the dusk that was falling like a scarf over a lamp. Soon it would be dark, and there was no time for them all to make it back to Montehue Manor safely.

Abner added, "The abbot told me that it's supposed to be a secret."

"Something is a secret? Or someone?" Celestia asked, staring at Nicholas.

Nicholas stood, his heart heavy. "The baron cannot be looking for me. He has sent me on the road he wants, and," he gestured to the knights who still wore blue and gold, "he even sent his own men to make certain I get there."

The knights protested that they'd sworn fealty to him, but Nicholas shook his head. "Why would the baron burn the monastery?"

"No!" Abner said, rocking from side to side. "No, the baron's men were there to rescue the abbot from the flames of retr, ret—" Abner's face reddened. "I forgot."

"Then who did it? Who is responsible?" Sir Forrester put his hand on Abner's shoulder, as if that would hasten the telling process.

"Don't know, the abbot just wanted to warn you, he said," Abner's eyes widened, "to beware."

Nicholas turned, staring at the woods around him. *Beware of what?*

Celestia did not care for the hunted look on Nicholas's face. "Well, that is a cryptic message, if I've ever heard one. Do you like puzzles, my lord?" She kept her tone light, and walked over to where Nicholas stood as still as a deer in the woods.

She slowly brought her hand to his sleeve and let it rest there, sending what soothing thoughts she could.

His cheeks were pale beneath his tanned skin, and she surmised that he was grieving for those lost or injured in the monastery. "I will go to Abbot Crispin, and heal him myself. In truth, mayhap we should all go back to the manor. It will be safer than pushing forward, with an unseen enemy at our backs."

"Nay," he pushed her fingers from his arm. "You belong with me."

"I will go," Lady Evianne said. "My place is there. It was a longing for adventure that brought me on this journey, and now I've had enough." She laughed. "I vow that Sir Petyr will be sorry to see me go, but I'll have Abner with me."

"Gram!" Celestia looked up at her grandmother, who struck a pose upon the back of her horse.

"This makes the most sense, and if we leave now, just Abner and I, we can make it to the manor before midnight."

"Thieves won't hesitate to strike you, my lady," Sir Petyr said in a strained voice. "I will escort you back."

"No, I won't allow it," Celestia said, worried for her grandmother as much as she worried for Nicholas.

"I beg pardon," Nicholas said firmly, "but I will decide who is going where."

Celestia stepped back and tried to hide her frustration. Having a husband was inconvenient, if one had to ask to speak first.

"Lady Evianne is needed at the manor. Abner is with her, and can help protect her, if need be."

"Yes, my lord!" Abner grinned and puffed out his small chest.

"Lady Celestia will stay with the caravan. Or have you forgotten what is at stake?"

Celestia willed herself to think of calming thoughts, white puffy clouds and sunshine dappling through the trees, so that she didn't yell and behave unseemly.

"Nicholas, what will a few days mean to the baron?" She kept her tone reasonable as she asked the question.

He answered with unnecessary sarcasm, "As if I know? We are pawns, and I will have answers from him. Sooner," he glowered and Celestia saw just how terrible he could be, "rather than later."

"I see." Her voice rose as she tried to make her point. "So you would send my grandmother home alone in the dark to satisfy your need for speedy answers?"

"Must you argue?"

"Yes!" Was he so focused on his own quest that he would send an old lady and a boy on their own through the night forest?

"Stop tapping your toe at me, my lady; the ringing

of those damn bells annoys me. If it means so much, Bertram can escort them home." He arched his brow as if she were being ridiculous.

Folding her hands primly at her waist, she breathed in deeply and said, "Thank you, my lord. That will be much more to my liking." She was not being difficult!

"It would be my honor to go," Sir Bertram said gallantly. Celestia saw that the knight had won Abner's admiration and her spirits lifted, just a little. "If we leave now, I can meet you by tomorrow evening," he said to Nicholas.

Celestia reached up to kiss her grandmother goodbye, tears blurring her vision. This was all happening so fast. Her grandmother's company had offered security, and without her, Celestia would be forced to make her way as a wife and mistress of the keep without help. Not to mention that she was now left with many unanswered questions regarding the curse on the Peregrine name.

Five days ago she'd had a vision, and now here she was on a path much different from what she'd planned for her life. Saving Nicholas, being forced to wed, coming to terms with her own dreams and desires, only to realize that she had to give them all up in order to save her family, and even Nicholas. It was all so overwhelming that she could cry. She bowed her head into the horse's warm side.

She felt the weight of her grandmother's kiss at the top of her head, like a blessing. "There is no turning back, Celestia. What's done is done. Make him love you."

"It is not that simple, for a man to love one such as me."

"You need to open your heart, 'Tia. Or how can love find its way inside?"

Chapter Six

Celestia stared into the flames of the large bonfire before her, squirming a bit on the log she was sitting on. The mouthwatering scent of freshly cooked venison made her stomach rumble and took her mind away from the tight knot of her marriage. Satisfied with her new plan, if she had but the courage to implement it, she tossed the last crust of bread into the fire.

At least her brothers would be safe.

She stood, stretching her back and glancing around the tiny village. They'd arrived just as dark was falling, and the villagers, who had been warned by Sir Petyr that they'd be coming, had already cleared an area in a vacant field for them. They'd shared their wood, and their water from the communal well. In return, she'd helped a woman in childbirth, and Nicholas, with some of his men, had hunted. The villagers were too poor for fancy weaponry, and seemed in awe of the men's armor.

Nicholas gifted them with fresh meat.

Her husband. Nicholas. Lord Nicholas Le Blanc. He was fascinating, but unpredictable, and he'd been avoiding their tent all night.

She tried, discreetly, to stretch her legs. The ride had been exhilarating, and a bit tiring—not that she would admit it. Celestia had always made it a point to keep up with her family, even if she had to work twice as hard.

Willy and Sir Geoffrey were laughing over mugs of ale, and she didn't know any of the others. The villagers had all gone to bed, and Celestia sorely missed the company of her grandmother. Especially since Nicholas was ignoring her.

Gram said that she had to make him love her. She scoffed, walking around their party's encampment. She lifted a hand to Stephan, Petyr, and Forrester, who were getting supplies from the back of the Montehue wagon, well, not the Montehue wagon anymore. It belonged to Nicholas, who'd stated that he preferred his own surname to that of his father.

Stubborn man, she thought with a surge of unwanted pride. The emotion brought to mind the heat that traveled between them like lightning, and she considered it might be desire; what if she acted upon that?

She was not schooled in the art of seduction. Her nerves bounced up from her belly to her throat at the idea. Nicholas was a handsome man, a worldly knight, who'd likely had scores of lovers. Would he find her innocence tedious?

It galled her to realize that she should have listened

more closely to those damn minstrels and their inane tales of love.

Sending a prayer to Saint Agnes, the patron saint of betrothed couples, strengthened her resolve until she remembered, with a laugh, that darling Agnes was the patron saint of chastity, as well.

Mayhap I'll have to resort to visiting the village wise woman for a simple love spell. Me, a magical healer, and I can't encourage my own husband's affections.

"We've readied the tent, my lady." Bess and Viola giggled as she came closer to the large green-and-white striped dome. Montehue colors.

Waiting outside, the two maids were fresh-faced and pretty. Bess, plump, and Viola thin. They'd flirted all day with the knights, and Celestia felt a pang of homesickness for her own sisters.

"Will you need us anymore tonight?" Bess asked, her full lips turned up at the corners.

"We will be right here, my lady, if ye do," Viola said, gesturing toward the fire that Celestia had just left. Turning back, she realized that while she'd been sitting there, the other members of their party had gathered elsewhere. Now that she was gone, everyone mingled around the fire.

She exhaled, wondering at why such a small thing could hurt. When would she be accepted for who she was? Ever?

"I'll be fine. Good night, girls."

"We've left out some sweet wine, and bread with cheese." Bess giggled.

"For if you get hungry, later." Viola dipped her head and blushed.

Then they bobbed their heads in unison and dashed away, their eyes bright with anticipation.

Celestia decided to find Nicholas before she went to bed, but found her gaze returning to the tent again and again. What was she going to do? In order to free her brothers from the baron, she had to produce a child. She sighed. Even she knew that meant having sex with her husband, which didn't require true affection.

She walked to where the horses were stabled and found Ceffyl, who was tied next to Brenin. The two seemed content. Celestia reached her hand out to the mare. "I haven't anything for you, my sweet."

Ceffyl neighed, as if in sympathy, and Celestia swallowed hard. Her anger at Nicholas seesawed with hope for a future, although his reaction to her healing ability, his rejection of her body on their wedding night, and his numerous other humiliations stuck in her throat.

She might not want his love, but she needed it in order to stay who she was.

Could she put on such an act that he wouldn't see through her façade? She was a healer, not a storyteller, she thought with a shiver of apprehension. And Nicholas's gray eyes were penetrating.

"Good night," she whispered to the horses. "Wish me well." They snuffled softly as she made her way to the tent she'd been avoiding.

Pushing the flap aside was hard to do.

The girls had outdone themselves, creating a bower

of romance within the fabric walls. Plump pillows and colorful blankets beckoned. A flask of wine sat on the table, and even though she'd already had plenty to drink, she picked it up and took a large, soothing swallow.

Then she stood at the entrance of the tent, holding the flask and watching her husband from afar.

He stood so casually by the fire, yet she could tell he wasn't at ease. Nicholas was tall, and darkly handsome. While her father had broader shoulders than her husband, Nicholas was trim about the waist and hips. The borrowed tunic flattered his physique. Petyr had called him a hero, back from the Crusades, and his injuries told the story of how beaten down he'd been—yet to live, how strong he must be. He was a knight, but he could read and write and he spoke of his youth at the monastery as if it were a haven. Who was Nicholas Le Blanc?

Warrior, or monk?

She huffed, feeling like a scavenger crow gathering what bits she could, since he wouldn't tell her anything himself.

He turned then, and his strong profile was shadowed against the flames. Her blood heated, just looking at him. What had happened to him, to wound such a man?

Celestia had heard stories, not that she took much stock in rumors, but sometimes there was a grain of truth amongst the lies. Her father thought that King Richard was a brilliant strategist, but a butcher on foreign soil. He'd muttered something about King Philip and King Richard and the fall of Sodom, and then he'd issued a warning that the king's own brother was not to be trusted. One of her father's friends had laughingly pointed out that in the royal family, nobody could be trusted.

She had no patience for politics. War was a man's game, and one she didn't fully comprehend. What good could come of death and mutilation? She was a healer, and determined to fix what England had broken.

Nicholas reminded her of a caged panther. She'd seen one once, all sleek strength just waiting for a chance to escape its bonds. Or perhaps he was more like the falcon of his mother's family. Strong, quick, and deadly.

Shivering, she vowed to do her best to make him love her. She'd be sweet of voice, quick of wit, and conscious of his comforts. She'd be . . . fortunate if she didn't yell at the poor man for not washing his hands before a meal.

Nicholas still stood with the others around the fire, but away from them, too. It took a moment for Celestia to realize that even in his relaxed stance, he was guarding the camp.

Why couldn't he trust the other knights?

Baron Peregrine's men, now Nicholas's men, were present, as was Sir Geoffrey. Nicholas said something, and they nodded. Stephan yawned and made a show of walking over to his sleeping roll near the fire. Viola giggled while she and Bess finished the last of the dishes, signifying the end of the evening. Two of the knights took their posts at opposite ends of the small camp, while the others readied for bed.

Nicholas's gaze touched upon each of them, as if making certain that they'd do their job to protect the ones who slept. He turned toward their tent, met her stare, and then glanced away as if she was just another chore.

He had no plans for bed, she thought with a start. She'd noticed, while healing him, that Nicholas fought sleep. Mayhap that was when his inner demons came to torment him. Saint Cosmos help her; she could make him rest.

Celestia glanced around the tent until she found the tapestry bag that contained small vials of her most commonly needed herbs. She never went anywhere without it.

Letting the flap drop behind her, Celestia grabbed the bag, unrolled the top, and reached for the vial filled with pure opium powder. "Perfect," she smiled, wanting to help him before he relapsed into fever. "He'll relax, and mayhap let me close enough to touch him. Then," her cheeks flushed as she imagined what might happen next. His lips to hers, his hands on her bare skin . . .

She swallowed, her fingers trembling as she took the vial and uncorked it. Taking a goblet from the low, square table, Celestia dropped a few grains inside. Just enough to make her husband get the rest he needed.

And if it made him amenable to sharing her pallet, then what of it? They were wed, and she needed to get with child even if Nicholas could never care for her. *But it felt wrong.*

Love or no love, at least her brothers would be free. Her pride ached at the thought of being without the magical power in her hands, but Gram was right. She knew enough herbal lore that she could earn her way, and still help others. Her throat was sore with repressed emotion, so she poured wine into her own goblet and took a sip.

She wanted so badly to find a common thread between them, so that they might have a future to knit together. He could be shy when it came to women. Mayhap he had another love interest, or, she sipped at the sweet wine until her head swam, mayhap the Crusades had left him unmanned.

Oh heavens, she pressed her hand to her rolling stomach. The baron had demanded a healer and a wife for his only son. Which had to mean . . . pity rose to the surface like water. She'd seen him, all of him, and he hadn't looked—but if there was something—something she hadn't known about?

Sweet Jesu, and all the saints. The healer in her wanted to mend what was wrong, while the feminine side of her wanted to feel his lips upon her own and heal him in a way that only a woman could. She stared at the goblet. *Where had that thought come from?*

Setting the wine on the table, she rolled up her bag and put it to the side, then she got up, determined to catch Nicholas's eye. How could she get his attention? How could she ask her husband if he couldn't perform as a man?

Suddenly the way he pulled away from her made perfect sense. His self -deprecation, the blackness and despair.

She smoothed her hair, then adjusted her tunic. Chewing a sprig of mint for fresh breath, Celestia faced the tent flap and told herself to charge out there and get her man.

Her slippered feet refused to budge.

It was just as well.

The flap flew open and Nicholas stood before her.

"Ah!" she shrieked, her hand to her throat.

He spun around, his hand on the hilt of his sword as he looked behind him. "Who's there?"

"No, so sorry, oh," Celestia cringed. "You startled me."

Nicholas turned all the way 'round, then let his hand fall away from the sword. "And you, me, my lady. I was worried that I'd walked into the wrong tent."

Celestia's knees were shaking so hard that she couldn't move. She gathered her courage. "We have the only green-and-white tent."

"'Tis bigger than some of the villager's homes."

"I noticed that, as well." Celestia could feel the hot color staining her cheeks as she watched Nicholas take in the tent's interior.

His jaw muscle clenched, and she saw anew that the floor was piled with thick, sumptuous furs and large pillows. The low table was covered in a crimson cloth, stacked high with food and wine. Saint Mary Magdalene's mercy, but it looked like she was planning a seduction.

Gulping her fear, and feeling especially penitent, she stepped in front of the intended wedding bed. She said in a high voice, "The girls, Viola and Bess, got carried away, my lord."

"You had nothing to do with this?" His ebony brow quirked.

"Nay," she answered, determined to get past her embarrassment and at least let her husband rest. "The bed is comfortable," her tongue tripped over itself at the double entendre, "I mean, if you are tired?"

"Your face has turned the color of one of the roses in your garden. Please, don't fret over what was done out of kindness." He stepped farther into the tent, and the flap closed behind him. A fleeting expression of panic crossed his face, and Celestia wished again that she'd paid attention to the minstrel's instructions on how to win a lover.

"There's drink," she said as she walked over to the table. She paused before pouring the sweet white wine into the goblet dusted with opium.

It was for his own good.

But she'd not seduce him while he was drugged. Celestia could not do so; it went against every moral she had. Her brothers would be saved another night, and it was more important that Nicholas get some sleep.

She would guard him herself.

The pressure to be someone she was not, namely, a seductress, fell away and she was able to stop her damnable shaking.

Turning, the goblet in her hand, she caught Nicholas staring at her backside. Her body immediately warmed, no matter her best intentions. She held the wine out to him until he reached forward and took it. Their fingers brushed, and the tingling returned. She recalled the sight of their joined hands during the wedding ceremony, and the feel of his lips against hers. Her breasts grew heavy, her nipples tight and sensitive to the linen gown beneath her tunic.

The room swayed. Had she thought his gaze cold?

The gray orbs were smoldering, like banked ash. What would those eyes look like once the fire caught, and raged out of control?

Celestia dropped her hand to her belly, her thighs trembling with desire instead of nerves. The reaction was so instantaneous that she didn't have time to rationalize her feelings, nor fight against them.

All she could think about were his hands caressing her bare skin. Would his chest be hard beneath her touch? She already knew that his body was covered with a smattering of dark hair, it had fascinated her—the way the curls crossed his chest, only to taper downward. She lowered her eyes and prayed that he couldn't read her unseemly thoughts.

"No." His voice was gruff, and it doused her feelings like a plunge into the lake. "I'll not have it."

It could be that he found her simply undesirable, that she was experiencing things he was not. Fate could be cruel, but she'd not lay her heart at the feet of a man who would trample it—for her, love and lust had to be one.

She lifted her chin and met his eyes, striving to find that cold place Nicholas lived in.

"Is the wine not to your liking?"

Nicholas brought the goblet to his lips, never taking his gaze from Celestia. She was like a dream, her pale beauty against the vibrant fabric behind her. He hadn't felt the hot burning of desire in so long, and yet these past two days, just laying eyes upon his wife brought him close to bursting. "'Tis nothing. The wine is fine, my lady."

Gesturing toward the low table, she said in a clipped

tone, "We have roasted hare, bread, and cheese." As if he wasn't there, she began unlacing the bodice of her tunic.

Nicholas fought for and found his self-control. "We should talk. I've told the men I would take first watch, but they forced me to come to, uh, you." He cleared his throat, his ears burning at the ribald jokes the men had made regarding the wedding bed.

He noticed her fingers knot a lace, and she muttered what sounded like a curse. Surely not? He did not know her well, but she was a lady, forced into a situation not of her choosing.

"It will be difficult to keep up the illusion of being wed, with so many witnesses." He took another drink of wine.

The tunic fell open, revealing a sheer linen undergown. Feeling perverse, but unable to stop himself, he stole repeated glances. The pink of a pert nipple was visible, as was the dip of her belly. She said, "I've changed my mind."

"What?" Nicholas's penis stirred at the news.

She pointed to the bed. "Would you sit, please?" Celestia shrugged off the tunic completely so that she stood before him in the practically invisible linen gown. He was reminded of the crackling, mind-numbing heat between them on their wedding night. It had taken all of his will to stand his ground then, and he didn't know if he was strong enough to do it twice.

"I don't think," he blustered, draining the remnant of his wine despite the bitter aftertaste. "I suppose that, well, the annulment can't happen if we consu—" she brushed by him on the way to the pallet, her hair a beacon as he choked out the words, "consummate our," she lay back against the pillows and patted the spot next to her.

His body told his head to take a jump off the nearest cliff.

He covered his face with one hand, as if that would block the image of Celestia supine before him, her unbraided hair spread out behind her. He croaked, "Why, have you changed your mind about us doing, er, it?"

She closed her eyes, mumbling something. Nicholas found himself enamored of her golden lashes as they fluttered against her porcelain skin. What would they feel like, if he ran his fingertips over them? Soft, delicate as silk. "I can't come to bed," he said, stomping across the tent floor and taking a seat on the single low stool, as far away from Celestia as possible. He crossed one foot over the opposite knee. "Boots."

Shifting, she rose to one elbow on her side, her gaze pinioning him. "Would you care for help?" She spoke slowly, her voice a melody to his ears. "I've not been prepared to be a good wife, Nicholas, but I am willing to learn."

He groaned and tugged the boot off his foot, then switched legs. Teaching, learning, lovemaking—no. "The annulment is for the best."

"But what if the baron says no? My family is relying on me to save them, and I . . . I have feelings for you, Nicholas, that I would be willing to explore."

Nicholas tossed the boot to the corner, then stood, his entire body humming with the need to bury himself deep within his wife's sheath.

He picked up a slice of bread and took a ferocious bite. "I am not worthy of anyone's feelings, my lady. I've told you before," he chewed and swallowed, "I am going to confront Baron Peregrine—"

"Your father."

"He is not that to me," Nicholas welcomed the anger that took the edge off of this unseemly attraction. "I will confront him, and you can return home, as pure as you are now."

The open expression on her beautiful face fell, and he wondered if she was keeping a secret from him.

"I am a healer, my lord, if, uh . . ." she stammered as she looked pointedly toward his groin, "if there is anything you want to tell me?"

Nicholas reached for the goblet of wine, but found it empty. Had she been implying that there was something wrong with his manhood? Come to think of it, her father had been asking many pointed questions, as well.

He saw her take a deep breath before she lifted her eyes to his. Nicholas coughed on a stone from the bread, wondering if he could choke to death on embarrassment.

"There is nothing wrong with my, er, parts." He took a piece of cheese, eating because he didn't know what else to do. His head felt fuzzy, and his tongue thick. He was desperately thirsty, so he poured more wine.

"I am so glad to hear it, my lord."

Was that a tremble in her voice? "My reasons for keeping you untouched are noble ones. Why do you tempt me with something I do not want?"

She sat up, pulling a blanket around her shoulders, the roses gone from her plump cheeks.

His fingertips itched to touch her hair, to trace the shadow between her breasts. Why did he feel like he would jump from his skin for the merest chance to be inside of hers?

His voice shook as he said, "I told you before that I won't be consummating this marriage, my lady. It doesn't concern you."

He'd not seen such a sudden flash of temper, as she exploded upwards from the pallet, her fists clenched at her sides. "Not concern me? Is this a new humiliation for me? You are so repulsed by my healing gifts that you cannot even lie next to me? I'd changed my mind about seducing you tonight, but now—I don't care if I ever reach beyond your cold exterior! I care not for your reasons, by God. What shall I tell my maids? That you are not a man? What shall I say to my family when I don't get with child? That I will never save my brothers because it is *none of my concern*?"

Nicholas gripped the goblet, taken aback by her anger, nay, not anger, fury. His own irritation rose to the fore in answer. "I am a man, my lady, but my own. I won't be dictated to—I married you to save you from being burned as a witch, not to beget children." He glanced at her from the corner of his eye. "It has nothing to do with your healing magic."

Her eyes widened, and she tossed the blanket from her shoulders as if preparing for battle. The shy lady he'd wed was nowhere to be found in the woman before him.

His belly clenched as she stepped closer to him.

"Am I too ugly for you?" Her eyes blazed blue-green, firing him to the core. Her hair swung like a golden curtain he wanted to plunge his hands through. "Too small for you?" She ran her fingers over her breasts, breasts that begged to be cupped, then down to her slender, flared hips, hips he could circle with both hands. She pinched her cheeks until they were pink again, as pink as the bud of her mouth. "Too pale for you?" She snorted with scorn. "Too *female* for you?"

"What?" At that prod, Nicholas crossed the floor in two giant strides. He grabbed her by the back of the hair and smashed his lips to hers. He lifted her by the hips and sank with her into the cushions, pressing his hardness into the covered apex of her thighs.

She wrapped her arms around his neck as if she'd been held in a passionate embrace a hundred times before. Her lips parted to accept his tongue. Responsive and sweet, Celestia was warm, she was lush, she was beautiful. Nicholas cupped the perfect mound of her breast, tweaking the peaked nipple underneath the linen gown. Had a woman ever smelled so good? He buried his face in her hair, then kissed each delicate fingertip on each of her hands. Orange, cinnamon, and opium.

Opium?

"No," he groaned, banishing Leah and her dark ways from his memories.

He rolled to the side, seeing Celestia smiling uncertainly at him, tempting him on purpose. The scar at the base of his throat throbbed. She had a knife. No, that wasn't right. Nicholas shook his head to clear it.

Celestia was not trying to kill him.

He was not a prisoner. This was not Tripoli. He was in England, and he'd almost lost complete control of this bizarre situation.

"Nicholas?" Celestia's eyes turned questioning. Had she felt his shame? Had her strange talents allowed her to see the blackness of his spirit?

He refused to look at her. He got to his feet, opened the tent flap, and made a large production of adjusting the front of his tunic and hose. He turned back. "There. That should satisfy whoever is asking about whether or not I am man enough."

He tied his belt. "You are free to tell them what you wish. I don't want you to have to be *humiliated*. And Celestia," he paused and tossed her a quick glance, "never do that again."

She'd not cried herself to sleep since the Lord Riddleton incident.

A thrashing noise pulled Celestia from a troubled slumber. Frightened, she clutched the fur around her shoulders and stumbled to her feet. Moonlight filtered through the seams in the tent, and she saw her eating knife on the low table. Bess and Viola had slept in the wagon, so as not to disturb the newly wedded couple.

Wincing, Celestia wouldn't tell them they needn't have bothered. The thrashing sounded again. Louder.

Against the rear of the tent.

What if it was a bear drawn by the leftover food? Grabbing the knife, she eased the flap open. She let her eyes adjust to the night, and listened intently for the next sound.

She heard panting, then a low growl.

Her body was poised for flight, or a fight, depending on the size of the animal. Celestia tiptoed around to the side of the tent, her eyes scanning the deep dark of night. A pain-filled yell came from her left, and she spun around, her knife out. Behind the tent? Without thinking of the danger, she ran to save whomever had screamed so. They were under attack.

Heart pounding, mouth dry, she turned the corner and then stopped in mid-stride. Nicholas was tangled up in a sleeping roll, one pale bare leg visible and glowing like the moon. Her mind quickly thought through and then rejected many ideas. Had he hoped to save her embarrassment by sleeping out of sight of the others, yet save his chastity by not sleeping inside with her?

Then his hips rolled beneath the blanket and her mouth went dry. Confusion surged as she stepped forward, the knife outstretched. "Nicholas?" she whispered. He rolled back and forth, as if trying to subdue someone. She stopped again and licked her dry lips. What if he wasn't alone?

What if he was with another woman?

Nay! He gave another muffled yelp, and she leaned down and flicked back the top blanket. Nicholas was gasping for breath, holding his hands in front of him as if they were tied together and he was shielding himself from a deadly blow. Celestia bent over to look, but nothing bound him.

"Nicholas," she said again as calmly as she could. When he was ill, he'd responded best to that. Just like she'd thought, he was on the verge of relapse and fever.

He spewed something in a foreign language, then whispered harshly, "You rotten bastards, let me go, damn you to all seven layers of hell—I'll not be your whore!"

Celestia hopped back just as Nicholas lashed out with his foot. She swallowed uncertainly. Nicholas's voice was choked and raw, as if he were fighting for his soul. The demons he fought were so real, no wonder he avoided sleep.

Dare she intervene?

"Damn you." He kicked out again, his brow furrowed as he fought his tormentors. She knew that he uttered words he wouldn't want anyone to hear. Her hand hovered over his head as she sought to calm him without disturbing his fight. Gram said that ofttimes a person worked through their tragedies while sleeping.

How many ungodly things had happened in the holy fight for Jerusalem? Tears pricked behind her lids as she spoke as soothingly as the situation would allow, "Nicholas, wake up. Open your eyes, Nicholas, you are safe in England. 'Tis only me, Celestia . . ."

She removed the fur covering from her shoulders and dropped it over his thrashing, mumbling form.

His eyes whipped open, and she covered her mouth to stifle a scream. They were twin pits of despair, eerily unfocused and thoroughly black. His hands were in fists, and his body trembled with rage.

"Oh, Nicholas." She was about to reach out to him despite the damage it would do to her own body, when Petyr, along with Henry and Stephan, came running around the tent, swords drawn.

"My lord," Henry panted, "we heard shouting."

Celestia realized that Nicholas was not yet capable of answering; he was fighting his way back to reality. She bent over him, shielding his body from his men with her own. She plucked the fur she had thrown down to wake him from his nightmare and wrapped it around her shoulders, affecting what she hoped was a feminine pose.

"I'm sorry, sirs." She looked down and giggled. "We were, uh, sleeping, and I thought I saw a bear in the trees. Please, go back to your beds, it was nothing."

She kept her eyes lowered, as if shy. With her hair loose and dressed in only her shift, she hoped that she and Nicholas had just perpetuated their lover status. She laughed adoringly and dropped to her knees to snuggle on the bedroll next to her husband.

"Sorry, my lady," Henry said, his eyes wide until Petyr cuffed him on the back of the head.

Nicholas blinked, and Celestia could tell he was coming around. She took his hand in hers and dropped a kiss on his nose. "The men are worried that you've been attacked by the bear I thought I saw," she giggled inanely. Somehow it sounded better when her sister did it.

He sat up, raking a hand through his hair. "I think ye knocked me cold in your exuberance," he laughed, then waved the men away. "As you can see, we are fine, although I think we might move back inside. Eh?"

He stood, and Celestia noticed Petyr realize that Nicholas was completely dressed. The knight flicked his eyes to her, but said nothing.

Nicholas pulled her to her feet and chuckled with the men. "I don't think I could get back to sleep," Henry snickered, and when Celestia sent him a disapproving frown, said, "I can take the next watch."

Petyr shrugged, not hiding his suspicion. "The fire's almost out."

Celestia tugged on her husband's hand, determined to get him inside the tent and get some answers.

Nicholas wiped a hand over his forehead, as if to clear his mind. "That phantom bear has me wide awake. Besides, it is only fair that I take a turn on watch. I've had my," he smiled down at her with his lips, but his eyes remained dark, "entertainment for the night."

Henry laughed appreciatively, which irritated Celestia, although she couldn't deny the statement without creating a bigger problem. For certes, this husband business was most annoying.

"Don't be so stubborn," Celestia pleaded with Nicholas.

Petyr smirked. "Stubborn? I say tenacious. The man is so single-minded that he doesn't see beyond the end of his rather large nose."

Nicholas sent Petyr a glare that didn't seem to affect the blond knight overmuch, as he grinned and walked away, taking the two other knights with him.

The entire time they had been talking, Nicholas had handily steered Celestia toward the tent flap. His fingers pressed hers, and then he kissed her forehead before shoving her inside. "Stay there, Celestia, and sleep. We can talk in the morn."

No, she thought rebelliously, watching the flap drop closed. She would give it an hour, and then she would go to him. They needed to talk tonight.

Chapter Seven

Nicholas stoked the low burning embers of the fire with a long stick. How much had she heard? Had he hurt her when she'd tried to wake him? Brother Mark had told him that sometimes he yelled clearly when in the throes of a nightmare, but other times he yelled gibberish. Gibberish. The man hadn't understood Arabic, thank God.

He smiled before remembering that Brother Mark might be dead. If Baron Peregrine had anything to do with the burning of the monastery, then—Nicholas paused in poking at the fire. Then, what? The baron was already going to die, in order to avenge the deaths of the innocent men on the caravan. Nicholas grimaced. There was death. The memories of torture were fresh in his mind, thanks be to the nightmare he'd slipped into. And then there was *death.*

He'd have to make the sacrifice to Saint James large

enough to cover a multitude of sins. He tapped a fiery log, watching the sparks fly upward. "Falling prey to the ambush. Losing the sacred relic. I should have been more vigilant." He tapped the log again, harder this time. "I should have fought Leah harder, from the beginning." His belly cramped with shame. She'd withheld food, and water—she'd kept him chained to a wall. Her husband's men would beat him close to death during the day, and she—she would come at night, an evil succubus with opium and sex.

He threw the entire stick into the small flames. He didn't want to see pity in Celestia's beautiful light-filled eyes. Vengeance moved him out of the clinging past. Searching his spirit for anything good made him ill, and he didn't have the strength to manage it. The idea of the baron's neck beneath his sword pumped his blood and got him moving. Revenge first, redemption later.

Pah! Being saddled with a wife, a retinue of knights, and a keep he would need to fortify for battle weighted him under with obligations. What would happen if he died without meting out earthly justice on behalf of Saint James, and, yes, Nicholas gulped over the lump in his throat, even God?

The fire lulled him into reliving his mistakes. Oh, aye, he thought with a heavy heart. He'd made a thorough accounting of where he had gone wrong, and losing the relic was only the tip of the stack. By not reaching King Richard, he'd compromised the win of the Holy Land—he alone had survived the ambush; the rest had all been slaughtered. His chest squeezed painfully. And worse, despite the torture she'd done him, he'd murdered a woman in order to save himself.

Nicholas sighed in weary defeat. It might have been better if he'd let her kill him first.

Abbot Crispin said he had to forgive himself, but each time he tried, he remembered how hot the day had been. The sand was in each eyelash and, God's bones, he'd been tired from drinking the night before.

He should have been paying more attention to the caravan, but he'd allowed himself to be lulled into a doze by the boiling sun and monotonous sand. He'd had one duty, to deliver the relic to King Richard on behalf of Baron Peregrine. The artifact from Saint James could turn the tide in a holy war!

He'd failed. Bitterly.

The memory, even now, was so real that he could feel sand gritted between his teeth, and smell the metallic scent of freshly spilt blood.

Nicholas threw on another log. His defenses were down tonight, more than likely because he'd started to open his heart to Celestia.

"Nicholas?"

He jumped from the log he'd been sitting on, his hand on his hip though no sword rested there. "What are you doing here?"

Her eyes beguiled; her smile tempted. Celestia was innocent and clean, and he didn't deserve the compassion in her gaze. "I brought water."

"Nay."

"Surely you must be thirsty?"

He was. He had been. Stubborn, he sat back down without taking the waterskin.

She sat next to him, smelling of oranges and cinnamon. He ignored the soft press of her arm against his as they sat, each staring into the low burning fire.

"You don't take direction well," he finally said.

"No," she agreed with what sounded like true regret in her voice. "That's never been something I've succeeded at, more the pity." She laughed softly. "'Tis the terrible truth that I am much better at giving instructions."

Nicholas chuckled, grateful that the darkness inside his head was retreating before Celestia's light.

"What are you thinking that has your brow scrunched forward, my lord?"

"None of your concern," he paused. "What did you hear?"

"Much that made my blood run cold, and then thirst hot, for the chance to avenge the wrong done to you."

"What? You would go to battle for me?" He drew back, studying her face.

"Aye. It was wrong, what happened. *She*, this Leah, was wrong, too."

Nicholas couldn't breathe. For what seemed like eternity, he was back in the cell again, being tormented for a sick bitch's pleasure.

The cool press of Celestia's bare fingers against the nape of his neck eased the panic, until he could control the direction of his thoughts. Then she circled her other hand around the scars on his left wrist.

Rape. Nicholas blamed the heat in his cheeks on

the jumping flames from the fire. His captor's wife had raped him repeatedly during his captivity. She'd needed a child to keep her husband from setting her aside, and since he was not providing her with one, she was willing to try other measures in order to save her own life. Lovely Leah, with the lush curves and ebony hair, had given him opium in order to control him, and then manipulated his body to achieve her goals. After nine months, she remained barren.

He remembered the tears that had fallen from her coal-black, almond-shaped eyes, how she had held him close to her and whispered her love. That was when he'd felt the tip of the sharp blade at his throat. He had perversely decided he was not ready to die after all.

"Nicholas," Celestia cried softly. "I am so sorry."

Something in her tone pulled him from his memories, and brought him back to the present. He found the courage to look at her, and his heart thumped as he saw the tears glittering on Celestia's face, twin rivers falling over her cheeks. The dancing flames colored her, surrounding her in a bewitched web. "I'm sorry, I didn't know."

The dread returned to the pit of Nicholas's stomach. "You could see what happened? Just now?"

She hiccupped, and brought her fingertips to her lips. The calm demeanor she usually wore like a satin cloak was gone, replaced by borderline hysteria.

"I, she deserved to die, praise be that you survived. She sedated you, and abused you, and told you that she loved you—I'm terribly sorry, Nicholas."

Uneasy over many things, the first being that

Celestia just saw his shame, that by touching him with her bare hands she could see into his inner self, made him back away. Mayhap he had been wrong, and she was a witch. He'd heard of those who could perform supernatural tricks.

"Sorry? Calm yourself. It isn't like ye did it, my lady."

She stood, wringing her hands as if she'd committed a crime and he was the executioner. The dread climbed from his belly to his chest.

"But I did, Nicholas."

He stilled. "You did? You did what?"

Crying, his wife said, "I drugged your wine, just a little, to help you sleep—and then told you that I cared—and I do," she dropped her hands to her sides. "I was going to seduce you, and then I could not, and then—between us, surely you feel the attraction there?" Her odd eyes reflected the flames of the fire.

He was in hell.

Nicholas felt the blackness racing for him like a swarm of sand beetles. He wouldn't bow under; he dare not. It had taken everything within him to survive it once. *She* reached for him, this demon witch masquerading as an angel.

"Be gone!" he yelled, and because that didn't seem adequate, he threw back his head and roared his rage to the heavens.

Celestia was no mewling, toddling babe afraid of her own shadow. But when a fat raindrop landed on her nose like a heavy spider; she squirmed in her saddle and bit back a feminine squeal.

By all the saints, she was exhausted. So tired that she would swear shimmering ghosts leered at her between heavy, wet tree branches and hunchbacked monsters lurked beyond every turn of the thin trail. She pulled her hood farther down over her forehead and glared at Nicholas's back.

He didn't seem to notice the rain that fell in solid sheets from the sky, the thunder that roared with evil portent, nor the wickedness that shadowed them in the forest. She wondered what it would take to bring him back into the world of the living. He'd hardly uttered more than a single word for the past three days, and she'd noticed even Petyr had grown weary of his lord's surly monosyllabic grunts and groans.

If it weren't so unbearably wet and mucky, she would walk alongside her mare. Her thighs had never been so sore. Her bottom was chafed and her back ached and it hadn't stopped raining long enough to be able to build a fire for either warmth or hot food.

Dry clothes? She made a loud noise through her nose, and Ceffyl gave a sympathetic neigh. The canopy of tightly woven oak and pine branches over the trail was the only thing that had kept them all from drowning. They'd been plagued by tortuous weather, broken wheels, and bad luck. She trained her eyes on Nicholas; at least her anger at her aloof husband served to keep her warm.

She probably had no right to be angry, she admitted once again. But Nicholas refused to let her explain what had happened. It would soothe her injured pride if she could slander his character, but she knew in her heart that he was a good man. She'd inadvertently done him a deep wrong.

Goose bumps raced up her arms, and a foul chill settled at her nape. Celestia looked over her shoulder and searched the trees, uneasy. Huffing, she told herself firmly that it was much too wet and miserable for spirits to be roaming the woods. Still, she slowed Ceffyl's pace, angling closer to the wagon and her shivering maids.

When Bess, who had been riding one of the packhorses in order to lighten the wagon's load, claimed that her horse had picked up a stone, it was Nicholas who had helped her down, as if he were a Knight in Shining Armor and Maid Bess the most delicate of women. She sniffed. If Ceffyl had been the one to pick up a stone, Celestia just knew they would still be hobbling down the trail, more the pity.

Even though Nicholas left Petyr in charge of the retinue, he partook of his share and more of the nightly chores. She knew, for certes, that he never failed to check on the group's welfare before he rolled himself up in his woolen blanket; not that he slept. She was reluctantly awed by his stubbornness.

How long could he continue to deprive his body of rest? He would close his eyes for no more than a quarter hour; it was as if he had trained his body to jerk awake the moment he fell too close to a true sleep.

What had Petyr called him? Tenacious? She smiled from the deep recesses of her sodden cloak. Nicholas had been charged with seeing them all safely to Falcon Keep, and that was exactly what he was going to do. Stubborn and single-minded, that was her husband.

Ceffyl started as a branch whacked her on the nose, causing Celestia to slide to the right of her saddle. She grabbed the pommel and adjusted her seat, lifting her eyes just as Nicholas looked back at the noise. He stopped, his grayish-black eyes shadowed beneath his hood, yet she could feel the probe of them as he ascertained her welfare. She raised a gloved palm to let him see she was fine, and felt strangely bereft when he turned and continued on behind Henry.

All of the horses were sliding on the muddy trail, and Celestia was surprised that the wagon had been stuck but once, not counting the time they'd stopped because the left wheel was broken. Bertram had caught up with them, but hadn't brought the sun.

According to Petyr, they were only a day's ride from Falcon Keep. She ignored a stab of homesickness and thought of a hot fire, warm clothing, and a decent meal. There would be a great hall with a large fire pit, and friendly servants. The castellan would be kind, and offer to stay on until Celestia could learn her duties at the keep. She'd been reluctant to arrive, but that was before she started to mold.

Celestia's teeth chattered, and it was not as simple as the wet, cold weather. Dread surrounded her like a fog, and she tried to pinpoint from whence came her fear.

She was old enough to know that most ghosts were a product of an overactive imagination or too much wine, but she was smart enough to accept that sometimes they were spirits bent on communicating, whether the person was willing or not.

Just then she heard a rustling to the left of the trees, and then she saw an arrow, a very real arrow, fly through the line of men. She heard Nicholas give a shrill whistle, saw Petyr slow his horse and turn, just as the arrow landed with a loud thunk in his saddlebag.

Thinking only of Nicholas, and her vision of his injury, Celestia kicked her heels into Ceffyl's flanks, shouting to Viola, "Get my bow and arrow! Bess, take cover, we are under attack!"

She accepted the challenge without thought of failure, catching the bow and quiver from her terrified maid, and notching the arrow as her father had taught her. A calm pervaded her body; she was quick, but not rushed.

Scanning the bushes and trees, she waited, but all was silent. Even the birds were hushed, which told her that the intruders, *human*, were present.

Celestia glanced toward Nicholas, saw him with his sword drawn, his face intent and hard. She abruptly turned her gaze away; she couldn't afford to be distracted by her husband, not if she was to save his life.

He sat atop Brenin like the warrior he was, his back straight, his eyes trained forward. It eased her fear for him, although her heart beat madly at the sight.

Sir Geoffrey was also armed with a bow and arrow, but hidden within the confines of the wagon covering.

Bertram, Willy, and Forrester had their swords drawn and pointed to the trees, protecting the wagon and the maids.

Celestia didn't trust the unnatural stillness of the forest. She could see that Nicholas felt the same. Petyr and Henry had slowly brought their horses closer, until they were almost all within the safety of the group.

Nicholas whispered harshly, "Where's Stephan? He should have been bringing up the rear."

Petyr made a move to see, but Nicholas held him back. "Wait. Give it a bit more . . ."

Celestia swallowed and her stomach tightened. The mock battles with her brothers hadn't prepared her for a real attack. She forced herself to think rationally and to listen deep. There!

Her arrow flew fast and true through the thick of the trees. They heard a scream, then a rustle of branches as they all stayed as if made of marble and waited. Would they be under full attack? Who would dare?

An arrow with white feathers, the same as was stuck in Petyr's saddlebag, flew with a whistling noise and landed at Ceffyl's feet. She heard Nicholas shout, "Celestia!" just as she let another arrow loose.

Petyr rushed his horse through the tangle of bushes and trees after the arrow, using his sword to forge a trail. They all tensed, looking around for the next point of attack. Where was the enemy? How many were there?

Three more arrows flew in quick succession from the forest around them. Sir Forrester, the one knight who'd shown her any kindness, dove into the trees after Petyr. "Beware, I'm coming for your head! Ya hoo!"

Celestia stood firm as an arrow nicked her cloak and buried itself inside the tough leather hide of the wagon. Sir Geoffrey's warning faded as the blood gurgled around the arrow in his throat. Viola was at his side before he hit the ground. Nicholas yelled, "To the wagon!"

They huddled there, in the rain, for what seemed like hours. Celestia's arms ached with tension from holding the bow in place for so long. They heard a rustling, and all prepared to fight, but it was only Petyr. And he was alone.

Celestia cried out, "You are bleeding."

Petyr wiped his face with his hand and grimaced in pain. "Aye, my lady, but 'tis only from the branches and thorns. I couldn't find any of them, the rogues."

Nicholas lifted a black brow. "Not even a bloodstain?"

Petyr wiped his nose with the back of his hand. "In this rain, it would have been washed away before I'd gotten to it. Bloody forest!"

Nicholas, his voice scratchy, faced the group. "I say we ride hard for the keep. We should be safe there." He turned toward Viola. "How is he?" he asked, pointing to the Montehue knight.

Viola stood and wiped her blood-reddened hands on her apron. "He's unconscious, but alive, Lord Nicholas." She started to cry, and Bess jumped down next to her. "I can drive the wagon. He can ride in the back, with Vi."

Celestia, her knees shaking with stress but still astride Ceffyl, instructed Bess to get her herbal bag from the back of the wagon.

"Aye, Celestia, you can ride in the back with your

man," Nicholas said.

"But I—"

Nicholas held up one of the white arrows. "It seems you have kept many secrets from me, my lady. I don't wish to hear them now."

By the time Viola had reduced her tears to hiccups, the remaining knights had made a pallet for Sir Geoffrey and Celestia had started the healing process. She cleaned the wound, but felt that there was a piece of feather, or shaft, mayhap, that she wasn't getting.

"I can do better once we reach the keep," she told Nicholas. He'd dismounted, in order to help lift Sir Geoffrey to the back of the wagon, and then he'd stayed close to her as she'd worked.

"What, you can't just snap your fingers and heal him?"

Celestia lifted her chin, mostly so that she wouldn't cry in the face of Nicholas's sarcasm. "Nay, which is unfortunate. Perhaps then you'd have proof enough to call me a witch yourself, eh?"

His eyes narrowed, and she swallowed hard but didn't drop her chin.

He pointed to her bag of herbal medicines. "You have opium?"

Hearing the underlying fear in his voice shook her to the core. She looked down and began fidgeting with the ties on the pockets of her bag. "Yes. 'Tis especially good for injuries of the eye, but it also numbs pain at the site of the wound." She looked up and longed to take away the haunted shadows in Nicholas's gaze. "I've recently learned something," she said cryptically, in case any but they two could hear, "about opium, and all of its derivatives, even poppy tea. If one," she made sure to speak calmly, as calmly as if she were talking about plum pudding, "has been taking it for a long period of time, then the effects change. What once ended pain, now magnifies it."

His right eye twitched, but he was listening, so Celestia repeated, "It is very common to give poppy tea to someone who is having difficulty sleeping. Many healers would offer this to a patient."

Would he understand that she hadn't been trying to poison him?

It looked as if he would say something, but then she heard Forrester and Bertram shouting in the distance. Celestia scooted to the edge of the wagon and jumped down, running after Nicholas and toward the sound of the voices.

They slowed to a stop, and she edged closer to Nicholas, grateful that he wasn't glaring at her, and grateful that the men had finally returned. All of them except . . . "Where's Stephan? He isn't here."

He flattened his lips, and then he leaned in close, close enough that she could see his ebony eyelashes. Her stomach knotted so hard she wondered if she'd be sick. "But he is, my lady. His horse returned him, while you were working on Sir Geoffrey."

Confused, she followed the direction he'd nudged his head. Stephan's horse was at the back of the line, calmly chewing grass. Something lay draped over the back of the horse, a shape covered by a blanket. The dead knight's hand could be seen dangling close to the ground.

"Oh," she brought her hand to her throat, hoping to stop the sudden surge of bile. "Are you certain? I could . . ."

Nicholas expelled a deep sigh. "You don't need to see, unless you can bring spirits back from the dead?" He didn't give her a chance to answer, as if he were afraid of what the answer might be.

"I thought it best if I didn't call much attention to it. We can give him an honorable burial once we reach the keep."

Celestia was oddly touched that he said "we." It was more than likely a slip of the tongue, but she would take it. She sidled closer. "Poor Stephan. He was at our rear? I haven't seen another person in days, and even then it was only a party of priests."

"This is empty, wet, miserable country," Nicholas said with the first bit of life in his voice that Celestia had heard in ages. "A small caravan seemed an easy target. Bastards. Once we reach the keep we can send out some fresh men to scour the woods and find the petty thieves who are responsible."

"Aye," Celestia found she had a taste for vengeance, too.

"It sounded like you hit one of them. They didn't realize they were attacking a wagon protected by the goddess Diana, eh?"

He actually chuckled, and Celestia's pulse raced.

"Where did you learn to do that?" Nicholas continued.

She wanted to drown in the sound of his laughter, or at the very least, give him good cause to laugh often. Her vision blurred and she looked away. "I stole my brother's bows when they first left to be fostered. I tried to make my own arrows, but ended up shooting one into the toe of my slipper. My father caught me, and insisted that my grandmother teach me properly. In Wales, it wasn't considered unladylike to know how to shoot."

"You are much like your grandmother, then."

Celestia snickered. "I am hardly a bit like my family, no matter how much I wish to be so."

Nicholas crossed his arms over his chest. "You ride like you are part of your horse, you shoot a bow and arrow better than most archers, you have the gift of healing . . . and I'm not quite sure how you *all* ended up with that stubborn chin."

Celestia paused and bit her lip, surprised that he had noticed so much about her when she thought he'd been preoccupied with other things. "Aye, well, I am hardly a goddess, at any rate."

"None of us should aspire so high, me thinks," he said, rubbing the back of his neck.

Celestia put her hand on his arm, careful to keep her fingers on his sleeve. "I was wondering what it would take for you to speak again. I feel awful that it took an attack, and the loss of one of your men."

Nicholas jerked away from her touch. "Not one of mine, really, one of the baron's. Why should I speak when I don't have anything to say?"

Celestia was almost sorry that she had ruined the fragile peace between them. But not sorry enough to stay quiet. "Conversation between people is a way to get to know one another, to build up friendships and loyalties."

Nicholas slid her a look of rebuttal. "And if I had gotten to know Stephan, then when he died, I could have hurt over the loss?"

Celestia blinked back tears, but blamed the blurriness on the rain. How could he be so unyielding? "Aye. And you would have the warm memories, mayhap, of a friend."

"His death is another black mark against my soul, and naught more. I should have been attentive, and not lost in my thoughts."

Seeing a chance, she took it. "It is no great surprise that your mind wanders as it does. When was the last time you slept?"

Nicholas inhaled loudly and then set his jaw. "That is not your concern."

Celestia bristled. "You do love telling me what is mine to be concerned over. We are married, you and I, and that makes you my concern."

She tapped her foot, glancing around to see that their conversation couldn't be overheard. "I will never tell a soul of your nightmares, and that is my promise to you. You need not fear me. I am a healer, as well as your wife. I can make you an infusion of valerian, lavender, and vervain that will help you sleep dreamlessly, no opiates, now that I understand. I have been praying to Saint Raphael the Archangel on behalf of your nightmares. You should pray to him, as well."

She bravely reached out to place her hand upon his forehead, bare skin to bare skin—knowing before he did it that he would pull away. "Trust me, Nicholas. You can."

Nicholas's expression slammed shut like a door in her face. "Nay, and I will not have this conversation again. We ride for the keep, Celestia. I told you before not to waste your wiles on me."

He was scared. She understood that. It didn't matter to her breaking heart. Celestia didn't bother trying to hold back her temper. Taking a deep breath, she shouted to his retreating back, "You are as stubborn as a goat, Nicholas!"

She stuck her nose in the air at the men's good-natured chuckles over what they assumed was a lovers' squabble and stuck her fist on her hip. Nicholas mounted Brenin and took off at a fast clip, spewing chunks of dirt. Her first instinct was to get on Ceffyl, and gallop behind Nicholas until she caught him good. She'd sit on him, and force him to listen.

Since she knew that wouldn't work, she'd have to settle for hoping that Nicholas fell off his abused horse. Maybe a dousing in the mud would change his attitude.

She didn't worry that he would hurt himself. His head was too hard.

Nicholas's adrenaline was racing through his blood like poison. He lived off of that energy, needed it so he could stay awake and alert even as he denied his body sleep.

Reaching Falcon Keep with all of his group alive had become a goal that seemed more insurmountable each day. The rain, and the misery of traveling slowly in foul weather, was enough to drive a person mad. While not completely crazy, he wasn't entirely sane, either, and the blasted rain didn't help.

He kept his body bent low over Brenin, pushing the stallion through the unknown trail. The horse was massive, yet fast—bred in peace, but born for war. On Brenin's back, it would take him but half the time to get to Spain, and deliver the baron's head to the tomb of Saint James.

Nay.

He'd not take Celestia's gift and use it for such a purpose.

He heard Petyr following on his heels and spurred Brenin on.

The blond knight was proving to be a valuable asset to their party, not that Nicholas would tell him so. *Damn it all, why had he sent Stephan to ride the rear of their caravan?* Stephan had seemed seasoned enough to guard them, while keeping a sharp eye out.

But those woods were strange. Nicholas felt a shiver trail across his shoulders. He felt it, in his gut, and wondered if the others did, too. Too bad for him that the one person who would understand what he was talking about, was the one person he had to avoid at all costs.

Strange or not, the threat to the caravan had been human—he'd heard the yell when Celestia had hit the enemy.

He had thought himself too numb to be struck with such strong fury. Nicholas had learned to disassociate himself while captured, and he'd not gotten out of the habit yet.

Sinking his heels into Brenin's flanks, Nicholas trusted the horse to find the right footing. It occurred to him that he trusted the horse more than he trusted anyone else, including himself.

The damn arrow had hummed practically beneath his nose and he'd twisted in his saddle, his first thought to protect his wife. He ground his teeth in frustration. By Saint George, she hadn't needed his bloody protection.

He had turned 'round only to find Celestia at the wagon, fearlessly defending their party. When the white arrow had landed so hard that it splashed mud up her mare's legs, he had thought he would choke on his terror.

He'd feared Ceffyl would throw her small, dainty rider to the forest floor and stomp all over her with those deadly hooves.

He'd waited in vain. Celestia had guided the large mare with naught but her knees, and the mare remained as calm as any war-trained battle horse. When would he learn that nothing she did was expected? Healer or witch or simply a woman?

"Lord Nicholas! Nicholas, slow down before you break the tired beast's legs, I beg you," Petyr called over the thump of the hooves against the mud.

Nicholas slowed to a canter, and the knight drew alongside.

"What is it, Petyr? I took point, you were to lead them after me. What are you doing on my ass? I'll have your head if the caravan is attacked again."

Petyr's mouth thinned into a straight line before he said, "The wagon is going to lose a wheel, or worse. Bess hasn't driven a wagon so fast before, and Viola is hard-pressed to keep Sir Geoffrey quiet, with all of the jostling. Your lady is guarding them. I'd trust her at my back."

Nicholas lowered his chin to his chest and exhaled, not wanting to think about Celestia in danger. She was fearless, and it terrified him. "This means that we'll be forced to make camp again, one more night."

"Probably so, but if you keep the lead at such a breakneck pace, it might be days before the wagon is fixed, once broken."

"You're right," he conceded. Nicholas gestured to the emerald green forest around them. "I keep waiting to recognize something, but I don't. I don't remember this road, and I barely remember my mother. I have a vague memory of a large, peaked tower and some apple trees. I think."

"I've never been to Falcon Keep, but your f—, the baron, sent a retinue of ten knights ahead. They were to prepare everything for you and your lady wife."

Nicholas perked up. He would feel much better about his failure with Stephan if he could get the rest of his people safely tucked away. "Think you then that there will be a welcoming party?"

"Aye, and why not?" Petyr relaxed a little and grinned. "A large fire, and dry clothes would be most welcome."

The weight on his shoulders eased. "I'll be happy having everyone protected behind solid stone walls. But you are right, I was going too fast." *Trying to outrun Stephan's accusing ghost. Or a different ghost entirely?*

He rubbed his face and caught Petyr staring at him. "What?"

Sighing as if he had the troubles of the world on his back, Petyr grouched, "Ye've shadows beneath your eyes so purple and mottled that you look like you've been in a fight. And lost."

Nicholas glared.

"I've never seen you sleep for long, and ye don't eat much. You kind of stay to yourself, eh?"

"And what of it?" Nicholas asked rudely.

"You married a fine lady."

"Not afraid of her 'magic' anymore?" He deliberately

lifted his upper lip in a sneer. The last thing he needed was a friend. Although the knight had proven himself over and over again on this trip, never shirking a duty, Nicholas couldn't afford to care.

Petyr grunted, and Nicholas wouldn't have blamed the man if he'd ridden off. Instead, Petyr explained, "That was most odd, Nicholas, but not bad, not evil, you know. It was more like," the blond knight stumbled over the words, "sunshine."

Nicholas hadn't been expecting that, and a snort escaped him before he reminded himself to leave the embarrassed man some dignity. "Sunshine?" He blew out a breath of air, but remembered well the warm feeling of Celestia's dainty hand in his during their wedding ceremony. "Aye, it is a bit like that."

Petyr shook his head, spraying drops of rain like a dog. "I wouldn't mind the sun about now."

"I don't remember the weather being this dreary when I was a child."

"You said you didn't remember *anything*." Petyr ducked beneath a branch before it hit him in the head.

"That's true. Do you have the map?"

"Nay, I left it with Celestia, just in case there was a problem."

Smart, Nicholas thought. He wouldn't trust the man completely, but mayhap he wouldn't dismiss him out of hand, either. "It's raining too hard, and it doesn't make sense to push on. We can go back, and decide on where to make camp. I saw a small clearing a ways back, just big enough to pull the wagon off the road."

"Whatever you say," Petyr said with a nod.

When they caught up with the wagon, Celestia had already found the little clearing and she was just setting camp. She had Henry and Willy starting a fire, or trying to, and Forrester, with Bertram, was trying to set up the green-and-white tent.

Celestia looked delicious, even dripping wet in the rain. Her hair had escaped her braids and hung in heavy locks down her back. Her dark green tunic was sopped through, and she'd spread her sodden cloak over the wheels, underneath the wagon.

"I doubt that you'll get a fire going," Nicholas said, guiding Brenin to a tree near Ceffyl. He dismounted, feeling as if he should apologize.

But once he started, he might not be able to stop.

"Negativity breeds negativity, or at least that's what Gram likes to say." She made a weird "humphing" sound, and proceeded to the back of the wagon.

Nicholas followed her, hoping for a private word, but Viola was wringing out wet blankets, as the wagon was not meant to be watertight, and poor Sir Geoffrey was practically floating in the rear.

"I'm sorry for being such an ass," he said loudly so that he could be heard over the thunder. Luckily for him the thunder stopped rumbling and his apology was heard throughout the forest.

Celestia poked her head out of the wagon. "I beg pardon?"

"I'm sorry."

She crawled out and peered at him, looking him up

and down. "Did ye hit your head? Are you hurt?"

He ground his back teeth. "Nay. And you don't need to look at me as if I've grown two chins. You were right. But that changes nothing, Celestia." She opened her mouth to argue, and without thought, he leaned in and kissed her.

Her lips were cool, but her breath was warm, and yes, she tasted exactly like sunshine. "I'm still off to see the baron, as soon as you're safe at the keep."

Celestia's eyelids lowered a fraction, and a spark of lust hit Nicholas like a rock upside the head. "How do ye do that? Nay, I don't want to know." He walked away before he kissed her again.

Forrester and Bertram, unable to erect the tent, had instead made a roof of sorts, like a giant green-and-white striped sky. The two looked most proud of themselves. Celestia, who had followed behind him, came to a sliding halt.

"Oh, my," she said with a gasp. "Well!"

Nicholas scratched the back of his neck, wondering how she was going to react to having her precious tent maligned in such a way. It looked nothing at all like the square bower from the night before.

He needn't have worried that she'd be upset. Celestia glanced up at the large portion of tent they'd somehow managed to affix to three trees, creating a ceiling over the wagon so that Geoffrey would stay dry. Then she took in the two sides that they'd hooked from the tallest branch to the ground, creating walls so the travelers would be protected from the worst of the wind. The other two sides of their camp remained open to the elements, which was wet and cold, but it allowed them a fire.

"Just perfect," she said with a smile. "Not at all the way the tent maker designed it, but this is much better. We'll be able to see who's coming, and protect ourselves from attack, as well as stay mostly dry, and out of the worst of the wind. Thank ye," she clapped her hands.

Perfect. Nicholas saw that she'd won over all of his men. Well, not "his" men, but his father's men. Which was exactly what he wanted. He scratched the back of his neck again. Wasn't it?

Before long, Petyr had crouched next to the low fire providing the only light and warmth in the dark storm. The confounded rain had reduced itself to spitting in sporadic bursts, and they were able to heat water to drink.

Sir Geoffrey moaned from within the wagon, and they all jumped. Viola sniffed, "I want to press on, afore something bad happens to Geoffrey."

Bess stared at Celestia. "Why ain't ye healin' him, my lady?"

"I'm trying," Celestia said, poking at a foul-smelling brew she'd concocted. "I need the right instruments, and a clean environment for surgery. I feel like there is something still beneath the skin. I heal him, and the wound breaks open again within hours. It could be the jostling of the wagon, but I don't think so."

Celestia's eyes clouded, and Nicholas could see how heavy her burden lay.

"We might arrive at the keep by dawn, if we're willing to put the horses and wagon at risk." Petyr's reproachful voice gave his opinion of the folly loud and clear.

Nicholas tugged at a loose hank of hair, wishing he had magic of his own. No wonder Celestia had gotten so angry when he'd mocked her; it *would* be easier to snap fingers and be done with it. "We can't chance the wagon breaking. Then Sir Geoffrey would have no way of getting to Falcon Keep at all."

Celestia stuck the tip of her finger inside the bowl, then put it to her tongue and grimaced. "'Tis true, more the pity."

"We must stay and make our shelter here, for the night." Nicholas waited for at least Petyr, if not Celestia, to argue with him, but neither did. Instead, all eyes went to the puny flames that fought for life beneath the drizzle.

Celestia set aside the stinky herbal medicine and rubbed her fingers together for warmth. "I've made a topical ointment for Geoffrey that will hopefully draw the ill humor out." She slowly got to her feet, every inch of her body stiff and cold. For once she was grateful for her short stature, as there was less of her to freeze.

Viola made to rise, as well, but Celestia waved her back down. "Sit, Vi, and get warm. This will but take a moment."

"I still wish to go on, my lady," the maid said wistfully.

"And get caught by a border patrol? Or worse, the Scottish rebels we're supposed to be avoiding?" Celestia was only half-joking.

Petyr smiled, his white teeth brilliant in the dark. "It's a rare sight to see the Scottish and the English get along. King William may have bought his country back, but he wants more. It might be easier to explain our business in the morning light."

Nicholas looked as if he would say more, but eventually he just nodded. "So be it. For the final night, we shall wrap up in our stinking blankets and eat hard bread. Pass me the wine, Bertram, you old lush."

Celestia laughed with the others, touched by Nicholas's rarely used charm.

She backed away from the others and looked in on Sir Geoffrey. His pallor worried her. It had been a very long time since she'd lost a patient, and Celestia was willing to do everything in her power to keep Sir Geoffrey alive.

Hearing the others talk and laugh as she climbed into the back of the wagon kept the ghost fingers from creeping up her back.

She could feel the restless spirits in these woods. They didn't scare her nearly as much as the malevolent energy, human energy, that was watching them, as well. There was simply no way to climb into the back of the wagon with grace, so Celestia simply hitched her tunic and hiked up, glad that Nicholas was still by the fire.

Kneeling by Sir Geoffrey's side, she carefully pulled the bandages away from the wound in his throat. It was a testament to her skills that there was a smallish gash left in the skin instead of a gaping hole. But it should have healed completely.

She placed a hand across his brow. No fever. Exhaling, she sat back on her heels, reluctant to join the others while she was feeling so unsettled.

The fire outside suddenly raised high, and it illuminated the inside of the wagon. She noticed the broken arrow shaft. The white feathers, some stained red from the blood of Sir Geoffrey, were bright in the near gloom.

The arrow from her vision? It hadn't hit Nicholas. Had it been for her? Reaching down for the prayer beads beneath her tunic, she pulled out the gift from Nicholas.

The rosary glowed with high intensity, like a shooting star, and it burned out just as quickly—leaving behind the scent of apples.

"Hail Mary, full of grace, oh, my," she said, her heart beating wildly. The vision had showed her the shaft. The rosary smelled like cider. There was a mystery here, and it revolved around her husband. Didn't it?

Celestia knew in her soul that he was not out of danger. Neither was she.

She took the shaft out of the wagon, but there was no moonlight by which to see. Running her fingers over the silky edges, she noticed a notch of feathers missing. What kind of feathers were they?

Not one to let a puzzle go long without a solution, she put the broken shaft in her medicine bag. She couldn't name from what bird the feathers came just yet, but she was certain it would come to her.

Glancing toward the horse that carried Sir Stephan's dead body, she remembered the unease she had felt prior to the attack. The hair on the nape of her neck tingled, and she crossed her arms around her waist. "Stop being such a ninny!" she whispered aloud. After waiting in perfect silence for any type of sound that could be out of place, she forced a smile on her face and joined the others around their pitiful fire. "I will be glad to reach Falcon Keep on the morrow," she said in general as she took a seat on a blanket roll.

A chorus of "ayes" answered her, and Nicholas, who appeared to be in a mellow mood, thanks to the wine and good company most like, said, "I do hope you will be happy there."

"Were *you?*"

He tossed a twig into the fire. "I don't remember."

The rosary grew warm next to her skin, and she scooted back from the fire.

"Tell us about our new home, won't you?" pleaded Viola with a pretty grin.

"Yes, do!" agreed Bess.

Nicholas closed his eyes, and Celestia wondered if he would shut them out, as he'd done before. She wished she'd taken a seat next to him, so that she could lend him her strength. He needed to open his heart . . .

Hadn't her grandmother told her the same thing? That wily old bird, Celestia thought with a smile.

"I was a boy when I left. Maybe six, I don't remember. I think there was a river, and mountains. Hills, and caves, secret places that I wasn't supposed to go," his voice trailed off, and he looked as if he was concentrating hard on a memory that wouldn't stay. "And apples. Yes, lots of apples."

"I love a hot apple pie," said Bess. Forrester agreed by rubbing his belly.

"Did you have lots of servants?" asked Viola.

"I don't remember."

"And horses?" asked Henry.

"I, uh, don't remember."

Celestia met her husband's eyes across the fire. She saw such despair that she feared he would sicken from it. How did he manage to breathe and eat and pretend to be human with all of that pain inside of him? An uneasy silence had fallen amongst the group. Celestia stood, stretched, and grinned as if she were the happiest fool to ever come to the English-Scottish border. "For certes, your childhood home will be lovely and most welcoming."

She winked at him. "Especially compared to this."

The next morning, Celestia's teeth were chattering so loudly that Sir Bertram was able to find her through the thick blanket of fog that wafted all around them.

"Good morning, Lady Celestia."

"Are you certain that 'tis morning? How can you tell?" Celestia was too cold for her temper to get more than middling warm.

"Sir Petyr claims to have heard the chirping of a bird." Sir Bertram's snort told what he thought of that story.

They made their way to the rear of the wagon, where Bess and Viola sat coddling Sir Geoffrey.

"It's supposed to be morning!" Celestia quipped.

"Sir Geoffrey, welcome back to the world. You gave us all a scare."

The Montehue knight, his grizzly gray beard even more of a mess than usual, grinned wide. "Aye, and it's glad I am, as well, Bertram. I feel well enough to drive the wagon again, and I thank ye, my lady, for all yer kindness."

Celestia rubbed her blistered hands together. She'd sat the night through, her hands over the wound in his throat, putting forth all of her healing energy in addition to the ointment. "I found the culprit this morning. A piece of feather," she explained to them all. "Poisoned."

Viola burst into tears and rained kisses over the knight's face.

"I'd like to catch hold of the weasel bastard," Sir Bertram groused, "who shot it."

"The fog seems to be thinning, so let's see if we can find our way out of the woods first, eh?"

"Aye, my lady. The sooner we're out of this cursed forest, the better. I swear I heard spirits all night long."

"You drank spirits, which is why," Celestia pointed out. She left them laughing around the wagon, and went to share her good humor with Nicholas. Healing Sir Geoffrey had put her back to rights. She found him standing by Brenin, looking weary and worn. His black hair was damp from the fog and curled around his ears and neck, and he was so handsome to her that she had to clear her throat before she could speak. Sir Petyr was gesturing at something on the map.

"Good morn, Nicholas. Sir Petyr."

Both men turned and gave her greetings, but it was Petyr who said, "We are waiting for the fog to burn off a bit more, my lady, and then we're on our way."

"Wonderful news, Petyr." The knight nodded and left, leaving Nicholas alone with Celestia. He didn't look pleased.

"I shan't bite," she said crossly, wondering at how one man's surliness could affect her own mood. It was possible that Aunt Nan had the best of it, living with her cats.

Nicholas jerked his eyes to hers, his lips twitching reluctantly. "Probably not, my lady. Unless provoked."

She arched a regal brow, as she'd seen her mother do time and again. "And do you plan on provoking me?"

"Not intentionally, Lady Celestia. But I have noticed you have an uncommonly sharp tongue."

Celestia blushed and lowered her eyes. "You have? That is a shame . . . I was hoping to hide that flaw until you knew me better."

"I find you fascinating, flaws and all."

Celestia's gaze flew to his, but she could already tell that he regretted his words. She turned away to hide the sting of hurt. "I didn't mean to disturb you, my lord," she said sarcastically. "I was only curious as to when we would be on our way."

"Now."

Celestia lifted her chin and said, "The sooner the better."

She regretted her haste a while later.

"I can't see a blasted thing," she complained to Forrester, who was riding next to her.

"This fog is unnatural, I can sense it," the young knight agreed.

"Forrester, there is no such thing as witchcraft! Have you learned nothing from me on this journey?"

He stared at her with adoration on his face, and she

realized she'd need to be careful. Galiana would know how to flirt just the right way, but she, alas, was not her beautiful sister.

"You are magical, my lady."

Celestia deliberately wrinkled her nose, something her mother said a lady never did. "No, my young friend. I am blessed by God, and I heal whomever I can." She made a show of looking up at the sky. "Nay, this isn't at all enchanted. Just dreary."

"Mayhap a powerful sorceress is trying to block us from reaching the keep," he said. When he didn't get the reaction he wanted, he shrugged. "Although you can tell from the abundant foliage that it rains much in this forsaken land. You realize we have yet to see the sun?" He nudged Ceffyl with his horse. "I've seen you heal."

"I don't believe in sorceresses," she laughed lightly, moving her horse so they weren't so close. "My family's gifts are a natural phenomenon; I imagine others could be born with similar talents. My youngest sister, Ela, can roll her tongue and I cannot."

"That's a talent," he said, grinning and sticking his tongue out, rolled.

Celestia ducked her head to hide her grin. "Nicely done."

"I think I'll ride ahead, my lady. I just wanted to say, well, that," his face was red beneath his short leather helmet, "I am proud to be your champion!"

He galloped ahead, and Celestia finally allowed the smile to take over her face. She would never, ever betray her husband—even if she remained a maid for life. But still, the young knight's declaration was a salve to her pride.

So far the trip had been daunting. She was wet and bedraggled, her nose ran, and her hind end was sore. Not a very alluring new bride, even if her husband had been so inclined. She'd need to freshen up, for certes, before they reached Falcon Keep, lest she scare all the people away from her new home . . . a darkness shrouded her thoughts. She could not envision what her life would be like as its mistress.

Not that she had the second sight, for she didn't. The occasional vision, mayhap, and perchance because of her healing gift she was more open to intuition than others. And she was frightened by what she wasn't seeing.

Nicholas and Petyr rode flank to flank. "If the baron sent knights, then where are they? Shouldn't they have a few men on patrol?" Unease sat behind him like a second rider.

Petyr nodded, his brows drawn. "This place is too bloody quiet, and we should have reached the outer bailey by now. According to the map, we have to go through that, then there's a large pasture. A stream big enough to support a mill. Then the gatehouse."

Slowing Brenin to a trot, Nicholas peered out as far as he could. He'd expected a spark of recognition at the very least once they'd left the forest. *Nothing.*

It didn't seem right.

"We've got what looks to be a motte-and-bailey-style

keep, easily defendable, if this is correct."

Nicholas finally pulled Brenin to a stop on the wide, yet deserted road. "We should have passed the outer fence by a large round boulder. Either we got lost in the damned fog, or someone has taken down the boundaries."

"The map got soaked through, mayhap," Petyr shook his head even as he tried to find an explanation.

Nicholas held his body upright in the saddle. Apprehension tickled the back of his neck. The lack of his childhood memories bothered him, but not overmuch. He had long ago put his mother from his mind; he'd thought himself a bastard with no other kin.

The past few weeks had turned his life topsy-turvy, and he was no closer to redemption. He had a lot of fine reasons for feeling unsettled, he mused silently, but he knew that this particular feeling had more to do with Falcon Keep than his miserable excuse for a life. "The fog's lifted enough that we can see, although the clouds won't uncover the sun." Nicholas laughed harshly. "At least the rain has stopped. I say we go forward."

Celestia rode up behind them. "Well? Where is it?"

Nicholas said, "What? The keep?"

Petyr grimaced. "We don't know."

"You've lost an entire castle?" Celestia burst out laughing.

Nicholas and Petyr each sent her forbidding looks, which she blithely ignored. "May I have a peek at the map, Sir Petyr?" Celestia asked sweetly.

Petyr gave it to her, with reluctance. Celestia looked at the map, and then around her. The fog receded farther, and she said, "Ah! There is the mill! We are here." She pointed to a place on the map, and Petyr groaned in defeat.

Nicholas bit the inside of his cheek. "I didn't even see it, as it was broken and lying on its side. Where's the bloody stream?" Was this more of her witchery? Or a trick?

Celestia glowed.

Petyr took back the map and rustled it like he knew what he was doing. "That puts us a half league away from where the gatehouse should be."

"Wonderful! But where are the sheep? Nicholas, is it supposed to look this deserted? Where's the village?"

Nicholas gritted his teeth together. He'd been wondering the same things. "I don't know. I don't know."

He studied the smart and vivacious woman who was his unwanted wife. "When did you learn to read?"

She grinned, her eyes twinkling in a rare ray of sunshine. "We all learned how to read. Gram insisted."

How would he convince her to stay behind? He had an inkling that she wouldn't willingly stay. What really chapped his hide was how enthralled he found himself by the timber of her voice. Her temper, which was loud and quick, even though she tried so hard to control it—her face and her figure.

Her.

His sudden realization caused his knees to tighten, and his horse lurched forward. How had his defenses crumbled so far? Nicholas was attracted to his own wife!

Saint James, preserve me. He watched her, with some horror, from the corner of his eye as they rode along. Her slender back was straight, and her face shone with good health despite the terrible conditions in which they'd been traveling. She and Petyr exchanged some story, and his eyes followed the way she used her hands to talk. He loved her laugh.

He did?

His chin sank to his chest. A match between them would never work. He would only hurt her in the end. He was doomed, without a soul, on a mission to kill the man who'd given him life . . .

Within the blink of an eye, he accepted his feelings, and rejected what they meant. Nicholas knew he was the last man on earth to deserve a chance at such happiness. He would see to it that she was as content as she could be. He would make certain that she had all he could give before he left her forever.

His heart was so heavy he was surprised that Brenin could carry him. A short while later, Celestia shouted, "I see it!" She turned in her saddle. "Do you, Nicholas? Over there."

He had been too busy thinking of ways to tell Celestia good-bye to see the keep. But as he followed where her finger pointed, he saw a tall tower emerge from the clouds and a brief flash of sunlight sparkled over the moat.

The very dark, very disgusting, green moat. As they rode closer, a foul smell wafted through on a breeze.

They grouped together on the edge of the pasture that had grown wild around them, with weeds as tall as his knees. The knights, the women, and the wagon.

He didn't want to go on.

He noticed Celestia touching something at her chest.

"It feels wrong," she whispered under her breath, edging her mare closer to Nicholas and Brenin. She faced him, her eyes filled with concern. "Don't you sense it?"

Forrester's glance was sharp as he shielded his brow with his hand. "Aye, that it does."

Nicholas did feel it, but he couldn't admit to it. He accepted the weight of responsibility and turned to the others. "Nonsense. I'll ride ahead, and let them know we've arrived."

He waved Bertram toward the wagon, and the man answered with a clipped nod, casually moving his horse, while readying his sword.

"Keep the wagon there, Sir Geoffrey. Petyr, Forrester, and I will go ahead to scout the area. I'm sure we will be back anon, but be cautious just the same." He stared at his wife as he spoke the last words.

He didn't think to tell Celestia to stay put, so the fact that she followed them was more than likely his own fault.

When he'd opened his mouth to tell her to go back, she'd sent him a look that simply said she was not going to listen to his order. She withdrew her bow; her arrows were already slung across Ceffyl's saddle. Nicholas gave her a blank stare, then turned away.

What would he do if anything happened to her? Her face was set, but she didn't complain as they silently cantered toward a keep that was not at all prepared to welcome its new mistress.

He looked over his shoulder, and saw that Sir Bertram and Sir Geoffrey were prepared to defend themselves and the wagon.

Slowly the four of them approached the drawbridge, which was down, for all the good it did. It was gouged with holes and missing pieces of lumber.

The moat gurgled with green algae and noxious wildlife. The stench burned his nostrils, and still Celestia didn't complain.

Her face was pinched with concentration, and she stayed at his back "Will we take the horses across?" Petyr asked Nicholas deferentially.

Nicholas continued in his role as leader, even though he was a fraud. "Nay, leave the horses. We will tether them here, where the others can watch them."

They all glanced at the wagon, which had come suspiciously closer as the four had gone forward. Nicholas waved them back.

"They should be here by the time we come out again," he said dryly.

He held out his hand to Celestia, helping her dismount while she kept her bow in one hand and the quiver of arrows at her back. She could have done it herself, more than likely. But Nicholas simply wanted to touch her.

Skin to skin.

Just in case.

She was wearing gloves.

Chapter NINE

"Come. Be quiet, and stay aware." Nicholas's terse warning was all he offered in the way of a plan. Celestia found herself singularly unimpressed.

Danger. Had this been the danger hinted at in the vision, or was this some new danger for which she was completely unprepared? Nicholas led the way, his dark face set and stoic, his steps light and sure. Petyr was directly behind him. Celestia, wanting to be as close to Nicholas as possible, resented the blond knight's placement, but bit her tongue.

Forrester tailed her, his feet following hers exactly, as they made their way across the rotted boards of the drawbridge. Celestia swallowed convulsively as a piece of wood splashed into the green ooze and a pair of snapping jaws emerged. Giant fish? Eel? Monster?

Whispering a prayer to Saint Kathryn for courage—quickly adding that she had no desire to be a virgin martyr herself—she shivered and kept on.

Nicholas paused by the stone doorway and held a finger to his lips. Reaching around Petyr, he held out his other hand for Celestia. She grasped his fingers, anticipating the spark of warmth as their hands touched, secure in knowing that Nicholas would keep her safe. Even if he didn't really want to, his noble nature demanded it.

She kept her eyes open, determined to not be yet another obligation for Nicholas. Her knees shook as they entered the dark and abandoned front hall; being brave all the time was wearing on her nerves. She'd make an infusion of cowslip, and add extra oats to her diet. Forget being brave, mayhap it was being *wed* that was causing her upset.

Petyr was so close behind her she could feel his warm breath. Her head grew dizzy and a chill started at the nape of her neck. Now was most definitely not the time for a vision, she thought sternly.

Really.

Celestia gripped Nicholas's hand tighter as they entered the main room. The dreary weather kept the sun away, and what light did manage to break free from behind the clouds was not near strong enough to brighten the interior of the keep.

Dust motes caught the occasional puff of breeze through the slitted windows, none of which held any glass. Her husband's body stiffened, and Celestia's heart cracked anew at the pain he was feeling. This was Nicholas's childhood home, and it was a disaster.

Tables were overturned and broken; dog feces and mouse droppings littered the floor. Everything was decayed. Celestia's sorrow was overwhelming. Nicholas's emotions ran the gamut from disappointment, to sadness, to fear. It didn't matter how much it hurt her to accept his feelings, she would not release his grip. His face gave away nothing, but he squeezed her hand.

Like thieves instead of the rightful owners of the keep, the four stayed close to the thick stone walls and tiptoed through the debris. They said nothing, as if they all sensed that they weren't alone.

Celestia peeked up at Nicholas as they paused near another room, possibly the kitchens. His outward expression hadn't changed, and she worried that he showed no visible emotion. He was a master, it seemed, of hiding how he felt. She sensed that the key to healing his inner turmoil lay with what happened in Tripoli.

Nicholas pointed down a hall, and Celestia noticed a stairway leading up. Thinking that he wanted her to go that way, she stepped forward, accidentally kicking a brittle joint bone across the filthy floor.

Her heart jumped to her throat, and her eyes felt ready to pop from her head. She glanced at the knights, and both Petyr and Forrester looked wary, but Nicholas—he simply held a finger to his lips, and pulled her back behind him.

No enemy came pouring from the upstairs or the kitchens or the cellar.

"Mayhap nobody's here," Petyr whispered.

Celestia didn't believe that, and all she had to do

was remember the attack on the wagon to stay on her toes. Ghosts didn't shoot arrows at innocents. Bad people did.

Using his shoulder, Nicholas pushed open a door that hung on one leather hinge, his sword drawn and held before him in his left hand, his right hand still clasped in Celestia's grip. Cupboards, open and bare, and herbs so dried that if she touched them they'd turn to dust. *The kitchen.* Light from the jagged, open roof poured down onto the large pine table, as if all the angels in heaven were illuminating the atrocity below.

Two knights, dressed in blue tunics with gold edging, lay pinned as if bug specimens. Arrows with white feathers pinioned their arms, while their feet had been tied tightly to the table legs.

Flies buzzed over their sightless eyes and open mouths, and Celestia's stomach rolled in protest that such cruelty could be done apurpose. She'd no desire to touch the men, as they were beyond whatever healing she could do.

"Don't look," Nicholas warned in a scruffy voice.

She averted her gaze from the grisly sight. Forrester coughed, and Petyr gasped in rage.

"They've been tortured." Nicholas released her hand, and Celestia almost fell. She hadn't realized how much she'd relied on his strength.

"Oliver de Montry and John Gains." Petyr cleared his throat. "They were good men, Nicholas. If you had secrets to be kept, they would not have given them away."

Nicholas turned his anger on Petyr, and Celestia

backed up, too. "Aye, but I have none. So why would anyone do this?" He took great gulping breaths of air, fighting for that control he prized so dearly.

She must have made some silly feminine sound, because suddenly his gaze locked with hers. The night she'd woken him from his demonic dreams his eyes had been like this—despair so deep it was unfathomable. Beyond frightened, Celestia reached out, scared to touch Nicholas even though he needed her desperately. He backed away, into the dead men on the table. An arrow dropped to the floor, clattering against the stone.

For the blink of an eye, the look on his face was so vulnerable that it stole her very breath. She inhaled, getting nothing, no air, and her vision blurred. Bringing both hands to her neck, she massaged her throat to coax the airway open, but she only became more light-headed and nauseous.

She couldn't break eye contact, and everything Nicholas was feeling came at her tenfold.

"My lady!" Petyr caught her as her knees buckled and she sank to the floor, overcome with her failure. Her husband's pain and buried rage was too much for her to carry.

"Celestia." Nicholas shook his head, clearing it so that he could damn well think. He'd heard Celestia's small mew of distress just as she'd started to collapse, but he'd been powerless to catch her.

Petyr had, thank all the saints, before she banged her head against the stones. Nicholas took her from Petyr's outstretched arms. "We can't stay here," he said, dashing from the foul kitchen before he lost his mind.

What was left of it.

Holding her to his chest, listening to her struggle for air, Nicholas begged for another chance to do right. He retraced his steps across the drawbridge without hesitation, certain that if he could just get her away from the crumbling pile of rock, she'd be fine again.

Her head lolled to the side, and her lids fluttered. He hit the rocky dirt running, and called for help.

"She can't breathe, get her medicine bag, hurry!"

As he'd predicted, the wagon was parked to the side of the uncleared field, a few wagon-lengths away from the keep. He sank to his knees in the grass, Celestia still balanced in his arms.

Please, he thought.

His heart pounded madly in his chest as he caressed her silken blond hair. Her lashes lay like feathers along her pale cheeks, and he ran his finger over her lips. "Come back to me, 'Tia."

"That place is not fit for an animal; I say we burn it to the ground." Forrester's voice was shaking with anger.

Nicholas couldn't spare the time to calm the young knight. He rocked Celestia gently until Bess brought a blanket and spread it out over the grass.

"Here, my lord. 'Tis smooth, you can set her down, Viola's getting her herbs."

"Do you know what's wrong?"Nicholas asked.

Sir Geoffrey said, "We don't know what happened, my lord."

Petyr explained, while Nicholas eyed the blanket. He didn't want to let Celestia go. "They had tortured two of the baron's knights, and left the bodies for us to find. My lady fainted."

Bess puffed out her plump cheeks. "Lady Celestia fainted? Nay, I don't believe it."

Viola felt for Celestia's pulse. "Steady and strong. Mayhap it was the unexpected death? She's sensitive, she is, to things like that."

"Blood and pus, now, that don't get to her none." Bess looked around at them all, nodding. "Our lady is no weak little miss. What really happened in there?"

"Aye," Sir Geoffrey growled menacingly. "Tell us the truth, what happened to our lady?"

"That was the truth. The keep is deserted, and filthy." Nicholas bowed his head, resting his forehead to Celestia's. He never should have let her follow him. "She's strong, aye."

"Even I wanted ta puke," Forrester insisted. "But it was something between my lord and lady, that's what made her fall."

Nicholas raised his head. "What?"

"You, and her, you have a connection. 'Tis obvious, being married and all. I didn't understand what was happening, but it was like she could see inside your head."

"Witch," Bertram mumbled.

Viola jumped to her feet from where she'd been kneeling next to Nicholas and Celestia. "Take that back, you stupid sod, else I'll run you through," she threatened.

"With what?" Bertram laughed uneasily.

Sir Geoffrey stood next to Viola, his hand over the hilt of his sword. "I'll do it, love," he said. "I'll not let anybody speak of our lady like that."

Nicholas spoke so that all would hear. "My wife is no witch, and she is still out cold. Bertram, mind your tongue and apologize to the lady's retainers, and to me."

Would he? Nicholas watched the man carefully. Someone had been sabotaging their journey, and just possibly it was one of "his" own men.

"My apologies," Sir Bertram bowed stiffly.

Viola and Sir Geoffrey stood down, and the tension refocused on Celestia. Forrester had taken off his cloak for an added blanket, and Petyr had bundled his own for use as a pillow.

Nicholas had no choice but to release her, which he did, as if she were precious porcelain from Asia. Why had he not thought to shield her from such a sight? And if it was true, and she'd seen inside his head, no wonder she'd fainted. Seeing those men tortured had catapulted him back to his time as a prisoner.

"I'm sorry, my lady," he whispered into her hair. "I'll never be good for you, will I?" What remained of his soul was too dark, too black, for one so full of light. For certes, Saint James would be hard-pressed to be kind to him, even if he brought him the baron, piece by piece, on an offering of gold. The sacred relic of Saint James the Apostle was gone.

This was no place for a lady of breeding, but he had no place else to go. His plan to leave immediately for Peregrine Castle was moot. He could not, in good conscience, leave her here among the haunted ruins of his childhood.

Forced into a position of leadership, he took a deep breath and sought to change that which he could hold on to. Souls and hearts and mysterious, intangible connections were more than he could handle.

"Petyr, we must bury those men, and Stephan, too." He swallowed a maniacal laugh. "I should have realized that this 'gift' from my father would be tainted. The ladies can't sleep there, so we will have to make do with another evening outdoors." He couldn't even find a hard smile for the maids. "Just until we can find something habitable."

"But—" Bess started to complain.

"We'll do what needs to be done, my lord," Viola cut in, rummaging through the vials in Celestia's bag. "Susie fainted once, one of me friends, and," she took the cork from various bottles and sniffed delicately. "I think my lady used," Viola inhaled, "aye," she scrunched her nose and nodded. "This is it. Turns out she was pregnant." Viola blushed. "Susie, not my lady."

Nicholas's belly warmed at the immediate image of Celestia bearing his child, and he crushed the thought. "Now what?"

"A little pinch here, beneath each nostril, and we wait . . ."

The strong scents of ginger and black pepper made Nicholas's eyes water, and apparently, the stink was enough to bring Celestia around.

"Ah, ah, ahcoooo!" Celestia sneezed, her upper body jerking forward so fast that Nicholas hadn't time to get out of the way.

Her forehead thunked into his nose so hard he saw spots. She cried out, and he steadied her, grabbing her upper arms.

"You fainted," he said.

"You're bleeding," she cried in alarm.

"You hit me."

"Liar!" Her eyes flashed. "I would never do such a thing—unlike you, I keep my fists to myself."

Everyone broke into relieved laughter, with Petyr's being the loudest of all. His heart slowly returned to its normal beat, and Nicholas longed for nothing more than to hold her close again.

She became aware of their audience and flushed a brilliant red, even to the roots of her braided hair.

"Would you like some water, my lady?" Forrester asked, offering his waterskin.

"I'll see to my lady, thank ye," Bess said impatiently, shoving the young knight back while taking his waterskin. "Humph!" She knelt down on the blanket and offered it to Celestia. "Water?"

Celestia took a sip, but the strain remained around her eyes. "Mayhap you should lie down," Nicholas suggested.

"I never lie down in the middle of the day. 'Tis unproductive."

Nicholas watched as she gathered that incredible inner strength she relied on and she said, "The keep is a mess."

"I'll clean it."

Shadows passed over her face, but that stubborn

chin went directly upward. Now he remembered why he couldn't keep her from following them inside. He embraced her then, whispering in her ear, "I hurt you."

She pulled back, surprise clear in her expression. "Nay, it wasn't you."

"It was."

Resolve to do right by her filled him. She was not the only one who could focus amidst chaos. The sooner he followed through on his quest to kill the baron, or at the very least, find the truth as to what really happened on that hot, miserable day in Tripoli, the safer Celestia would be.

He got to his feet, brushing grass from his leggings. To Petyr he said, "Take Willy and scout the rest of the castle; make sure that it is truly empty, and that there are no more, er, surprises. I shall meet up with you shortly."

The warmth of Celestia's fingers entwined with his calmed him, but he couldn't be drawn away from his true goal.

"Yes, my lord." Petyr's face was grim. "May I suggest that the main room at least can be cleaned until . . ."

"Cleaned? I doubt it. A good fire is the only thing that will cleanse this rotten heap."

Petyr ducked his head, his lips pressed tightly together. "Come on, Forrester, Willy. We have much work to do."

"We'll try our best." Viola and Bess gathered buckets and rags, which left Sir Bertram, and Sir Geoffrey, with Celestia and Nicholas at the wagon. One look from Sir Geoffrey, and Sir Bertram followed the rest to the keep.

"Don't let the women in the kitchens, the main room, only, Petyr . . ." Nicholas yelled at their backs.

Celestia's face was pale again, and he wondered what she was thinking. She probably wanted to risk the woods and make her way home to her family, no doubt. He'd promised to keep her safe, and he hadn't.

He was angry. No, he thought, scratching the back of his neck, he was bloody well pissed off. He blamed his father, hell—he even blamed God. What had he, a learned knight, a decent man, ever done to deserve such a fate? The baron would pay, and mayhap all could have a happy ending.

"I'm sorry," he said again, unable to look at Celestia.

"Stop apologizing, would you, please?" She tugged at his hand. "It's annoying."

Nicholas looked down and noted the small lines of irritation between Celestia's fine blond brows.

Finalizing his decision to leave her made him want to touch her all the more, so he pulled her into a side hug before letting go. Off balance, she fell back, and those green blue orbs spit fire. "Clumsy?"

He laughed, mostly with relief. "You're fine. Do you fall over like this often? Next time, simply mention if you need a rest and can't keep up."

He knew that would get a rise from her, and he was much pleased by the pink gracing her fair cheeks. Anything but that waxen white.

"Not keep up? With you? Ha! I remember challenging you to a horse race once, when we first met, do ye remember? And you were so afraid of losing that—"

"'Tia!" Nicholas put his hand over her pretty mouth. "I will take ye up on the challenge, but I have work to do, and a keep to burn. And now that I see for myself you're," he winked, wanting to see her smile, "returned to *your* pleasant self, I can be off. Go ahead and nap."

"You cannot burn Falcon Keep, Nicholas," Celestia shouted up at him, shaking her cute little fist. "Are ye daft, then? It needs be cleaned, that is all! A nap? I told you I never nap. This was your home, you stupid man, and there is something to be salvaged from it."

Nicholas's adrenaline skipped like a rock over a still pond. Celestia's eyes thundered and flashed, her petite body shook, her blond hair shone like a crown. She would save him from his own folly, if she could.

The sight warmed him, and he fought the urge to kiss her senseless. It was getting harder and harder to stay away from his wife.

Grayish black clouds suddenly covered the entire sky, and goose bumps raced over his skin. He remembered Celestia fainting, he remembered the pain of being betrayed, and he remembered, God help him, what he had to do in order to win his soul. He could not relax his guard again.

"Salvage away, my lady, as you are the one that will be living here." He deliberately hardened his voice, along with his heart.

"I will be away before the end of summer."

Celestia sneezed and swatted at a large spiderweb in the corner. "This reminds me of when I decided to turn the dungeon at home into an infirmary."

"Aye," Viola agreed. "That was an awful mess. At least it wasn't haunted, not like here."

Bess let out a nervous giggle. "'Tis downright spooky, what with all the little bones on the floor and not a single person anywhere. Not a living one, anyway."

Chills gathered at the nape of her neck, reminding Celestia of the vision she'd had while in her "faint." Nicholas hadn't known what it was, and none of her family had been around to tell him.

Considering how strongly he reacted to her "talents," it was probably just as well. She'd have to tell Viola to use a lighter hand on the fainting powder, though. It wasn't harmful, just strong, and now she had a craving for gingered beets.

"The mouse bones are gone, as is most of the first layer of dirt. We'll need clean rushes, scattered with fresh lavender, and this room will be fine."

"I'll go!" Bess volunteered so quickly that Celestia had to laugh.

"Fine, but get Forrester to go with you into the woods."

The plump maid raced from the large main room like she was escaping a bad marriage. Viola lowered her head and continued sweeping, but Celestia could tell that the maid was unhappy.

"Bess was quicker than us, Vi," Celestia jested.

Viola sniffed and swept, obviously upset about more

than the missed opportunity to get outdoors.

"I don't think the keep is haunted, not really—just dirty."

"There were men murdered here!" Viola cried, and Celestia envied the maid her tears. But she was the mistress of this pile of stone, and she couldn't cry. There wasn't even a place to take a hot bath, with some of Gali's soothing oils, where she could pretend the tears were steam.

"Aye." She sighed and piled up the broken odds and ends that were left around the main room. "But now our very own knights have given those men a proper burial, and their souls will be at rest."

"Really?" Viola's thin face lifted with hope.

"Oh, yes," Celestia nodded.

"So who do you think killed those poor knights? Will Baron Peregrine blame Lord Nicholas?"

Celestia stopped poking at spiderwebs. Nicholas to blame? That was an interesting thought. "Nay, we all know that Nicholas didn't do any wrong. As for who killed the knights? Mayhap the Norsemen on the western shores, or the Scots." She picked up a pillow her mother had sewn and gave it a nice shake. "Rumor has it that King William is forming a rebellion."

"Me mam says that the Scots aren't happy until somebody is dead, or at least bleeding a lot."

Celestia looked around for a place to put the plumped pillow and snickered. "She must have known a few."

"Her first husband, my lady," Viola giggled back, at last relaxing.

Needing to think about the Nicholas and Baron

Peregrine connection, Celestia suggested that Viola find Bess and Forrester. She could concentrate better without having to keep up mundane chatter at the same time.

"Ye don't mind, my lady?"

"No, no. I'd like to go through my herbals, anyway."

Viola leaned the broom against the wall, and out the front of the keep she went. Celestia's days of skipping chores were over, and she knew it. She was the lady here, even if it was in name only.

She picked up her herbal bag, and put everything back in its place after the disarray Viola had left when she searched for the fainting powder.

Giving someone the wrong herbs could be deadly.

Her hand hovered over the powdered poppy, and the stronger opium.

Nicholas had been drugged, often, and the guilt he felt because of what he'd done, and been forced to do, was—to him—an insurmountable black mark on his soul. His addiction to the substance that he'd been force-fed—oh, Celestia forced her fingers to relax, terribly furious at the injustice done.

If the bitch wasn't already dead, I'd kill her myself, she thought—and without all of the worthless guilt from which her honorable husband suffered.

"What are you doing in here alone?"

Speak of the devil, Celestia thought and smiled. "Thinking."

"You're not to be by yourself." Nicholas narrowed his dark eyes at her.

She shrugged. "'Tis lucky for me that I am not."

He looked around, and so she said with a wink, "You are here."

"Ah," he sighed instead of smiling, which was too bad. Celestia was forming an attachment to the curve of his lips. "This room is clean." He paused, realizing that he'd brought more dirt in. "It was clean."

His face flushed, with embarrassment and hard work.

"I'd offer ye a drink, but the kitchen is off limits."

"The bodies are gone, but it still needs to be scrubbed down, floor to ceiling."

Shivering, Celestia said, "The arrow feathers from the kitchen? They're similar to the ones that were shot at us."

"I'd noticed that, too. They're unique."

"Exactly!" Celestia tapped her foot. "Different from other arrows—it's the feathers. Not a duck, not a peacock, not a hen . . ." Her brow furrowed as she groped for the elusive answer. "Mayhap if we knew why the murders happened, we could find out *who* is behind them."

"Most likely it was the Scottish rebels. We're too far inland for the Norse to care about this old place." Nicholas paced the floor, leaving a track of muddy footprints.

"I suppose that might make sense. Kill the knights, find out the keep will be inhabited once again, go back and collect the treasure a new bride would bring to a home." Celestia tied the medicine bag, and set it aside. That scenario didn't seem right. She wished she could tell Nicholas of her visions, so that he could stay alert. He was still in danger.

They all were.

Celestia pointed to a pile of broken pottery. "We have more to go outside. Did ye want to look at any of these pieces? Mayhap something will start your memories flowing."

Nicholas shook his head, barely glancing at the rubbish. His dark hair held the odd twig, and she thought him ruggedly handsome. "You would think that something would come. Shouldn't it? By now?"

Hearing the underlying anguish beneath the question made Celestia pause.

"Perhaps." She wondered, too. What if it was all Peregrine men who were cursed?

She believed, with all of her spirit, that her family's gifts were blessed. However, she also accepted on blind faith that some phenomena did not have a ready explanation. Her duty was to keep Nicholas safe, and heal him from the inside. They were going to have to talk about the curse, eventually.

"Will we have our own bedchamber?" She'd not gone up the stairs, having been distracted by the disaster on the main floor.

Panic flew across his body. If it wasn't so painful, Celestia lifted her chin, it would be most amusing. "I only ask, my lord, because I would have a conversation with you in private."

Nicholas shoulders slumped, then he slammed his fist into his open palm. "Do you think me an idiot?"

"What?"

"I've been given everything a man should need, and

I cannot accept it."

"*That* sort of an idiot. Well . . ." Celestia gave up trying to stay distant, and walked to him, with her hands outstretched.

He didn't accept them. "Something happens between us when we touch. I can't be ruled by lust, nor magic, nor anything that is not of my own choosing." His strong voice broke, and his gray eyes grew stormy. "I wish ye would stay away."

He meant it, Celestia realized with a gasp. He, in his deepest heart, believed that she was a witch who controlled men's emotions, and that he could not trust himself around her. Her heart was much more fragile than she'd realized, and when it plummeted to her stomach, it made her ill.

She would have run, but she had nowhere to go.

Geoffrey and Bertram came in, then, carrying bundles from the wagon. Quickly gathering her chaotic emotions, Celestia plastered a bright smile on her face.

"What have you, there?" *Please, please, no tears. This is the drek the minstrels sang of, heartache and heartbreak.*

"It was excellent foresight on your father's behalf to send the wagon full of goods." Geoffrey beamed at the clean walls and frowned when he noticed the muddy footprints on the floor. "We'll need rushes," he said.

"The maids went with Forrester to go and get some." Celestia took some dishes from Bertram's arms. "We will need everything in the wagon! Ah, candles—it is so dark in here, I feel as if the walls are moving closer and closer each time I turn around."

Her voice cracked. The tears were coming whether she wanted them or nay. She had to leave before she shamed herself, and Nicholas, with her unseemly crying.

"I think I'll go find them, mayhap they'll need help bringing the rushes in—just set the things wherever you can."

Nicholas called, "Wait for me, Celestia, I'll go with you."

She waved her hand, unable to look at her husband. "Nay, nay, I wish to be alone."

"Take these, my lady," Sir Geoffrey interrupted, handing her both an empty basket and her gardening dagger on her way out. "I saw some spring berries at the side of the keep nearest the tree line. Nothing like sweet fruit to lift the spirits!"

"Thank you," she said, then she walked very fast out the front of the keep. Tears blurred her vision, so instead of going over the drawbridge, she carefully made her way around the stone walls to the right. Turning the corner, she found a tall hedge of thorns and a gate of the same height. She could see nothing beyond, but she heard men's voices.

She pushed at the heavy wooden barrier until it finally gave way. Stubborn as she was, the gate never stood a chance, she thought with satisfaction as the door swung wide. Especially when she was in a temper.

Wiping away the tears that overflowed at will, she stepped into the rear of the keep, and almost dropped her basket.

"Oh, sweet Mary Magdalene!" She tightened her grip on the handle, amazed at what was hidden behind the keep's walls. The entrance to Falcon Keep had been falling down and rotten, disguising its true treasures. The moat didn't go clear around, so the noxious smell was hardly noticeable.

The back of the yard butted up against a grove thick with birch, beech, and oak trees on the left, and a large, forbidding cliff protected them on the right. The perimeter was handily fenced with stone and wooden palisades.

She was duly impressed with the fortifications. The rear of the keep opened to the yard, and she searched until she found what she thought might be the kitchen garden.

Neglected and lonely, some herbs that grew wild, and needed no coaxing, were barely visible. Her fingers itched to dig in the dirt, to fix what could be mended. Then she heard Nicholas's voice, and she forgot about the garden.

Willy, Henry, and Petyr, still wearing blue and gold, were stabling the horses with fresh hay and setting things to rights while Nicholas himself was chopping wood in front of a large barn.

She stomped over to him, telling herself with each step that ladies did not stomp.

"Nicholas," she demanded his attention. "How is it you beat me here?"

"I came through the kitchen."

He was all surly male, making a pronouncement that he couldn't be with her, and then pouting when she didn't wait for him to walk with her. Well, she refused to cry in front of him. He could not know that he'd hurt her so badly.

Swinging her basket, she asked, "Do my eyes deceive me? Is this the same place?"

"'Tis not quite as bad out here, my lady. Although it is just as deserted."

"Did you find the other eight knights your father, er, the baron, sent?"

He pointed his axe toward the very last shed. "Four of them were in there, dead. We've looked everywhere else for the other bodies, but . . ." he shrugged and Celestia followed the line of muscle across his shoulders. "We'll have to drain the moat."

Celestia lowered her eyes, her entire body suddenly chilled as she thought of the poisonous green water winding in front of the keep like a deadly snake. Her vision had centered upon it, and she was sure that they would find more bodies there. "I would not wish that upon any man."

Nicholas's jaw clenched tight. "I would find who committed these crimes, and hold them accountable," he set the axe head down, holding the wood.

Thinking only to comfort him, Celestia put her hand on his wrist, realizing too late that she touched scarred skin. She found it difficult to breathe as she absorbed the heat of him; her pulse pounded erratically. His tunic was rolled up at the sleeves, untucked from his breeches and open down the front of his chest. She gulped and stared at the play of muscles upon his flat stomach.

She slowly brought her eyes up to his face, aware of the burning in her fingertips. Her breasts heaved with emotion, and she stepped closer to the source of her confusion. *Nicholas.*

She flicked the very tip of her tongue over her dry lips. If only he would try to care for her, too!

"You are hurting me . . ." Nicholas told her as he gently removed her hand from his forearm.

Not understanding, she looked down and saw that her fingertips had burned their print upon his skin. Her eyes filled with stunned tears, and she dropped the empty basket.

Reaching forward to place her palm along the burn, to heal the wound she'd unwittingly inflicted, she pulled back, terrified of what had gone wrong. "I have never . . ." Celestia hoped that he would see the innocence in her eyes as she pleaded for him to forgive her. "I wouldn't hurt anyone, and *never* you."

She stumbled over her words, her hands fluttering ineffectually. "I've never caused harm, never . . ." She bit her lip and took a few faltering steps back, almost tripping over her neglected basket. It had to be the Boadicea legend. She'd been married without love, and this was the price she was paying.

Nicholas took her by the arm, careful to avoid skin-to-skin contact. "Celestia, calm down, I've never seen you like this—the burn was nothing, the marks are clearing already, do you see?"

She shook him off. In trying to heal his despair, she'd been unprepared for the devastation she felt now at the impending loss of her identity. "It is my turn to warn you, Nicholas, stay away—for your health, do you understand?" She ran for the forest, a wounded animal going to ground. "For your health!"

Chapter TEN

Celestia thrashed through the trees like a crazed rabbit being chased by a hungry red fox. She ran until her side cramped, and then she walked, caring little where she was going. She paid no heed to the height of the sun, nor the direction she went.

All she could think about was hurting Nicholas. Was this the first part of losing her gifts, as the legend predicted?

Somewhere in her mad dash, she'd twisted her ankle, and she was limping by the time she heard the sound of a stream. Her emotions had ranged from shame, injured pride, anger (at herself), irritation (at Nicholas), to regret. She eased her aching body onto a large, flat rock and cried some more.

The tears she had been denying ever since she had met her husband had been flowing steadily since her flight from the keep. She cried over leaving her family, whom she loved and missed; she cried because she would never know the love her parents shared, or the love between a man and a woman. "Especially not if you burn him whenever you touch him," she scolded herself out loud.

The chirping of the birds was her only answer, and as silence reigned around her she began to feel foolish for running. Nicholas would never have chased after her; he would never give in to that kind of emotion.

She rubbed at her sore eyes. What was it to her if her face was puffy and red? Normally not one for self-pity, she was not sure what to do with her feelings. At home, if she was unsettled, she found someone who needed her.

The serfs at Montehue Manor were decidedly healthy.

Now she was married to a man who believed her to be a witch, and how could she deny such an accusation when she burned him with her healing touch? But the cruelest jest of all was the knowledge that she'd gone and fallen head over heels in love with her husband.

He was a good man, despite the demons haunting him. She wiped her eyes with the back of her hand, grateful that Gali was not there to see such an unladylike act.

But the thought of her sister's absence brought on more tears, and she lay back against the rock, using her arms as a pillow. She closed her itching, watery eyes and prayed for her husband's soul, and her own salvation.

It was late afternoon when she woke, startled by a cracking branch. Celestia sat up so fast that she fell off of the rock where she had been napping and landed on her rear.

Not for the first time in her nineteen years did she

wish for more womanly curves. She slowly got to her feet, rubbing her backside and looking for any sign of danger. Rationally, she realized that it must have been a deer or some kind of woodland animal that was, hopefully, not hungry.

She couldn't see anything, so she wandered to the stream and knelt on the banks, cupping the cold water in her hands to sip before leaning over and splashing some on her face and neck.

A twig snapped behind her, and she whirled, her panicked heart beating triple time. That was no deer, maybe a boar? "Who is there?"

She glanced around, her eyes darting wildly from left to right as she searched for intruders. She saw no one, but sensed she wasn't alone.

Celestia cautiously made her way to the rock where she'd slept. Her stomach hitched to the back of her throat as she spotted the arrow lying in the exact place her head had rested. No wild boar carried a quiver of arrows—had she been watched—was she still being watched?

Debilitating fear threatened her usual pre-Nicholas composure, so she deliberately slowed her breaths until she regained her balance.

Her father had always said she was the most logical of his brood, the one most likely to calmly react. So she would think . . . She ran her thumb over the white feathers. It was getting dark, but there was enough dusky light flitting through the tree cover that mayhap she could pick her way back.

"Fool!" she muttered angrily. It was her own fault

for running through the forest like a wayward brat. Her sense of direction was completely off-kilter, and since she'd never been here before, she had no landmarks to guide her.

Mayhap it would be smarter to wait until morning before trying to find her way back to the keep?

Nay, she chided herself. Whoever had been watching her was still out there. Weren't they? Why would they leave her alone now, unless they were toying with her as a cat does a mouse—and what was the point of the arrow? A threat? A warning?

"Where are you, Nicholas?" Her whispered voice echoed eerily in the twilight. He was more than likely thanking the heavens that she was lost and praying that she'd been eaten by a wild badger. One less responsibility forced on him.

She brushed her hair off of her face. Sternly reminding herself that she'd never been a coward, Celestia lifted her chin, located as many of the broken branches she'd torn through as she could, and started walking.

Nicholas could not stop staring at his wrist. The burns had faded, just like he'd tried to tell Celestia before she'd darted away from him and run for the cover of the trees.

He hefted the axe, flexing his sore muscles. He didn't use to be so weak, but the fever, as well as weaning himself off the opium, had abused what was left of an already sore-used body.

Abbot Crispin said that he'd never be well until he looked to his soul.

He swung down, inhaling the scent of freshly chopped pine.

Nicholas would offer the baron's head to Saint James in return for his soul—vengeance would be just and right.

There was no time for emotional attachments. They couldn't be trusted, for one thing, and for another, they got in the way. Celestia was dangerous, his wrist was proof of that.

With her kind of power, she'd see into his secret self—a place where even he didn't dare to look. She'd fainted at just a glimpse of the darkness he lived with every day.

He might have fooled an ordinary woman into thinking they could be happy. Celestia would know the truth. *Damn.* He swung again.

He'd not imagined what had happened, and Nicholas refused to dwell on what couldn't be explained. His heart bade him run after her and wipe the tears that had welled in her brilliant eyes, just as his head insisted that he stay away, for both their sakes. She even had his innards at cross-purposes.

What had she meant—to stay away, for his health?

He worried, and picked up another log. It was getting darker by the minute, and she hadn't returned.

Celestia made him feel things he would rather not. Like hope. He tossed another chopped piece of wood to the growing stack near the kitchen garden.

If he'd followed her, he would have kissed her until they both forgot the consequences of making love. He had no right to take Celestia's virginity, nor her heart, not when he knew he couldn't give her what she sought.

He shivered and almost sliced his foot in two. *Her eyes grew luminous in passion, and she stared at him as if she knew him, as if she could love him, despite his many flaws.* His groin pulsed with lust. He'd not missed sex, but she'd reawakened desire.

Nicholas sank the axe into the chopping block and watched the handle quiver. Control. He needed to control the lust she inspired within him. He'd not give up everything that had kept him going as he'd crawled back from Tripoli.

Revenge.

That could keep a man's blood hot, as well.

Viola and Bess, who'd started scrubbing the kitchen after laying the fresh rushes, came out to empty a bucket of dirty water.

"Where is Celestia?" Viola wiped her wet hands on her apron.

Nicholas walked away from the stack of wood, his gut heavy.

"She didn't return from the forest?"

"No," Bess said, her eyes searching the tree line. "Sir Geoffrey said she was gathering berries, and we—"

"We thought she was with you, and, oh, no," Viola said.

Nicholas closed his eyes, and ran his hand over his forehead, calling himself ten times a fool. "She ran, she was upset, and I just assumed that . . ."

Bess, obviously forgetting about or not caring about, the differences in their rank, yelled, "You let her traipse off into the woods alone? In a strange place, with a band of mad Scots roaming around?"

Nicholas, red-faced, could hardly explain that he was trying to control his baser urges. "One would think she had more sense than a puppy." He knew he was in the wrong, but he couldn't stop his mouth. "Actually, she should have stayed inside, doing a woman's work, rather than running around after a few berries."

The maids both gaped.

Petyr cleared his throat, startling Nicholas. He'd been so lost in his own misery, he'd forgotten the knight was there."Lets go find the lady, eh? It's not getting any lighter," Petyr said.

Nicholas cursed the falling darkness. "Aye, get the men, would you?"

Petyr snorted. "One day ye'll have to claim us, or let us go."

"I've enough to worry about at this moment, don't you agree?"

Sighing, Petyr went off into the keep, and within moments, came back with all the knights in tow. Forrester, Henry, and Willy all stood with military precision as Petyr handed out torches.

Geoffrey stood shoulder to shoulder with Bertram without bickering. "We'll search all night, if need be," Bertram said grimly.

"Excellent." Nicholas shrugged off his feelings of guilt; he hadn't the time to dwell on mere emotion. "I want bonfires at the edge of the property, something to draw her toward us."

Petyr nodded. "Henry, Willy—it looks like Lord Nicholas was preparing for such a disaster, so take what you need."

"We'll help, my lord. The sooner we get to the trees, the better," Geoffrey said as he and Bertram each grabbed armfuls of wood. "It seems a long time to be gone, collecting berries."

"She doesn't know these woods, not like she does the ones at home," Viola said, picking at a thread on her apron.

"I thought she was avoiding me, and that mayhap she'd slipped around the front of the keep somehow." He'd needed the time alone to sort through his contrary feelings. It was not easy coming to terms with warring emotions, and Celestia sent his entire system into battle.

Bess looked at the woodpile, then she sent him a forgiving glance. "Aye, and so you were going to cut down all the trees in the forest while ye waited for her to come back?"

Nicholas scratched the back of his neck. Celestia needed him. Suddenly he knew that with every bone in his body.

"We can't wait," Nicholas grabbed a torch and set the resin tip alight. He gave up trying to control the fear that tore at his gut. If he had only chased after her, then she wouldn't be in danger, and for certes, he knew that she was in danger.

If he had but listened to his heart, instead of his head.

He thought of her stranded alone in the dark, perhaps with her ankle twisted in a fox hole. Or maybe she had fallen, and hit her head on a gnarled tree root. He couldn't stand it anymore. "Let's go find my wife."

Petyr grunted. "It is about time ye claim her, at least. Let us find the lady then, and mayhap our cursed luck will change."

Nicholas didn't argue.

They made enough noise to alert any wild animals to their presence, but since they weren't hunting, Nicholas didn't care. "Celestia!" His voice grew hoarse from shouting.

Wandering for what felt like hours, Nicholas came to the conclusion that he wasn't dead to feeling after all. Each step he took, he imagined something worse, and yet he couldn't give up.

"Over here." Petyr pointed to a hunk of long blond hair caught on a branch. "She must have come this way."

Nicholas charged forward through the concealing brush without a thought to his own safety, only to plummet down a hidden ravine, rolling and feeling every stone and stick until he landed out of breath on the hard turf.

"My lord! Are you all right?" Petyr's voice bellowed down at him as he lay on his side, taking a moment to decide whether or not anything was broken. "Nicholas?"

Nothing ached, besides his pride, which had been taking a beating anyway. He shouted back, "I'm here, Petyr. Unhurt."

Nicholas looked around the deep valley, startled to see sheep sleeping in the spring grass. They looked like woolly rocks in the dark. His head was still spinning, and he focused on a scrap of blue. The same shade as Celestia's tunic.

His breath caught in his throat, and his voice came out as deep as a bullfrog's croak. "Celestia?"

Rolling to his feet, he ran to where she lay as still as death. It was obvious that she'd fallen down the same steep hill. Had she broken her neck? He ran his hands over her hair, noticed the grass clinging to her clothing, saw a vivid scrape on her cheek, but she was breathing, and he thought her the most beautiful thing he had ever seen.

"Celestia!" He shook her shoulder, willing her to wake.

Her eyes opened, startling them both. "Nicholas? You came for me? Oh, dear, I hope you didn't fall . . ."

"You little fool—why didn't you come back to the keep?"

She lowered her eyes, and her voice was a whisper as she said, "I fell asleep."

Nicholas sat back on his heels, her answer not at all what he'd expected. "In the forest?"

"On a rock."

"A rock?" Was she that naïve? Didn't she know she could have been eaten by a bear? Or killed by marauders? Fear, more than anything else, drove him to raise his voice. "Were you born daft, or do you just try exceptionally hard?"

Her chin snapped up. "As a reminder, my lord, I happened to be upset over burning your arm. I can see now that I shouldn't have worried. May I touch your tongue next? Mayhap the nasty thing will fall off!"

Her temper fanned his own. "Are you not even one whit sorry that you had us all worried while you lay like some princess in a fairy tale, lounging in the forest? Do you not understand what could have happened to you?"

She gave him a sly look and stood on shaking legs before him. She pulled the arrow from her pocket in triumph and shook it under his nose. "Aye, I ken quite well understand what could have happened whilst I was sleeping, my lord. I could have been killed. And where were you, pray tell? Finishing all of your knightly duties so that you can abandon me in your moldering keep without guilt?"

He gritted his teeth.

"I knew it!" She glared at him.

"You are too quick for anyone's good, Lady Celestia. My life would be less complicated if you were . . ." he searched for the perfect word that she couldn't use against him.

"Idiotic? Sheep-brained? Dull-witted?"

He sighed in exasperation and plucked a blade of grass from her tangled hair. "Aye, any of those would suffice." He held up a single digit before she sliced him yet again with the sharp side of her tongue.

"But since you are none of those things, I suggest that we talk about our future—like two reasonable adults."

"Ha!" Celestia crossed her arms and stared at him in disbelief. "I'm quite reasonable, but I have serious doubts where you are concerned. If you can give me one good, sensible reason for leaving me behind, then I might listen. But I get nothing from you except that you seem to think it is for my own good." She stuck her fist on her hip. "That's very condescending, Nicholas, and I won't have it."

"It is for your own good," he said, wanting her to understand.

"You're afraid of our desire. Why? That it might lead to caring? Or, God forbid, love? Are you pledged to another?" She fired accusations one after the next, a tiny, righteous cannon, with him as the target.

"Nay!" he shouted, and then winced as his voice boomed around them in the ravine. "There is no other, damn you."

Petyr's voice yelled down, "I am most pleased that you have found the missing lady, Lord Nicholas. Might I mention though, that I, along with the rest of the forest, can hear every word that you both are saying? Whilst we would like to listen, we are growing tired. Perhaps you can argue while we walk back to the keep?"

"Oh!" Celestia's hands flew to her cheeks in mortification. "Why didn't you tell me we were not alone?"

Nicholas exhaled and slapped his knee in disbelief. "So now this is my fault?"

"Aye!"

Nicholas was in awe as she stomped toward Petyr's voice, taking steps as large as his own. He hurriedly offered his assistance to regain the hill, but he was not surprised when she refused his help. Instead, she grabbed a handful of wild grass and pulled herself up, as nimble as a mountain goat.

Nicholas, once again openmouthed, could do nothing but follow, ready to catch her if she fell.

She didn't.

Two solid days of raining misery did little to endear Nicholas's childhood home to her heart. Not that she was speaking to him—if she was going to lose her touch, so be it, but she was not going to hand her pride over on a gilded platter, as well.

"I never realized how much I would miss home. All it ever does here is spit water. The sun hides its face in shame, more the pity." She knew she sounded churlish, and so attempted a smile that made her maids laugh. "I wish I could have gone hunting with the men."

"It's not that bad, being the lady of the keep, is it?" Viola bit off a piece of thread and tied the end in a knot. "I fancy a nice roasted lamb, with a neat mint jelly." Her brown eyes grew dreamy, and she licked her lips.

Bess giggled. "It's been too wet to even fish the stream, oh, anything hot and fresh. I'm tired of pottage and pickled herring."

Watching Bess put the finishing touches on a lace drapery, Celestia agreed. "We shouldn't complain, I know, for at least we have a not-so-leaky roof over our heads in this miserable weather. Still," she shrugged her shoulder, "'tis hard to remember our blessings. Being a lady of nothing is just that."

"I even miss Father Harold."

"Bess! That cantankerous old priest?" Celestia cupped a hand around her ear and glowered as she mimicked the elderly man. "What was that you say? Eh?

Celestia, I told you not to climb trees—when God wants you, he will come to you. I saw you pilfer that hot bun, Celestia. Do you think God wants a thief in his kingdom?" She leaned over as if her back were crooked and shouted, "Seven Hail Mary's and no meat for a fortnight, young sinner!"

"'Tis true," Viola said with a smile, "that you vexed the poor man terribly, 'Tia. Thank the Lord above that Father Jonas came along. He saved you plenty of harsher penances."

"Aye, and in return, he has to handle Ela. I think he made a bad bargain."

Viola and Bess agreed, tittering behind their teeth, then Bess gasped. "Oh, no—Lady Celestia, you've done it again. That is the wrong color green thread on that pillow. See, how it is a lighter green at the bottom?"

Bess took the fabric away from her mistress with a mew of dismay. Viola clucked, "I don't know why you persist in trying to learn to embroider, my lady. I believe you must be color-blind."

Standing to stretch her sore back, Celestia admitted, "Nay, not color-blind, just disinterested."

"I don't blame Lord Nicholas a bit for making you stay inside the keep, my lady. He was wrought with worry when ye got lost in the forest," Viola said.

"He was only worried about losing face in front of his men. What manner of knight loses his wife in the forest?"

Celestia walked to the arrow slit and peered down. They were in the only habitable room on the second floor of the keep. Though they had all been trapped inside for the past two days, they had only been able to scour through this upstairs solar and the main floor. Though it had been cleaned, they all avoided the kitchen.

She should roll up her sleeves and investigate the north tower and the other two chambers, so long as she stayed away from the holes in the wood, but she couldn't summon the desire. Even though the sun was sparse, at least it wasn't drizzling. Celestia tapped her foot against the wooden floor. "I will die if I stay inside. Truly, it should remain dry for at least another hour, do you not think so?"

Viola and Bess exchanged a knowing look. "Why don't you see if the kitchen garden can be turned, or if it is still a puddle of mud," Bess suggested.

"Yes, I will—I can go now, before it starts raining again."

"Vi owes me a foot rub. I wagered ye'd not last 'til the men came back."

"Ye like the dirt, my lady, and we don't. Me and Bess would rather finish the curtains for this room, and then work on the master chamber."

Caught, Celestia cautioned, "Beware the floor. Nicholas said it needs to be repaired. Are you certain you don't mind?"

"Me thinks Lord Nicholas would appreciate having his own chamber," Bess giggled. Blushing, Celestia laughed along, keeping up the charade that she and Nicholas were wed in every way.

The midday sun peeped from behind the ever-present clouds and shone brightly through the loopholes. Joy filled her spirit, and she wished that she could gather the sunbeams and put them in her vials for days when she needed cheering.

She leaned forward on tiptoe, looking to see as far as she could. The magnificent view of the bountiful forest made her grateful that she'd been found at all, and the sheerness of the craggy cliff both amazed and frightened her.

The palisades around the back of the castle served as a boundary for keeping wild animals out, as well as protected them from any human enemy who might come through the thick tangle of trees. She remembered the arrow on the rock and shivered in the brief sunlight.

Viola said, "If ye're going out, I found some old pelts that you could throw on the fire pit, my lady. Heaven only knows what vermin are alive in those nasty furs."

"I will take them, then." Her stomach rumbled, and Bess glanced at her with surprise. Celestia grinned. "Once I knew the men would be able to hunt this morn, I didn't break my fast with boring pottage. I vowed to wait for fresh meat." As her stomach roared again, she laughed. "I may regret my hasty decision. What shall I do if they can find naught?"

"All the animals in the forest will be glad of the sun, as well, so I would place another wager that you shan't starve." Bess helped Viola gather the musty pelts and furs and rolled them in a large, stained linen sheet so that the bugs living in the furs wouldn't find a new home on Celestia. "Here you are, my lady."

"Lord Nicholas will thank you as well . . . I've noticed he has an uncommon aversion to crawling things."

Celestia smiled and recalled the incident Viola referred to. Being cooped up together below stairs, all of their party had visited and talked in front of the fire for many hours on end, building camaraderie. Nicholas had not said much, and she remembered how tired he had looked in the unkind shadow of the hearth.

An industrious spider, who had somehow escaped the brooms and cleaning of she and her ladies, was spinning a web from the corner of the ceiling to the mantle above the fire. The single strand of gossamer web caught the light from a flame and Petyr had pointed out the spider as it was dangling above Nicholas's head.

Nicholas had scrambled to his feet as if his hair were alight and begun beating at his clothes. "Spider? Where? Where is it?" he'd yelled.

Everyone had laughed, thinking he was jesting, but Celestia had caught the real alarm in his voice before he covered it with more jokes.

She dragged the rotted furs down the stairs. Nicholas kept himself shaved and trimmed as if he didn't care for facial hair. Celestia assumed that this habit, and his dislike of bugs, came from his time in captivity, but she didn't ask him about it. It would lead to an argument, as did every conversation they had lately. The bundle came to rest on the last stair with a thump. He would mock her, which would only anger her, and the last thing either of them needed at this point was her ire.

It galled to know that it was in Nicholas's best interests to leave her. He'd spent so much time pushing her away, and now he didn't need to.

If she could just get pregnant before he left, then at least her brothers would win something from this awful game. She'd let him go—for even though she'd come to love him, he dared not care for her. Her powers were already misfiring. If she told him that she needed his love, he would pity her, but even that wouldn't be enough to satisfy Fate.

Aye, she was becoming a veritable candidate for sainthood. Her heart twisted, but she resolved to cling to her pride. She hauled the load out through the kitchen. Her pride would be all she had to hold on to in the lonely life ahead.

She entered the yard just as Forrester and Willy rode through the gate, shouting victoriously and showing their youth. Her eyes were drawn to her handsome husband as he cantered in behind them, sounding more at ease than she had ever heard. "It was a great shot, Willy! That buck never heard you coming."

Forrester carried the brown and white buck, which was the size of a small pony, over to the shed to be cleaned and dressed. "It will feed us for a week, and for certes, 'tis better than the dried fish we've eaten so much of."

Celestia knew a pang of guilt. They had been eating what her father had packed in the wagons, in addition to the few root vegetables they'd uncovered from the kitchen garden.

Then the torrential rains had come, and all had been forced to stay inside. The men sounded so relieved to have something else to eat that she realized she should have been trying harder in her role as mistress of Falcon Keep. She eyed the shed and thought of all of the venison that would be available, then cringed. They would be so sorry if they gave their prized buck over to her inexperienced hands!

Well, she could learn, couldn't she? She grimaced as she remembered all of the failed cooking lessons she'd had until her mother had finally thrown up her hands in defeat. If it didn't involve an infusion or a decoction, she was hopeless.

Bess and Viola were lady's maids, although they had been pressed into other work since their arrival here, and she wondered if either of them could cook something besides toast.

She gnawed her lower lip and carried the furs to the lively fire, which had been steadily burning the keep's refuse all morning.

Swallowing her pride, she approached the men, who were elbow deep in gore. As a healer, she didn't mind blood. However, her stomach rebelled at the slaughter, and she had to swallow again before asking, "Do any of you know how to cook that?"

Nicholas, a carving knife in his hand, glowered at her. "I know you are angry with me, but would you refuse to cook meals for everyone out of spite?"

"And if I told you that I don't know what to cook?"

"You have a book of recipes, my lady, which you insisted we bring along. Surely you can find something there?"

Hurt that he would think her so mean, she didn't correct the misunderstanding. Her recipes might clear the sinuses, but they'd hardly feed the keep. "Of course.

I would happily feed an entire troop of Scots rebels before cooking for you." She turned her back on the knights, all of whom had been kindness itself, and knew she couldn't walk away from them.

Lifting her chin, she turned back and approached Forrester instead. She cleared her throat and said, "I am worried that the ovens are not yet clean enough—perhaps we could roast the meat outside? I would be happy to turn the spit and, uh, season the meat." She dearly hoped Bess and Viola could help her not make a fool of herself.

Forrester blushed at being singled out. "Aye, my lady. I would be pleased to build a low fire and set up a pit. Anything to be of service."

She nodded her thanks and ignored the snort from her husband. "I will make certain that we have some suitable side dishes for when the meat is finished." Smiling at the knights, she glared at Nicholas and stalked back into the kitchens. Now what? She barely knew the difference between a boiled parsnip and a mashed turnip.

While she was glad that the knights had burned the pine table in the kitchen, Celestia found that she didn't have anything for a work surface.

Gazing at the four stone walls, she wished she'd been more adamant about taking the second wagon. Then she stopped in mid stream; her subconscious was determined to be fair.

Nicholas had a valid reason for not wanting the second wagon, and mayhap he'd been right. If there had been two wagons, perchance the thieves might not have left until all were killed.

She hadn't thought to pack furniture from Montehue Manor, and they'd all been eating in the main hall in front of the fire, seated on various pillows and rolled-up blankets.

Her chin quivered. *I'm horrible,* she thought. No wonder Nicholas wanted to leave! She bit her lip until the trembling receded. If hard work was needed, then she was up to the task. By Saint Jude, she was finished with tears. Aye, murder had been done here in this room, and it was true that they had all been avoiding it. But a kitchen was the heart of the home, and the ghosts needed to be purged.

A chill settled at the nape of her neck.

Or not. Would that they had cooking recipes, she'd even invite them to stay for dessert.

Chapter ELEVEN

She would start with another dose of soap and water, and see if she could remember any of the recipes her mother had tried to teach her.

Celestia was up to her elbows in suds when Forrester found her.

"Ye're busy, my lady, should I come back?"

Glancing over her shoulder, her rump moving in rhythm with her arms, she said, "Nay, nay—my grandmother says that idle hands are a devil's helpmeet. I suppose that makes me quite immune to Satan's wiles today."

Celestia tossed the rag into the bucket, well pleased with the gleaming stone floor and the iron pots she had located behind the oven. "I was hoping for a miracle. The men are hungry, and most tired of anything potted or salted."

"I've set the buck on the spit, for roasting, my lady, and I was just wondering if ye had some extra salt?"

She got up and nodded, leading the way to some of

the packed crates in the main room. "Aye. Salt, dried basil, onion, and," Celestia dug around until she found what she was looking for, "parsley."

Noting the dubious look on Forrester's face, Celestia flushed. "I've got gold plate and fine linens, but no table. I've got goblets, but the wine is gone. And, oh, I may as well confess." She lowered her eyes in shame. "I don't know how to cook."

She waited for his disparaging remarks, but when she raised her eyes, he was nodding with sympathy.

"No one liked to say it, but me mam wasn't a cook, either. Me and my brothers had to learn to cook, or learn to love burned stew." He smiled shyly. "I hate burned stew."

Celestia laughed with relief.

"If you could help me, Forrester, I would be forever in your debt." She rubbed her lower back. "I am a healer. I can clean and garden and do the scullery work, but God help us all if I have to do anything besides toss a few raw vegetables in vinegar."

"You can hire a cook."

Celestia stopped laughing. "And where would I find one of those?"

"There has to be a village close by, no more than a day's ride, surely."

"That is a brilliant idea." But it spoke of permanence, and she didn't plan on staying here long enough for it to matter.

Viola and Bess danced into the kitchen, their expressions playful. After sending a flirtatious nod to Forrester, Bess said, "The entire second floor has been reinforced, and is now as clean as can be. We have beaten the rugs, brushed the draperies, and put fresh linens and rushes in each room. Including the master's chamber."

Celestia blushed. "Oh. Well, I thank you, and for certes, Nicholas will thank you, too." She was certain of no such thing, but she could hardly share that with her maids.

Oh, for certes, she could say, *I want his love, but he refuses mine, so I am afraid that I will kill him with my anger and adoration*? Nay. She'd keep up the pretense that all was well.

"It will be wonderful to have a real meal," Bess said, batting her eyelashes. "I saw ye, from the window, making the fire pit."

Forrester's face flushed, and he stared at the floor.

Viola said bravely, "My lady, if ye would like to prepare for dinner, ye'll have privacy now." She pointed to Celestia's head.

"What?" Celestia brought her fingers to her hair, remembering the old cloth she'd tied around her braids. "I'm cleaning," she said defensively.

"Lady Celestia," Bess said, grasping her mistress's hand. "Look at how red and chapped these are; Lady Galiana would have a fit. You have a peasant's kerchief wrapped around your head, your skirts are tucked between your legs, and your feet are bare. I know that you are working hard, but so is Lord Nicholas."

"I think ye lovely, my lady," Forrester said with bright red cheeks.

Bess smacked his arm. "A few strokes of the brush, my lady, and ye could remind him of how lovely ye really are."

Shouts came from the back, and Forrester hurried to open the kitchen door. Willy shouted, "We have visitors!"

"Visitors?" Celestia pressed her hand to her belly. She was in no way ready to meet anyone as the lady of Falcon Keep. And the last time she'd heard someone announce visitors, she'd ended up married. *Danger.*

Viola plucked the kerchief from Celestia's head, and smoothed down her tunic. "Cover your toes, my lady. We don't want them to think ye a maid."

"Maid? We have been doing the work of ten maids. Do I have time to change?" Celestia hissed the question between clenched teeth.

"Nay, here." Bess reached over and pinched Celestia's cheeks. "For color."

"Are ye ready?" Viola asked, her brow scrunched with dismay.

"I'll escort ye, my lady." Forrester gallantly held out his arm.

Bess huffed.

"I'm ready," Celestia lied. "Wait, a quick prayer to Saint Agatha Hildegard."

"Who?"

"She was a model wife, and I have much to learn. I don't even have anything to offer anyone in way of refreshment!"

"They'll need nothing but water," Forrester soothed.

Celestia allowed the young knight to walk next to her as they left the kitchen and walked into the yard. "I forgot, we have a cask of the baron's burgundy."

"I put the last bottle of sweet wine from Montehue Manor in your chamber, but I could get it," Viola said.

"So long as we serve our guests outside, we shall be fine, and mayhap they won't have to know the extent of our . . . poverty." The logical half of her brain reasoned that any visitors would be understanding, but marriage had turned her into an emotional disaster.

"Mayhap they will know of where we can hire some servants. Or better yet, mayhap we can find the former servants from Falcon Keep, and get them to return."

Celestia stopped her nervous chatter when she bumped into Nicholas's back. "I beg pardon . . . I wasn't watching where I was going."

Looking up, she saw the clearest pale green eyes she had ever seen. They were set in an oval face, surrounded by waving locks of ebony black hair. Warm, rosy lips dimpled in a devastating smile that was not directed at her, but toward her speechless husband.

The woman was beautiful, more beautiful than anyone she'd ever seen before, and considering that she came from a gorgeous family, that was saying a lot.

Celestia hated her on sight.

Nicholas could not remember ever seeing a woman of such timeless beauty. She was like a painting in a church, a Greek marble statue, a work of art that left him chilled.

He knew that he should return her greeting, but he couldn't move. Her dark hair and voluptuous body brought to mind Leah, with her veiled charms and naked threats. The sling holding her arm to her chest did nothing to detract from her loveliness.

Celestia fumed at his back, and he was grateful for her presence.

Petyr filled the void of his bad manners. "Welcome to Falcon Keep," he said, with a widespread gesture including all of the keep's inhabitants. "Good day to you! We welcome you, and beg you to not to judge us too harshly." He grinned. "We arrived but a few days past, and though it may not seem so, we have accomplished much."

Petyr used his mythical blond looks to coax another smile from the young beauty, and Nicholas was impressed as his chief knight first bowed to the crone next to the beauty, and lastly to the tall silent man who stood behind his womenfolk.

'Twas obvious that the younger two were brother and sister, so alike were they in their features. Nicholas, following Petyr's lead, bowed, as well, but it had nowhere near the grace of Petyr's.

"I am Petyr Montgomery, chief knight to Lord Nicholas Peregrine."

"Le Blanc," Nicholas muttered low enough that only his people could hear him. He raised his voice, but kept his face a polite mask. "Indeed, welcome, and though our hospitality may be rough, we invite you to stay and dine with us. As you can see, we have plenty." He slid his glance toward the pit where the venison was skewered and browning on a rack.

The beauty lowered her eyes shyly, and the crone stepped forward. "Greetings, and welcome to Falcon Keep, Lord Peregrine. I am called Grainne Kat, and these are my children, Maude and Joseph. We bring you a gift of bread and jams."

She handed the basket to Viola with a throaty chuckle. "Welcome, mistress."

Celestia's maid accepted the basket graciously. "Our thanks; I'll give these over to Lady Celestia."

The crone pressed, "Ye're not the mistress?"

Nicholas watched the fleeting emotions cross his wife's face. He could tell she wanted to dig her toes in the dirt and hide.

He compared Viola's brushed hair and clean tunic with its crisp white apron to Celestia's garb. 'Twas obvious she had been interrupted in the middle of some chore. He was about to come to her aid, when she hefted that dainty, stubborn chin and walked forward with her hand outstretched.

"Welcome, I'm Lady Celestia. Thank you for the lovely jams."

She stood regally, and Nicholas cringed as all three pairs of the visitors' eyes raked over her disheveled appearance. He had never been so proud.

She kept her gaze steely and refused to flinch, even as the beauteous Maude sought to hide a giggle behind her hand. The crone didn't try to be polite. "Oh! I certainly didn't see you standing there, how tiny you are. If I would have noticed you, which I didn't," the crone assured her, "I would have thought you a child. But, no, I see now that you are full grown."

Smiling, the old woman showed her blackened teeth. "Certainly you are too small to bear sons for such a large knight?"

Celestia pursed her lips and straightened her shoulders, but Nicholas prevented what might have been a blistering tirade by placing his hand upon her shaking shoulder. "I find her perfection itself, Grainne Kat."

Taking the brunt of attention upon himself, Nicholas dipped his head and continued, "And, if I was a man to notice such things, and I am, I would say that you are definitely old enough to mind your tongue—or perhaps such things are not important here in the backwoods of civilization?"

The old woman's eyes popped wide, and her son took a threatening step toward Nicholas. Grainne Kat laid a gnarled hand on his arm and gave a hearty laugh. "Oh—that is true, that is true. The backwoods? Indeed, they are, and, no, my good lord, such fancy manners are not needed. Although I know them, and though they be rusty, I shall do my best to remember them. And curb my tongue," she laughed, a horrible rusted sound, and said, "I beg your pardon, my lady."

The old woman tried to curtsy, and Petyr caught her before she fell all the way over. Celestia nodded her forgiveness, sending Nicholas a shy glance that warmed him.

Nicholas hoped that he had soothed his wife's ruffled feathers enough that she wouldn't scorch the side dishes apurpose. He was ravenous for anything besides pickled herring and boiled greens. He answered the thankful glance from Celestia with a jerk of his head toward their guests.

She sighed, then smiled. "Won't ye please stay and join us for a bite to eat? Your bread and jam would go nicely with the meat I am sure you can smell roasting." Her eyelids flickered as if she refrained from accusing them of coming for the food on purpose. "We have been cleaning nonstop since our arrival," her hesitation conveyed that she resented the interruption, "but we would deeply appreciate your company."

Nicholas gave her an approving smile and she discreetly rolled her eyes.

"If you would sit," she gestured toward the trio of stumps the knights had been using as chairs, "we will bring out refreshments. I see, Maude, that you've been injured? Poor child."

Maude bared her teeth in a smile and quickly unwrapped the scarf from her neck. "It's nothing, a scratch."

Celestia, though shorter, managed to look down her nose just the same. "Nicholas, perhaps you could find a way to make some sort of table to accommodate a feast?"

"Would you like it in the main room?"

Celestia pursed her lips. "Being as that is the only room that could fit everyone, my lord, it will have to do." She turned to the side, so that her unwanted guests couldn't read her lips. "Unless the shed would be too uncomfortable?"

Nicholas shook his head and playfully pushed her toward the kitchen. "Get to work, wench."

As she gave him an exaggerated curtsy, baring her naked toes, he grinned, quite liking his wife—again, damn it all.

Celestia sipped her wine and wondered why she felt such a ridiculous sense of pride in her position as the lady of the keep.

The spitted buck was juicy perfection, but she hadn't done it. Bess and Viola had found some wild watercress growing by the stream, which she'd washed and tossed with oil and vinegar while they boiled and mashed some turnips. The single bottle of sweet white wine from Montehue Manor had been opened, as well as the cask of burgundy from the baron.

She sipped again, feeling magnanimous enough to admit that the bread and jam were a perfect addition to the first real supper at Falcon Keep in what she'd calculated to be over twenty years.

Celestia eyed the long table, which was actually the back of the wagon settled on the three stumps from the back of the courtyard and draped with a fine linen cloth. Her family's gift of silver and gold plates adorned the top, with golden goblets shining in the candlelight. She smiled. Perhaps it wouldn't be up to her parents' standards, but it wasn't bad, considering what she had to work with.

She tilted her head to the left in order to get a better view of Nicholas. He was eating, and flirting uneasily with their beautiful guest. Nicholas was not Lord Riddleton, and she could tell that he was merely being polite. Celestia couldn't blame him, she supposed, but it rankled.

Tightening her grasp on the goblet so that she didn't

throw it at Maude's dark ringlets, her heart ached at more evidence of Nicholas's kindness. For a man who did more brooding than a pregnant woman, he was the very ideal of knighthood.

His valor in coming to her defense today had only deepened her love; he was a man of honor, temperate in food and drink. He worked as hard, if not harder, than the other men. And he was so very handsome. Her pulse jumped in her throat as she watched him lick a piece of meat from his thumb. She narrowed her eyes, irritated, as she saw Maude flutter her lashes.

Celestia had never backed down from a challenge, and facing a woman who had no qualms over acting the flirt with a man, in front of his wife made her angry enough to scream.

She'd taken the time to wash and change before eating. She'd brushed her hair out, and it fell to her hips in waves once released from the tight braids she'd worn. Pinching her cheeks, powdering her nose, these were all things that Galiana would make her do. She'd even applied her favorite perfume.

No one had been more surprised than she to find out that she was feminine enough to want to compete with Maude, the fair-faced beauty, for her husband's attention.

Picking her favorite blue kirtle and her low-heeled embroidered slippers, she added ear bobs of blue sapphire, which glittered against her hair. A matching ring with a huge stone flashed upon her finger. She had done her best, but her husband had barely glanced her way. He was too busy staying away from Maude's quick fingers.

She sighed and popped a candied almond in her mouth.

Nicholas was saying, "Ah, it was so long ago, I hardly remember a thing."

Grainne Kat asked, "What about your mother? Do you remember her?"

Nicholas drank deep from his goblet. "Nay." He changed the subject. "I am most curious as to what happened to the people here. The north tower has been boarded and mortared, and the rest of the keep reeks of neglect."

"Well, now." Grainne sucked her rotten teeth. "After your mother died, and the peasants realized that no one was coming to govern them, they stole most everything. Between them and the raiding Scots' border patrol, this shell is all that is left." She waved a hand to indicate the mostly barren interior. "It used to be grand, you know. Your mother's family lived here, afore she married the baron." Coughing, she added darkly, "He wasn't a baron, then, though, was he?"

"Did you work here at the keep, Grainne Kat?"

Celestia detected the woman's slight hesitation before she laughed. "Me? Nay, Lord Nicholas. I am but a simple woman who knew your mother. Half-English, half-Scot she was, and all alone here amongst the Scottish folk who considered her a traitor—with the exception of yourself, and you were just a babe."

Celestia didn't care for the crone's ingratiating laugh. In truth, that laugh was alarming.

"And if it's workers that ye need, why I've got two for ya, right here," she said, pointing her gnarled finger to her children. "There's a small English town along the border, a day's ride to the west, where ye can find more. By my reckoning, them that wasn't killed by the raiding Scots fled to the village there."

"What have ye heard of a rebellion? And the Norsemen, are they as fierce as rumor says?" Petyr leaned forward, trying to keep Maude's attention on him. "We're far enough inland from Solway Firth that I don't see this keep as being pivotal to the enemy."

Joseph spoke up behind a hunk of meat, "Aye! The raiders are bad men . . . when you hear the thunder of hooves, you must hide. But we live deep in the woods, deep. I can see them, but they can't find me."

Grainne Kat cackled and tapped his hand. "Oh, Joseph, no sense being maudlin. We've had a good life, haven't we?" She spoke to Nicholas, "My boy's a wonder at hunting the small animals in the forest, a fine touch with curing the skins to sell at the village on fair days. We get by, we get by."

Nicholas posed a question as he crumbled a piece of bread, "Why did the peasants leave the place fallow? It's obvious that they'd worked hard to clear the area for grazing the sheep and growing crops. What happened to the mill and the stream? It seems odd that they left it, rather than wait for the baron to send more men after my mother died."

Nicholas tossed the crust to the table, confusion clearly writ upon his face. "Why would they abandon their homes? Could they not defend themselves against the Scots?"

It was about time he started asking questions, Celestia

thought. Mayhap he'd stay, if he could but remember.

Joseph tore a large bite of meat off the bone, chewed, and gulped. "I'll tell ya why. It's haunted, this place. I've got me charm against spirits, I do, so none can bother me. But everyone else left 'cause of the screaming from the north tower."

This time Grainne's tap was more of a smack. She made an apologetic sound, and looked down at her plate. "He's not right in the head, mind, not bad, like, but not . . . right."

Celestia straightened and discreetly looked Joseph over. Her abilities to heal did not include the mentally deficient, but she'd not sensed anything off about him. He was a big man, and tall. His eyes were not as bright as the sparkling orbs of his sibling, yet he seemed intelligent.

"The north tower? It's haunted?"

Maude giggled instead of answering Celestia's question and dabbed at her mouth with her napkin. "Be good, Joey, and remember, we don't talk about ghosts." Her eyes danced encouragingly at each of the men around the table.

Joseph nodded his dark head. "Hail Mary and alleluia! There are *no* ghosts."

Goose bumps rose on Celestia's skin. It was no wonder that the crone did most of the talking, with her son a good-natured simpleton and her daughter a flirt. She rubbed her arms. She was a firm believer in ghosts and spirits, having befriended them all her life. For the most part, they were harmless.

Petyr raised his glass in an obvious effort to divert the turn of conversation. "A toast!"

Celestia picked up her goblet, as did everyone else.

"Here's to good health and good fortune, and to the new lord and lady of Falcon Keep."

Bess giggled from too much wine and stood. "As a gift for the both of you, we've readied the master's chambers. For the first time since your wedding night, you will have a feather mattress and some privacy!"

Viola laughed aloud before clamping her hand over her mouth, and Celestia found her gaze drawn to her husband once again. Her eyes, she was certain, would never look at anything else, if left to their own accord. Would he think she had, once again, deliberately arranged to seduce him?

His surprise was fleeting and was gone before she was certain it had ever been there. He stood and bowed like the chivalrous knight he had been trained to be. Smiling, he met her eyes and said, "Now *that* is a reason to drain your cup!"

Maude chose not to drink to that and tipped her goblet over, "accidentally," Celestia was sure, drawing all attention to her.

"Oh! How clumsy of me!" Maude pouted prettily as she got to her feet, rubbing the spill of white wine farther into her tunic. "Oh, dear, 'tis ruined."

Celestia bit her tongue to keep from calling the wanton chit horrible names. Maude's breast was clearly outlined beneath the wet fabric, and the more she rubbed it, the perkier her nipple became. Celestia looked around the table, and the only male eye not watching the show belonged to Joseph, the wench's brother.

Mustering her dignity, Celestia stood to her full

height, and jerked the sopping linen, clanging the platters and plates together. "Quite right, it *is* ruined. This cloth came down from my mother's family—however am I to get the stain out?"

Viola choked on a laugh, and Grainne recovered her wits as the sensual web was broken. "Cover yourself, girl." She immediately draped her own shawl over her daughter's shoulders. "The hour is late, and we must be getting home."

Nicholas cleared his throat, reminding Celestia of her manners. Since when had she needed so many reminders?

She smiled while glaring at Nicholas. Did he find Maude attractive? In her duty as chatelaine, she couldn't refuse hospitality, no matter how jealous she was. "It is late, and while I cannot offer you a *bed*," she defiantly met her husband's eyes, "we have blankets aplenty if you'd care to sleep here in the hall by the fire."

Maude shot her a look of venom as Grainne held her daughter by the elbow. "Thank you kindly, my lady, but we'd know our way through these woods blindfolded. We will come again, and if I hear of anyone looking for work, I will gladly send them this way."

Celestia bobbed her head, noting that the old woman didn't offer her children's services again.

"Henry, fix them a torch, won't you, for the walk home?" Nicholas edged them toward the back door as he thanked them for visiting.

Once the trio left, the rest of the party sat back down at the table. Willy, the youngest of the knights, chewed a slice of dried apple. "Pretty maid, weren't she?"

Forrester nodded, Petyr blushed, and Henry said knowingly, "She may be pretty, but I warrant she's the kind that leaves a man bleeding on the floor when she's through with 'im!"

Sir Geoffrey coughed and gave the knights a pointed look to mind their tongues. The older and wiser knight continued loyally, "Aye, but she weren't half as fine to look upon as our own Lady Celestia."

Celestia blushed as the men all hurriedly agreed. Forrester hastened to add, "The lovliest lady ever, that's the Lady Celestia."

Bertram sighed and drained his ale. "We cannot forget the lovely Viola."

"Or the beauteous Bess," Willy said.

Bess asked, "All chivalry aside, my dear knights, but have you ever met an *ugly* woman in the dark?"

Holding her stomach from laughing so hard, Celestia said, "Stop, before I fall off the bench." She placed her hands on the rickety table.

The table was cleared, the fire was banked, and it was time for bed. Celestia had never known such an awkward moment, and from the way that Nicholas was shifting from foot to foot, he felt the same.

Petyr stood and stretched. "I'm exhausted, but what a day, eh?"

Willy yawned. "Nice buck, nice meal."

Bess set her embroidery hoop to the floor. "Will you need me help, my lady, readying for bed? Viola and I took the chamber down the hall, if ye need us."

The men slept in the great room, and she had to leave

if they were to sleep. She was being ordered to bed by her maid. Celestia slowly got to her feet, finding Nicholas behind her, ready to take her arm. This was strange and ridiculous, she thought as she murmured, "I'll be fine this eve, thank you," with a dry throat.

She bid everyone a good night and led the way up the stairs on shaking legs into the cleaned chamber. Her eyes focused on the brightly made bed, and her knees buckled.

Candles perfumed the room and gave off a romantic glow. He'd think she was seducing him, for certes.

Nicholas steadied her, his hand confident beneath her arm.

"My lady?"

She swallowed. "I . . ." she gulped. "I didn't put the girls up to this, Nicholas."

"I can see that."

"Yet," she managed to whisper, "'tis lovely."

He released her arm and sighed, then poured them each some water from a cool jug. "I'm nervous as any bridegroom."

Celestia accepted the goblet with trembling fingers, wishing they'd not run out of wine, and sat on the edge of the bed. "Bridegroom?" Her voice cracked. "Do you mean to sleep with me after all?"

Nicholas coughed, his brow furrowed. "I was but referring to the circumstances, nothing more."

"Oh." Celestia damned her flaming cheeks. "Nicholas, I . . . I am mortified beyond reason, so I might as well forge ahead and ask." She knew he could think her stupid, or foolish, but she had to take the chance. "Have you considered making me your wife in truth?"

Nicholas sank to his knees and clasped Celestia's hands between his. He rested his forehead on her knees, and her pulse beat so rapidly she wondered how she could survive it.

Was he gathering his courage to break her heart? She couldn't stop her hand from caressing his ebony hair as another crack formed in her heart. "'Tis all right, Nicholas, you don't need to explain."

He looked up, and all of the despair she had ever sensed in him was there in his gaze. "I must. I have feelings for you that I thought were long dead and buried, yet you have resurrected them. You, Celestia, have come between me and my desire for vengeance."

"Vengeance? I thought you wanted absolution, from Saint James."

"My pilgrimage to Spain and Saint James involves more than my begging forgiveness."

"For killing that woman, when she had been torturing you?" She caressed a lock of hair off his forehead. "Would be that I could take my poisons to her and make her suffer, but she is dead, and she deserved to die."

His briefly closed his eyes. "You defend my actions, yet that is not all."

Celestia took a deep breath. "I know you don't like to hear it, but I felt what you felt, when I touched your wounds. I knew your pain as you were tortured, and sorely abused, poor Nicholas." She'd pledged to stop her infernal crying, but he was hurting her fresh.

"God's bones, 'Tia." He ground his back teeth together. "I've made a vow before God that I will do this thing—I must have answers, and those lie at the feet of Baron Peregrine." His voice broke. "I don't want to want you, but I do. And I know that by fulfilling my vow, I will hurt you. It cannot be avoided."

He said so much, she thought, without making anything clear. He stood, obviously uncomfortable with baring his emotions. She took his hand, reveling in the warmth there, and pulled him down to sit beside her.

"Nicholas, you've been given a harsh lot in life; there is none who would deny it. There is good in this world, too. But would you push aside all that is good only to focus on the bad? You test yourself beyond endurance—your body requires sleep. Your mind needs the rest, and your soul, Nicholas, cries for peace. Let me help you. You won't hurt me."

She picked up his arm, remembering how she'd burned him. "I am afraid that it is I who will hurt you."

He was quiet for a moment, and then he once again rose to his feet. She followed his every movement, captivated by him. He removed his tunic, then rolled up the sleeves of his linen undershirt. He showed his wrist where she had touched him. "See? There is no mark." He spoke slowly. "I am healed."

No burn mark, thank Mary Magdalene for another miracle, she sighed with relief. "I'd worried that I'd left a scar, since you've kept your arms covered."

"For this reason." He showed his other wrist to her. "I didn't want to answer questions, if anybody noticed." His other wrist was still covered with scars.

Celestia felt her eyes widen as she realized what had

happened—she wasn't losing her gifts—instead, she'd healed an old wound, something she would have sworn upon Boadicea's grave was impossible.

"From the manacles used to chain me to their damned walls," Nicholas continued in a strangled voice. "I could hardly believe it, yet the old scars disappeared, right before my very eyes. I was chopping wood, and then you ran."

Celestia caught her breath, then brought her finger to her lip. "I thought I had burnt you out of anger." She lightly caressed the smooth skin on his wrist, overjoyed that the marks, and the pain, were gone. "Because of great grandmother's curse."

Nicholas gathered her hands in his and kissed the backs. "I've heard my father is cursed. Ye say your family is cursed. Joseph says the north tower is cursed." He kissed the fingers on the right hand, and Celestia's body responded with an acute awareness of the texture of his lips, of the warmth of each breath, of . . .

"I know of no curse, my lady. I say you have a powerful gift, indeed, if you can smooth old scars."

Her stomach clenched as his lips brushed each sensitive pad on her left hand.

"I'm not a witch, Nicholas," she said as she leaned over, dropping a soft kiss on the top of his head. He was still on his knees before her. His elbows leaned on either side of her body, and she leaned in, wanting to be closer to him . . . to the way he smelled, of pine trees and fresh air and hard work.

"I know. Though ye've bewitched me."

He lifted his head, and his eyes were stormy gray

and turbulent with desire. Heat shot from his gaze to hers, and her breathing became shallow gasps. Their eyes stayed locked to one another, and the air between them sizzled with need.

Only he could soothe her trembling heat.

"Then stay with me."

"I cannot."

"I want you, Nicholas." She rubbed her hands over his shoulders, thrilling in the play of muscles beneath her fingers. She scooted to the edge of the mattress, parting her thighs so that Nicholas could come between them.

He did, inching closer a breath at a time.

His linen undershirt was open in a deep vee, and she dropped a kiss at the hollow of his throat. Images of Leah, and her knife at his throat, angered her, and she growled like a feral cat. She would do what she could to protect her man.

"She's gone, Nicholas; let this memory be better than the old one." She flicked her tongue against his skin, and he sucked in a breath.

He grabbed the back of her head, lifting her face as if he needed to study the truth of her yearning. "I made a pledge, to God and Saint James," he pleaded with her to understand.

My noble man, Celestia thought, catching the sob in her throat.

"We're wed, and even though you must leave me, I would wait, Nicholas, for you to return." She realized the truth in her words as soon as she spoke them.

He crushed her against him, and her cheek rested

against the warmth of his broad chest. Hope blossomed in Celestia's heart, and she rained kisses along his collarbone.

He kissed her forehead, her brow, the tip of her nose. "You've lovely hair. I've wanted to touch it since that first night I saw it down." His breathing was fast and hot against her ear, and the air seemed to travel straight to her belly.

"I would have let you," she whispered, unable to keep from pressing her lips to his. This was glorious, and no wonder the minstrels and troubadours sang of it, it was a wonder that people did anything else. *Love.*

Her hands fisted in the loose linen cloth of his undershirt. "Would you think me too bold to say I want to take this off of you?"

Nicholas paused in his exploration of her back and neck and groaned. "'Tia."

"I want you, and I think you want me, too, aye? We're married, and I would wait for you to come back from your quest to Spain. This can't be wrong, Nicholas."

She pulled at the shirt from the back, then tugged at the front, wanting to see him bare-chested. Even in the short time they'd been together, he'd filled out his once too-thin body.

"Here." She pulled at the sleeve that covered the once-scarred wrist and then placed her lips against the healed skin. Then she took the other wrist, and her heart broke at the scars there.

Red, angry welts that looked painful. The manacles were gone, but the memories of why he had them still lingered, and would, for as long as they were there as a reminder.

She started to touch him, hovering her hand over the scars, faltering for a heartbeat as she waited for his consent. Dare she try again?

In a leap of trust, he nodded.

"I'm afraid, Nicholas."

"Don't be. I am ready, if you are willing."

She took the trust he gave her as if it were more precious than all of her jewels combined.

Covering the irritated scars with her fingers, she set her mind free to focus on the injury. Once pinpointed, the warmth came slowly, from the center of her being, as she concentrated on absolving his pain.

The wound pulsed, crimson red. Bright, vibrant colors splashed in her mind as she worked over his wrist. Angry crimson, light burgundy, brownish-red, grayish-brown.

Celestia refused to give in to the weariness that drew her. Gram warned that to give in to that while healing would injure both her and the person she was working on.

Concentrating, she focused on the colors until rose and mauve appeared, and she was soothed by a healthy pink and light blue aura around the scarred area. She exhaled and released the negative toxins.

She had only begun to relinquish her grip both mentally and physically when suddenly she became bombarded with more pain—anguish for which she wasn't prepared. She had no choice but to absorb it into her own body.

Black.

The deepest, darkest black she could fathom came at her in waves, crashing like fluttering bat wings against her weakened psyche.

Chapter TWELVE

Nicholas did not know what to expect as he watched Celestia close her eyes and place her slender fingers on his wrist. He was prepared for the burning sensation he had felt before when she handled his scars. He braced himself so that he wouldn't move or pull away. He'd not scare her again.

This time, however, the feeling was different.

There was warmth, a pleasant heat that reminded him of the high summer sun when he'd ridden at the abbey, a time before he went on crusade. Celestia's grip never tightened, but remained loose over his scars, which began to pulsate beneath her touch. Nicholas's eyelids grew heavy, and he found he was tiring, even though he was doing none of the work. Rather, she was drawing out his injuries and pain with her personal energy.

He'd never imagined that his internal wounds had substance. When he'd given it thought, which wasn't often since he was a warrior, by God's bones, he thought the pain to be a figment of his mind.

Like a man who swore he could still feel the itch on a hand that had been lopped off in battle, he would feel the damning narcotic pull of opium in his blood.

And he raged for it.

He'd learned that the madness would come for him in his deepest sleep.

Did Celestia take the dark need into her healer's body and break it apart, as if it never were? What if she was stealing his life force, as well? Nicholas did not move a muscle as she worked her magic. He made himself stay calm—he trusted *her*.

He chose not to examine how that had come to pass.

Nicholas lost track of time, rousing as he realized her healing touch was cooling. He opened his eyes, which he hadn't remembered closing, and saw that the red, aching scars were gone. *Gone.* A smile flitted across Celestia's face, and he could see that she was finished.

He opened his mouth to thank her, expecting her to release his arm, when all of a sudden she grasped his wrist in a rough hold. Her gaze met his, and he read the confusion on her face. She was trying to let go, and yet could not. Her fingers were fused to his skin.

Concerned, Nicholas tried prying her hand off of his arm, but it was bound tight. Celestia's brow creased, her mouth twisted, and a warning moan came from the back of her throat. *Oof.* Nicholas jerked back—something, mayhap the same invisible something that bound the two of them together, had slammed into the middle of his chest. He gagged, choking on fragments of memories. Rats with pink eyes and scrawny bodies in his cell, lice in his hair, bugs in his food, and Leah . . . Leah, with her inky sloe eyes and sensuous body, plying him with opium and raping him to satisfy her own carnal desires and need for a dark-haired babe.

Every ugly thing in his past threatened to suffocate him. He coughed and fought against the images—he had escaped before—he would not let his foulness drown Celestia.

Summoning the remnants of his pride, he could think only of saving Celestia. He loosened her grip from his wrist and shouted, "No!"

She fell back onto the bed, her eyes wide open and unblinking, her mouth pursed as she battled confusion. Nicholas ran his hands through his hair, bitterness enfolding him once again. He'd been a fool to think he could move beyond his past. "I am sorry, so sorry. Sweet Jesu, 'Tia, are you hurt?"

She sat up, her blond hair tumbling in disarray around her shoulders, her eyes wide.

"Nay, I am not hurt," she said in a whisper. "But, Nicholas, you are. I have never felt such pain. You can't keep it locked up inside you. 'Tis a foul humor and it will poison you, surely as the opium once did."

Nicholas backed away from her outstretched hand. "Never mention that again—do you hear?" He struggled against her empathy.

"I'm sorry, Nicholas, please, come to me." Her pale face was drawn, her brilliant eyes shadowed.

It would be too easy to bury his hurt in her accepting

body, her forgiving heart. But he'd not chance causing her more pain by giving in to her beseeching arms. He bowed his head and searched for the resolve to walk away, knowing it would be one of the hardest things he'd ever done. "That is none of your concern . . ." He flinched at the sudden anger in her gaze.

She deserved more than that.

Nicholas stalked over to the table holding the water and poured them each a cup. He handed one to Celestia, and swallowed his in a single gulp before pacing back and forth in front of the bed.

"I went on crusade, for God and king, like many other knights. We followed the codes of honor, and fought for our country—to win control of Jerusalem for the glory of God and Christianity. My duty was to protect the sacred relic of Saint James the Apostle. We had strict instructions to carry it directly to King Richard, who believed he needed a certain number of relics in order to win the war."

The memories were still sharp, and he poured himself another goblet of water.

"My father sent it as a vassal price instead of going on crusade himself." Nicholas briefly met her eyes and turned away from her compassion. "And me, his unclaimed son. I was also part of the price he paid, although I only knew it that night when Leah told me." He couldn't think of it, of the type of man who would send his only living son to death. Why?

Anger pounded in his temples. "I was not vigilant enough, and we were ambushed by the enemy. All were slaughtered, all but me. I had fought hard, as had my men, yet they lay dead and bleeding around me. The Saracen leader kept me for ransom."

His voice shook, and he took a deep breath to keep it steady. *Sand, wind, blood, and gore. The loss of a holy relic that could have turned the tide for King Richard. And God.*

Nicholas wet his dry mouth, but he couldn't forget the blistering hot day of the attack, the screams of the horses, the blood from his slain comrades.

He looked at his wife, who was watching him with tenderness, damn her. He would spare her the gory details, except he had a feeling she'd already seen them. *His fault.*

"I was held for a year, until I finally escaped." He stomped across the carpeted floor of their chamber, wishing he could carve the image of dead Leah from his head. "I prayed, Celestia, with all my might. But the day of the slaughter, God stopped listening to me. He could not forgive me my foolishness, nor for losing a great relic to the infidels." He pierced her with his gaze, expecting to see condemnation.

He saw none, and sought to make her understand the severity of his sins.

"I was raised in a monastery, I could write, I could reason—but I could not get God to answer my prayer for death." Nicholas detested the ache in his chest. It was a weakness, and he pounded at it with his fist.

"I tried to bribe the guards for poison so that I could commit the sin of suicide. I gave up every shred of dignity, living, finally, for the visits from Leah and the opium she brought. I wanted to die, thinking it would be my fate to rot in that stinking, filth-infested cell. But their doctors knew how to keep me alive for eternity."

He lowered his gaze, shame heavy on his back. "Then she told me her husband grew suspicious, and she had to kill me. I begged," his voice tore as he remembered the bitter taste, "I begged her to ransom me."

Nicholas tugged at his hair, agitated with painful memories. "That was when she told me that the man who hired her husband to ambush the caravan and steal back the relic was the same man whom I thought would send the ransom money." Nicholas laughed, but there was no mirth in the sound.

"Yes, Celestia, why would *my father* want me back alive?"

"Nicholas, oh." Celestia started to rise, but he waved her back. He couldn't bear her touch just now, not when he was so bruised and barely hanging on to his sanity.

"I felt the prick of her blade against my throat." He touched the scar that Celestia had blessed with her kiss.

"And I realized that I was not ready to die after all. She thought I was too far gone, but it's amazing how fast nearly dying can bring a man back from the brink of ecstasy. My shame, Celestia, is that I knew it was wrong to lie with Leah, just as I knew it was wrong to forget about life with drugs—I knew this. My shame is that I did it anyway, and God forgive me, sometimes that joy was all that kept me going."

Nicholas dropped to his knees and bowed his head. "I took the knife away from her, and I slid it into her neck as easy as a blade through butter. She'd left me unbound, which was *her* final mistake."

He heard Celestia crying, but he couldn't comfort her. He would tell the story this one time, and then never again. "I escaped. I ate scraps, and I'm sure I scared a few good folk, but there were some who helped me, too. Gave me clothing and water."

He leaned all the way over, his forehead touching the floor as if praying to their God, Allah. "I made it to the monastery and the abbot, and the rest you know."

Standing, he felt empty. Numb.

Deserted.

Celestia listened to Nicholas's story with mounting horror. He was so strong, blessed be. She didn't regret these tears she shed, for they weren't weak, but shed on behalf of Nicholas's pain. He'd not want to see her pity, and she knew it.

She could not hold back the love she felt, not when he needed it as he did. "You are a good man, Nicholas Le Blanc. Now I understand why you hate the baron so. I hate him, too."

Nicholas looked up, the gray of his eyes so dark they were black.

"You survived, and I'm so glad that you did. Verily, I can't imagine my life without you in it. Do you hear me?"

She shuddered as his blank, black stare was turned on her. "I am a murderer. I have killed and I have slaughtered in return for what was done to me. Would that I could find that relic—but it's gone."

"Nay." Celestia jumped from the bed. "Nay, you just said that Leah told you that the man who had hired them to steal *back* the relic wouldn't pay your ransom—that means that the baron must have it!"

His olive complexion faded to white. "I said that?"

Celestia ran to where Nicholas was kneeling and helped him to his feet. "We need to see the baron immediately. I'll go with you. There are so many questions to be answered, and he holds the key to them all. No more, Nicholas, until we find out what he's really up to." She'd been tugging on his arm with no effect.

"No."

"What?" She stared at him and stomped her foot in frustration when she saw him clench his jaw. "No, *what?*"

"Stop jingling! You'll not be going anywhere near the man. He's dangerous, now you know how dangerous. What if I can't protect you?"

She shook his arm, which was solid muscle. "You did not cause the ambush." Celestia sensed that her words, and the inflection of them, would be most important. She spoke calmly, "You did not want your men to die." She searched his face, hoping he could hear her.

His stare was so hot she feared she would melt like a ball of snow on the floor. He'd been raised in a monastery, raised with the theory that God's wisdom ruled all. "Nicholas, mayhap God is the one who gave you the strength to survive your captivity."

The look that flashed across his strong face broke her

heart in two. She saw a flicker of hope before denial and despair settled on his stricken features.

"I was not strong, Celestia, I was weak in body and soul. And if that was a test of my faith, then I failed there, too."

Celestia wrapped her arms around his waist, wanting to love him in any way she could. She kissed his chest, and reached up on tiptoe to kiss his mouth.

"Nay." He pushed her away.

She understood that he couldn't accept her compassion, yet he didn't want her passion, either. Lowering her eyes, she walked to the edge of the bed. "Nicholas, please, please just come and sit down. I will watch over you as you sleep, and perhaps we can find an answer come dawn. Let me at least give you that, if you will take nothing else from me that I would freely give."

Nicholas raised his hands in the air and strode across the floor with pounding steps. He stopped with his hand on the doorknob.

"Weren't you listening? Nothing can help me now, and that includes you and your healing. I could have killed you with the sickness that lives in my soul, and you—you would take it in until you choked of it, too."

"I care for you, Nicholas, that is why I would try!" Celestia stepped between him and the door, knowing that she might lose him forever.

He placed his hands on her shoulders, and she cried out at the depth of turbulent emotion in those gray eyes. Gray aura, gray seas—drowning . . .

She was startled as he dipped his head and caught

her lips with his in a searing kiss that shook her to the core. Without a single reservation she threw her arms around his neck and kissed him back with all of the love in her heart.

If she couldn't heal him with her hands, then mayhap she could touch him with her love. She knew even as he pulled away from her embrace that it wouldn't be enough to hold him.

He unwound her arms and said, "I couldn't resist . . . which is why I have to go. If I stay here with you, we will both regret it."

Celestia didn't recognize her own voice as she cried, "You are my husband—I will regret nothing."

He clasped her chin and brought his face so close she had to close her eyes or lose focus. His breath was warm as he whispered against her cheek, "I don't deserve such a gift, and how can I explain to you that you will regret even those words by morning's dawn? You make me want to be a man you could be proud of, but I cannot guarantee for how long that noble dream will last. I made a vow, at first it was in desperation, aye, but it was a pledge I will honor. I will kill the baron for his role in the ambush and bring his heart to Saint James. I will beg the saint for the cleansing of my soul by offering the real culprit behind the ambush. *Earthly justice*."

Celestia gasped.

"Before I murder the lying sod, I will take care of your family; your brothers will be safe. I will send them here. You can have this place, or go home, I care not." Nicholas shut his eyes. "God knows that man owes me more than this. Damn him."

Seeing that he believed everything he said, Celestia knew that she'd not sway his mind by pleading. She straightened her arms and lifted her chin.

"If you cannot see the goodness that surrounds you and revel in it, then I cannot open your eyes. I will say this one last thing—you are not beyond redemption, Nicholas, no matter what you have done. I could not love an evil man."

She watched with sadness as he moved away from her. She had severed the tenuous cord that bound them with her declaration.

"Love? And I thought you an intelligent woman."

She couldn't hurt any more if he'd run her heart through with a sword. Sticking her chin farther in the air, she flared her nostrils to keep those tears from falling. She would, by Saint Agnes, survive.

She winced as he slammed the door.

Nicholas slept. He'd not meant to give in to sleep, but honor would not let him leave Celestia until Falcon Keep was safe. She couldn't love him—he didn't deserve it. Dreams of the fires of hell were so real he could feel the lick of flame against his cheek and smell the odor of burning wood.

What was burning? He forced his eyes open and sat up, sniffing the air like a hound before the chase. No scent. A dream. Where had the fire been? His heart raced beneath his undershirt.

The danger still felt real. A cough alerted him that he was no longer alone. The mocking noise also told him who it was.

"Yes, Petyr?"

"I find it most odd that a man of your station is so comfortable sleeping in a mound of hay."

"Station? I am a bastard, and bastards are always completely happy in the stables."

"I beg to disagree, my lord. You are not and have never been a bastard in any way, except perhaps, in temperament."

"One day, Petyr, you will speak to me with respect, but I won't hold my breath."

Petyr snorted. "I was patrolling the eastern fence when I heard shouting. It was you, of course. Alas, you awoke before I could throw this bucket of water on you."

Nicholas eyed the pail swinging from the knight's fingers with alarm. "I believe I know you well enough to say that you would have enjoyed dousing me."

"You misread me. Now that I can see that you are all right, would you like to go back to your screaming—er, dreaming? I assume that your nightly terrors are the reason you aren't safe and snuggled abed in your newly cleaned chambers? Did my lady have the good sense to kick you out so that you didn't disturb her rest?"

Nicholas lazily stretched, then shot to his feet for the axe that had been set in the corner. "I wonder about you, Petyr. How well do you serve my father?"

Petyr stood his ground; in fact, he laughed and set

the bucket down before crossing his arms and leaning against the wooden frame of a stall.

"Oh, you shouldn't be worried about me. I am loyal to a fault. If I were a worrying man, then I would choose something else to concern myself with. Like, for example, sleeping through the night."

Nicholas dropped the axe on its head, his hand comfortable around the wooden handle. "No doubt my father wanted to get rid of you, and foisted you on me as another of his sick gifts."

Petyr kicked the pail. "No doubt."

"Tell me of the baron, then. Do you know why he sent me to Jerusalem?"

"Aye, to guard the sacred relic of Saint James the Apostle. You were to give it to King Richard in the Holy Land so that he could have yet another good-luck charm and win the Crusade."

"And when he heard that the relic had been lost to the infidels?"

Petyr tugged on his golden mustache. "Hmm, that was rather odd. He laughed."

Nicholas grew cold. "And when he heard that I was being held for ransom?"

The knight's shoulders flexed. "We had heard that you were dead, along with the rest of your men. I did not know that you were the baron's son until that very night when your father drank too deeply of his burgundy. 'Twas most strange, for he went on and on about a curse. That mayhap with you dead, the curse would end."

"I have heard too much in the past day about curses.

So, he wished me dead?"

Petyr looked uncomfortable, but he proved his loyalty to his new overlord. "It was a sennight after that he lost his two toddling boys and wife to a pestilence in the castle. He was furious. He ranted and raved for months, saying that now he had no heir at all, thanks to the bloody curse. But I could never find out what curse it was that he meant. Your father is normally most close-mouthed, my lord."

Nicholas exhaled and struggled to sort through the tangled weave of his emotions. His father, who had gone to great trouble to arrange his marriage with a healer, had first wanted him dead. What had changed?

"Petyr, did he ever talk about my mother? Why did he leave her in this castle all alone?"

"I don't know, Nicholas. He was not one for confidences, and I only came up in rank after he sent his other men to Jerusalem with you. Methinks he carries many secrets close to his chest."

Nicholas realized that he could not hold off on seeing the baron for long—who knew when the man would decide he was better off dead, again?

"I think, Nicholas, you should settle in here at your home with your lovely wife. Forget the man who sired you. You are your own man, and perhaps better for it."

Nicholas frowned at Petyr. "You are always filled with advice, but this time I will thank you to stay out of my affairs instead of punching you. Tell me where I can find my father. A visit is long overdue. I will need a sharp sword to pierce the man's black heart—what is one more murder to me?"

Petyr opened his mouth as if to argue, but they were interrupted by a piercing scream of terror. Nicholas pushed Petyr out of the way, knocking him into the bucket of water. Celestia needed him.

Celestia had never been so glad to see the dawn. She had alternated between praying and yelling all night, determined that one way or another, God would hear what she had to say. She had called for the blessings of all the saints she could think of, and thanks to cantankerous Father Harold, she could think of many. She was tired in mind and body.

She knelt at the oriel, the broken bay window was spiderwebbed with cracks, and peered out at the courtyard below. She tried to imagine what Nicholas's life had been like as a child. When the courtyard would have been humming with activities and not deserted. She had a view of the north tower; its base of ashlar building stones seemed solid. Dirt, or soot, licked up the tower's exterior, and Celestia added a good washing to her list of chores. No exterior stairs were visible.

Why had the entrance from inside the keep to the tower been boarded over with thick planks and then mortared?

What had Joseph meant last night at dinner about screams in the tower?

Celestia rubbed her arms as a sudden chill swept

through the room. She hadn't felt any spirits or ghosts. Her lack of sleep was making her nervous and edgy.

A wailing scream of pure terror resounded through the keep's thick walls. Celestia jumped to her feet, ran out of the room and down the stairs before the sound subsided. Viola saw her and screamed again. Her maid's cap was sideways on her head, and she was pointing down at the moat.

Celestia's first concern was Nicholas. Had he foolishly tried to leave during the night and drowned in that noxious pool of poison? Her vision of the moat returned, and she could taste the foul water at the back of her throat.

She ran to Viola, desperate for news. Keeping her voice calm, she asked, "What is it? Let me see."

Viola fell to her knees at the entrance. "'Tis Bess. She's in the moat!"

Celestia was out the door and down to the berm in a flash. The small mound of earth betwixt the keep and the moat was spongy and rotten, but she didn't pay it any heed. She dropped to her knees and grabbed Bess by the leg to pull her out of the stinking water. The body was heavy, and her hands slipped, sending her closer to the edge. She took a deep breath and tried again.

She protested weakly as she was gently moved aside. "Let me, Celestia. How long has she been here?"

"I don't know, Nicholas. I just heard Viola's scream. She's dead, Nicholas, she was facedown in the . . ." she swallowed bile, "in the water."

Celestia's stomach heaved as Nicholas pulled Bess

out of the moat; it wasn't water, but thick—her belly protested—like vomit.

Nicholas flipped Bess over and Celestia backed away, then leaned back in, her illness momentarily pushed aside. The maid's apron was tied about her neck; her tongue lolled out of her mouth, and her eyes were wide open, locked forever in fear.

She turned to the side and retched. Nicholas handed her a clean handkerchief.

"She's been murdered," he said, as if he had to hear it for himself.

"I can see that!"

"What shall we say to the others?"

Celestia pointed to Petyr, who was standing behind Nicholas. "Ask him. I can't think . . . I just need a moment." She was a healer for a reason; death was not her strong suit. But murder? Who would kill Bess?

Petyr pointed to the knights above. "They can see everything from there, and your voice carries. They already know."

Nicholas exhaled. "Celestia, gather everyone in the hall. Petyr, will you help me carry Bess around to the back? We will give her a quick burial."

"Nay!" Celestia put her hand on Nicholas's arm. "I will bathe her first. The others will want to see her." *She'd been so friendly, so pretty, so flirtatious.* Mayhap that had been the issue. A jealous suitor?

Nicholas must have heard the edge in her voice. "What are you thinking?"

Celestia shrugged off his hand, and wished she were

better at lying. "'Tis nothing, my lord. I simply want to do the proper thing."

She ignored his shrewd look.

"Fine. Follow us, then." He called to Bertram, "Can you gather everyone together in the main room? We will be in shortly."

Celestia's hands were shaking by the time they had laid Bess out in the shed. The doors were open, so she had plenty of light. "You don't need to stay," she told the men.

Petyr left, but Nicholas remained. "What are you looking for?"

Celestia sighed; she knew how sensitive her husband was, especially to *this*. "Bess was a pretty young woman. She has on no shoes, nor stockings. I am going to see if she, er, had, well . . . Hmm." Her cheeks flamed. "You know."

Nicholas glanced toward the door where Petyr was standing and then back. He whispered, "You think she had a lover?"

Exasperated, Celestia tapped him on the sleeve. "Nay. Bess was a flirt, but a very good girl, as well." She plunged in. "I am looking for evidence of rape, my lord."

"Rape?" His queasy face immediately flushed with anger. "You think one of these men would resort to such brutality? I'll not look away from such a despicable act."

Celestia bravely touched her bare fingers to his smooth wrists. "I know."

He calmed beneath her touch, and Celestia was reassured that her healing powers were not gone yet. While she still had them, she still had time to make him love her.

"Now," she said, "would you at least turn your head, so that I can do this? I swear to Saint Edward that most newly wedded couples talk about nice things." Seeing Nicholas's blank look she suggested, "Dancing, meals . . . a family. Not curses and death."

"Which Edward was he?"

"The third. Patron saint of difficult marriages." She lifted Bess's dress.

Nicholas left the shed.

Mayhap a quarter of an hour had passed before Celestia was washed and ready for the meeting. She carried a mug of hot lemon and honey, to help stop the lingering nausea. Lemon and honey were also used to cleanse the palate, but the tart sweetness did not erase the stench of death in her nostrils. She drank again.

She took her place next to Nicholas, who was sitting at the head of their makeshift table, and looked at each of the keep's inhabitants. All she saw were faces filled with sorrow. Geoffrey's eyes were red from tears; Viola's face was puffy and raw. Forrester and Henry were subdued, while Petyr tapped his finger against his thigh, and appeared to be deep in thought. Bertram and Willy sat like soldiers, their faces set in grief. Nicholas looked . . . guilty?

Why was she surprised? The man took everything that could go wrong as a personal affront. "Unless you killed Bess, my lord Nicholas, this situation is not your fault. Kindly bring yourself from your moment of self-pity and help me solve this crime."

Nicholas got to his feet, his face white with fury.

"What?"

Celestia calmly sipped her hot drink. "You heard me, my lord. We need your brains, sir." She wouldn't look at him and turned to the rest of the group. "Bess was knocked on the back of the head, and then choked to death with her own apron."

Viola sobbed, "Who would want to kill poor Bessie?"

Celestia met her husband's angry, accusing eyes. "It could have been *any one* of us. The only injuries I found to her person were the ones I just described."

Nicholas exhaled, his relief evident. "When was the last time anyone saw Bess?"

"We all went to bed at the same time last eve," Bertram said.

"I was tired, and slept through the night." Forrester glanced at Nicholas. "Well, most of it."

Her husband studied the trussed ceiling of the hall.

Petyr said, "Nicholas, you slept in the barn. Did you hear anything?"

Celestia hid her smile as Nicholas glared from Petyr to the rest of knights. Forrester sent her a knowing grin, which she immediately frowned at.

"Well, Petyr, as you know, I have trouble sleeping, and I did not wish to disturb my wife. But no, I did not see Bess, nor hear anything amiss."

Celestia intercepted a look that Nicholas sent Petyr, and if she read it correctly, it was a look that promised retribution. She looked at Petyr, but his nose seemed fine. Nicholas crossed his arms over his chest.

Petyr finger combed his mustache, as if unconcerned.

The bottoms of his leggings were wet, yet he hadn't gotten in the moat. *What was going on?*

Celestia looked to Nicholas and cleared her throat to remind him he needed to take control. "Well, my lord? What are we to do?"

Nicholas almost broke under the weight of so many needy stares. He had no bloody answers. He paced the main hall, thinking. He was lord of this pile of rock, and it was his duty to care for everyone in it.

He could leave, go to the baron, and tear the bastard limb from limb. But not while there was a murderer loose and Celestia was in danger.

Fate.

He crossed his arms and ground his back teeth. He made eye contact with each person. "Bess left the castle sometime in the night, and none of us heard her or noticed her missing."

Viola raised her head. "I awoke to, er . . . well I just did." Her red cheeks let everyone know she'd had to use the chamber pot. "I might have wakened Bess, for it was after I was," the red flamed from her cheeks to the tips of her ears, "finished, that I thought I heard rustling. I assumed Bess had a similar need, and I went back to sleep."

Celestia touched Viola's hand. "'Tis all right, Viola. So you don't know if she went outdoors instead? For more privacy, perhaps?" The pretty maid shook her head.

Nicholas paced, his boot heels clicking against the stone floor. "Let us say, then, that she must have left the solar of her own accord. What made her go near the moat? Who had the watch last eve?"

This time it was Willy who colored like a rosebush. "It was me, Lord Nicholas. But I . . ." The young man straightened his shoulders and said, "I fell asleep."

Petyr shot to his feet. "Nay! You did what?"

"All was quiet on the battlements! I saw nothing, and the wine at dinner . . . I fell asleep at my post, sir."

Willy straightened his shoulders, certain that he'd be given twenty lashes. Petyr cuffed him upside the head and looked ready to follow through with another tap.

Nicholas grabbed Petyr's fist. "Not in here amongst the women, Petyr. There has been enough violence already. Discipline him outside."

Petyr bowed an apology, as did a shamefaced Willy.

Nicholas lowered his chin and resumed the mantle of duty. "Did anyone here kill our Bess? I don't think so. Are any going to now confess of the deed?" He glowered at them all, but none admitted to murder.

Instead of guilt on their faces, he saw hope—the belief that he would somehow keep the rest of them safe. The burden was heavy so he expelled a sigh and admitted, "Last night, I was going to leave the keep."

Celestia gasped. "Leave?"

"To find my father."

"Oh!" Her dainty, work-roughened hands clenched tightly in her lap, the pulse in her throat leapt. He had no doubt she believed she cared, and it scared the piss out of him. He hadn't wanted any responsibilites.

"But now I will go to the village that Grainne Kat mentioned. There should be a priest there, and we can bring him back to properly bury Bess. He can say a blessing for the others, too."

Celestia nodded, her face proud. "I shall go with you."

"Nay. I can go alone."

She pushed back from her bench seat and walked to him, unmindful of his towering height. He could see that she'd slept, or rather didn't sleep, in her dress from the eve before. She was disheveled, her hair tangled, and her heart confused. She faced him like a warrior as she pierced him with her blazing mismatched eyes.

His heart beat louder in his ears, and his mouth dried. "Would you argue with me?"

"I will go, Nicholas. We will go together. You need me."

His groin tightened. "I don't need you," he lied.

"Aye, you do; you are just too stubborn to admit it. I am coming, Nicholas, even if I have to sneak out and follow you!"

Visions of Celestia using bedsheets to climb out of their chamber to the ground below buckled his knees. The woman had no sense of her own mortality. He yanked at his hair, frustration in every bone of his body. "Fine."

Nicholas didn't know whether to laugh or howl when she gave him a curtsy meant for a king and said in that sweet voice, "Thank you, Nicholas."

Chapter THIRTEEN

Brenin and Ceffyl—chestnut and white, stallion and mare—got along better than their human riders. Nicholas was afraid to point out the similarities.

"Why do you never do as I say?"

Celestia glowered at him. "You should ask me to do something worthy, and then I might."

"I am capable of bringing back a priest on my own, Celestia. Believe this or no, I used to be quite able to care for myself."

She jerked her chin in the air. "And how long ago was that, my lord?"

Nicholas wanted to throttle the wench. For once, wallowing in his guilt was not near as important as making her see reason. He cantered forward. She caught up, refusing to let him take the lead.

They rode into the village, bristling like hedgehogs. Celestia quietly asked, "Can you stop frowning? Who will talk to us if you frighten the children?"

"Would be that there were children to frighten. Is this entire country deserted?" Nicholas sought calm, but it was nowhere to be found. His life had been remarkably easier when he hadn't cared at all, about anyone or anything.

He eyed Celestia, who looked like a fairy queen in her dark green cloak. Her hair flowed down her back, almost as white as Ceffyl's mane. "Why didn't you braid your hair? Or wear a veil? Have you no modesty?"

"Aghh! You said you were leaving without me. I was lucky to get the tangles out."

Nicholas ground his back teeth together.

Neat and tidy huts lined the road, smoke curled from various chimneys, but no people showed their faces. "We don't look like the bloody Scottish patrol, so why is there no one to greet us?"

"For once I agree, Nicholas, this is more than passing strange. Let's go to the church over there on the corner."

He found the steeple and turned toward it, at his wit's end. The churchyard was fenced and whitewashed, and inside were a few pigs and chickens. An elderly man in a black robe came around from the henhouse and into the front yard.

"Good day," Nicholas called out.

The priest looked up, and fright immediately covered his age-lined face. He dropped his eggs on the cobblestones and didn't seem to notice when they oozed yellow yolk over his toes. "Baron Peregrine!"

Celestia rode forward. "Good day, Father."

The priest turned to Celestia and clutched his heart. "Oh, God in heaven, a fairy witch!"

She laughed, as if she was accused every day, and used to it. "I am no witch, nor a fairy. Just small." She dismounted and held out her hand to Nicholas.

"Nicholas," she whispered from the side of her mouth. "Nicholas. He only has one eye, stop staring."

Nicholas was not staring because the priest had but one eye, no, it was something else. A tip of something, mayhap a memory.

The priest pointed a shaking, gnarled finger at Nicholas. "I told ye, Baron, that I know nothing about a curse. It was the Lady Esmerada's doing."

Celestia tugged on Nicholas's tunic hem, and he was hard-pressed not to shake her off. "Nicholas. He thinks you are your father . . . say something! Can't you see he is scared to death?"

Nicholas blinked and swatted at her hand. "Um, yes. Priest! My name is not Philippe Peregrine. I am Nicholas. Nicholas Le Blanc. And I remember you. You are Father Michael."

Celestia looked at him in awe. "You know him?"

"Aye. Do you not remember me, Father?"

Father Michael shuffled his feet forward until he came to the short fence and tilted his face so that his good eye could see clearly. "Nicholas? Nicholas! Not the father, but the son."

Nicholas slid off of his horse, and the priest opened the gate. Celestia stayed by his side, quiet for once, but he saw the happiness on her face, for him and for the return of a memory, and he forgave her for arguing.

"You're handsome when you're moody," she teased.

Father Michael led them into his small quarters on the side of the church. "Would some ale be welcome?"

Nicholas answered nay, but Celestia smiled and accepted a leather mug, as regally as a princess born, Nicholas thought. She settled comfortably on her bench, as if readying for a childhood story.

Nicholas felt like a giant in the small room, and he had to duck his head until he sat. "What happened to you, Father Michael?"

The priest waved his hand. "'Tis an old wound."

Nicholas looked at Celestia, wondering if she could heal him, but she shook her head no. He nodded. The eye was gone, so what could she do? Funny, how little time it had taken for him to expect miracles from her.

"What curse were you talking about?"

The priest shifted uncomfortably and took a large gulp from his mug. He changed the subject. "It is time that you're here, Nicholas. Where are you staying?"

Nicholas scratched the back of his neck, startled by the question. "The keep, of course. Where else? We are living in the parts that are habitable until I can get to the rest. As to why I am here in the village, one of our maids was murdered. We came looking for a priest so that she could have a proper burial."

The priest sucked his bottom lip, his one eye wide. "Murdered?"

"Aye. She was hit on the back of the head, and then strangled with her own apron strings."

"Shame." He made the sign of the cross and bent his gray-haired head in prayer.

"Have ye caught the brute who did it?"

"Not yet, but we will."

Father Michael stared into his mug, as if he'd rather join the dead Bess than journey to Falcon Keep. "I'll come, then."

"I thank you." Nicholas made no move to get up. The priest held answers to his past, and mayhap it was time to ask questions. "What do you remember of my mother?"

The priest winced.

Nicholas's gut clenched and he tapped the table top. "I've changed my mind, good father; I'd like some ale after all."

Father Michael looked uncommonly nervous as he went to get ale, and Nicholas wondered what secrets the old man was hiding. After more drink, the chances were greater that the priest would give away information as freely as chickens laid eggs.

Nicholas glanced at Celestia, who was contentedly sipping from her mug. He put a finger to his lips, warning her to be quiet and to let him speak.

Father Michael returned and handed Nicholas a mug with a shaking hand. He sat, fidgeting uncomfortably, repeatedly smoothing the black robe over his thin legs.

He looked to Celestia, who sent him an encouraging smile.

Finally the priest cleared his throat. "Your mother . . . she was a lovely woman, she was."

Nicholas had the sudden urge to keep the past within

the past. He'd tried, with Celestia and her healing hands, to move ahead, and how much pain had that wrought? He got up, banging his head on the low ceiling so hard he saw stars.

The priest looked alarmed as dust fell to the table.

"Nicholas!" Celestia captured Nicholas's sleeve and urged him to sit back down. "Father Michael, Nicholas cannot remember much of his childhood. He was a lad of six when he arrived at the monastery. Don't you find it odd that he has so few recollections of his life before then?"

Father Michael hid his face in his mug and slurped his ale, but not before Nicholas saw the fleeting expression of guilt cross his brow.

"Father? What do you know?" Nicholas decided to let her badger the priest a while. Asking Celestia to still her tongue had been a futile effort anyway. His head ached, and he swore he could smell apples. He plopped his elbows on the table.

Father Michael sighed and set his mug down with a thump. "How often our sins come back to haunt us." The elderly man closed his one eye and said, "I told a small lie, but for the good of dear Nicholas. He was just a boy. And a monastery has no place for toddlers. Too young to work, too much trouble. But not our Nicholas, he was a strapping lad, big for his age."

Nicholas narrowed his eyes but held his tongue. Celestia tapped her finger impatiently against her tankard, her gaze unrelenting as she stared the priest down. Nicholas would have told her everything, had she ever used that gaze on him. No, wait, he reflected, he had already spilled all of his secrets with but a touch of her hand.

"And what small lie would that have been?" she prodded.

"Hmm," the priest said quietly, looking away from Celestia to speak to Nicholas. "It was for your protection, mind, that we sent you so far away. I'd heard of a monastery run by Abbot Crispin, a man with a more than fair reputation. You were in danger here, so in the letter I sent to the abbot I said that you were six, when in reality you were but four. "Tis no surprise that you can't remember. And mayhap that is just as well, my son."

Nicholas closed his eyes. His name was not his own, his age was not his own. His entire life was a lie. It took all of his courage to stay seated, knowing that he would finally hear the truth of his past. The soft nudge of Celestia's foot against his reminded him that at least he wasn't alone.

The priest drained his mug dry, then smacked his lips together. "Let me see, now, the year was 1169, or was it '68? No matter, our Lady Esmerada—your mother," he said with a tip of his head toward Nicholas, "was a fetching lass of sixteen years. Half-Scot, she were, and half-English. She lived with her parents at Falcon Keep, which was her mother's property. Her mother being the Lady Margaret, who had inherited the keep upon her own father's death."

Waving his hand as if that was just the bones of the story and not Nicholas's family history, the priest continued, "After his demise, Lady Margaret was alone in the world. Frail and lovely she was, a pure English rose. But no matter her goodness and beauty, she was but a woman, and all know that a woman cannot hold a keep by herself."

Celestia opened her mouth to protest, but the priest rambled on, having found his speed. Nicholas found the look on her face endearing.

"Afore long, she found herself wed to the Scottish brigand, Brinden McCarthy, and not long after that, she bore our Esmerada. Are you following along, Nicholas?"

Nicholas nodded, feeling dazed. Margaret, his grandmother, and Esmerada, his mother. He had Scots' blood.

"Your grandsire, Brinden McCarthy, was an enterprising man, and remained loyal to his Scottish clan. Ye'll have followed Solway Firth a ways before coming inland to the keep? Aye, Falcon Keep is too far from the water to be used as a port, but Brinden, he found a use for it—he grew crops and raised sheep, all to give food and money to the Scottish rebels."

The priest's brows furrowed in concentration. "The borderlands were being torn up by King Henry and King William. Each king wanted more than what they had. Scotland's never been rich, but King Henry wanted land for his sons to inherit." He chuckled, as if impressed by the old king's audacity.

Nicholas broke in, "Aye, but King Henry won the argument, did he not? Forced King William to sign the Treaty of Falaise."

"Good lad, to know your history!"

"I was raised a scholar, before becoming a knight."

"Ah." The priest nodded with approval before turning to Celestia. "For fifteen years Scotland was under England's thumb. The country was beggared and pillaged by the Scots and English alike. 'Twas after Henry died and Richard the Lionhearted became king that Scotland reverted back to King William."

"King Richard sold it to him, his own land," Nicholas scoffed. "Richard was already looking for coin."

"It was said he felt great guilt over his part in his father's death."

Guilt? Nicholas understood that motivation quite well. And like Richard, he would pay his penance *after* doing the dirty deed.

Celestia smiled pointedly, "Nicholas's grandfather?"

The priest colored, "I digress . . . Back when Henry was king he found out what old Brinden was up to. Falcon Keep was English, on English soil, and Henry vowed to put a stop to the Scottish McCarthy's traitorous ways. However, your grandsire, me boy, was never of a mind to do as he was told."

Celestia giggled. "A family trait, Nicholas?"

Nicholas looked over his nose at her before turning to Father Michael, fascinated by his own history.

"So when Brinden got the missive stating that his lovely daughter, Esmerada, was to be married to an Englishman, a lord favored by King Henry, he weren't happy, and that is the God's honest truth. Nor was Esmerada, for she was in love with the Scottish rebel, Robbie MacIntosh. She fair turned her nose up at her mother and her English ways; her wild heart was pure Scots."

The priest looked sadly at Nicholas.

"Now it is my opinion that the good lady Margaret died of sorrow, for what her no-account Scottish husband had done to her keep and king, and for her daughter who had followed his ways. None but God knows for certain." The priest wiped his watery eye. "I'll tell you, Nicholas, Lady Margaret was a good woman, and I was sorry when she passed."

Nicholas found himself sorry, too. The good Margaret had been his grandmother, and he had never gotten to know her. "What happened then?"

"The day came when the Lord Peregrine arrived, young and cocky. You look most like him, but not so, er, *vicious*, around the, er, eyes," the priest stammered and hastily took another pull from his empty mug. He set it down with a reproachful glare and continued, "Brinden was not so foolish that he thought he could deny the English king's order. Did I mention he was an enterprising man? Aye, what he did was plan something else for his daughter's wedding day, something that was to have suited them better. I remember that the sun shone that day, how rare, eh?" He smiled at Celestia's nod. "A rarity it was, and lucky too, as the wedding was to be held outside. You'll have noticed the large field in the front of the keep?"

Nicholas grunted. "The vacant acres of grass and weeds, you mean?"

"Yes. Away from the safety of the keep walls, but in all of nature's splendor. There were a hundred trees at one time, apple trees."

"I said I remembered apples," Nicholas said to Celestia, his belly tight.

The priest frowned. "Your mother, the Lady Esmerada, and your father, the Lord Philippe Peregrine, were wed beneath God and before witnesses. Barely were the vows finished when the Scottish rebels arrived over the mound, ready to slaughter your father and all of his knights."

Nicholas reached for Celestia's hand, and the gentle warmth of her fingers curling over his calmed him as he absorbed the horrible tale.

"The English knights, though taken by surprise, had been better trained; they were not so wild and unruly as the Scottish warriors. They stayed in their formations and fought until the grove ran red with blood. By the time the battle was finished, the lord and his knights were victorious. Unfortunately, Brinden McCarthy and Robbie MacIntosh were both dead. Esmerada fell over their bodies, crying. Her heart had been trampled, as well."

Nicholas took a deep breath. He could not remember his mother's face. He tightened his grip on Celestia's hand.

"And?" His wife was relentless in her pursuit of the truth, and Nicholas knew he should be grateful, yet his head was spinning with too much truth already.

Father Michael looked away. "She shook her fist and cursed your father. She told him and all the servants and guests left alive that she had loved Robbie MacIntosh with all of her body and soul. She vowed she would never be a wife to Philippe Peregrine, that she would never submit to him. Then she ran back toward the keep, and your father chased after her. He was a ruthless man, and Esmerada *was* his wife. He pulled her up over his horse and continued on for the keep. He left the next day."

"The next day?" Celestia squeaked in surprise.

Nicholas could not believe his ears. "My father raped my mother on her wedding night?" He stood, remembering to duck before he slammed his head against the rafters. "No wonder she gave me away."

Father Michael pulled Nicholas back down on the bench. "Nay! She never gave you away; we took you."

"You what?" Nicholas exclaimed in confusion and disbelief. Celestia sidled closer to him.

"Let me explain." The priest held out a placating hand. "Esmerada, when she found she was with child, hoped that the babe would be Robbie's. She was happy, she sang and napped beneath the apple trees, dreaming of the future." Father Michael deepened his voice and leaned close. "She was not content to wait unprepared for the lord's return. She fortified the keep with extra men, and posted spies to watch the roads. Lord Peregrine was not to be allowed inside Falcon Keep's walls."

The priest continued sadly, "But he never came. You were born, and she realized that you had to be the baron's get, so she sent word to him. He ignored her summons. Esmerada planned and plotted on how she could take her revenge against him. During that time, she allowed no English, nor Scots, in the keep. She began to spend most of her days in the north tower."

The priest ran his hands over his drawn face. "As

the years went by, she grew more pale and thin. Her anger was bitter, and it was poisoning her from within. I begged her to forgive and move on with her life, but she could not."

He sighed, choosing his words carefully.

"Then she burnt down the apple trees, catching fire to numerous huts and frightening the peasants who worked in the fields. She had a friend who acted as your nursemaid during the times when she was, uh, not herself."

"Who was she? What happened to her?"

"Ah, Nicholas, I am an old man. It was too long ago. A plain woman, as I recall. It was she who took you to Abbot Crispin." The priest stared at the floor.

Nicholas shifted on the bench sensing that priest kept a few secrets still. "My mother was a madwoman? And that is why you took me from her?"

"We had to, my son. Were you not listening? Her dementia became worse. We worried that you would be in danger, because she could not forgive you for being Philippe Peregine's child."

Nicholas tightened his jaw, grinding his back teeth in frustration. Celestia elbowed him.

Father Michael stood on wavering legs and poured more ale all around. He took a healthy swallow, and gestured for Celestia and Nicholas to do the same. Nicholas pushed his mug away. "I cannot understand all of this. My mother came to her wedding already bedded by Robbie MacIntosh?" He felt sick.

"Aye. Your father, mayhap, had a reason to be angry. Forced to wed away from court at his king's command,

Lord Peregrine is attacked by his new wife's lover as soon as the vows are pledged. What was a man to do?"

"Did he ever come back?" Nicholas sat forward, folding his hands over his knee. Rape and murder and curses. Revenge had driven his mother crazy. Would it do the same to him?

The priest squirmed uncomfortably in his seat. "It seems that Esmerada sent many letters to her lord, telling him to claim his progeny. Lord Peregrine, well, he became a baron soon enough, was angry and determined not to dance to Esmerada's tune. He ignored the both of you."

"So you sent me to Abbot Crispin—yet you didn't tell the abbot that I was legitimate, and you didn't tell him my proper age. I believed I was a bastard, with no value other than what I could earn for myself."

Nicholas swallowed a surge of bitterness. What would his life have been like, if he'd grown up acknowledged as the baron's son? He doubted that his father would have ordered him killed. His gut churned again.

"I did what I thought best," Father Michael said firmly. "The letter I sent to the abbot gave your father's name, but we insinuated that you could be in danger from him. Your mother was insane and had tried to throw you from the battlements; I did not want her to find you. I had to put my trust in God that all would be right in the end. The baron had already shown he didn't believe you to be his, and we worried that he might have you killed. 'Accidents' happen, Nicholas, and we wanted you to survive your childhood so that you could come back and claim your birthright. Falcon's Keep has been in your mother's family for generations."

"Some legacy. Nothing but madness and murder." Nicholas rubbed his eyes, then scratched the back of his neck. His knee started to shake, and he had the overpowering need to punch someone or something.

"Why didn't you contact me sooner?"

The priest ran his thumb over the long scar on his face. "I was waiting for you to be stronger than your father, strong enough to take your inheritance by force, if need be. It was best to have limited contact with the abbot on your behalf."

Nicholas growled low in his throat. Damn his father. Celestia placed her hand on the nape of his neck, her fingers soft and soothing against his hot skin.

"I'm truly cursed," he said, staring at his wife. "Both of my parents have tried to kill me."

"You cannot blame your mother; she was ill," Celestia spoke softly. "Before her dementia, she loved you very much—the good Father said so, did you not hear?"

Was there no end to a man's capacity for pain? "When she thought me another man's child, aye, she loved me then."

Father Michael interjected, "Which brings me to Esmerada's curse."

"Am I not cursed enough?" Nicholas slammed his fist down on the table so hard the top cracked.

"After you were safely taken away, Esmerada became more agitated. She walked the battlements of the north tower every eve, her white gown billowing in the wind, her hair flying about like black bats around her face. Esmerada was so pale and fragile, yet she fought the elements and stood on the crenellations shouting her curse, night after night. 'Tis no wonder that the peasants thought her a ghost. They said she was already dead, that her unhappy spirit roamed the north tower. All of the servants, left Falcon Keep."

"And what was the curse?" Nicholas sounded weary even to himself, and his shoulders slumped.

"That your father, Philippe Peregrine, would never have another living heir so long as he didn't claim his first-born son. *You*. And you had to have a child of your own, ensuring that Esmerada's bloodline did not die out."

Nicholas nodded, some of the tension in his neck gone, thanks be to his wife's magical hands.

Father Michael spread his hands wide. "That is the whole tale. Now, answer me this. Why have you come to Falcon Keep after all this time? The abbot had written to us that you were a knight, and preparing to go on crusade. I'd heard nothing since."

"I suppose he left out the fact that my liege lord was Baron Peregrine?"

Father Michael's face lost its ruddy color.

Nicholas longed for his small cell at the monastery–but mayhap that place was not the haven he'd thought it was. He wanted darkness. He needed time to think. His past was full of jagged pieces of half truths. Crossing his legs at the ankle, he tried to appear as if he was not overwhelmed.

Celestia said in a husky voice, "You never answered Nicholas's question, Father Michael–did the baron return?" Father Michael pointed to his empty eye socket. "Aye. He returned."

Her chin went up as if she readied for battle—Nicholas had never been so glad to have a champion—in truth, he'd never had a champion. "Speak clearly—no more riddles," she said."

"Baron Peregrine came back immediately after King Richard sold Scotland to King William. He said he was missing something from the keep and demanded to know where it was. He was not forthcoming in what the object was; he seemed to think we were deliberately hiding it from him in retaliation for his neglect of Lady Esmerada."

What other bad news could the priest possbily have to impart?

"That was when he heard *all* of Esmerada's curse and began to believe it was true. I don't know who told him of it first, mayhap the villagers. Though I doubt they'd have the courage to taunt such a man. When I could give him no information on his missing object—would that I even knew what it was—nor could I release him of Lady Esmerada's curse, he grew angry. He and his men tried to burn down the church, and I stepped in front of him. He slashed at my face, and I lost my eye."

"The baron did that?" Celestia gasped in outrage.

Nicholas closed his eyes, filled with sorrow and regret as his suspicions were confirmed.

"I may have provoked him." The priest looked discomfited. "I may have taken great relish in telling him I could not release the curse. And of telling him that his son was, indeed, his. He said he'd heard rumors, but he'd never gone to the monastery to see for himself. He was a fool, and I told him so."

Celestia covered the old man's hand with her own, amazing Nicholas with her capacity for compassion.

"I paid for my foolish tongue with my eye."

"I owe you gratitude, Father Michael, for protecting my husband as long as you could."

"The two of you are married?"

"Aye, I am Lady Celestia Le Blanc," she said proudly.

Nicholas shifted. How did she do it? Her infernal optimism annoyed the hell out of him.

"How long did the baron stay at Falcon Keep the second time he came?" Nicholas wondered if the joyous news that he had a living son was when his father decided to have him killed.

"A fortnight, perhaps. Not longer than that. He knocked the mill down, chased away the last few stray sheep, and left. He has not been back since. Now will you tell me why you are here?"

Nicholas looked toward the heavens. If this was all God's plan, as Abbot Crispin had taught him to believe, he did not understand. Nothing about his past made him feel any better about his future. He moved away from Celestia, who had so proudly stated that they were husband and wife.

The more he learned about himself, the clearer it became that his wife deserved better than he. Much better. He looked at the priest, then back at Celestia. It was time to tell the truth, and end this farce of a marriage.

"My father sent me here on the pretext of protecting the keep from Scottish rebels. He coerced us," he jerked his head toward Celestia, "into marriage. She's a renowned healer. Now that I have heard Esmerada's curse, it's clear that the baron needs me to have a child, thereby freeing him to father living heirs of his own."

"A healer. Has she helped you, Nicholas? Were you injured on crusade?"

Nicholas would rather walk back to the keep on his hands than talk any more this day.

Celestia whispered, "Don't give up, now, my lord."

He thought of the months of torment he'd spent fighting back the longing he'd had for opium and the horrible nightmares that meshed with his memories. How Celestia had reached within his spirit, to try and draw out the cravings as if they were a tumor.

Had she helped him? Even now, her fingers rested against his skin, soothing him.

"Aye. She cured me. Mentally, I was—well, I was not in the best of health. I was not," he searched for the right words, "well, Father, after what I did to escape my capture. I killed. A woman."

Father Michael winced. "During a holy war it is sometimes necessary to stray from the commandments. Have you prayed for God's forgiveness?"

"Aye. But He has not chosen to hear me. I am not worthy, Father Michael."

The old man frowned. "Not worthy? How so?"

He thought of his mother, who had been raped and gone mad. Her journey into madness had taken years. Would that happen to him? He had to make his father release the Montehue family from their obligation before he turned the bend.

"I plan to kill again."

Nicholas knew without a doubt that he would be the one to mete out justice to his father, and he was willing to take the stain against his already blackened soul.

Father Michael glanced from Celestia to Nicholas. "I see. Is there no other course for you to take, my son?"

Now more than ever Nicholas knew he had to be his father's slayer. It was balanced—a life for a life. "No."

Celestia removed her hand from the back of his neck, folding her fingers around her mug.

"Celestia will never be safe so long as he breathes. He plots and schemes . . ." Nicholas ground his back teeth together. "For what? I still don't know."

"Money, most likely–and power. Land to give his heirs." Father Michael sighed. Now that he knew the history of his birthright, Nicholas would be content to never see Falcon Keep again.

"You take a risk of dying yourself," Celestia said softly.

But could he live without seeing Celestia?

Celestia *hated* the look of determined hopelessness on Nicholas's face.

She leaned forward and pointed at the priest with her mug. "The baron had promised King Richard a sacred relic from Saint James the Apostle as part of his vassal price toward the Crusade. We think that the baron then paid the enemy to attack the caravan, and make it look like it was a Holy Fight—all so that the relic could be 'stolen' and returned to the baron. Don't you find that odd?"

"Celestia," Nicholas warned. But sometimes her husband was too noble for his own good. She would find the answers, for both their sakes.

"Wait," she said, keeping her attention on the priest. "The baron knighted his son, and sent Nicholas to lead a retinue of his own men. To protect the false relic."

The priest rose to his feet, excited. "The finger bone of Saint James! Of course. King Henry had given it to Lady Margaret's father, Lord Harbotten, as payment for a piece of land or something—it isn't important—some men hoard holy relics, thinking that it will get them closer to God. Lord Harbotten was a relic collector."

Celestia slid a glance toward her husband, who studied a bruise on his thumbnail.

She continued, "So King Henry originally gave the relic to Esmerada's grandfather?"

Father Michael nodded. "Aye. Lady Margaret held it dear. Legend says that sacred relics, especially those from such a venerated saint as Saint James, can turn the tide in battle. Old Henry loved a good fight, but he either forgot Harbotten had the relic or else he was waiting for a worthier battle to use it."

"But King Richard knew enough about it to ask for the relic specifically, and he knew Baron Peregrine was the only one who could possibly have it, as Esmerada, and all her family, were dead." Celestia tapped her lower lip with the pad of her index finger.

Nicholas glowered. “What if the Scots, er, Brinden McCarthy, stole it?”

“I don’t know why they would,” the priest said doubtfully.

“For coin, to support the rebellion, naturally. But I don’t think that’s what happened. The way I see it,” Celestia loved to solve puzzles and she felt as if this might be the thread they’d been missing, “Baron Peregrine lost the original relic. That’s what he was looking for when the monastery burned.”

“What?” Father Michael leaned against the rickety table. “I’m sorry, Father,” Celestia said, quickly placing a soothing hand on his. “Abbot Crispin survived the fire, but the monastery is lost. He sent a secret message to Nicholas, warning him that the baron was searching for something. ‘Tis obvious it’s the relic.”

“The baron is evil,” the old man said in a shaking voice.

Celestia picked up Nicholas’s hand and kissed the knuckles, knowing that her next sentence would be hard for him to hear. “What if the reason he destroyed the caravan and had the relic stolen was to protect the fact that it was already gone?”

“So my men, the men he’d given me to lead, were all killed to protect a lie?” Nicholas asked skeptically. “I don’t think so.”

Father Michael sat back down with thud. “My God.”

Nicholas’s fingers tightened upon hers. “He would have killed me, in order to cover up a secret.”

“A sacred relic can’t be used for ill. The baron should be cursed a thousand times over,” the priest said, rubbing at the scar above his empty eye socket.

"It's my fault."

"Nicholas, ye've been sore used in this life, but you're not responsible for your father being a blight on humanity. Ye say ye feel great guilt over killing a woman? A woman who tortured ye. Well," the priest made the sign of the cross, "I absolve ye. Some people deserve to die, and it is our human hand that metes out God's justice." Father Michael continued, "If your lady is right, then no sacred relic was lost, and again, ye are absolved."

"And if my carelessness is at fault?"

Father Michael slammed a fist down on the table. "I absolve thee!" he shouted. "But all the forgiveness in the world will not be enough if ye don't forgive yerself."

Celestia's chest was tight with unshed emotion. The goodly priest had told her husband exactly what he needed to hear. Whether or not the stubborn man would listen, well, that was another basket of thread entirely.

She rubbed the pad of her thumb over the tops of his knuckles, sending what comfort she could.

"I wanted to live," he said quietly.

"Did you have another choice, Nicholas?" Father Michael made sure that he had the younger man's attention. "Did you enjoy killing her?"

Red flags of guilt flushed Nicholas's cheeks. "Aye, I did enjoy killing the foul, rotten whore."

Celestia pulled her hand free so that she could applaud his revelation. "As well you should have. Let the guilt go, Nicholas," Celestia said, deliberately covering the new smooth skin where the scars from the manacles used to be. She shivered, thinking his thoughts with him to lessen the impact. *He'd been drugged, held down in the beginning, but toward the end, he lived for the opium and the pleasure that woman had brought. Anything to forget that he was locked in captivity and tortured at the enemy's whim.* She didn't blame him for wanting relief from the pain, and she wished he would stop blaming himself. It was only because his shame went so deep that she'd gotten such a clear image when she'd first healed him. Now she could at least soothe him for periods of time without absorbing his despair.

"You are strong, strong enough to survive what would have killed a lesser man. Now live again, aye?" The priest reached out to pat Nicholas as if he were the four year old boy he'd known so long ago.

Her husband was breathing like a tourney horse, deep from his chest. How long before he saw what she and the priest could see? God had not turned his back on Nicholas. Instead, Nicholas had plugged both of his ears with his fingers, unable to accept forgiveness.

She hated to see him struggling. "It's been a long day," she finally said calmly, using her words and the softest touch of her fingertips to sooth him. "Bess's death," her breath caught in her throat, "the revelation of your past, and now you're wrestling with something that you've convinced yourself is true. But it doesn't have to be."

Leaning over, she kissed the side of his face. "You are so strong that you can make your life whatever you want it to be."

She bowed her head, hoping for their future, if he could just forgive himself his past.

Nicholas kept his head buried in his hands.

Enough was enough. She was a person who needed to fix what could be fixed. Celestia stood and lightly trailed her fingers over the back of Nicholas's smooth, ebony hair. "Come. It will be dark soon, and poor Bess unburied. You have been most kind, Father Michael. You'll stay the night at the keep? We've no beds, but blankets aplenty."

Nicholas followed her as she led the way outside. Breathing deep of the fresh air, she exhaled, wishing she was truly a witch so that she could cast a spell and make her husband happy. His expression was grim as they waited for the priest to bring around his own mount.

He shut her out with his silence, and it hurt. "So much information, and yet still no answers. We can talk more of this later, in private, Nicholas."

"Enough talking has been done to last a lifetime," he growled.

The priest came around the side of the small house, his old horse laden with bags, the greens of a carrot dangling from the nag's mouth.

Celestia's stomach rumbled, and she smacked her hand against her forehead. In all of the emotional upheaval, she'd forgotten a very important question.

"Do you, by any chance at all, know where we can hire a cook?"

Chapter FOURTEEN

It was the sound of her husband's heavy boots clomping on the stone floor as he tried to sneak out that caught her attention.

She looked up, noticing the faint bruise on the side of his cheek. Willy said that Nicholas had lost his balance while working on the drawbridge, and that it hadn't been the first time he'd done so. Even Petyr admitted that Nicholas was more surly than usual, and walked around in a daze. Fear for him made her angry. She but wanted a chance to help, and she was the last person to whom he would come.

Celestia threw the hated embroidery hoop on the bench. "Nicholas, you do not need to go into the village again. We have supplies, food, and servants. In the past week you have done the work of ten men."

Nicholas paused in front of the open keep doors, and Celestia caught her breath as a sudden shaft of light surrounded him like a halo. She stuffed her project into a willow basket next to her chair.

He pushed an overlong strand of thick black hair off his forehead. Celestia's knees trembled with a spike of uncertainty. Why was being in love with one's husband so difficult? He'd neatly managed to avoid her and the bedchamber by taking the midnight watch. He looked so tired. She was not sleeping, either, concerned as she was for his health.

She knew he would not appreciate her worry. "I have planned a picnic," she said.

Panic darted in his eyes. "I am too busy to lie about and eat."

He was avoiding her, but she would run her prey to ground. "Nay, I have already checked with Petyr, and you can be spared for the afternoon. Beatrice has made some tasty meat pies that will melt on your tongue. I found some wild strawberries and have chilled some wine."

She babbled on, trying to put him at ease. "Beatrice must have been sent by Saint Martha—she's the saint of cooks, although she couldn't help me, more the pity—but that Beatrice. Do you know she can make a marzipan cake shaped like this very keep, all while cleaning the bed linens and dusting the corners?"

Nicholas laughed, then caught himself and bit his lip.

Celestia skipped up to him and shook her head. "Too late, my lord. I saw you smile." She smoothed down his tunic sleeve. "Besides, it isn't raining for once. I know Ceffyl could use a canter . . ."

She flirted with her husband like a shameless hussy. "Oh, I forgot. *Maude* came by yesterday while you were out hunting. She said she'd seen you in the forest, and she'd promised you some more of that jam you *just loved?*"

Obviously recognizing the danger signals, he stammered, "What else was I to say, 'Tia? She had me pinned up against a tree!"

"Oh, she did?" She quirked one brow up, while keeping the other straight. She knew that Nicholas wasn't fond of the beautiful Maude, but if she had to trick her husband into a picnic, then so be it. He was too honorable to dally.

"Not like that. Just, ah, Celestia, the woman is wicked."

She pointed her finger in the middle of her husband's chest. "Mayhap she is, but she wants you."

Nicholas's mouth gaped open, and Celestia stuck her fist on her jutted hip. Did he not understand how alluring his gray eyes were? His lashes, his noble nose? His body had strengthened with all of the manual labor he'd been doing, and his skin was burnished gold by the sun.

How could he not *know* this?

She narrowed her eyes, watching closely as he tried to find a way out of spending time alone with her. Celestia tapped her foot and quirked the other brow expectantly until he wisely gave in.

"When are we leaving for that picnic?"

Since she'd gotten her way, she decided not to hold a grudge against him for something like Maude's unwanted advances.

"Now. Before you change your mind."

Celestia called for Forrester, who brought Ceffyl and Brenin around from the stables. The new drawbridge was sturdy, and the horses didn't shy from crossing it.

She waited until they were each over to the grass, then turned and tossed out the challenge, "A race, my lord? Or are you afraid to lose to me?"

Clucking her teeth, she sped off, letting Ceffyl have her head. They tore through the large field, then past the old apple grove, where a few trees had managed to grow and blossom. The sweet perfume called to her, but she didn't stop. Instead she continued on to the grassy meadow where the old mill lay in ruins. Nicholas was right on her heels.

"I win!" she said, her breath coming in quick gasps.

"No fair, you never told me where the finish line was," he laughed, shielding his eyes from the sun.

"We can race back, my lord. Mayhap you'll have a chance, then." She slid from Ceffyl's back. "I'm famished, aren't you?"

He didn't answer, just dismounted and looked around. "'Tis too bad that all this is laid to waste. You could find no place closer to the keep for a picnic?"

"I liked the apple trees, but the mill beckoned. Besides, this area is pretty, too, don't you think?"

"Not especially." His voice was grim. "The stream has dried up, and the mill is tipped over on its side, rotting in the weeds. No, I don't think it is 'pretty.'"

Determined to change his mind, Celestia twirled around like a little girl. "Pah! The grass is soft and fragrant, the wildflowers are in bloom, and the mill makes for an excellent conversation piece. For certes, if we were to look closely, we might even find the remnants of the stream."

"Why must you always argue with me?"

She tossed out the blanket until it was positioned just so, then put a bag on each corner to guarantee that it stayed. "A difference of opinion is hardly an argument, my lord." She put her finger against her lower lip, deliberately drawing Nicholas's eyes to her mouth. "You try being the smallest in a family of giants, and you'd be 'arguing,' too."

He smiled, relenting a little. "Aye, and would I be as stubborn?"

She raised her chin, but kept her tone light. "Focused. It's all in how you see it."

Nicholas stepped closer, as if drawn to her energy, which was good—since she was putting all she had into charming him. She held out her hand. "Will you walk with me to find the stream?"

"And if it isn't there?"

"It will be!"

"But what if it isn't?"

"Then I shall owe you a forfeit."

He stopped in his tracks. "And if there is?"

She laughed, low and husky. "Then you shall owe me one, my lord."

He looked like a hare caught in a trap, and she reveled in her feminine power, something she'd never realized that she had. She'd believed that her only strength was her ability to heal. *Fate.* Celestia had learned how to love, which meant that she could now lose her heart, in addition to her healing hands.

Not to mention the welfare of her brothers.

She led the way to the tipped-over mill, and Nicholas followed. Reserved at first, it wasn't long 'til he was laughing as freely as she'd ever heard. Her spirits rose as they explored the mill and the meadow like children, creating an ease between them that but needed a chance to grow.

They'd ventured far into the trees when she finally stopped and cupped her hand around the curve of her ear. "Listen," she said, "over there."

"What?"

She grabbed Nicholas by the hand and pulled him forward. Waiting until she was certain that he heard the trickling sounds of a slow-moving stream, she announced, "I found it!"

Nicholas groaned aloud, but she could tell that he was glad that she'd won the forfeit. His glance was hot, and her body hummed with anticipation.

Since the point of the picnic was to get him to relax, she supposed that she could demand a nap. He couldn't tell her nay.

But how boring would that be?

Her toes curled within her half boots at the thought of being encircled within Nicholas's arms. They could nap together, and that might be more fun.

"Come, Nicholas, the water tastes sweet."

He joined her and they knelt side by side, scooping up the cool water in their hands to sip. Her leg tingled where it brushed against Nicholas's, and she wished that someday he would come to feel for her what she felt for him.

She sighed and patted stream water on her cheeks in an effort to cool her desire. Then she scooped up another handful and playfully tossed it down Nicholas's back.

His look of surprise warmed her heart, but the look of revenge had her running as if her life depended on it.

Nicholas chased after her, but even his long-legged stride did not catch her before she fell to her knees on the blanket. She tilted her face up to his and laughed, "I am safe, my lord!"

"You cheated, wench. I didn't even know we were playing a game of tag." He, too, dropped to his knees.

They faced each other, their chests heaving with exertion and physical awareness. She reached out her hand to touch his cheek. The work he had been doing around the keep, as well as the time spent training with the knights, had chiseled his features. "You take my breath away," she whispered.

His ebony brows arched perfectly over his smoldering dark gray eyes. The shadows beneath them worried her, but she would do what she could to fix that. His shoulders had broadened, and his arms were more muscularly defined beneath his tunic. His jaw was stubborn, but she didn't care.

She had that same trait.

Leaning forward, she caressed his smooth chin. He was so honorable, and yes, apprehensive. Gram had said that he lived and breathed fear, and mayhap that was so, a week ago. But now he was coming to terms with his past.

After getting a glimpse of his life, she was simply grateful that Nicholas was alive—no matter his moodiness.

He could eat with his toes and she knew that she would find it endearing. When had she turned into a silly female? She didn't even mind being small with Nicholas at her side; she knew he would protect her. Wouldn't Galiana love to see her laid so low?

Nicholas stayed very still as she brought her mouth to his. Celestia placed a tiny kiss at each corner of his sculpted mouth before sliding her lips along his. She closed her eyes and nipped lightly at his full, lower lip.

She didn't protest at all when he clasped the back of her head, angling her mouth so that he had better access. He separated her lips and taught her the wonders of his tongue as it dueled with hers. She crawled closer to him, wanting to feel his body flush against her, knees to knees, breasts to chest. If she was being brazen, she didn't care. Being with Nicholas was all that mattered.

Sliding her hands up his arms, she marveled in the play of muscle beneath her fingers. She traced his collarbone, and slid her fingers down the open vee of his tunic, following the path her fingers took with light kisses.

With a groan, he pulled her across his lap so that her bottom brushed his manhood. The feel of rigid male, even through her clothes, was enough to send a pool of heat to the apex of her thighs. She tore her lips from his in frustration. As much as she would like an afternoon of seduction, Nicholas's health came first.

She jumped up and giggled like a fool.

"I forgot to get our basket."

Narrowing his eyes, Nicholas sat back, his face an

unreadable mask as she dropped a napkin over his lap. She pretended not to notice the bulge; instead, she handed him a plate of meat pie and strawberries. "Eat up, my lord. We have plenty." *Oh, Nicholas would think her a nitwit, no doubt. But it was for his own good.* Her heart beat erratically, and her belly burned with longing.

Nicholas accepted the dish. "Are you trying to fatten me up for a feast that I don't know about?"

She giggled *again* and brought out the wine, filling his goblet to the very top. "I made this spiced wine myself. I do hope you like it."

Fluttering her lashes, she hoped he would drain the cup. He did. "Well?"

"It tasted, uh, spicy?"

She dropped her shoulders and pinched a thin piece of skin on her arm until water welled in her eyes. "You didn't care for it?" Sniffing, she hid her face in her hands.

He quickly held out the empty cup. "Don't cry, 'Tia! I thought it was an excellent wine. I doubt you brought enough to satisfy my thirst."

She blinked her eyes a few times for good measure. He was so predictably honorable. The wine contained thyme and valerian, a combination that would give him sleep, with no opiate at all to send him battling demons instead of counting sheep. "I can make you more, if you find that you truly like it, my lord. A glass of wine helps me to sleep."

Suspicion dawned in his sharp eyes. "Sleep?"

She scooted back on her heels, hoping to hide her nervousness. "Aye, sometimes I find I am overexcited after a busy day, and a glass of wine relaxes me."

He looked at her goblet, which hadn't been filled. "Where is your wine?"

She pleated a napkin in her hands. "The water from the stream refreshed me, my lord."

"Have some wine, Celestia."

She giggled and waved the napkin in the air like a flag of truce. "If you feel so strongly about it, I will join you in a cup." She poured herself a small amount.

"Drink it."

His eyes bored into her as she pretended to sip.

"Come here, Celestia."

She knew from past experience that there was no reasoning with him once his jaw was set like that. Walking on her knees across the blanket, she stopped in front of him, determined to hide her fear. The vein at the base of her neck jumped. What would he do to her?

"Open your mouth."

She tightened her lips, then exhaled and did as he said. Would he understand that she had drugged the wine for his own good? Considering his past, probably not.

He leaned in and sniffed her breath. He cocked his head to the side and took a swallow from his own goblet. Before she could protest, he kissed her, sharing the mouthful of wine between them.

She pounded her fists on his chest, but he didn't release her until she swallowed the wine. "Nay!" How could she stand guard while he slept if he drugged her, too?

Nicholas forced her to lie back, her head pillowed on one of his arms. "Are you trying to kill me, Celestia?"

His voice was a low whisper, and his eyes were twin orbs of iron.

"No." Her voice came out as a squeak. She cleared her throat. "Nay—I was but trying to help you sleep." Her traitorous fingers traced the hard lines of his face with love instead of anger, pausing over the bruise on his cheek. "You work so hard, and fight your rest. What would happen to me if you were hurt? I thought to help you, as a good wife, and healer, should."

"You know my past, and yet you betray me anyway?"

"It's not a betrayal," Celestia argued in self-defense. "You need to sleep before you kill yourself, and I won't have that, Nicholas—I won't!"

Nicholas's hard gray eyes turned to onyx. "You argue, wife."

Celestia pressed her body to his, reveling in the weight of him. "Would that I could be your wife in truth."

She lifted her head to meet his mouth in a kiss as hot as fire. His lips ravaged hers, yet she pulled him closer, harder, wanting to be absorbed into his heat. Nicholas wrapped her hair around his hand and tilted her face so that she had no choice but to look into his eyes.

"You know that I would give you the choice. Why do you make this so difficult?"

He nipped her upper lip with his white teeth, and then licked the spot with a flick of his tongue. She ran her hands in small circles over the muscles in his back, memorizing the feel of him. She would pay the penalty for this act later, she knew, but for now she had what she wanted. Nicholas in her arms.

"I warned you not to play your games with me," he growled into her ear. She shivered, but did not let go.

"I am not playing a game, Nicholas." She lowered her eyes. "I love you."

Nicholas lifted his head and took her chin in his hand. His voice was controlled and matter-of-fact. "You have forced yourself to think of me with love in order to save your family. I'll not be used like a stallion for stud."

She protested, but he stopped her with another searing lip-lock that she felt all the way to her toes. Stud services? From the hard length against her thigh, she could well imagine what that might entail. Lifting her hips, she struggled against the pull of the sleeping herbs.

"Mayhap my feelings started that way, but I pledge to you that what I feel for you is true." She slowly guided his hand to her aching breast. "Do you not feel my heart beating?"

He molded his hand around the plump curve and exhaled, leaning his forehead down against hers. "'Tia! No matter what else happens between us, I am getting an annulment from the baron. Your brothers will be safe, I promise you that."

Her eyes were heavy, as was Nicholas's voice. The warm sun beat down on them in benediction. "I made my choice, Nicholas."

What would he say to that?

"Nicholas?"

His body was heavy on hers, his head cradled between her shoulder and neck. The length of his body relaxed against hers. His breathing was steady, his eyelids closed.

She was too sleepy to laugh.

The sound of horse's hooves and shouting roused Nicholas from the deepest sleep he'd had since the last time Celestia had drugged him. He rose to his elbows, reluctant to move from her warmth.

Her angel eyes fluttered open, and Nicholas wondered what it might be like to look into them every morning of every day.

He knew that she thought to protect him, and perchance, considering how light-headed he'd been lately, she was right to worry. He wished that she didn't think she loved him. He knew very well that she wanted to save her brothers. Celestia was a woman who saw something that needed doing, and then took the most direct route there.

While such forthrightness was a good quality in many ways, it also led to self-sacrifice on her part. A sacrifice that he, in good conscience, could not allow her to make.

He'd made a pledge to avenge the men his father had killed, and he would do so. Just as he would save Celestia's family before taking the baron's heart and going to Spain.

"I'm sorry," she whispered, her brilliant eyes filling with tears. "I was going to stand guard while you slept, but you kissed me with wine."

"You're sorry I kissed you?" He stared down at her face, reluctant still to get up, even though the horse was coming closer.

"Nay," she flushed. "Sorry that I let you down."

She made him want to forget about his previous pledge for vengeance, and that wasn't at all right. A knight who didn't stand true to his oath was no man at all.

She turned her head, finally realizing that someone was approaching. He watched the emotions cross her face. Disappointment, surprise, irritation, and—it stayed at irritation.

Pulling herself from the cocoon of Nicholas's arms, she got up and waved to Petyr as she marched across the grass to meet him away from the blanket.

"My lord Nicholas was sleeping—what could be so bloody important that you interrupt our tryst?"

Nicholas arose, noticing Petyr's eyes flicker. "My apologies, my lady. Viola has been laid out by an arrow. It is deep in her side, and she is calling for you."

Celestia's hands flew to her cheeks. "Saints forgive my sharp tongue, Petyr. Get the horses, will you?" She turned to Nicholas. "You'll have to chastise me later, my lord. Will you ride back now?"

Nicholas ran to where the horses were tethered. Falcon Keep was one nightmare after another. There'd been no leads as to who had killed Bess, and now Viola?

If the women were being targeted, then only Celestia was left. The baron's heart was safe for a while longer. Nicholas would stay and protect his wife.

Celestia must have come to the same conclusion,

that she was the last of the three women in their party, because suddenly fear shadowed the brilliance of her eyes and her stubborn chin quivered.

Nicholas handed her Ceffyl's reins, and he knew that Celestia was out of sorts because she accepted his help to mount.

"I had thought that I would never speak to you again, Celestia, but I find that the extra sleep has calmed my anger. Not that I am thanking you for your treachery, but I will forgive it. You are a healer, and I suppose you couldn't help yourself."

"Thank you, Nicholas."

"If you do it again, I will beat you, as is my right as husband."

She kept her eyes lowered. "Yes, Nicholas."

"Is the wound life-threatening, Petyr?" Nicholas asked as the three of them flew neck and neck toward the keep.

"It looks to be, but mayhap our lady will think it not."

Nicholas had noticed that all of his knights had accepted Celestia on her own merit. He wished that he could be so free.

His breath caught in his chest as she rode Ceffyl to the edge of the drawbridge, only to dismount before the mare came to a complete stop. Nicholas followed her, calculating how he could best be of help.

They ran upstairs to find Beatrice wringing her hands outside Viola's chamber.

Celestia panted for breath. "Why are you standing out here? Why aren't you with her? Is she? Oh, no—"

Barging past Beatrice like a five-foot-tall Roman soldier, she halted at the edge of the bed. Nicholas would have hired her on the spot for mercenary work.

Viola's face was a bloodless mask. The maid's lank brown hair lay lifeless against the pillow.

Opening her eyes, Viola said, "My lady, I waited for ye." She lifted her hand and whispered with a lopsided smile, "I tried to tell them to get your bag, but they didn't."

Nicholas focused on the one thing he could do. "You need a bag? What kind of bag?"

Holding up a dainty hand, Celestia pulled back the sheet. She said calmly, "You did fine, putting clean cloths to the wound. You've learned much from me, but you have a natural talent, too."

The maid looked pleased at the compliment, and Nicholas recognized the soothing manner that Celestia used with her patients. She used it on him a lot.

Dropping the sheet, she turned to him and said concisely, "Nicholas, I need two buckets of hot water. Beatrice, my medicine bag should be in the solar by the window. Forrester, more clean linens please. Petyr, clear everyone out, would you? This is not a show at the fair."

Petyr nodded with tight lips, as if annoyed, but then he shooed everyone back. "Everyone to work."

Nicholas delegated his bucket duties to Willy and then came in to ask Viola some questions. "How are you feeling?"

Celestia rolled her eyes, but the maid answered with a quavering voice, "Like I am dying, my lord. But now that Lady Celestia is here, for certes, I'll be fine."

"Of course, you will," Celestia said.

"It was the Scottish rebels, my lord."

Nicholas pulled a stool over to the pallet and sat so that he wasn't towering over the injured maid. "How do you know?" His pulse sped.

"I saw a plaid," Viola whispered, her big brown eyes wide with fright. "And then I heard a 'thwack,' and then I saw I was hit. The edge of the forest should be safe, Lord Nicholas. I was but looking for berries."

"I see." Nicholas hated not being able to protect his people, and he folded his hands over one knee. Then he saw the discarded cloak on the floor by the bed. Bloody and torn, Nicholas's gut knotted as he picked the thing up. "Celestia, isn't this your cloak?"

Viola tried to rise from the bed. "Lady Celestia said I could borrow it against the chill, my lord. I didn't steal it!"

"Calm yourself, Viola. Of course, you didn't steal it."

Nicholas looked up and saw the warning in Celestia's eyes. She was right, again. Viola needed to stop dying before he could question her so hard.

"Nicholas, would you go see what is taking so long with the water, please? Beatrice should have had some boiling in the kitchen. Two separate buckets." She turned from Viola's side, pushing Nicholas toward the door.

She tugged his head down, and whispered in his ear, "I will use my hands to heal the wound, but not in front of the new servants. They know me not, and I won't harm you by people saying that I am a witch."

Even in the midst of a crisis, she thought of him. He took her by the shoulders and kissed her nose. "Would you not concern yourself about me and my reputation?

Heal Viola, as only you can. I have grown used to her."

Because wherever Viola is, Celestia was near at hand. And, indeed, just knowing that made his blood warm, he realized with a start.

"Go, then! I have much work to do. But only you or Petyr can enter the chamber once I begin."

"I don't want Beatrice in here," Viola agreed weakly. "All she did was wring her hands and cry. If anybody is going to cry around here, it is going to be me."

Celestia pushed Nicholas out of the room and shut the door, certain he would follow her orders.

Trusting he would keep them all safe.

She didn't know how much time had passed as she worked over the maid's wound. It was deep and ragged, and it tore in exactly the same way that Sir Geoffrey's wound had.

Celestia took extra time cleansing the area, looking for the poisoned pieces of feather. She couldn't think about who was behind the attack, not yet.

A healer had to concentrate. She'd given Viola an infusion of coltsfoot, balm, and yarrow, to help with internal bleeding and pain. Her family was not certain how their gifts worked, only that they did. Whenever possible, they combined their powers with herbs.

Whispering a prayer, she rubbed her hands together. She visualized the four humors of the body, then focused on the tear in Viola's side. When her hands were warm, she placed them over the wound. Bending her head forward, she prayed to all the saints to help her heal Viola. She frowned; the wound was deep.

The crimson red of the gash pulsed with gray. Celestia went deeper into her own spirit, moving her hands over the afflicted area, time and again. It was a challenge, and she had to reach deeper and deeper until she wondered if she was using the last of her powers.

But she could not let Viola die.

She kept rotating her hands in a circular motion, hovering a half inch over the skin, until finally the gray burst like a pus bubble and dissipated. Sighing with relief, she wiped the sweat above her brow. "My thanks," she whispered, keeping her warm hands over Viola's side until the tissue was a healthy pinkish-red and her hands cooled.

A ceramic pot crashed to the floor. Startled, Celestia rocked back on her heels, neglecting to cover Viola's healed wound in her surprise. Beatrice stood at the door, her hand over her mouth. Her eyes were wide with terror, and Celestia could do nothing but stare at the new cook. Where was Nicholas?

Beatrice opened her mouth and shouted, "Witch! Ye're a witch, I knew it. I heard that you practiced the black arts, and now I've seen it with me own two eyes. I should never have listened to that addle-pated priest—a woman can sense evil. Witch!"

Nicholas ran to the door and stopped behind Beatrice, a look of intense displeasure on his face. "She's no witch. Stop your yellin', woman."

But it was too little, too late. Celestia sensed the malevolence in the air as if it were a foul smell. She quickly covered the sleeping maid. The new servants, the ones they'd paid extremely well to come work at the "haunted" keep, had heard every word and were fighting to get into the room and look.

Beatrice gloried in the moment, her small brown eyes gleaming with accusation as she faced her fellow villagers. "I saw it all, I say." She glared at Nicholas. "The apple never falls far from the tree, my lord. Your mother was crazy, and you must be, too. They say that the Baron Peregrine isn't even your true father. A bastard and a witch, a match made in hell!"

The servants all listened with their mouths gaping open.

"My healing is a gift," Celestia tried to explain, knowing that she was wasting her breath.

Celestia heard the clatter of shields and swords as their knights came up the stairs, drawn to the ruckus.

Petyr pushed his way through until he met Nicholas's gaze, then he glanced at Celestia and Viola. "What is going on here?"

Beatrice drew herself up tall. "She is a witch—I demand that you bring her to the priest."

Viola chose that moment to wake from her herbal stupor. Before anyone could stop her, she stumbled from her bed with the blanket wrapped tightly around her shoulders, her face as pale as death, her brown hair clouded around her head. "What goes on here? Can't a woman get some rest?"

Beatrice shrieked as if she'd seen Viola rise from the dead.

Celestia sighed and looked to Nicholas. "Do you see why I hate to meet new people?"

Chapter FIFTEEN

Reclining against the propped-up feather pillows, Viola sniffed. "I'm so sorry, my lady. How was I to know that everyone was standing there?"

Nicholas jabbed at the fire with a poker. "Who would have thought those servants could be so damn sneaky?" He rubbed the back of his head where a thin stream of blood showed through his ebony hair.

Celestia finished wrapping Viola's side in linen. "Who would have thought that people have been calling me a witch all through the village? Do you think that Maude started those rumors?"

All three sighed out loud.

Nicholas's stomach growled. "I'm getting hungry. What are the chances those vile peasants will allow us bread and water?

"Would you really want to eat anything from Beatrice now?" Celestia huffed. "And to think I admired her marzipan!" She stalked over to Nicholas and bade him sit down.

"I'm too furious to sit," he grumbled.

Celestia tugged on his arm. There should be a patron saint for difficult husbands, she thought with a sigh. "It will take but a moment to fix this." Celestia lightly touched the back of his head.

"Do you think that the villagers won't notice that I no longer have a cut on my head after they brained me with a rock?"

Celestia burst into tears.

Nicholas pulled her into his lap and held her close. Since she liked it there, she stayed, letting the rumble of his chest beneath her cheek comfort her.

"I'm sorry, Celestia. This is my fault. I never should have walked to the end of the hall . . . I was simply stretching my legs as I waited. I never even heard Beatrice walk up the stairs. This marriage has been a disastrous union from the start."

Hurt anew, Celestia sprang from his lap. "Father Michael will be here shortly, and this whole mess will be sorted out."

Viola scrubbed at her leaking eyes. "So long as he doesn't demand to see my wound, we'll be fine. I won't let them burn ye at the stake, my lady, I won't."

Knees trembling, Celestia raised her chin. "Thank you, Viola. I appreciate that."

Nicholas was up and pacing the room, so Celestia followed him. Perchance pacing was a good way to sort a mind humming with one chaotic thought after another.

"Are you following me?"

He turned and stopped so that she ran nose-first into

his chest. "Ouch!"

"What were you doing?"

"Don't yell." Celestia rubbed her sore nose. "I'm pacing, if you would get out of my way." She pushed against his stomach, which was as hard as his chest.

His lips twitched, and his dark eyes, for a mere second, glittered with amusement. He looked, heaven help her, very full of the devil.

She blinked, then turned and ran for her herbal medicine bag. Celestia rummaged through some of the tissue-wrapped herbs until she found a dried sprig of angelica. "Mayhap this will help save us."

The sound of the door opening had them all hurrying back to position. Viola affected a wan look as she lay back against her pillows, her hand to her brow. Nicholas glared at the doorway, retribution sparking from the ends of his hair. Celestia sniffed into her handkerchief, hoping that sorrow and sadness emanated from every pore. She sent a quick prayer to Saint Vitus, the patron saint of actors and troubadours, that they could pull the wool over everyone's eyes.

Beatrice entered the room, looking smug. "See, Father Michael? We have them locked up, just like I said."

The old priest shook his large cross in front of Beatrice's face. "Beatrice. How often do I have to tell you not to meddle? You've done it this time! It will be the stocks for three days, woman, no matter what your husband has to say."

Father Michael walked quickly to Celestia, who quit sniffing long enough to give him her limp hand. "My lady. I apologize for this disruption. Please forgive my overzealous flock. Your maid was shot with an arrow?"

Viola lowered her eyes demurely and said in a weak voice, "It was just a graze, good Father, a lot of blood, but not too deep."

He got up and knelt by Viola's side. "Where were you, dear?"

"At the edge of the forest." She grabbed his hand, her large brown eyes filling with tears. "It should be safe enough there, Father, to gather berries for a pie. I had Willy and Bertram with me for protection." Viola cried with more enthusiasm. "To think that they could have been hurt, as well—oh!"

Celestia found it very difficult to keep a straight face at her maid's antics, but one look at the severe expression on Beatrice's face kept her from so much as smiling.

Father Michael awkwardly patted Viola's hand. "There, there."

Then it was Nicholas's turn, and he groaned loudly enough to get Beatrice and Father Michael's attention. He touched the back of his head, making certain that his hand came away covered in blood. "Father Michael, Celestia is no witch. If she were, she could have healed me, for God's sake." Nicholas stared at Beatrice. "I will find out which one of you hit me from behind."

Father Michael stood, his old knees creaking as he sent a dark glance to Beatrice. The servant was white around the mouth, with anger or fear, Celestia couldn't tell.

Not to be outdone, Celestia played her role with gusto. "Let me get something for your head, Nicholas. Why didn't you say it pained you?" She grabbed her bag, lifting up various herbs. She made sure that the woman and the other servants could see her handling them. She said aloud, "Angelica, garlic, horehound . . . Viola, where are the blackberry leaves so that I can stop the bleeding on Nicholas's head?"

Viola said, "You used the last of them on my wound. We will have to gather more tomorrow."

Father Michael's face was bright red with anger. "Angelica, you said?"

"Yes, Father Michael," Celestia answered, lifting her head.

"And horehound?"

"Why, yes." She handed him the neatly tied bunches of dried herbs.

He took them and showed them to Beatrice, whose entire body was now pale. "Do you see this? If there were any witch's test, this would be it. It is common knowledge that witches cannot handle these herbs. I am ashamed of you, Beatrice, ashamed."

Turning around, he splayed his hands in supplication and said, "My lord Nicholas, I beg your pardon for recommending such a woman to work for you." He returned the herbs to Celestia and shrugged. "She has a way with marzipan."

Nicholas's lips curved into a slight smile. "So I've heard, Father."

Celestia's shoulder's relaxed as she sensed the crisis was over. Not being burned at the stake was a cause for celebration, but when she looked over at Nicholas to share a smile of relief, her knees buckled.

He was furious.

There was no way to ignore the sharp, cutting gaze he was sending to the servants in the hall. If she read him right, he would like to tear them limb from limb. Each step was deliberate, each blink a promise of retribution. Celestia gulped. The servants quaked.

"Downstairs." He didn't raise his voice. He didn't have to. Celestia noticed how they all snapped to attention. "*Now.*"

Celestia had never seen Nicholas so driven by emotion of any kind, well, she thought with a blush, except for the few kisses they'd shared that had been enough to curl her toes.

The knights held themselves stiffly as they surveyed the group of servants. They looked disciplined, yet angry on behalf of Nicholas–he'd truly become their lord, proving himself by word and deed. Yet their tunics of blue and gold were a miserable reminder of Baron Peregrine, and his strangle-hold on Nicholas's life. Her husband had forced the men to stand down after he had been locked in Viola's chambers, wanting to prevent bloodshed. Thank all the saints he'd had the presence of mind to send Petyr with Beatrice for Father Michael before the villagers trussed Celestia up with rope and tossed her in the moat to see if she sank.

She shivered and rubbed her arms as a chill settled against her nape. *No, no, not another vision.*

Nicholas stood on a stump at the end of the great room, his anger making him appear even larger than he was. She'd never seen him use his size, nor his looks, to intimidate others before. He looked like the king of his castle. Celestia smiled. It was, for certes, time.

Like his shoulders, his confidence in his own abilities had grown through hard work and exercise. Was it any wonder that she was so very much in love with him?

He kept his voice low, yet it boomed off of the stone walls, commanding the attention of all who listened. "I am searching for one good reason not to flay all of you in the courtyard."

Celestia's smile drooped. Nicholas's dark gray eyes stopped at each shuddering peasant. The knights grinned and flexed their fingers. "So far the only one coming to mind is that then my wife, the *healer*, would feel honor bound to care for you. I would as soon never see you again. Ingrates."

Shy Sally, who worked as a scullion in the kitchens, slowly raised her shaking hand. "Lord Nicholas, we came to work for ye, 'cause ye paid us well." She paused, and her friends urged her on. "We'd heard that yer wife was a witch. She has a pointed chin and two different-colored eyes!" The encouragement got louder. "But some of us was so desperate for work that we had to come anyway."

There was a chorus of agreement, though most stayed cowering under Nicholas's stare.

Beatrice was not willing to give up her time in the sun. "And we heard that she used magical spells." She lowered her voice theatrically. "We heard she ensnared you with magic, my lord. Why else would you have married such a wee thing?"

Celestia decided that Beatrice would look much

more attractive with a fat lip. Petyr grabbed her by the shoulder. "Have faith in your husband, my lady. Give him a chance to prove himself."

She shrugged off Petyr's hand and stayed put, but barely.

Nicholas turned his scowl full force on the arrogant, misinformed cook. "If you ever speak of my wife in such a manner again, you will live to regret it. Where did you hear such nonsense?"

He gave Beatrice no quarter until she stammered, "The wise woman, me lord." He started in surprise, but covered it by turning toward the peasants he'd hired. "My wife is no magician," he spread his hands, "nor is she a witch. An enchantress? Mayhap. She is beautiful. Her eyes? One blue, one green. They beguile, for certes. But she is not evil. Her chin, yes, it is rather pointed, but if she were perfect, then she would not entice me half as much."

Nervous laughter filled the room. Father Michael tucked his rosary inside his cloak after kissing the cross. He asked piously, "What will you do with these gossipers, my lord? I am much ashamed to say that they are from my flock. Perhaps I have not been a good shepherd."

The peasants looked frightened. Even Celestia wondered if Father Michael might desert them in their time of need.

Nicholas jumped down from the stump and walked amongst them, his arms brushing theirs. He stopped in front of Sally. "Why were *you* so ready to believe my wife was a witch?"

She reddened, two dark blotches against her pale skin. "Me lord!" She scanned the group nervously for aid, but none came forward. She wouldn't meet his eyes and whispered to her shoes, "Everyone knows the north tower be haunted, me lord. And if ye allow spirits in yer castle, why not a witch for a wife?"

The others gasped aloud—certain they would all be missing the skin off of their backs come dawn.

Two tears leaked from the corner of Sally's eyes as she glanced at him. "I am so sorry, but ye asked, ye did."

Hmm. Nicholas folded his hands behind his back and rocked on his heels. His volatile fury had spent, leaving a quieter anger that had nothing to do with these uneducated folk. What to do with them?

He scratched the back of his neck. He'd like to send them all packing, without pay, mind, but he knew Celestia well enough to know she wouldn't agree to it, despite the fact they'd wanted to drown her but an hour prior.

His wife tugged on his sleeve. "I know a way, Nicholas, that we can dispel these rumors forever. Would you hear it?"

She was clever. Bringing out the angelica and horehound had been cunning and effective. Filled with pride, he placed his hand on her shoulder, drawing strength from her goodness. If she wanted them hung by their thumbnails until they recanted, by God, he'd see it done. "Aye."

All eyes were focused on them, and Nicholas became aware for the first time what a contrast they made. Celestia was so petite and fair, and he—he thrust his chest a bit, he was so large and dark. He felt her hand slip into his, and knew that they could conquer the world, or at the very least, this room full of peasants.

"Tomorrow we will open the north tower. You will see that neither ghosts nor witches reside here at Falcon Keep."

Nicholas felt a shimmer of doubt, but he could not think of a reason to halt the plan.

Father Michael clapped his hands together in applause. "What a wonderful solution, my lady. I have wanted to dispel that ghost nonsense for years." He appealed to Nicholas with his one good eye. "And if you don't mind, my lord, my 'flock' and I will spend the night in the courtyard, on our knees. We will pray for God's forgiveness, pardon for our loose tongues and closed minds. We will ask your forgiveness on the morrow, as well."

Nicholas dipped his head. "We will discuss this in the morning. All are welcome to remain but Beatrice. I cannot look past the harm she has done here today, and for the past week, if I understand correctly. 'Tis too bad that I will never taste her marzipan."

Beatrice turned green, then red, then white. She looked as if she would dare argue, but Father Michael shook his cross at her. "Aye, me lord." She muttered under her breath. "Damn that Grainne Kat!"

Nicholas followed Celestia up to their chamber as naturally as if they'd been sleeping in the same room for fifty years. "How are you feeling? Of course, we won't keep those servants. They'll be turned out immediately after we open the tower."

Celestia turned 'round and poked her finger into his chest. It was like being smacked by a cat, though he chose not to tell her that. "Nay! Nicholas, the others were simply following Beatrice's lead. She instigated the entire episode. Did you know that Sally has four babes to feed? I vow she's learned from her mistake."

Nicholas shrugged, although he was delighting in her defense of the villagers. Aye, he thought with an inner grin, their children would be warriors. "Sally would have watched you drown in a witch's test rather than come forward. Your handling of those herbs in front of Father Michael was incredible. You constantly amaze me with you quick-witted thinking."

She blushed, and the sight warmed him. *He could not have her.*

"Thank you, Nicholas." Celestia lowered her eyes, and he wondered if he'd embarrassed her somehow. Mayhap she was unused to compliments? Impossible!

He sat down on the cushioned trunk at the foot of their bed, his gaze taking in the embroidered pillows. Things that made a keep a home. What would happen to her if he died before achieving his quest?

"Did you hear Beatrice? She said the wise woman told her I was a witch." She rubbed her arms as if she were cold. Nicholas longed to pull her into his embrace.

"Perhaps I should pay a visit to Grainne Kat—what say you?"

Celestia wrinkled her nose. "I doubt the woman seriously believes I'm a witch, but it's no secret that Grainne Kat has not approved of me from the first she saw of me. I know that I am not as beautiful as her Maude, but marriage shouldn't be based on the matching attractiveness of two people, should it?"

Nicholas cocked a brow and looked at his wife, whom he felt was ethereal in her angelic beauty. Was she jesting? Had he been so caught up in his own troubles that he'd not seen a hurt in his wife? "Celestia? Come here."

She walked toward him, her natural grace evident in the way she held her head.

"Who says Maude is more beautiful than you?"

"Everybody?"

"Give me names."

She stammered. "'Tis nothing."

"You mean that you judged her to be more attractive, and so believed everybody else must think so, as well?"

She wouldn't meet his eyes.

"'Tia!"

Nicholas took her hand and led her to the full-length polished silver mirror she'd used as a cloak hanger. He removed the garments and tossed them on the bed. "I want you to look in that mirror and tell me what you see."

"Nicholas, release my hand—I know very well what I look like."

He could not believe his ears. How could she be so beautiful and not know it? "Tell me, then."

"This is strange, Nicholas. We have more important things to discuss than my looks."

"Nay. Indulge me, Celestia."

She blew a piece of hair off of her forehead in exasperation. "I have done nothing but indulge you since we met. You are severely trying my patience. Have done, *please!*"

Nicholas turned her shoulders so that she was facing the mirror with him standing behind her. "Then let me tell you what I see."

She struggled, but he held firm. "I see a woman of delicate stature who carries the weight of the world upon her slim shoulders. A gifted woman, with a loving heart three times her body size."

She stilled in his grasp.

He caressed her hair, his fingers lingering in the soft locks. "I see a young woman with long, waving blond tendrils—the kind that men dream about having wrapped around them during the night."

Kissing the top of her head, he continued in a husky voice, "I see a beautiful lady who looks like a fairy princess come to grace mortal man with her smile."

Celestia held his gaze, spellbound as he stroked her cheekbones with featherlight touches. "Why are you doing this?" she asked in a shaking whisper that came from her soul.

His chest tightened as he finally heard her inner pain. "This is what I see when I look at you. You are worth ten thousand Maudes! Your beauty comes from within and shines throughout, your eyes are beacons of light that cast compassion wherever they land—*look*."

She did. "But I am nothing like my parents or siblings, and they are beauty to me. You, too, are vibrant and alive in your coloring and features, whereas I am pale and small in comparison. Lord Riddleton even said so."

Nicholas's heart stopped for a single beat. "The odious toad?"

She laughed nervously. "'Tis nothing. He said he loved me, he said that I was beautiful, and I thought I could love him to protect my healing gifts. But then he . . ."

"Yes?"

Her face was hot with remembered humiliation. "He changed his mind. I overheard him say that he would rather have the younger, comely daughter, as the eldest daughter looked like a twig with odd eyes. He made mention, in great detail, actually, of Galiana's beautiful curves compared to my lack of them."

Nicholas set his jaw. "And when was this?"

She whispered, "A year past. He was speaking with his friend in our hall and did not see me until it was too late."

Nicholas's heart thundered on behalf of his wife. "And then what happened?"

Her eyes widened. "There was an embarrassing display, in which Lord Riddleton called off the engagement, in front of everyone." She shook her head at the memory. "I was already going to turn down his suit, as I didn't like his kisses."

"That's when he attacked you in the barn. Don't try to put a ribbon on the tale when it doesn't deserve one."

She met his eyes, and he saw gratitude in them. That angered him even more.

Celestia put a hand on his chest. "He didn't realize I would fight back. I bit his tongue until I tasted blood and ran. I made the mistake of running to my garden instead of directly to my father. Lord Riddleton thought I would be meek and accept him anyway. I didn't."

"I'm proud of you." Nicholas unclenched his tight fists. "You say you had already rejected him? He was getting back at you, that is all. If he could tell his friend that he didn't want you, then he does not look bad, do you see?"

The heat in her cheeks faded. "I am small . . ."

"Petite." Nicholas whirled her around so that they were nose to nose. "You are an angel. Beauty comes in many guises; the differences are to be appreciated. Your sister can be beautiful, and yet so can you. I find that I prefer petite blonds."

He dropped a kiss on her slightly parted pink lips. "Yet before you get a swelled head from all these compliments, I want to remind you that you are not perfection."

She inhaled and met his eyes.

"You do have a pointy chin."

She balled up her fist and punched him in the stomach before capturing his mouth in a shy kiss. "You are not perfection, either, Nicholas. I had thought you were, but I was mistaken."

"Oh, really?" His heart thumped beneath her palm.

She lowered her eyes. "If you were perfect, Nicholas, you would love me."

Nicholas knew it was late, but he headed through the woods anyway. He had an idea of where Grainne Kat's hut was, thanks to a small talk with Shy Sally. He held his torch high, looking for the worn path that had brought the village women to Grainne Kat's door for years.

She sold simples and small enchantments for love to the women in exchange for food stuffs or coin. Her daughter, Maude, had joined her enterprise. He could think of no reason as to why the two women would try to put the villagers against Celestia.

Grainne Kat had said she'd known his mother. Now that he'd had time to think over what Father Michael had told him, he had more questions for the wise woman. She had to be home. Where else could she be this late at night?

He finally found the path. He parted the low-hanging branches of the maple tree and stepped forward. The trail leading to the back of the hut was dirt-packed from the many feet that had traveled it. There was no fire or candlelight glowing from within, yet smoke curled from the roof.

One would think that the majority of love potions would be sold in the dark.

He walked as stealthily as he'd been trained and knocked on the back door. No answer.

Knocking again, he called softly, "Grainne Kat? 'Tis I, Nicholas."

He waited, but his instincts told him the hut was empty. Manners dictated that he should come back in the morning. Residual anger at the fact that she'd been slandering his wife made him push the door open. It wasn't locked.

Peering into the dark recesses of the hut, he kept all senses alerted to sound.

He jumped nigh out of his skin as Celestia whispered behind him, "Is she not home?"

Turning, he put a finger to his lips. "How did you

follow me?"

"I was but pretending sleep. I told you that my family was protective, my lord. If I didn't want to be left behind, I had to be quick. If you would have slept on the bed, instead of in front of the door, I may have been fooled." Celestia's hair shone like moonlight, and he quickly pulled up her hood.

If he would've slept on the bed, he wouldn't be here now. He'd have broken all personal codes of knightly honor, but been a sated man.

"Nicholas, if she is not here, we should not be going inside."

He ignored his wife and stepped farther inside the hut. She stuck like a shadow to his back.

The glowing embers of a recent fire in the grate gave a soft and eerie light to the gloomy interior. Three rooms had been partitioned off as sleeping quarters, and the central area had a long table with three chairs around it. A basket of sachets, fragrant herbs, and fabric sat by the fire, as if someone had been in the act of filling the simples for sale.

"They were just here." Nicholas eyed the room again, his gaze pausing over the mantle.

"We should go." Celestia tugged at the hem of his sleeve.

Curiosity might have killed the cat, but nothing could have dragged Nicholas away from the stone shelf over the fireplace. His heart banged against his chest, and his throat dried. "Dear God," he muttered, stumbling forward with his hand outstretched.

"What is it?" Celestia placed her hand on the small of his back. "Nicholas?"

Nicholas could not believe what he saw. It couldn't be. His fingers shook and his breath came in quick bursts. So very carefully, he lifted down a square box covered in royal purple velvet. Amethysts and pearls had been attached for decoration; the seal of King Henry was embossed on the golden handle.

His knees buckled, and he gasped for breath. "Nay. It cannot be." He stumbled into a chair at the table like a drunken man, his lungs constricting.

Celestia stood beside him, as she placed her cool fingers at the back of his neck. His chest eased.

Tears blinded him as he gently lifted the lid of the box. Blinking, Nicholas saw that it was true. The relic, praise God. Inside, a long finger bone lay nestled within swaths of linen. The bone still wore the ring of Saint James the Apostle.

Celestia gasped. "Nicholas?"

"I thought it had been lost forever." His heart started to beat again, a painful reminder of his past sins. Was this a sign, at long last, from God and the saint? He wiped his eyes, afraid that the precious relic would disappear yet again from his grasp.

Celestia took his hand. "This is the exact relic you lost?"

Calm pervaded him, and he was able to breathe deeply as he studied the box again. "Nay. It cannot be . . . The relic I carried had not worn such an elaborate ring. But in my heart, Celestia, I know that this is the true relic. It is a sign that I must return it to Spain. I have neglected my vow, dear God, forgive me. Is it not holy, 'Tia?"

Celestia tightened her grasp on her husband's hand. "Aye, Nicholas. It does indeed look holy. But answer me this—if you are holding the holy relic, what then were you carrying to King Richard?"

He released her hand. "You had the right of it. When we were talking with the priest, remember? My father had lost this relic, mayhap my mother hid it from him to keep it within the family, and so when King Richard wanted the relic back, my father had to come up with something false. But he knew that his lie would be caught out."

Celestia exhaled and stepped back. The words had the ring of truth, and Nicholas had that brooding look on his face that she disliked intensely. It meant that the friendship they'd been building together was about to take another blow. Goose bumps ran up her arms, and the embers in the banked fire glowed brightly. The chill at her nape urged her to flee.

"We must leave, Nicholas, now!"

He didn't question her, but he wasn't leaving without the relic. He stuffed the velvet box beneath his cloak. "The way we came?"

Celestia shook her head, her nose detecting the fragrance of wild apples, but she didn't see any. "Nay! I think there is a different entrance. Quiet, now." She led the way as if she'd been in the hut before. Grainne Kat's sleeping chamber had a separate door. "Here . . ."

She practically pulled Nicholas out behind her, and they found themselves in a small yard. Celestia gagged. Grainne Kat had said that her son, Joseph, had a talent for hunting small animals in the forest and selling the skins at the fair. Skins hung to dry on racks everywhere she looked. She did not deal well with death. "Ah!"

Nicholas covered her mouth with his hand. "Ssh, 'Tia. It will be all right, but we must leave now. I, too, sense there is danger here."

She nodded, and he released her. Leading the way, she followed a path that most likely led to the village, but Celestia didn't follow it. Then they passed a pen of arctic geese, snowy white-feathered birds that came to rest on Scotland's shores during the winter. The sleeping geese looked docile, but one wrong step could have them squawking like guard dogs.

Celestia wrapped her cloak tighter about her shoulders and tread on wraith-like feet until they reached the safety of the forest's edge.

Then she clasped Nicholas's hand and they ran like the devil chased them until arriving at the back gate of the keep.

Chapter SIXTEEN

"Heaven help us, Nicholas, but those woods are haunted with restless spirits. I know you felt it, too."

Nicholas leaned over to catch his breath. He pointed toward the southern part of the courtyard, where Father Michael was sleeping with his "flock." "Praying must have been too exhausting with that group," Nicholas muttered as he led Celestia toward the north tower.

"Stop jesting—what was that?"

"I don't know. I prefer flesh-and-blood enemies."

"The sense of danger was so strong, Nicholas."

"I don't believe in ghosts. The worst harm ever done to me was by human hands."

She patted his forearm. "Did you smell apples? Apple pie, or a tart, mayhap? All I know, Nicholas, is that the warning came through very clear. And I've never been to Grainne Kat's house—how, for certes, did I know how to find that secret door? And yet the feeling in the backyard was malevolent. Pure evil. Even you felt it, you said so. Why on earth would they have penned those geese? For food? Pillows?" She took a deep breath.

Nicholas's eyes twinkled at her like diamonds against a black cloth. "You are babbling, and I don't blame you overmuch. The hanging skins were enough to make *my* skin crawl." He scratched at his chin. "Ugh!"

Celestia exhaled and stared at her husband in the intermittent moonlight. "What do we do now?"

"We? *We* do nothing! I am leaving at first light. I'm going to return this sacred relic to Saint James and beg a boon. My soul, for starters." He pounded his fist against his chest.

She'd been afraid of that.

"Think for just a moment afore you go chasing off. Why would Grainne Kat have the relic? Why would she get the villagers in arms by telling them that I was a witch? What does she have to gain by it all?" Celestia kicked a rock with the toe of her boot.

"Would that I knew. But this . . ." He gave the hidden relic a pat. "This was a sign, 'Tia. I should never have let my feelings for you distract me from my purpose."

She bit her lip to keep from crying out. How was it that he had the power to hurt her so badly? "And what of the baron?"

He clenched his jaw, and Celestia winced as she heard the bone crack. "I will leave by morning's light." He punched his left fist into his right palm and lowered his voice. "I knew that nothing good could come from caring for you, or any of this." He flung out his arm, encompassing the entire keep.

It was clean, organized, and looked much improved, thanks to Nicholas's caring and hard work. Still, he negated everything with a dismissive wave. "Saint James will forgive me, aye, the instant I return the relic to his tomb. I'll walk, crawl if need be, to make amends. Mayhap this means that I need to forget vengeance, lest it drive me as mad as my mother was."

Celestia's heart broke in two at the naked hope on Nicholas's face. How could she compete against God?

He was leaving her.

She felt it deep within her being. Some of his despair had worn onto her, and now she ached with it. Celestia had known the day would come, yet still the hurt was almost more than she could take. Losing her healing gifts could not be nearly as debilitating as this awful wrenching of her heart.

Damn love. Damn minstrels, for they sang of this, too.

She blinked back those stupid, female tears and met Nicholas's imploring gaze straight on. "Of course you should go. If your responsibilities can't convince you to stay here, then who am I to try?"

His eyes narrowed into slits of iron.

Flipping her hair back as though she didn't care, she hefted her chin high. "Just the woman whom you married *out of honor*. Your father forced this union, and again your damnable honor kept you from trying to make a blessing from a curse."

Her voice broke, and her good intentions fell to the

ground. "If you make it back from your pilgrimage, Nicholas, then I tell you now, I will not be waiting like the docile good wife." His gray eyes widened. "I may take a lover to satisfy these feelings you have awakened in me. Yes, a lover."

Nicholas stepped back, his hands fisted before him.

"I may not even live here at this stinking keep. I hate it! There is no love here. The only happiness in this hole was what I felt for you. So go, then. I shall get over you in a trice." She snapped her fingers beneath his nose, then turned and ran for all she was worth.

"Celestia, wait!"

She was gone as if she'd never been there, yet the deep hurt in her eyes was forever branded in his mind. Nicholas couldn't breathe past the sudden ache in his chest. His eyes burned, and the relic weighed heavily in his tunic.

Pressing the jeweled box closer to his heart, he agonized over going to Celestia and soothing her, as she had soothed him so often. He could beg her to wait for him to come back, a whole man, one healed in spirit as well as body.

But he had no right to do so.

He'd been honest with her. He'd been honest in his desire for revenge.

Sighing, Nicholas wondered if he was moving too fast. He'd promised Saint James the baron's heart on a gold platter. If he returned the relic without the pledged death, he was, perhaps, failing another test of faith.

Celestia threw the bolt on her chamber door, knowing quite well that Nicholas wouldn't even try to open it. She picked up her sewing basket and withdrew the new tunic she'd been pouring her love into. Bess, she quickly caught another sob in her throat, and Viola had been making matching tunics for the other knights. She sniffed and held the garment up to the candlelight.

The fabric was ruby red, a perfect foil for Nicholas's midnight hair. She'd pricked her fingers many times applying the silver trim to the hem, but she had wanted to do herself. She'd had Willy draw her a falcon, and she'd used it to create a pattern of the bird with its wings outstretched in flight. To think and she'd hoped Nicholas would want it for his personal insignia.

All she had left to finish was the gold embroidery on the talons.

She sniffed again, gathered her needle and thread, and bent to complete her task. How could she let her husband travel to Spain in hand-me-down tunics? A man as proud as Nicholas needed his own colors.

Her eyes were sore from bad light and unshed tears, but the tunic was finished by dawn's arrival. She packed a knapsack with Nicholas's essentials, and carefully folded the crimson fabric inside. Celestia straightened her shoulders and rubbed her weary back, then firmly told her breaking heart, "This is the last thing I will ever do for that man."

Nicholas adjusted the saddle over Brenin's back. He was alone in the courtyard of the keep, and as dawn broke, he noticed that the work they'd done was beginning to show. The dirt was raked, the firewood stacked, the stables clean.

Satisfaction welled within as he fed the stallion an apple he had collected from the kitchen, along with the food he'd need to start his journey. He carried the relic safely within his tunic.

Father Michael had already gathered his parishioners inside to eat a small meal before the opening of the north tower and the banishing of his mother's supposed ghost. The urge to stay was overwhelming, but after creating such a scene last evening between he and Celestia, it wasn't possible. Not if he wanted to hold on to his pride. Nicholas would leave quietly, without fanfare or trumpets. It felt like he was sneaking away.

He had left written instructions for Petyr regarding Celestia's well-being.

Brenin's nose tickled his palm. "Sorry, boy. That's all I have for you. Are you ready?"

Nicholas knew, deep down inside, that he'd avoided speaking to anyone of his quest because it would take very little to convince him to stay here at the keep.

He wanted to stay. "Fine," he sighed aloud and Brenin chuffed in sympathy. "Maybe I'm curious about this 'haunted' tower." He told himself that this was not his home, Celestia was not his soul mate, his men were not his to command.

It wasn't working.

More than salvation, he wanted his wife. He never wanted to see such heartbreak on her face again.

"Ouch!" Nicholas clasped his hand to his aching head then looked down. His knapsack lay at his feet. He'd thought to leave it here, since he hadn't dared to breach the locked door of Celestia's chamber.

He'd tried once already, thinking to get her approval, but the knob hadn't turned and then he'd heard her crying.

Nicholas could withstand torture and take on ten knights at a time, but those tears made him tuck his tail and run.

He tapped the sack with his toe and looked around. Where had that come from? Alone in the courtyard, he looked up and saw the very person he had been thinking about waving gaily from the window at her chamber.

His heart tripped over itself with joy. She'd ask him to stay, surely. "Did you throw that?"

"Aye."

He grinned, forgiving her his aching head.

She stuck her tongue out. "I want no reminders of you here, so I thought I'd help you pack."

His temper grew, and he clenched his fists. "Did you have to throw it so hard?"

"I know how stubborn you can be. I simply wanted to gain your attention."

"You have it!"

"I wish that were true. Good-bye, Nicholas. Safe journey."

Nicholas stayed rooted to the ground and watched her disappear into the confines of their, her, chamber. Then he foolishly waited for her to come back so that he could drink in the sight of her, hoping she would ask him to stay. But after a few moments, he realized that she was not returning.

He picked up the knapsack, mounted Brenin, and left the courtyard without looking back. Why did he feel like a coward?

Brenin's steady gait left him time to contemplate his actions. Was he doing the right thing? The honorable thing? He remembered Celestia's earnest question last eve. Why exactly had the relic been in Grainne's possession? How had the poor wise woman come by the holy object of Saint James? Mayhap he needed to swallow his pride and think before leaving Celestia alone, with Bess's murder unsolved and Viola's attackers uncaught.

His pride.

It was getting in the way of doing the right thing. "Let's head for home, Brenin."

He heard hooves pounding behind him, and his heart leapt with anticipation. Had Celestia come after him? He grinned like a love-struck fool as he turned the stallion around. He and Celestia could make the best of their situation—what had she said?—they could turn the curse into a blessing, and turn the pilgrimage into a thing of love instead of hate.

Hope died. "Petyr—what are you doing? You are supposed to be back at the keep, taking care of Celestia. I left you instructions."

"I'm wasting time, chasing after your pathetic hide, that's what I'm doing." Petyr brought his horse to a halt, the horse's hooves kicking a little dirt on Brenin. "Here," he tossed a wrapped packet that Nicholas caught with one hand. "Yer wife said ye forgot it, again."

He opened the folded cloth and inside was his mother's rosary. The worn wooden cross seemed to pulsate with warmth, and heat flooded his face as he remembered that his wife was quite used to him acting the fool. She'd remembered that he'd forgotten the talisman when he'd left on crusade, and she thought to protect him. *Could she love him?*

"I read your instructions, my lord. You are making a mistake."

Nicholas put the rosary around his neck, carefully tucking the cross beneath his tunic. "I am going on pilgrimage, Petyr. It is a journey I need to make alone." *Or with Celestia.*

Petyr scoffed, his fair skin turning red. "Pilgrimage? Escaping from your duties, more like. Your wife scares you because she makes you *feel.* You enjoy wallowing in your self-pity. Holdin' everyone at arm's length. So you suffered in the Crusades. Lah-de-dah. Well let me tell you something, me lord Nicholas." Petyr's horse came nose to nose with Brenin, who snorted and rolled his eyes back.

"You weren't the only one to suffer. My brother was one of the men in the ambush on your caravan who died. It was you leading those men, and you who led them into a trap. Aye, I see the guilt still eats at ye."

Nicholas swallowed the bile in his throat. *Sand, sun, blood. Men's—screams, hoarse and gruff before they were silenced forever.*

"Would that my brother could have been returned to me, I doubt that he would have spent his remaining years lamenting his captivity—nay, methinks he would be kissing the ground for his very life."

Dizzy, Nicholas pressed his knees into Brenin's barrel chest. His voice was barely a whisper as he met Petyr's stern blue gaze. "How can you not blame me for your brother's death?"

Petyr hawked and spat. "*It was a trap.* I never heard of you. It was rumored, very softly, around Peregrine Castle that the baron had to have God's worst luck when it came to babes and wives. And that somewhere he had a grown boy—nobody knew where."

Nicholas couldn't move as Petyr unraveled another knot in his history. "It wasn't 'til the night he thought ye dead that he drank too much and spilled the secret of your identity."

"You believe in the curse?"

"I'm surprised if that evil bastard only has one curse heaped upon his oily head." Petyr laughed, but Nicholas heard no joy in it.

"He let go another secret, too. That old relic ye were willing to die for? It was fake."

Nicholas gritted his teeth until it hurt.

Petyr puffed out his chest. "Well, my Lord Nicholas, this is the last of me secrets. Your father, Baron Peregrine, bought my loyalty with coin. My brother and

I were fostered at his castle, and raised to be knights. I," he grinned, "held on to honor, believing in right and wrong under God's law. Me brother, now, rest his soul, he believed right was the side that paid the most."

Unsure of where Petyr was going with this, Nicholas leaned over to rub his calf, as if easing a cramp, and palmed the small blade he'd hidden there.

Petyr's brow furrowed. "Before he left on that damn Crusade, he told me that not all things were what they seemed. He thought he was bloody funny, but would not explain the jest. He told me," Petyr looked Nicholas straight in the eye, "that he would come back from Crusade a richer man than Midas."

Brenin sidestepped, and Nicholas grasped the reins with his left hand, as the blade was still palmed in his right.

"Now what do you think he meant by that?"

Nicholas's head was reeling. "The relic I found is the true relic. It must be returned to Spain and Saint James." *What does the man really want?*

Petyr flung his leg over his horse and dismounted, and then he drew his sword. "Ye're bloody well deaf!" the blond knight shouted up to Nicholas. "Not to mention single-minded and stubborn. Come, let me beat some sense into you."

"You would draw a blade on your liege? You swore fealty to me, Petyr. You go against your knight's oath of honor." Nicholas, goaded by anger, jumped from Brenin's back, slipping the blade back into his boot and taking his sword instead.

"For your own good, my lord." Petyr didn't back down.

"Are you friend, Petyr, or foe?" Nicholas grinned, defending the first blow. "I'm tired of you always telling me what to do." With a roar, he attacked, his sword upraised, the relic strapped against his chest. It felt invigorating to be a warrior, to hold a sword and fight. Peace was good. Battle was great.

Petyr blocked the blow, then came at Nicholas with an answering growl. His blade of fired iron slid down Nicholas's sword and bit into the handle. Nicholas tossed the blade off, his eyes narrowing as he acknowledged the worthiness of his opponent before backing up, and positioning for the next attack.

"I'm older than you, and methinks a great deal wiser. Try again, pup," Petyr said with a huff.

"By a year, if that much." Nicholas lunged, his sword aimed for Petyr's heart. Petyr sidestepped and whacked Nicholas on the back of the shoulders, sending him to his knees in the muddy forest.

Nicholas regained his footing, fire in his blood. *Lunge, turn, attack.* But not to the death. He swung, bloodying Petyr's sword arm. Back and forth, until each had bones as soft as dough.

Blood trickled down the side of Petyr's golden face. Nicholas had a slash in his thigh. With a wheezing laugh, Nicholas called a truce so they could catch their breath.

"Are ye willin' to finally listen to reason?" Petyr heaved.

Nicholas slumped against a tree. "I'm too tired to move."

"Good. Ye fight well for a man who has been mired in the past. I can see why you survived the ambush.

Who trained ye, at the monastery?"

Nicholas wiped his sweaty brow. "Sir Edwin Palster."

"That explains much. He was a great warrior, one of the baron's favorite knights."

"What happened to him?" Nicholas wiped blood from his forehead.

"Died. Riding accident, his horse threw him, or so the baron said. It was but those two and me brother who rode into the forest that day, and just my brother and the baron who came out alive."

"What was your brother's name, again? I've each man's face carved in my memory, and I don't remember one who looks, or spoke, as you."

Petyr chuckled. "Bernard."

"Bernard?" Nicholas widened his puffy left eye and searched Petyr's face for a family resemblance.

"He had dull brown hair, Lord Nicholas, and was a short bit of a runt. I was the beauty in the family."

"Modest, too." He remembered the knight, and Petyr's description of his brother was apt. Bernard had always made the hair on the back of his neck rise; Nicholas recalled that, as well. "He was to kill me? And return the fake relic, but instead he was killed and the fake relic sent back to the baron, along with the note for my ransom. I'm sorry, I think."

Petyr shrugged and grinned. "His heart was as stubby as his legs, and he followed the baron like a puppy. Now," he scratched his chest, "if I were you, and I had a wife like the Lady Celestia awaiting me at home, I would want the quickest solution to me problem. I sure as hell wouldn't want to go all the way to Spain unless I was ready and my family safe."

Nicholas eyed him dubiously from beneath a fall of hair. "More advice. I'd hoped I'd beaten you enough to keep you quiet."

"And I must have knocked ye stupid. The baron is at the heart of all of this. Not Saint James . . . You said that Grainne Kat had the relic. Where did she get it? Think! Why were the baron's knights killed, after being tortured? Were they, perhaps, looking for something? The relic, mayhap?"

Nicholas groaned and got to his knees, his thigh throbbing. "I am a selfish fool. As if the state of my soul could be saved if I left Celestia, and those in my care, in danger. I am an idiot."

"Aye," Petyr agreed with a bloody smile.

"Where is he, Petyr? Where can I find my sire?"

"Now ye're usin' your noggin'! I've brought the map, and there's a shortcut through the trees, here. We can be there in a hard day's ride."

Nicholas nodded as a warm feeling spread from the rosary against his skin throughout his entire body. It was as if his mother was giving him her blessing for finally doing the right thing.

"You can find the truth ye seek, and be home to your wife in less than three days."

"She might have a lover when I come back," Nicholas stated, knowing he would throttle whoever dared to touch his wife's lovely form.

Petyr started to laugh. "The Lady Celestia sent me

after you, imbecile. She explained you were taking the true relic to Spain, but that she didn't trust you to get there without falling over your honor, whatever that means." Then he pulled out a crimson tunic with silver and gold trim. "She gave me this."

Nicholas stared at the gold falcon in flight. "She made that for you?" His heart pounded in protest.

"You are stupid, God help you. Look in your knapsack, the one she brained you with."

Nicholas found his fingers shaking like a silly twit's as he pulled his new tunic from the rumpled sack. He smoothed the folds of cloth, noting the occasional uneven stitch as if he were discovering a pearl amongst the sand. His throat was clogged with unwanted emotion as he remembered the look of heartbreak on her face. *He'd treated her so poorly.* "The gold falcon was to be our crest?"

Petyr nodded. "Aye. She said Willy helped her draw out the pattern. Fine work, eh?"

As Nicholas packed the tunic away, he said, "She deserves better than me, Petyr. No matter what else comes of this journey to my father, the Montehue family will be released from his tyranny. Celestia will get her annulment."

Petyr had been nodding and smiling like a proud teacher listening to a prized student. Until he heard the last part of the speech.

"Ye're bloody daft!"

Celestia hoped she hadn't made a mistake, sending Petyr after Nicholas. She didn't want her husband dragged home like a naughty child, but the thought of him journeying alone gave her chills.

The cloudy vision she'd had of him, trapped and miserable, could be something from his past – or, she paced the room with worry, something to come.

Chewing slowly, she supposed it was only fitting that she should give her heart to someone as bullheaded as she was. Finishing the last bite of omelet, she put her spoon on her plate. Beatrice had outdone herself on the egg dish, but it would not sway her mind. The cook had apologized and promised to behave, even Father Michael had interceded on Beatrice's behalf. Yet something about the woman made her uncomfortable. It very possibly had to do with Beatrice locking her in a room and calling her a witch.

Turning to Viola, who had a dreamy look on her face as she scooped up the last of her berries and cream topped with cinnamon, she ordered, "Stop that. Beatrice is not staying here. I should never have let her pleas sway me."

Viola licked her lips guiltily. "Aye, I know. She accused you of witchcraft. But anybody can make a mistake, Lady Celestia."

Celestia shook her head with impatience. "I'd always worry she'd try to poison me. I'll go and give Father Michael my final answer, and then, we are opening the north tower. We will put these ghost stories to rest once and for all."

Viola sprang to her feet.

"And stop that, too. You are supposed to be wounded, remember?"

The maid immediately slumped and rubbed the bandage on her side. "Oh, yes, my lady, I'd forgotten. Limp to the left, limp to the left," she repeated.

Celestia pinched the bridge of her nose. She hadn't slept well, and her body was as dry as the stream by the mill, thanks be to all the crying she'd done. Falling in love with one's husband was a stupid thing to do, and now she would pay the price for her folly.

Her healing hands would be no more; her life would be as empty as the north tower. *What a maudlin thought.*

Had her husband been pleased with the gift she'd made, just for him? She wondered if the single-minded, stubborn oaf had even found it yet. Well, once Petyr caught up with him and gave him his mother's rosary, which he'd forgotten—again—then, for certes, he'd see the tunic.

Arriving in the large main room, she eyed the other knights in their new attire. They stood straighter, prouder. They were Lord Nicholas's men now, and no longer belonged to the baron. Celestia sighed, knowing she had some decisions to make. The knights would not look quite as nice in Montehue green.

Pausing at the doorway, she accepted that she was now the person in charge of this cursed keep and things needed to change. She puffed up her chest, lifted her chin, and clapped her hands for attention.

She waited until everyone was looking at her, then

climbed up on a chair. Forrester quickly came to her aid. *As if she would fall, ha!* "As you all know, my husband has gone on an important pilgrimage to Spain. In the future, you will be dealing directly with me, or Sir Geoffrey, with any issues you may have."

She ignored the muttering voices as they questioned Nicholas's abandonment. "I had promised that we would open the tower and disprove the notion there is a ghost lurking inside." She'd not sensed any spirit activity, although she'd received many visions that didn't make sense. Scenes or images in quick bursts, as if the sender of the visions was being interrupted.

"We shall adjourn to the tower. Father Michael? Will you escort me?"

The old priest got to his feet and smiled, his good eye flashing. "I will, my lady."

Celestia didn't miss Forrester's brief look of disappointment when she nimbly hopped down from the chair without falling, or needing his aid. The boy was a man, she reminded herself. Ordering the knights to gather their tools, Celestia led the fifteen or so servants down the long, narrow hall leading to the north tower. It opened to a sitting area, where she sat them all back against the keep wall, where they could witness but stay out of the way. The interior door had been boarded over, and mortared.

Forrester arrived with a sledgehammer and an axe. Willy had an iron pick, as did Geoffrey and Bertram. Celestia looked around. "Where's Henry?"

"I'm here, my lady." Henry wore gloves on his hands

and carried two buckets.

A chill was settling on her skin like mist before a rain. Goose bumps traveled up her arms and down her spine. Was it a warning? Or a greeting?

"Let's begin."

The servants were forced back into the narrow hallway as the dust from the mortared ashlar stones thickened the air. Celestia felt a need to remain as close as possible to the tower, so she wrapped a veil of gauzy material around her mouth and eyes. Viola bravely joined her.

"'Tis too bad that Lord Nicholas couldn't be here for this." The maid had to shout over the pounding noise of the knights as they battled the rock.

"Aye. I wish that Nicholas could have held his journey off by a day to see it." But her husband was too stubborn, too focused on doing the noble thing to see that they needed him here, too.

Father Michael came to stand at her other side, and Viola bobbed her head and left, carefully limping to the right, then left. "Nicholas is going to Spain, my lady? In such a hurry that he leaves you to dispel the ghost of his mother?"

Celestia bristled at the disapproving tone in the priest's voice. Leaning over to whisper directly into his old ear, she said, "Nicholas found the original relic."

"What?" Father Michael's eye widened. "Where? Did he go to see his father?"

"Nay," Celestia swallowed, glancing around to make sure that nobody could hear her. "Grainne Kat had it. Nicholas took it from her hut."

Father Michael coughed as a heavy plume of rock dust came toward them. "Nicholas *stole* it away from Grainne Kat?"

She clapped her hand over his mouth. "Shh! How did she come by it? It was never hers."

He knocked her hand away. "Theft and murder, ghosts and plots. This has never been a peaceful village, my dear."

"There is a mystery here, and I want it solved. I'll not have Nicholas go on this journey to reclaim his soul only to come back to a deserted, ill-used heap of stone."

"So you'll not be leaving him, my lady?"

"Where did you hear that?"

He lowered his eye. "Gossip, it abounds. But some of us were awake when you screamed that ye would take a lover, my lady."

Celestia's cheeks flamed as she recalled the courtyard scene. "Oh." She put one hand against her churning belly. "Well, I just might do that. And I might leave, but afore I do, I would make things right for him when he comes home."

Father Michael broke into deep chuckles as he patted her on the arm. "Ye love him, then? It is not often that the scorned woman worries about making things 'right' for her man before she leaves him for another. Aye, ye love him, my lady, and you'll not leave while there is hope."

She clapped her hands over her ears in a childish gesture. Did the entire keep know that her love was unrequited?

She was a fool.

"Lady Celestia," Willy yelled with excitement. "We've broken through!"

Celestia coughed her way through the thick dust, waving her hand in front of her face, as if that would help. It didn't.

Forrester took her by the hand. "This way, my lady."

They had made a hole in the mortar the size of an oak tree trunk. She bent over and peered inside. The stairs leading to the top were dark, until her eyes adjusted. "Why is it so light in there? It's bright as day—how did I not realize how many windows there were?"

Father Michael called for quiet as the clamoring from behind increased. Everybody wanted a peek at the ghost of Lady Esmerada.

Celestia leaned farther in—first with her head, and then her shoulders. She didn't mind the dust at all. Excitement brought plenty of air to her lungs.

Inside the tower was a thin and crumbling stairway, and it was suddenly, urgently, imperative that she climb it. Celestia was halfway through the wall when Forrester pulled her back.

"Nay, my lady. It might not be safe. Let us finish clearing the debris, and then I will join you."

She wiggled out of his hold. "I will go now!" Where was this urge to scramble up those steps coming from? She felt as if she could find her way in the dark, or with her eyes closed and blindfolded. She knew that she belonged at the top of the tower. Apples. Sweet, yet with a sour twist that whetted the appetite.

A screech like a wounded owl penetrated her dream-like state, and she turned, ready to chastise whoever had broken the trance.

Grainne Kat barreled through the throng of servants, smashing her sideways, directly into Forrester's waiting arms. Grainne Kat fell on top of them, and the trio hit the stone floor with a thump.

Celestia struggled to her feet, her humiliation warring with the need to retaliate and beat the woman with a huge stick.

"Grainne Kat!" For certes, this woman could give her answers about the relic, and mayhap the baron, as well.

Henry helped the old woman to stand, where she wobbled as if trying to find her balance. She kept her gnarled finger pointed at Celestia, while screeching in a language Celestia couldn't understand.

Cool air swirled at her feet, and Celestia turned her eyes to Father Michael, who was as colorless as a corpse. "Father? What is she saying?"

Brave Viola pushed her way through the tightly packed bodies. "Move over!" She turned Grainne Kat around, spat on the ground, and forked her fingers against the woman's evil eye. "What are you saying, crone? If it be a curse against my lady, I'll knock ye flat."

"Not against Lady Celestia," Father Michael said, his voice trembling. "She's speaking of Lady Esmerada's curse!"

Snorting like a determined boar, Sir Geoffrey demanded, "What language is she speaking? And what is the matter with her eyes? Is she mad?"

Father Michael snapped his fingers under Grainne

Kat's nose. "She's not speaking in tongues, just the Scottish brogue, so thick that only another Scot can understand it. Grainne Kat!"

The old woman's eyes shut at the same time as her mouth, and she visibly shivered beneath the onslaught of wild rage.

The servants muttered, and Celestia knew that she'd have to forestall another riot.

When Grainne Kat finally reopened her wicked eyes, they were no longer dilated with fury. "What are you doing?" she rasped.

Celestia stuck her chin in the air, knowing she was being had. How was she supposed to defend herself against the wise woman? The servants, and even her knights, were petrified.

"We are opening the tower."

"Ye can't!"

Relying on her own anger, and the pain of some new bruises, thanks be to Grainne Kat's mad strength, Celestia furrowed her brow and crossed her arms in front of her. "This is my home. I wish to dispel the rumors there is a ghost in this tower."

The woman's face paled.

"Just as I will confront you about why you were creating rumors amongst the village about me being a witch. What did you think to gain from such nonsense?"

Grainne Kat seemed to shrink under the confrontational onslaught. She slumped her shoulders and tucked her chin into the folds of her cloak. All of a sudden she was no more than a pitiful old woman, and Celestia knew that the crone had won again.

Tossing the long ends of her veil over her shoulder, Celestia vowed to watch the dame like a cat watched a snake.

Grainne Kat lifted a trembling hand and said in a shaky voice, "Lady Esmerada's tower cannot be disturbed! Her ghost has been resting, until you came." She pointed a bent finger at Celestia. "Esmerada is not happy with you living here in her keep."

The group whispered.

"Now that ye've disturbed her in the tower, she'll haunt ye 'til ye die."

The peasants gasped in fright at the prediction, but they didn't move away. Father Michael had told them all he would no longer allow them succor in the church if they misbehaved, Celestia knew. "You lie."

Shy Sally said, "Beware, my lady, lest ye get cursed with warts."

Grainne Kat hissed, and Shy Sally shrank back. "You overstep your boundaries, me lady. I knew the Lady Esmerada well, just as I knew Nicholas when he was but a boy. I know much, Lady Celestia, that you do not. Take care that ye don't cross me."

"Cross you? What would it take for you to share some of those secrets, Grainne Kat? Coin? I have plenty of that."

"My knowledge is not to be bought or sold."

Knowing she was perchance playing with fire, Celestia sniffed. "Again, I say you lie."

The peasants were shaking from limb to limb, but they stayed. Celestia was impressed by the control Father

Michael had over his flock.

She instructed Forrester to hit the wall. "The sledgehammer, if you please, sir knight. I say this tower is going to be opened, and that Lady Esmerada's curse will be dissolved."

"Nay!" Grainne Kat wailed in fury.

Forrester swung back with all of his might and hit the stones. The muscles in his arms flexed beneath his red tunic, and Celestia gave Grainne a defiant smile. She was the victor here.

"Oh, oh, no. No, Lady Esmerada!" Grainne Kat brought her hand to her forehead and then collapsed in a heap of sodden cloak.

Forrester, chivalrous knight, dropped the sledgehammer and knelt at the old woman's side. Father Michael cleared the way through the crowd, and soon the crone was set up on a cushioned bench in the main room of the keep by the fire with a mug of ale in her gnarled hands.

Placing her hands on her hips, Celestia growled low in her throat. The tower was forgotten as everyone crowded around the wise woman. Grainne Kat had the audacity to wink at her when nobody else was looking.

She stomped her foot at the woman's daring before admitting that she might have a thing or two left to learn about the road to victory.

Chapter SEVENTEEN

Grainne Kat was the center of everyone's attention, and the old dame was loving every bit of it. Her customers from the village gathered around her feet to show their support for the elderly wise woman.

They were probably afraid of being turned into toads.

Traitors, Celestia thought as she edged closer so she could hear what the woman was saying. She was jostled from behind. "Beg pardon," Celestia said as she turned.

Maude grinned at her in a cocky way. "I'm sorry, me lady. I didn't see you down there!"

Celestia's vision turned red. "Listen here, Maude," she began.

Viola bumped into Maude with a plate of scones. "Excuse me," she trilled, "I'm so clumsy, I was trying to help, my lady, but mayhap my wound is not healed enough." She ineffectually brushed at the crumbled scone on Maude's tunic, getting more onto the fabric than off. "So sorry," the maid said, her lowered brown eyes twinkling with mirth.

"Perhaps ye need to control your staff?" Maude's pretty lips pursed.

Celestia took the tray from Viola. "You're flushed, Vi, go take a seat. If Grainne Kat wishes to give her guests refreshments, then her daughter can serve them." Celestia handed Maude the tray and walked to where she could hear better.

Viola giggled. "I don't like her, my lady."

Jealous thoughts chased 'round in Celestia's head. She knew Maude wanted Nicholas. "That makes two of us, Viola."

"Grainne Kat is about ready to tell of the curse," Shy Sally whispered as Celestia made her way to a bench seat near the hearth. A chill settled at her neck, and she got an immediate vision of Nicholas and her brothers and pink beady eyes.

Her brothers had been turned into rats?

She stood, noticing Forrester gazing at her. Perfect. "I'll be back in but a moment," she said softly to Viola.

Celestia hated the visions, especially when they weren't clear.

Her brothers could not be rats. Not really. And Nicholas? If he were caged again, he would, for certes, go mad. What man who had suffered captivity once could survive it again?

"Forrester," Celestia tugged at his arm until the knight leaned over. "You must ride in search of Petyr and Nicholas. I believe they are in grave danger."

He arched a handsome dark brow. "My lady?"

"You will have to trust me. Occasionally I have a, well, hunch. And sometimes I'm right. Ride to the baron's castle. Be stealthy."

"I thought my lord went to Spain."

"Aye." Celestia smiled and batted her lashes, hoping to charm her way past his arguments.

"Do you have something in your eye, my lady?" He peered at her with concern.

She sighed, and pinched the thin skin between her thumb and index finger until tears came to her eyes. "I'm worried about my noble husband. I won't sleep, for fear will keep me awake. I beg you, my chivalrous knight, to find my husband and warn him of this danger."

Celestia felt a moment's guilt for playing upon his youth. A jaded knight would ignore her silly plea, but according to the minstrels, a young knight simply lived for the next noble quest.

Forrester brought her hand to his lips. "Don't fret, my lady. You say you want me to ride to Peregrine Castle? I will do it." He gazed at her expectantly.

She waited.

Finally he asked, "Might I have a token?"

A token? She was going to have to pay better attention. "Of course." She bit her lip, thinking furiously, before bending over and plucking a small bell from her slipper. "Here you are, Sir Knight. Godspeed, and good luck."

Forrester looked taken aback by the tiny bell, but accepted it with good grace.

She supposed that she should have offered a lock of

hair? This chivalry business was almost as confusing as having a husband. Smiling, she reached up to kiss his cheek. His eyes lit, and he left to do her bidding.

Making her way through the throng, she took her seat on the bench, missing her sisters—all of her family—so much it hurt. Gram would know what to do about the servants, and Galiana would tell her how to capture her husband's love. She needed her parents, she thought with a sniff, because she was making a mess of running Nicholas's keep. She was a healer, not a wife. She sniffed again.

She'd hoped to open the tower and dispel the rumor that it was haunted. And yet, how else could she explain the light she'd seen, or the strong scent of apples, when she'd stuck her head through the hole?

Mayhap Ela, with her unique talents, could tell her how to get rid of a ghost. She folded her fingers together and held them in her lap, swallowing the ache lodged in her throat.

Family.

What if this ghost was all that Nicholas had left of his mother? She couldn't send his mother's ghost to the other side without his ever "meeting" her . . .

"Is all well, my lady?" Viola asked.

"Hardly." Celestia unfolded her restless hands and leaned around the servants all waiting patiently for Grainne to begin. "I'm fast losing interest in this story, old woman," Celestia waved her hand with a flourish, as if she was introducing a traveling act, and said, "Begin!"

Grainne cleared her throat five times more than was

necessary before starting with a surprisingly clear and, loud voice. Celestia barely refrained from rolling her eyes.

"Lady Esmerada was a truly beautiful woman."

Some of the peasants nodded, though none but Beatrice looked old enough to remember. Celestia pursed her lips. Would the woman never get on with it?

"She had hair as black as a raven's wing, eyes as stormy gray as the ocean itself. Her skin was white as new-fallen snow—"

Father Michael cleared his throat, and interrupted the wise woman's tribute. "'Tis true, she was comely."

Grainne narrowed her eyes, then smacked her lips before continuing. "Esmerada was a lass of sixteen, sweet and kind. She did her parents' bidding without question. And when she was told to marry an English lord, she did as she was told."

Celestia noticed that the wise woman's voice deepened into a Scottish brogue the further she fell into the tale. Who exactly was Grainne Kat?

The old woman's hands moved as she drew her audience in with her eerie tone. "Even though she'd already given her heart to a brave, braw Scottish lad! The day of the wedding came nearer, and though her Robbie begged her to run away with him, she would not. The English lord came for her hand, and she gave it, like a dutiful *dochter*."

She still didn't roll her eyes, though the urge was strong. Celestia noticed that the peasants ate the story up with a spoon.

"Strong winds came along with the Scottish warriors as soon as the vows were said. Brave Robbie was going to save his Esmerada from her cruel fate." The crone's face grew mottled with anger. "The lord ordered his soldiers to attack—and he killed Robbie MacIntosh in cold blood!"

A collective gasp came from her audience.

"And her *athair,* too!" She wet her lips, her keen gaze landing briefly on one person before grazing the next. "Poor Esmerada faced the lord over the bodies of her lover and her father. She cursed his foul deed, and denied the marriage!"

Grainne Kat shook her gnarled fist. "He took her to the keep and ravaged her. He beat her black and blue, and then he laid waste to the lands and left her in ruins."

The peasants sighed. Even Celestia was not unmoved.

"But that is not why she cursed him. Nay—he left her with child. The lord abandoned her with neither coin, nor protection from the Scottish clans that blamed her for Robbie's death." Lowering her voice, the wise woman whispered, "She went mad with grief. And that is when she summoned the devil's own help."

Celestia wasn't certain, but she thought she saw true tears in Grainne's eyes.

"She cursed the lord, denying him any living heir until he claimed his rightful son. Nor would he be allowed to kill off her own bloodline."

She paused, and sorrow flitted across her wrinkled face. "Esmerada locked herself into the north tower, vowing to kill Lord Peregrine if ever she saw him again. Each night she walked the battlements; each night she yelled her curse to the heavens! Until the night when she could take no more, and she threw herself from the tower, onto the craggy rocks below."

Celestia rubbed her arms against the sudden chill in the room. Was this the spirit of Esmerada at last? The hair was rising on her arms, and her pulse raced with alarm.

Thinking of Esmerada made her think of Nicholas, and she sent a prayer for his safety. He didn't believe in ghosts, but it was the only way he would ever meet his mother.

After getting lost during Petyr's "shortcut" through the forest and having to spend one night wrapped in a blanket with his knapsack for a pillow, Nicholas finally arrived at Peregrine Castle bedraggled and dirty from his wild ride.

Brenin was a stallion worthy of the name King. Foam flecked his nostrils, and he wheezed from exertion. Or was Nicholas himself making that noise?

Nicholas dismounted, his legs shaking. He gave the giant horse a pat on the nose and promised him oats and water.

Petyr dragged in behind. "Brenin was born small and sickly, did she say? I'd trade my best suit of armor and two horses for him."

Rubbing his sore thigh, Nicholas said, "I am not offering him for sale, Petyr. I, too, appreciate his strength. He was a gift, besides." *From his wife*.

"I don't know what was in that forest, but I'll not travel through it again," Petyr promised, his handsome face smeared with moss. "It was filled with haunts."

"There is no such thing as ghosts, Petyr. And even though we weren't hit with any, I swear I heard the notch of an arrow in a bow."

Petyr brushed his unruly blond hair off his forehead. "Well. We are here, now. Should we clean up, perhaps, before storming inside demanding answers?"

Nicholas wanted nothing more than to have his father's throat in his fingers. Nay, his hands did not need to be washed for such a task.

Petyr cleared his throat. "Nicholas?"

He stared at the castle, which was fortified mightily with several outer walls to be breached. They'd skirted the small village attached to the castle undetected, although they were close enough that Nicholas noticed the small huts in need of repair. The smell of refuse and garbage reached him, and when he looked out to the fields he saw thin women working alongside starved children.

His voice was deep with anger as he answered, "Aye. We're getting closer."

"Shall we wear Lady Celestia's tunics?"

Nicholas reached out one hand to Petyr, resting it on the knight's shoulder. "You say that you are loyal to me. You say that you bear me no grudge for your brother's death. Yet how does it feel to be back at the castle, knowing that we are here to bring down your previous liege? Can you stand before me honestly and claim you are my man?"

Petyr dropped to one knee in the dirt and bowed his head. "Lord Nicholas, I swear my fealty to thee. My arms are at your service, my honor bound to yours."

Hauling the man to his feet with a grin, Nicholas asked, "Did that hurt your pride overmuch?"

Petyr chuckled. "Not as much as I had thought it would. We had all been wondering when you would demand our vows, of your own accord."

"The other men are content to be at Falcon Keep?"

"We swore an oath to your father. We thought you a sickly, arrogant ass-wipe when we met you, but we have grown to tolerate your surliness. Ye treat us fair, my lord."

"I should know better by now than to ask you a question I don't want an honest answer to."

They cleaned up, and donned their fresh garments. He had his own man by his side, his mother's rosary around his neck, and he was proudly wearing the crimson and gold tunic Celestia had sewed.

He felt blessed.

His faith was still to be tested. Could he truly give Celestia the annulment and offer her freedom now that he knew how much he loved her? Choice was the only thing he could give her. The thought that she could turn him down without the threat of her family's ruin hanging over her head turned his blood cold.

Her family would be safe. Would she walk away from him, then?

He rubbed the hem of his new tunic between his thumb and fingers, noticing the uneven stitches of embroidery. His throat clogged with strong emotion, and he pledged to do right by his wife.

"Are you finished admiring yourself in the water's

reflection, Petyr? I would like to get this done with."

Petyr grunted. "Let us go then."

They rode through the gatehouse and the bailey, mixing in with other travelers. They were not challenged either time.

"Is that it?"

His father might not give much thought to the villagers, but, for certes, he cared about his castle.

It had four spiked towers and a large, square middle section made of ashlar stones that had been painted blue. The moat sparkled with clean water. The forest had been cut back to allow room for a practice field. Men in blue and gold jousted with covered lances; others perfected their swordplay. Maidens with high headdresses and matching gowns wafted across the patch of green grass, posies in their hands. It looked like a knight's dream come true.

"How could he be so evil and have all of this?"

"Mayhap he isn't as evil as you think, just . . . misguided."

"Misguided? Petyr, this is one time that I think you will be wrong."

They dismounted and handed their horses to a waiting stable lad. "Feed them well, boy, they have been ridden hard." Petyr tossed him a coin, which the lad caught deftly in one hand.

"Are you ready, me lord?"

Nicholas took a deep breath, his hand over the hilt of his sword. He was coming face to face with the man responsible for ruining his life. "Aye, Petyr. Let us find my father."

"Too late. I think he has found you," Petyr pointed

to the party coming toward them.

Nicholas found himself rubbing the hem of his tunic for luck. Since when had that become more important than the relic near his heart? He hadn't even counted it in the things that had made him feel blessed.

There was something the matter with him.

An imposing man with coarse, black, bearlike hair broke from the foursome he was walking with and Nicholas winced as he was enveloped in a hug and squeezed until he thought he'd pass out.

Nicholas took a step back, straightening his tunic and staring at his father in disgust. The man had food in his beard!

"Did we disrupt your lunch?" Nicholas made certain his voice and demeanor were haughty. The baron had much to answer for.

"Just a plate of bread and beef to tide me over 'til dinner. What a surprise! You look well, my son. The witch beat the curse, eh? Is she breeding yet?"

"No," he answered, stunned.

The baron slapped Petyr on the back. "Petyr, I have to say that I am impressed. I didn't think you would ever get Nicholas here."

Nicholas felt the blood drain from his face as he stared at the man he'd welcomed as a friend not an hour before. "Petyr?"

Petyr shrugged. "Mayhap coin is important, Nicholas. For certes, it is more important than honor. Give your father the relic in your tunic."

Betrayed!

"I thought Celestia sent you after me? Is she a part

of this scheme?" *Of course, she wasn't*, he immediately discounted the idea.

"I showed her your letter, and it was easy enough to play upon her worry. It helped that she wanted you to have the rosary."

Petyr had played them both. Were all the knights still loyal to his father? He'd left Celestia in a snake pit. He'd not go down without a fight. Nicholas reached for his sword, but Petyr beat him back, obviously expecting Nicholas to make such a move.

"Careful, Petyr! As my heir, he really should have the use of both hands."

The baron chuckled, his fat belly jiggling beneath the costly velvet expanse of fabric. He reached his jeweled hand inside Nicholas's tunic and pulled out the ornate box. He kissed it and laughed. "At long last I have it back! Almost twenty-five years it has been lost to me . . . damn your mother's soul!"

His voice remained jovial, as if he cursed Esmerada with joy every day.

Nicholas never sensed the blow from behind.

"Be careful with him, Petyr. I need him until he produces a child to end that damn curse."

Celestia woke from her nap with a start. The back of her head ached, and when she delicately probed the sore area, it seemed as if it should be bruised, but there wasn't even a raised bump. She didn't remember banging it.

She never napped, more the pity, so what was she doing in bed? Not sleeping, but escaping, she remembered with a shudder. *Grainne Kat.* The wily wise woman had set up camp for two days in the main room of the keep. Maude had been shadowing Celestia's every step. They said that Joseph was away peddling his furs.

If she'd had her choice, she would have picked the company of Joseph over either woman. Mayhap. Her stomach rebelled at the memory of animals skins stretched on the racks.

A knock sounded at her door. "Come in."

Viola entered the room with Shy Sally on her heels. Shy Sally's face was streaked with tears, and Viola, who used to be so even-tempered, looked angry enough to burst.

"My lady," Viola bobbed her head. "Grainne Kat must go. Even Father Michael cannot persuade Beatrice to get into the kitchen and work. The wise woman has them terrified of being here, in this keep, with you—a possible witch—argh!" Viola's brown eyes nearly crossed she was so mad. "And an angry ghost, and the spirits of the murdered knights in the kitchen—and Bess," Viola started to cry, "she says that Bess haunts the drawbridge!"

Celestia blinked away the last vestiges of sleep. "Nonsense. Father Michael blessed her grave himself. And you, Sally? Why are crying?" Celestia rose from the edge of her bed and put what should have been a soothing hand on the peasant woman's arm.

Nothing happened. She didn't feel anything, not even a splutter of energy.

It was finally happening. Nicholas didn't return her

love, and she was losing her powers to heal. Celestia fought her own tears as she tried to sympathize with Sally. "She blames ye, and says ye'r in league with the devil—when it's her tongue that has everyone riled."

She removed her hand from Sally's arm and swallowed hard so she wouldn't join the two women in a crying heap. "Viola, help me braid my hair, please? You are both right, and Grainne has to go."

Celestia searched within herself, wondering that she didn't feel as empty as a spilled jug of milk. Her healing hands, the only thing that marked her as a true Boadicea descendent, were no more.

Her chest ached as if she'd been stabbed, but she didn't have time to feel sorry for herself. She would fix what she could. Smiling for the two women, she bent her back and covered her chest with one hand, while putting the other to her forehead.

"'Tis prostrate with grief, I am, me lady, upset that ye've called down Esmerada's wrath; all of us here at the keep are in danger . . . bwah hahahahaha."

Viola's lips curled upward, but Sally—she still looked afraid that Grainne Kat would give her two noses. "She's good, for certes, just as good as some of the traveling actors we had at Montehue Manor, eh, Vi?"

The maid sniffed. "Aye. Not quite, but with a bit more training, she could take her act on the road. Away from here, anyway."

"I promised myself that I would open that tower. I was willing to delay, hoping that Nicholas would come home."

He wasn't coming. After three days, it was clear that

he was on his way to Spain.

Viola finished tying off the last braid. "He'll come for ye, my lady."

"Well, we can't wait any longer." Having had years of practice hiding hurt feelings, Celestia was able to lead the way downstairs as regal as a queen.

She came to a halt in front of the cushioned bed someone had brought for Grainne's comfort. "It is time for you to leave. I regret withdrawing my hospitality, but you are disrupting the entire keep. My Lord Nicholas would not be happy, Grainne Kat. I think you know you have overstayed your welcome."

Mouth opened to argue, the old woman must have realized that it would be a waste of breath. She got to her feet, her body shaking and trembling. "I only wanted to save you from the wrath of Lady Esmerada."

Celestia remained firm in her resolve to bring order to the keep. "I have no fear of the woman who bore such a fine man as my husband."

Maude came from the kitchens, holding a piece of toast. She walked toward Grainne Kat, ignoring Celestia completely. "Mother, get back into bed before you fall down."

Celestia stepped in front of her, bracing her feet to block the way. Maude came to a surprised halt as she bounced off of Celestia's small frame.

"It is time for you to take your mother home."

Maude's lovely eyes turned yellowish at the center, very unattractive, thank the heavens. "She's ill and cannot be moved."

Celestia didn't back down, not even one step. "She's no

more ill than you or I, as well you know. She is here to halt the opening of the north tower, and for no other reason."

"You mistake me intentions, Lady Celestia," Grainne Kat warbled. "I but fear for your safety. If you must open the tower, at least take Maude with ye. The Lady Esmerada knows her, and mayhap she can protect you from harm. She's a hard worker, my Maude."

Celestia looked over her shoulder at Grainne Kat. "I have yet to see her lift a finger around here. She browbeats the servants, and I won't have it."

When she turned back, Maude's lower lip started to tremble, and two tears slipped like lovely pearls from her eyes. The woman even cried beautifully, Celestia thought with disgust.

"Fine, Maude, come with me—I want that tower cleared today. Willy? Henry! Geoffrey!"

"Yes, my lady?" Sir Geoffrey headed up the line of crimson-clad knights.

Tilting her chin, she spoke calmly and precisely. "We continue with the tower. The servants are all dismissed, and I want a litter made to carry Grainne Kat back to her hut. I will not have my husband return to a keep filled with lunatics!"

She made certain to look at each peasant before her, letting them know her words were final. Most looked shamed by their behavior. Beatrice scowled. "Geoffrey, pay each of them what we promised, but they are finished here." Celestia paused. "Except for Sally. She can stay if she wants."

"Yes, my lady, I do want to stay," she dipped a fast

curtsy, missing the dark look Maude was giving her.

"Sir Geoffrey, do you or any of the knights object to opening the tower?"

The old knight shook his head, nay. Willy blurted, "No, my lady. I would slay any ghost for you."

Henry, not to be outdone, knelt and kissed her hand. "If there are ghastly apparitions to be found, I will save you, my lady!"

The rest agreed, although Celestia ignored the whiteness around Bertram's mouth, not wanting to call attention to his fear. "Let us finish this, then. Gather what you need, and Geoffrey, be kind when you let the servants go—but get them gone from here!"

Later, Celestia was so exasperated that she took the pick from Bertram and tore the stone from the wall herself. "If there is a ghost, Bertram, you certainly could not hurt them with your axe. Do you understand?"

He looked at the ground, his ears red. Maude stood over the crew as if she were the lady of Falcon Keep, and not Celestia.

It didn't help, Celestia admitted, that Maude looked fresh and lovely in a gown of green, while she wore an old brown tunic that was covered in dust and grime. She wiped at her brow.

The memory of Nicholas holding her captive in front of the mirror, his eyes caressing her as thoroughly as his hands and words had, warmed away the chill of jealousy.

For certes, the memories of her husband's kisses downright warmed her from head to toe.

She'd not had another vision, praise all the saints, but

that left her with a belly full of worry. Petyr had gone after Nicholas, and surely he'd had time to talk him into returning home. Obviously her husband didn't want to come. And poor Forrester, she'd sent the young knight on a fool's errand, twisting her wild imagination into some kind of warning that Nicholas was with her brothers.

Which meant Peregrine Castle.

Nay, she sighed. She was losing her mind as well as her healing touch.

She threw her weight behind the next swing of the pick—challenging one's strength felt good. It was no wonder men exerted themselves beyond measure.

"'Tis done, I say! There is plenty of room for us all to pass through without the wall falling down upon our heads."

Henry said, "But my lady, it will take just a bit more time for us to clear the rest of the debris. Your safety matters above all else."

Celestia looked at him, her blue eye opened wide as she squinted through the dust. "I'll risk it."

"Lord Nicholas would not be happy," he said, his arms crossed.

"Lord Nicholas isn't here, Henry, thank you. Do you smell that?" Apples. Spiced apples, from cider, or pie—it didn't matter. Her stomach rumbled, and she had that immediate need to explore the top of the tower. Invisible fingers pushed her forward, and she found herself through the hole and up three stairs before Henry could stop her.

Up and up she climbed the thin circular stairway, her hand against the stone wall so she'd keep her balance. Light filtered through the arrow slits that were everywhere. Had Lady Esmerada expected a siege?

She remembered that Father Michael had said she'd prepared for the worst, poor woman.

"I'm coming, Lady Esmerada, I'm coming." She finally reached the only room in the tower. The door was closed. A large lock prevented her from pushing it open. The lock appeared old and somehow accusing. As if the lady were trapped inside, and not of her own accord.

Celestia looked around for a key that would, mayhap, be hanging from a hook, but there was none. A chill went up her spine and she reached for the lock. Her fingers were not her own as she yanked down.

The lock opened beneath her hand and spilled to the floor in a puddle of rust.

Behind her, Maude screamed and pulled on Celestia's dress. Tottering on the edge of a thin step, she couldn't regain her balance, not with Maude clutching and pulling at her old tunic. The sound of cloth ripping echoed around her and she was falling. Down, down, and down. Her life flashed before her eyes as she hit each stone step, each curve of the sharp rock wall. Nicholas, she thought, Nicholas!

Nicholas.

Chapter EIGHTEEN

Nicholas thought he heard someone calling his name. Rousing himself from the light doze he was trapped in, he tried to answer back. "Celestia?"

She said nothing more.

He sat up from his prone position and hit his head on the short ceiling. Again. He blinked his eyes, but it remained dark as pitch. Shivering, he muttered, "God's bones, not again."

The smell of horse's dung assaulted his nostrils. He'd never dreamt of horse shit before. He stretched out his hands and touched rough wood. A wall? He traced the wooden planks, using his fingers to tell him what he couldn't see but was beginning to suspect.

This was no case of night terrors. He'd been captured.

His sodding father, and Petyr, a betrayal he should have expected. His hands flew to his tunic, although he knew damned good and well that the relic was gone. His father had taken it with his fat, ringed hand. And then he'd had Nicholas bashed on the back of the head.

How much more could his skull take? Sneaky bastards, hitting a man from behind.

His father and Petyr, cohorts all along. And the rest of the knights now had the keep under their control. He was a fool, letting hope come between him and solid revenge. If he'd but entered his father's castle with his sword singing, then it wouldn't be him trapped in a dark cage.

Damn it.

He had nothing to offer Saint James, and nothing to give Celestia. He narrowed his eyes, letting them adjust to the blackness.

His wife thought he'd deserted her to go on a pilgrimage to Spain. A worthwhile endeavor perhaps, but poorly timed, on his behalf. She had sent Petyr after him to keep him safe, and instead, it had been the perfect opportunity for Petyr to betray him.

Celestia had made the shattered keep a home, with her commanding presence, her jingling slippers and her laughter.

Then he thought of her all alone within those barren walls and he couldn't breathe. What would be Celestia's fate if Petyr and the baron killed him? Would they harm her in any way, or send her home to her family?

He had to escape. It had taken a miracle, but he had learned to love again. They'd been right. Abbot Crispin, Father Michael, Celestia—he had been plugging his ears like a petulant boy. He'd been bloody stupid, and not seen Celestia for what she was. A gift from God himself.

The rosary beneath his tunic warmed against his

heart. He was done with self-pity. Nicholas would die before letting anything happen to Celestia, which meant he had to get out of this vermin-infested pit and find his sire. If the baron were dead, then he would no longer have a hold over the Montehue family. That part of his original plan still held true.

He whirled. "'Tia?" For certes, he knew he heard her calling him. The hair on the back of his neck rose. "Wait for me, I am coming," he whispered in the dark. He had to get out of here.

But where was he?

He carefully got to his knees, ignoring the fact that insects and bugs crawled in the same space as he. He couldn't let that make him crazy.

Hooves clomping. Horse manure. Hay.

He was in the stables, or some part of them. He whistled. Horses neighed. Where were they? Could he reach Brenin?

Belly-crawling like a snake across the filthy floor, his eyes began to filter shadow from shape. Turning on his back, he looked up, and straw fell into his eye. Yes. He was below the stables, but this space was not deep enough to be used for anything other than storage.

He looked around and identified bundles of hay and bags of oats. A pair of red, beady eyes blinked at him. *Damn rat-infested hole.* Breathing through flared nostrils, his mouth clamped tight, he moved forward, determined to find his way out if it were the last thing he ever did.

As the hours passed, Nicholas could feel the familiar despair beckoning. He had been over every scrap of wood, both on the floor and the roof of his prison, but he couldn't find a damn door. Not so much as a loose plank budged. His hands were bleeding and raw from trying to scratch and pull his way free.

His old friend Useless threatened to visit, and Pathetic whispered how easy it would be to lie back and die in this hole.

He wouldn't give up. He hadn't then, and he wouldn't now.

How long had he been belowground? His stomach rumbled, and his mouth thirsted. He had rested his eyes when they blurred and he couldn't see, but he'd not given in to sleep.

Nicholas fought for his sanity, for his very soul. He would not lose another piece of himself; there was nothing left to give. The rosary warmed against his heart and he did the one thing he hadn't been able to do since his capture in Jerusalem.

He got on his knees and prayed.

His faith had taken a beating, and through his own stubbornness, he had pushed aside all help. Had he thought himself so godly, then, that he could not make mistakes? His pride had felled him, just as an axe could topple the tallest oak. His sin had not been his human fallibility—man was not perfect. His great sin had been his pride. Tears burned his throat. He had killed a woman, a woman who had drugged and raped him. The joy he had felt at her death had been the blessing of being alive. He had never killed for the sake of watching someone die. He choked on the bitter memories, but he looked at them and accepted them for what they were.

His past.

Nicholas wiped his eyes and took a cleansing breath. Leah had not stolen his worth. He had tried to bury the torture that had been done to him by opting not to feel at all. Unable to accept love, because he had been protecting his own shriveled heart.

Bowing his head, he gave thanks, and pledged to live his life a better man. "But I need to get out of here first, Lord. I am open to any suggestions."

He heard a whistle in the dark, and Nicholas sat back in surprise.

He looked around the dark hole in awe and whistled back.

"Me lord Nicholas? Is that you?"

"Yes, 'tis I."

One eye peered between the small crack in the roof of Nicholas's prison. "What are ye doin' down there, me lord?"

Nicholas growled. "I've been captured by the baron and Sir Petyr. Is that you, Forrester?"

"Aye! Petyr, sir? Are ye sure?"

Since Nicholas didn't trust Forrester's loyalty, he bit his tongue.

Another voice piped up from above him. "Who ya talkin' to?"

Exhaling, Nicholas curled his fists in disappointment.

"Nobody, boy, now mind yer own business."

Nicholas heard the thwack of a board hitting a man's

head, and dirt rained down upon him as Forrester's heavy body hit the boards. A tiny golden bell fell from the besotted knight's tunic.

Another knight sent by Celestia?

Nicholas was brought before his sire, his tunic stinking of manure.

He nodded to Petyr, who sat to the baron's left. Nicholas said nothing to the man who'd raped his mother and then abandoned her. Father Michael had clearly said that some deaths were meted out with earthly justice, and right now, he felt like the sword of God.

The baron drank deeply, pointing to the jeweled case holding the finger bone of Saint James. It sat on a crystal pedestal above the baron's plate. "You are to be commended on how quickly you found me the relic, Nicholas. Tell me—where was it? I tore that damnable keep apart. Do you have any idea what it's like to lose something that belonged to a king? I hope you slit their throats."

Petyr chuckled. "No need to slit anybody's throat. The old wise woman had it—I know not where *she* got it."

Nicholas answered, "Grainne Kat had it proudly displayed in her hut, velvet box and all. I don't think she realized what it was she possessed."

"Grainne Kat? I have never heard that name before."

Petyr looked into his goblet rather than meet Nicholas's angry glare, but Nicholas refused to let him go.

"She looks as if she has lived in the woods for at

least a hundred years." Petyr sipped. "Pretty daughter, though. Did you know that the ten knights you sent ahead to the keep are all dead?"

The baron paled beneath his drink-flushed cheeks. "Dead?"

"Aye. Tortured, some of them. We found two in the castle, four in the shed, and four in the moat. We were even attacked on the way to the castle. *Your son* handled himself quite well."

The baron spluttered and slammed his goblet down on the table so hard that the silver bent. Nicholas stood still, relying on his soldier's skills. His sire asked, "Why did you not send word?"

Petyr slowly buttered a piece of bread. "How was I to do that? The other men accepted being loyal to Nicholas. Unless you made the same devil's bargain with them as you did me."

"Nay! I but wanted the relic returned before any uncovered the ruse I'd played on King Richard."

Nicholas's jaw hurt from clenching it so tight. If his sire wanted a reaction, he wasn't going to get one. If he could but get that knife from the center of the table . . .

Petyr sent Nicholas a mocking salute with his bread. "Nicholas wants to atone for his sins and take the holy object back to Spain. It seems his year of captivity furthered him from his faith, or some such thing."

The baron laughed, pointing at Nicholas with a rib bone. "Fool, ye spent too much time at the monastery with that sissy abbot. I should have had ye fostered here with me."

Nicholas could hold his tongue no more. He stepped forward but his father's knights were there with their swords to hold him still. "Why didn't you?"

He patted his bulging belly. "I didn't know if ye were my son, now did I? Yer slut of a mother was in love with Robbie MacIntosh, the Scottish rebel King Henry wanted slaughtered. He was dark, as I was dark. She, though beautiful, was dark. How was I to know, until ye got older?" The baron tapped his nose.

"How did you find me?"

"I didn't have to look far. Abbot Crispin sent me a letter within months of your arrival."

Nicholas gulped, his jaw clenched. "You knew about me?"

"Aye." The baron laughed. "I paid a small stipend, and your mentor kept me apprised of your growth."

Betrayed by the abbot. "Hedging your bets, were you? You could watch me grow at the monastery, and interfere whenever it pleased you. Did you burn the monastery down?" Nicholas's hands itched to get a hold of anything that he could stab the baron with.

"Now, son—"

"Don't call me that," Nicholas said in a controlled voice that didn't match the boiling anger inside him.

"I thought the abbot might have the relic. And I wanted to know about you. He wasn't cooperating. The fire was but a warning that burned out of control. I offered to build him a new one."

Nicholas bowed his head, knowing that his father didn't see loss of life as something to fret over. *He wanted to know about me; he was searching for something else to hold over my head. Controlling bastard.*

Petyr leaned forward, his eyes darting from Baron Peregrine to Nicholas. "What about the babe needed to end Esmerada's curse? How are ye going to manage that?"

The baron glared at Petyr. "Go and bring the healer to me," he said carelessly. "Mayhap I can get a babe on the wench."

Nicholas could feel his gut jump to his throat, and a low growl escaped.

"Nicholas doesn't like that," Petyr sat back, holding his goblet. "What sort of father would send his son to be murdered while on crusade?"

The baron drew his knife. "Why are you asking questions, Petyr? You never needed answers before."

The knight swiped back his golden hair and smiled maliciously. "I find that I have a certain respect for Lord Nicholas. My conscience is telling me that I've made a mistake in selling him to you for a few paltry coins." He crossed his arms over his broad chest. "Did you plan my brother's death, as well?"

The baron wiped the beads of sweat from his brow with the back of his hand. "I could kill you, too, if you become greedy. Bernard thought too highly of himself. I can see that you, also, have a good opinion of your worth."

"You won't avenge your brother's death, Petyr?" Nicholas hoped that the two would snarl at each other, and give him an opportunity to kill them both.

"Petyr! Why are we arguing?" The baron laid the knife on the table. "You have brought both my son and the relic to me. I have your gold in my chamber. It is a contract that will be paid in full."

Petyr narrowed his eyes. "Aye. Our devil's bargain. I think that I will take my gold, plus ten percent for the death of my brother, and retire elsewhere. Methinks I would not enjoy my old age if I remained here in your service."

Sucking his teeth before spitting on the floor, the baron asked, "Ten percent? I hear France is nice."

Nicholas lunged for the table, but the baron's knights caught him before he could grasp the knife. The baron reached over and slugged Nicholas in the head. "Throw him back. The next time I see him, make sure he's been washed."

Joseph tracked the horses to the baron's castle. He stayed hidden in the forest, deciding what to do. He wanted his treasure back.

He pulled his worn cloak around his head, hiding the quiver of special arrows beneath it. He fell in with a group of peddlers and walked with them through the gates. He kept his head down and shuffled through the village, focused on reaching the castle itself.

He had no idea what he would do when he got there.

Joseph thought while he walked. He did his best thinking when his feet were moving—did Lord Nicholas still have the treasure? He frowned in confusion. He had thought Lord Nicholas to be a good man. His instincts had told him that Nicholas was as good at heart as even Father Michael.

Father Michael always had a kind word for him, even though he was big and stupid and the other villagers were afraid of him. He scratched his head, which was hot and sweaty beneath the heavy hood. If Nicholas was so good, then why had he stolen Joseph's treasure?

Joseph clearly remembered the day that he'd found it. It had been raining heavily, and the stones around the outer base of the north tower had come loose. Inside he'd found an oiled deerskin wrapped tightly around a pretty box. He grinned. His mother had laughed so hard she had cried! She'd patted him on the head and called him a good son. His heart raced. He loved his mathair, but usually she boxed his ears and called him daft.

Which was why he was so careful to do as she said. He was not supposed to go around the north tower; she'd told him it was haunted.

If his mother found he'd let Lord Nicholas take the treasure to Baron Peregrine, a man his mother hated above all others, he knew he would be in for it. He shuddered. She might even break his arrows.

He tried to prove to Maude and his mother that he was a good provider. He was a better hunter than the men in the village. Hadn't he killed all of the baron's men, just as his mother said? He had even pinned those two bad men to the kitchen table so that his mother could talk to them. Otherwise they would have hurt her, she'd said so.

He reached the end of the dirt road in the village and now he had to make a choice. Should he sneak into the castle grounds on his own, or should he stay with the group of peddlers?

Blending was the most important part of being a great hunter. He stayed with the peddlers. His mother said that Lady Esmerada wanted the baron to suffer for his many, many sins. His mother thought that making people suffer for their sins was her life's work.

He realized he'd fallen behind the peddlers, but at least he was in the castle courtyard. He knew it was wrong, some of what his mother did. But she was his mother, and Father Michael had told him to respect his parents. His father was dead.

He'd told his mother that he was off to sell furs at the next village. She hadn't noticed that the treasure no longer sat on the mantle above the fire. She had been too busy trying to make the villagers afraid of the pretty Lady Celestia.

Joseph had tried to make sense of his mother's ranting, but he only understood that his mother was fond of Lord Nicholas, yet hated Lady Celestia. He shook his head, confused about that. The Lady Celestia was beautiful and kind, much nicer than his stupid sister, Maude. Maude pulled the wings off of butterflies.

When he had come back from checking his traps that fateful night, he had seen the two, Lord Nicholas and Lady Celestia, running from his hut and into the forest. He was going to call to them, but they had looked frightened. Besides, Maude had called him inside, and that was when he'd realized they'd taken his treasure.

He'd been angry at first. His mother would get mad. But then he thought that mayhap the treasure really belonged to Lord Nicholas, since Joseph had found it at his keep. He remembered the finger bone with the ring and wondered if it was magic. He scratched his head again. Joseph would have given the treasure to Nicholas, if he had asked. But not if he had known that Lord Nicholas would give the treasure to Baron Peregrine—now that was something he really didn't understand.

Baron Peregrine was the devil; his mother said so. He stopped in his tracks. Mayhap the finger bone was magic, and Lord Nicholas needed it to defeat the baron! A smile grew. He had to find Lord Nicholas, and help him fight the devil! He shrugged his shoulders, reassured by the heavy quiver full of arrows.

He stepped against the shaded covering of the inner wall. Where would Lord Nicholas go? He thought and thought. He watched a tall youth take a horse to the stables. Yes! Lord Nicholas was most fond of Brenin. He would be certain to visit his stallion, sooner or later. Joseph edged toward the large, long barn.

He knew how to be patient.

Celestia heard Viola's crying voice, "I feel her heartbeat, but it is faint." Then she heard Sir Geoffrey round on Maude. "Ye could've killed our lady!"

Bertram said, "Nay, Maude didn't do it on purpose."

"No accident," Geoffrey said.

Maude cried, "'Twas an *accident!* The lock fell away like water beneath her palm. She is a witch—it shocked me so I screamed, and lost my footing on the stairs."

Willy sniffed. "Bertram, you should never have let her go. Why did ye allow her to run up behind our lady?"

Bertram yelled, "Lady Maude wanted to save the Lady Celestia."

Willy shouted back, "Oh, and that worked out fine—did it not? Your slut may have killed Lady Celestia! Lady Maude," Willy spat in disdain, "when did she get elevated above peasant's status?"

Henry asked in a subdued voice, "Will she live? Who can heal her, if she is the greatest healer of all, and she's injured?"

Celestia heard all of this, yet it didn't compel her to open her eyes. Viola said, "The Lady Evianne. We need Celestia's grandmother."

Grainne Kat shuffled close. "What is all the ruckus about?" Celestia, though she had her eyes tightly closed, could feel the malevolent gaze of the wise woman. "Didn't I tell ye? The tower is cursed! I told you not to let her open the tower. Is she dead?"

Celestia felt Viola leap over her prone body. "You old hag—what have you done?"

Geoffrey must have caught the maid, since Celestia heard Viola's grunt and her knight's huff. Then he said, "Get me the litter that was to take Grainne Kat back to her hut. We'll place my lady on it, and carefully carry her into the downstairs sewing room."

Willy said, "Shall I ride for Montehue Manor?"

Viola clapped, and sighed heartily. "Ride like the wind, and bring our family to us."

That was the best news of all, Celestia thought before letting the darkness take her.

Time had stopped.

There was no urgent need to do anything—nothing called for her attention. Celestia felt as if she was floating betwixt one world and the next. "I hurt," she told the lady with the raven-black hair.

The woman smiled kindly and caressed Celestia's blond waves, the only part of her that didn't ache. "Ye've been brave, lassie. But ye canna give up."

"Can you not ease this pain?" Celestia whimpered.

"I canna, *dochter;* to feel is to live."

"I would die, then, to escape this torment."

The woman smiled again, "Ye would not! Not when Nicholas needs you, yet." The smiling face changed into a mask of sorrow. "Beware the old woman."

"Where are you going?" Tears slid down the woman's cheeks, and Celestia reached for her as the lady disappeared into mist.

Her voice echoed, "Beware the *carlin!*"

Celestia longed for Nicholas.

She saw his strong, gray eyes, his noble nose, his ebony hair as clearly as if she was looking through a pane of glass.

He was trapped, for certes, as she was. But he was fighting to be free. Celestia wasn't certain she wanted to be free.

She felt the lightest touch of Viola, then heard her

lament, "I don't know what else to do. We've mended the broken bones in her arm and her ankle, but she will not wake."

Shy Sally sniffed. "How long until the family arrives?"

"Three days more, and that is only if they rode without stopping."

"Will she lie so still forever?" Shy Sally whispered, but Celestia could still hear.

Viola smacked the girl, most likely on the arm, Celestia thought, wondering at the maid's spunk. "I won't hear that kind of talk, do ye understand? She will come 'round! She has to. She is the lady here, and Lord Nicholas will not be pleased to find his wife ill."

She felt Viola sit on the edge of her bed, and then Celestia heard her pick up a brush. Viola gently pulled the bristles through Celestia's hair. Her maid sat, sniffing and brushing, brushing and sniffing. "Come back, Lady Celestia. Come back to us!"

Shy Sally started crying, and Celestia heard the sound of the woman's tunic swish as she left the room.

Viola spoke. "Grainne Kat is still here, my lady, and I know if ye could, ye'd tell her to leave. But she insists she's the closest thing to a healer we have, and unfortunately, she's right."

Celestia wondered if she should be alarmed, but in this odd state of limbo, she wasn't concerned about anything other than escaping a new hurt.

"She helped us set your ankle. That old dame's strong, and all of her pretending to faint antics—they are just that."

Celestia's pain was soothed by the sound of Viola's voice.

"Sally and I take turns standing guard over your pallet. I don't know how, my lady, but I swear that wise woman is responsible for your bad health."

This agitated Celestia, and she tried to open her eyes, but found she could not. They *wouldn't* open.

She opened her mouth to speak but it was sealed, as well. Panic flared. Was she paralyzed? Or crazy? She concentrated with all of her might but she couldn't move her arms or her legs. *Help*, she thought wildly.

The lady with the raven hair came back and touched her shoulder. "Sleep, Celestia. Grow strong. Yer body fights for life, just as the *carlin* tries to steal it from ye."

"I am so frightened . . ." Celestia said as tears slipped from her eyes.

"I am here, *dochter*, I am here."

"Who are you?"

Celestia thought the woman would not answer her, and she struggled against the invisible bonds that kept her from moving.

"You are a fighter, lassie."

"I am a healer."

"You are strong, stronger than I ever was."

Celestia's mind suddenly filled with images. *An apple orchard, a woman, and a toddler.* The woman was laughing, her sewing in her lap, a gold thimble on her thumb. "Nicholas!" the woman called. "Ye'll get dizzy if ye keep turning round and round like a dervish! Come, sit by me." The boy wobbled over to the grass and plopped down. "Yer a braw bairn, young Nicholas. Yer mam loves ye, remember that. Give me a kiss, son."

Celestia's heart thundered in her ears, but she was afraid that if she spoke the images would fade.

She watched as another woman, older than Esmerada but not middle-aged, walked over to the two. "Welcome, Katherine! Would ye care to join us?" The woman shook her head with sorrow. "Nay, Esmerada. 'Tis time for your medicine. Ye don't want to get worse, do ye?" Celestia knew that woman. Grainne Kat!

The sight began to dissipate like so many clouds. "Nay!" Celestia cried out. "Don't leave me!"

"Beware the *carlin* . . ."

Chapter NINETEEN

"Psst."

Nicholas rose from his semi-slumber. Day and night had become mixed as he lay beneath the stables. There'd been no more word from Forrester, and Nicholas hoped the knight hadn't died from a head injury.

He hadn't seen the bell again, either.

"Are ye there, me lord?"

Nicholas scrambled to his knees, not sure he'd heard correctly.

"Joseph?" The plot grew thicker and thicker, Nicholas thought with a wild laugh.

"Aye, I tracked ye."

"You did?"

"Ye stole me treasure." Joseph peered through the slat, looking like he might be settling in for a long talk as he laid himself out, full-length, across the floor of the stable.

Nicholas swallowed. "I'm sorry, Joseph, I should

have asked."

"I would a given it to ye—I figure ye need it to take down the baron. Me mother says he's the very devil."

"Your mom might be right."

"Who got ye?"

"Sir Petyr."

"I never liked that Petyr, too pretty. Though Maude thought he was 'heavenly.'" Joseph snorted. "Heavenly. What does that mean?"

"Not to rush you, but can you get me out of here? I can't find a door."

"I am so stupid!" Nicholas heard the sound of a palm smacking skin. "Of course ye'll be wanting out."

"Hey," a young man's voice said. "Who are ye talkin' to?"

Nicholas, remembering what had happened to Forrester, hoped that Joseph would have the sense to stay quiet, or at least lie.

Joseph answered proudly, "The prisoner."

Nicholas lowered his eyes, certain he was through.

"Prisoner?" the lad's voice squeaked. "Below the stables? Must be full a shit down there! What did he do?"

"Didn't think about that." Joseph laughed. "Is there piles and piles of horse shit, Lord Nicholas?"

Nicholas gritted his teeth. "Aye."

A second eye, this one a sparkling green, joined Joseph's at staring down into the storage pit. "Good day to ya! I never met a real prisoner. The baron usually just has the peasant's heads cut off."

Nicholas touched his neck. "I am rather attached to

my head, lad . . . will ye help me escape?"

The green eye widened through the crack in the plank. "Escape? I dunno, the baron would have *my* head then. We should ask me brother, Ned."

Nicholas dropped his chin to his chest. Was God the biggest jester of all time? "Ned? Would you be Ed, by any chance?"

The green eye grew suspicious. "And how would ye know that?"

"I know a lot about you, young sir. I am married to your sister Celestia. Now will you get me out of here?"

"Yer the reason that Celestia had ta get married?"

"Aye."

The suspicion remained. "And just why would the baron want ye to marry me sister, who is the greatest healer ever, and then throw ye beneath the stables?"

Talking with a clenched jaw, Nicholas said, "If you would help me escape, mayhap we could find the answer to that very astute question."

Ed jumped to his feet, pulling Joseph up with him. "Quick! Someone is coming. I'll show ye a grand place ta hide."

They left, spattering more dirt and straw down on Nicholas.

He wasn't naming names, but someone Up There had a wicked sense of humor.

When Nicholas had told his Lord and Savior that

he would be open to any suggestions, he'd had no idea that he'd be offered escape through the cesspit. Beggars could not be choosers, he supposed.

Ed had come back with Ned and Joseph. Ned worked inside the castle as a page, and had quick fingers. He'd nabbed the plans from the baron's private rooms and found the cesspit drain below the stables.

The drain was located beneath the heavy bags of molding feed, which Nicholas had not thought to move. The rats lived there, and he had been willing to leave them undisturbed. A live-and-let-live philosophy. He looked at the bags seething with rat bodies and bit back his nausea. Celestia needed him. He hated rats.

He crawled forward, uncertain as to how he could accomplish his goal without getting bitten to death. As he got closer, beady red eyes popped up everywhere he looked.

"How ya doin'?" Ned or Ed asked in a changing voice.

Joseph said, "I have an arrow, me lord, if that will be of any aid."

The boys scoffed. "What good is an arrow without a bow? Are ye daft?"

Joseph answered, "Aye. I but wanted to help."

"You can squeeze an arrow through that crack, Joseph?" Nicholas asked.

"I thought to widen it a bit, not so anybody would notice, and then pass it through. But it was a stupid thought, me lord."

"Nay! I have no weapon; even an arrow would be better than naught."

The boys apologized to Joseph, who didn't hold a

grudge. He let them help shave slivers of wood to widen the crack, then he slipped the arrow through.

Nicholas accepted it gratefully.

"Now what, me lord?" Ed or Ned asked in a whisper.

"I wish that I knew," Nicholas said, his jaw tight.

Joseph said, "It would be easier, me thinks, to take the planks from the floor and pull him out, then we can return the planks as if we'd never been here. We must hurry, though, the guard I coshed over the head ain't dead, you know, just sleeping."

Nicholas groaned. "I am glad you didn't kill him, Joseph. I hate rats, and I'm already covered in manure without having to crawl through a cesspit. I much prefer the idea of you pulling me out."

Ed pushed Ned into a pile of hay. "Yer brilliant, Joe! Ned! Makin' Lord Nicholas crawl through the cesspit—what were ya thinking?"

Ned cuffed Ed upside the head. "I was usin' me noggin for something besides pickin' me nose, bugger."

The sounds of the boys scuffling up ahead had Nicholas realizing he might never get out of his prison.

Joseph picked the two boys up by their arms. "Ye can fight over who is stupider after we free Lord Nicholas. If we use that empty stall over there, we can cover the hole up with hay if we need to hide in a hurry. Should I go back and slit the guard's throat, me lord?"

"Nay!" Nicholas quickly answered.

"Come, lads. Get to work."

Nicholas was out of his prison before noon.

"Ye stink!" Ed or Ned said as they waved their hands

beneath their Montehue noses. The boys were well on their way to being as gigantic as their father. One twin had blue eyes and one had green beneath blond caps of hair.

Joseph tapped his finger against the side of his nose. "Ye'll have to get clean, but then what?"

Nicholas knew he sounded like a whiner, anything but the heroic figure he wanted to be for his wife, but he pleaded, "Can we start with clean?"

The boys laughed and led Nicholas and Joseph to a stream tucked away at the edge of the forest. Nicholas jumped in with all of his clothes on. He scrubbed his face and hair, then his body. He finally came up for air.

"Yer a funny one, Lord Nicholas. How fares Celestia?"

Ed, the twin with the green eyes, repeated the question. "Aye, how is she?"

"Would that I knew—I must return to her as soon as possible, I feel she needs me." He had removed his clothing while in the stream, cleaning it as best he could. It was important that Celestia's tunic not be ruined. Before leaving the water, he donned his linen undershirt. He would not scare his wife's brothers with the scars on his back. He laid his hose and tunic to dry on a rock.

The gash on his thigh, a gift from Petyr, looked red and irritated.

"If she needs ye, then why did ya come here?"

Nicholas ignored the injury and sat down before the small fire Joseph had built. He warmed his hands. "I was a fool to leave her," he told them. "I thought that returning a relic to Spain was more important than telling Celestia how much she meant to me. And then, then

Petyr convinced me that the baron, my father, was the root of my problems."

Nicholas scratched the back of his neck. "I was the root of my problems."

The boys giggled and blushed. "Did ye tell her ye loved her?" Ned asked with an adolescent grin.

"Did ye kiss her before ye left? Hmm?" Ed waggled his lips.

They thought they were so funny that they laughed until they got the hiccups.

Nicholas enjoyed the fire and the camaraderie, content to bask in life while he dried. He'd been afraid of living for too long. "Oh—living—what happened to the knight that you hit over the head?"

Ned shrugged. "Don't know. When I came back with Ed, he was already gone. And then the baron wanted to see you—I wondered if it was because of the knight."

"It wasn't." Nicholas wondered what had happened to Forrester, or if the knight was safely ensconced within the castle, drinking ale with the baron.

Joseph turned his head so that the twins would not hear his question. "I know you stole my treasure to defeat the baron in battle. When are we going to confront him?"

"Joseph, allow me to apologize for taking the relic. I—you see, I had lost it once, and I thought that by taking it all the way to Spain that I would be able to ask a boon."

He could see that Joseph did not understand, which was fair, as he did not, either. "I was wrong to steal it."

"'Tis no matter, me lord. There is something about the treasure that makes me feel good, too." Joseph poked at the fire nervously. "I found it buried between the stones of the north tower."

Nicholas thought he heard wrong. "You found it there? Where?"

Joseph would not meet Nicholas's eyes. "There had been a lot of rain. The stones around the base of the tower came loose, and I found the treasure wrapped in an oiled deer skin and tied with pretty ribbon." Joseph peered into the fire and continued quietly, "I knew I shouldn't a been there; me mother told me the place was haunted by Lady Esmerada's ghost. But I liked the tower fine! I never really heard ghosties, not a once. I just said I did, 'cause Mother wanted to scare the villagers away from the tower."

Nicholas closed his eyes. He was going to be sick.

Joseph looked at Nicholas quick, then went back to studying the flames. "Ye ain't angry at me, are ye? I really would have given it to ye."

Forcing himself to be calm, he answered, "Nay, Joseph. 'Tis not you I am angry with." He patted the simple man on the shoulder. There was stupid, and then there was *stupid*. Nicholas put himself into the latter category.

He stood and pulled on his damp hose. "Boys, I want you to be prepared to ride with me from this place. The baron is a dangerous man."

Ned spat. "Leave? We can't. Our family has an obligation to the baron." Ed nodded.

Nicholas belted his tunic. "The obligation will be forsworn, trust me." He found the arrow inside his tunic, pulled it out, and handed it back to Joseph. "Here. Thank you for the thought, anyway."

His hands slid over the feathers and they caught his eye. He recognized that arrow! Swallowing hard, he glanced at Joseph. Had he been the one to kill the baron's men? His stomach turned. And Bess? He exhaled. Nay, he did not see Joseph as a murderer of women. The younger man had proven his worth; he would question the rest later.

Joseph accepted it and placed it with the quiver full of others. "I am a good hunter, Lord Nicholas. I will help you beat the devil back."

Eyeing his group he said, "Boys, this is no game we play. I want you to have Brenin saddled and be hiding in the forest here. I will come to you as soon as I have finished things with the baron, my sire."

Nicholas recognized the stubborn look that settled over their features. His wife wore an identical expression when she did not get her way.

Ned shook his head. "What? Ye plan on walking through the front doors of the castle? From what ye said, that didn't work in your favor before."

Ed made a rude noise through his nose. "Ye want to end up below the stables three times in a row? We will lose our heads as well, and there won't be a soul left to save ye."

Nicholas crossed his arms across his chest and said drolly, "You have a better plan?"

Ned pulled out the map of the castle from his doublet. "Aye, me lord, I thought ye'd never ask."

The problem with plans, Nicholas cursed under his

breath as his hand slipped on the ivy, was that they rarely took in all aspects of a situation. He slid down two feet on the twenty-five-foot-high wall. "I am beginning to think that going through the front doors of the castle was not such a bad idea."

"Not if ye didn't mind losing yer head," Joseph agreed. He was quite nimble for a large man and clambered up the ivy-covered walls with little effort. "Need a hand?"

"Nay." Nicholas blinked against the sting of sweat in his eye. "I'll get there."

He looked up at Joseph, who sat on the miniscule window ledge swinging his legs back and forth. "I think asking those boys for a plan may have been a mistake. They think of this as an adventure—the more challenges, the better. They don't realize that there are enough obstacles already." Nicholas pulled himself atop the ledge next to Joseph. Exhaling with relief, he turned and peered into the window.

The ledge cracked beneath their combined weight.

"Did you hear that?" Nicholas asked calmly, his gut in his chest.

Joseph's eyes widened in alarm and he pushed Nicholas on the arm. "Aye! Hurry, man, before we fall to our deaths. Boys—ye never should have listened to them!"

Nicholas slipped his knife from the belt at his waist, quickly sliding it upward between the paned doors of the window. The blade lifted the latch just as a piece of the ledge fell to the ground.

He swallowed and pushed inward. Nothing!

Now what?

"Try pullin' towards ye, Nicholas," Joseph suggested.

Nicholas would never refer to Joseph as "simple" again. Using his knife as a lever, he pulled the pane outward. It flew free, knocking him off balance. He tottered on the edge of the ledge, one hand firmly on the window frame. Joseph heaved him forward, and they both flew inside the room. Neither man missed the sound of the remaining ledge falling to the ground below.

"Thanks," Nicholas said between pants.

Joseph nodded with wide eyes. "Er, Nicholas?"

"Hmm?"

Joseph used his thumb to gesture behind Nicholas. "Ye might want ta look."

Nicholas slowly got to his feet. He expected nothing less than a full patrol of the baron's knights with their swords drawn, all pointed at him. He turned around, trying desperately to think of a way out of this situation and keep his head. "I can explain . . ."

The baron was sitting in his high-backed chair, his arms pulled behind him and his hands tied. He had a gag in his mouth, and his eyes bulged.

"What the hell is going on?" Nicholas demanded.

The baron kept jerking his head toward the voluminous velvet drapes surrounding his bed. Nicholas flicked his gaze down and saw two boots poking from underneath the curtains.

He searched the room, his eyes lighting on his father's sword. It lay unsheathed next to his father's feet, having obviously been knocked to the ground during a scuffle and then forgotten.

Nicholas snatched it up, admiring the blade, before settling the grip in his palm. The baron was desperately motioning for his ties to be cut, but Nicholas was not certain he was ready for that. "Joseph, keep an eye out."

He turned back to check on the younger man, but realized he had spoken with no need.

"I see you already have the situation under control." Joseph had his bow pulled back, an arrow notched, and trained on Baron Peregrine. "Good."

He walked to the draperies and pulled them back with the tip of his sword.

Petyr attacked, sending Nicholas on the defensive. Petyr aimed for Nicholas's thigh, which had not had a chance to heal since their last skirmish. He slashed, tearing the hose and piercing the skin.

"Agh!" Nicholas dropped to his knee in agony. This was not going to be a friendly fight, then. He shot up and jumped backward, avoiding the downward lunge of Petyr's sword. He had to find a way to distract him.

Nicholas asked, "Did you really think you would get away with killing a man of such stature as the baron?"

Lunge, parry, slice.

"Aye!" Petyr snorted. "And why not? It will look like you did it. Ye escaped from the stables—I couldn't have made it any easier for you, Nicholas. Ye broke in through the windows and killed your own father in a fit of rage. 'Tis perfect!"

Woosh! A lock of ebony hair fell from Nicholas's head.

Nicholas narrowed his eyes and pushed forward, slashing, aiming for the jugular. Petyr meant to kill him, but he would not go quietly.

"Not so perfect. There is a witness in the room, and the baron, he still lives."

Baron Peregrine's eyes popped wider as his son used him for bait.

Joseph's aim was steady.

"Not for long! What matter will it make if ye die two seconds before yer sire?" Petyr turned on his heel and reached into his sleeve, pulling out a blade. "I'll not tell and neither will the baron."

Joseph fired the arrow at the same time he was hit in the side by Petyr's knife.

The baron screamed, and Nicholas lunged, attacking Petyr fiercely and without remorse. The sound of blades clashing again and again as they met reverberated around the baron's chamber.

"Enough!" Nicholas shouted hoarsely. He focused on the enemy and whispered, "Enough." He aimed steady and ran forward, stabbing Petyr through the heart.

Petyr tried to pull the weapon from his chest but he could not move it. He fell to the floor, an odd smile on his face. "You win . . ." he said with his last breath.

Joseph bravely tried to lift his head, and Nicholas clenched his jaw at the gushing blood pooling beneath the young man. "Ah, Joseph."

He smiled. "I got the devil, Nicholas. Tell me mother I did good."

Kneeling beside Joseph, Nicholas clasped his hand. "I will, Joseph. I will tell her. Thank you, friend."

Joseph died smiling.

Nicholas stood and slipped in the blood and gore that stained the chamber. Was it just today that he had made his peace with God? A thumping noise came from behind and he whirled, weaponless.

The baron whacked his feet against the floor. The sound was oddly muffled, since the chair was sitting in the middle of a large bearskin rug.

"You are alive?" Nicholas went to his father and searched for Joseph's arrow. Philippe Peregrine was bleeding profusely from the neck where the tip of the arrow had pierced his skin to his chair. Nicholas reached forward and pulled. The tip came loose with an audible pop, and tears of pain filled the baron's eyes.

Nicholas stepped backward and stared at the man who had been the cause of so much sorrow in his life. There was an eating knife on the table, a halved apple on a plate. Petyr must have interrupted the baron during a snack. Nicholas picked the knife up and shifted it from hand to hand.

"I could kill you easily, and blame it on the others."

The baron's black eyes were wild.

Nicholas leaned forward and slit the gag from his father's mouth. He held up the small knife in warning. "One shout from you, and I will change my mind. I have many questions, Baron Peregrine, that it seems only you can answer. At the end of this, I will demand a boon. And you," Nicholas waved the knife, "will grant it."

Philippe nodded eagerly. "Whatever you want! Lands, money, my name—"

"'Tis not so simple as that." Nicholas gathered his

thoughts. Now that he had this man before him, and at his mercy, nothing seemed as important as getting home to Celestia.

But Joseph, he could not let Joseph die for nothing. He hovered over Philippe and said, "Tell me why you stole the relic."

The baron looked confused. "What are you talking about? I never stole it! King Henry gave it to me to hide, almost a quarter century ago. God only knows where he had gotten it from that it needed to be gifted to Lord Harbotten, in the wilds of England, but after the mess with the archbishop, I don't think he wanted any more fingers pointed at him for wrongdoing."

Nicholas shook his head. "But you stole it back from the caravan. You organized the ambush, and you wanted me to die."

Baron Peregrine flushed with guilt. "Now, Nicholas, 'tis true that I ordered the arranged ambush. But it was because King Richard had demanded the relic in return for my vassal price. He was collecting holy objects in order to win that damn crusade! He knew King Henry had given it to me for safekeeping."

Philippe went a deeper shade of red. "When I went to retrieve the relic from Falcon Keep, it was gone. What was I to do? I couldn't say that I had lost the cursed thing, now could I? So I had a duplicate made, and I was going to foist it off on the king. But then, I realized that mayhap the true relic would have powers, and this duplicate would not. It seemed the easiest thing was to have the relic 'stolen' on the way to King Richard. That way it wasn't my fault."

Nicholas swayed on his feet. "The fact that I needed to die, it didn't bother you?"

"Well, a man can always make more sons," the baron attempted to jest while studying the trees outside the window. "Usually."

"I've spent my entire life believing that I had no father. And then I found out, after a *very difficult time*," Nicholas deliberately kept his pain understated and was rewarded by his father's sudden paleness, "that I had a father, and that he was the very same man I'd sworn to kill, as vengeance."

The baron moved his gaze to the bearskin rug.

Nicholas laughed. He laughed and laughed and laughed. When he had himself back under control, he wiped his eyes and shook his head. "You are a piece of work, Baron. I will say that for you."

His sire glanced at him hopefully.

"Oh, nay. I am not finished with you."

"What else, then?"

"How about the curse?" Nicholas paced back and forth in front of his father. "How about, once and for all, I hear about this damn curse. You abandoned me, even at the monastery. And why Celestia, for marriage?"

The baron raised his eyes. "The curse."

Nicholas threw the knife into the table so hard that the apple fell from the plate. "You wanted Celestia and I married as a way to break the curse?"

"I wanted her because she is rumored to be a witch. And who better than a witch to break a curse, eh?" The baron chuckled, evidently pleased with his reasoning.

Nicholas sighed. "Celestia is not a witch, and I don't believe in ghosts or curses."

"'Tis true—yer mother laid on me the most evil of curses! I have been married three times, and I have buried many children. More than any father should have to. I am a rich man, Nicholas, and the older that I get, the more I want an heir to pass my legacy to."

"Because I didn't matter?"

"You were *hers*." The baron finally looked Nicholas in the eye. "Your mother was beautiful. I thought that I could come to love her, but she—she loved another."

Nicholas thought he heard what might be the truth, and told himself to hold on to that and none of the other drivel his sire spouted.

"What was the curse?"

"I would have no surviving progeny until I claimed you as my own. When I had ye knighted, I thought it would count, and then I had a babe who lived a full two years. I didn't need ye, then, and I thought to have done with the curse by having ye killed."

Nicholas thought the news should hurt more, but instead, it freed his mind, as well as his heart. He owed his sire nothing.

"The other half of the curse is that you need to have children—I didn't know that part until you were already on your way to Jerusalem. Esmerada didn't want her line to die out, either."

Nicholas let the blade of the paring knife rest against the pad of his thumb.

The baron cajoled, "I went against the promise I had made to a loyal family in order to save you, and us."

"It was convenient for you to do so--and you are the one who caused the hurt!" Nicholas scratched the back of his neck. "It makes no difference. I am ready to demand my boon. I want the Montehues released of any vassal obligation to you. I want the relic. I will return it to Spain where it belongs."

"Of course."

"I'll have it in writing before I leave, my lord."

The baron's eyes flashed. "Fine!"

Nicholas thought of Celestia at Falcon Keep and her twin brothers waiting in the forest for him and Joseph. Poor dead Joseph. "I want Joseph properly buried, and I am taking the Montehue twins with me to be squires under my tutelage."

"You'll hold the keep?"

"Aye. It belonged to my mother."

He searched the baron's writing desk for a quill and parchment, then quickly covered Joseph with one of his father's velvet drapes. Joseph had killed the baron's men, but he had paid in full for his crimes. He could not see Joseph behind the murder of Bess. He left Petyr where he was.

Nicholas slit the baron's bonds and said, "Start writing."

Celestia heard Sir Geoffrey say, "They should be here by the day after tomorrow."

Viola answered, "Aye, it's been four days now, since

our lady fell."

"Was dragged, ye mean."

"I'm worried," Viola whispered to the trusted knight.

Celestia shivered.

"There's no fever, and the bones are set—why isn't she coming to?"

Yes, Celestia wondered, *why am I not waking up?*

"Sir Geoffrey, will you stay with her while I brew some chamomile and rose? My head is beating in time with my heart. Would you like a mug?"

"I'll stay, but I don't want anything to drink. I'm sick with worry, to tell ye true, Viola. Why does she toss and turn some times, and then at others lie so still?"

"I wish I knew! My first thought was poison. But nobody is around her but Shy Sally, me, and now you—and nobody but me prepares her broth. It must be something inside her that is causing this distress."

Viola's voice broke on a sob. "Would that I could do more!"

Celestia felt horrible for her maid, and she tried so hard to get past the pain of breathing. Her lungs were on fire, and her limbs ached so that she would have cut them off, if she could but move.

"And where is Sir Nicholas? Surely Forrester has found him by now?" Celestia heard Viola's question end on a cry, and then she heard footsteps run from the chamber.

Sir Geoffrey's clomping strides followed the maid from the room, and Celestia knew a subconscious fear as she was left without her protectors.

Soft dainty footsteps stopped by the side of her bed.

Celestia wished she could see, as well as hear, however her senses were heightened and she could tell that whoever this was, they meant her harm.

Poison?

"Open," the voice urged, pinching the doll-like Celestia's mouth. The spiritual Celestia screamed and yelled for help, to no avail. Then the burning pain rushed through her body, numbing her and sending her back to the safe place amongst the sky.

"Ye can't stay here."

"Why not?" Celestia alternated between floating on clouds of white, or dodging bolts of lightning and fierce rain. Little by little she released her connection to her body, spending more time in spirit.

She was resting on a puffy cloud, contemplating absolutely nothing, when the Lady Esmerada said, "'Tis time for ye to return, lassie."

Celestia yawned. "Nay. I don't wish to go back. It pains me too much! I would stay here and sleep."

"Yer *Mathair* and *Athair* are waiting for you."

"Who?"

"Yer sisters are there, too."

Celestia opened her blue eye. "Why have they come all of the way to Falcon Keep?"

"For you. They are worried. Ye must go."

Struggling to get out of the soft cloud, she asked, "They are worried? What is the matter?"

Lady Esmerada smiled kindly. "Why don't ye go and see?"

Without thought, Celestia returned to her body.

Every nerve ending screeched with pain. "Nay! You tricked me! I don't want to go back."

Shaking her head with sadness, Lady Esmerada said, "Ye must. Nicholas needs ye, as does yer family."

She lay quiet. "Nicholas?"

Nicholas!

"I may not have the special healing gifts that you and Celestia share, but I know that my daughter needs me, Mam. Move along, please, sir knight—where is she?"

Celestia heard her mother's strident voice carrying across the keep. She heard poor Gram sputtering and imagined the chaos of her family arriving in one large untidy heap. Her heart filled, but she still could not move. Willing to risk the pain, all she did was hurt herself each time she tried to regain possession of her flesh.

"Viola?" Celestia heard her grandmother ask. "Why are you lying over Celestia?"

Deirdre burst into tears. "Mother's here, darling girl . . ." Galiana sniffed. "It smells in here."

"Who has been giving Celestia poison?" Ela asked. "Her aura is grayish brown—she is *dying!*"

It sounded as if Lady Evianne dropped to her knees in front of Ela. "What do you see? Tell me."

Frustrated, Celestia could only hear the pain in her youngest sister's voice. "Grayish brown, like the undersides of toadstool . . . 'Tis poison! Save her, Gram."

Lady Evianne said, "Viola, are you sleeping, what is

the matter with you, girl?"

Celestia wished she could burst free of her cage. If Viola was injured, she'd—she'd—what?

Thankfully, Viola's sleepy voice came to Celestia like music. "I went to the kitchens for but a moment. When I returned, Maude was placing a powder beneath Lady Celestia's tongue. I pushed her, but Grainne Kat hit me over the head with her walking stick. I tried to stop them, I did!"

"A powder?" Evianne bent her head and opened Celestia's mouth. She sniffed. "An Amanita mushroom. It causes deep sleep and paralysis of the limbs, until finally the victim dies." She snapped her fingers. "Galiana, gather my herb basket from my horse. Henry—bring me a pot of boiled water. The belladonna can save her."

Deirdre gasped. "But that is another poison."

Lady Evianne said, "Aye, but it may be the only way she will live."

Chapter TWENTY

Lady Evianne forced more of the belladonna concoction between Celestia's lips. Deirdre smoothed her daughter's hair away from her face.

"She's so hot, Mam. Should she be so hot?"

"Aye, and soon she should be retching." Celestia vaguely heard this, but she was so miserable she couldn't concentrate.

"Be ready. 'Tis the best thing for her. Did ye send Forrester for goat's milk in the village? And Geoffrey to Grainne Kat and Maude's?"

Deirdre trickled cool water over Celestia's wrists. "Forrester never returned from trying to find Nicholas, but Geoffrey is on his way for the milk. I feel so hopeless! If you could not save her with all of your healing power, then what chance has she of fighting this alone?"

"I think that Maude must have been watching for any moment when Viola had her back turned. It would take less than a blink of an eye to dab some of the powder beneath her tongue. I think that my healing gifts may have helped Celestia fight the poison if we'd gotten here sooner, but who knows how much, or how often, Maude has given it to her?"

Lord Robert stomped into the room. "Evianne, I have many questions, and I know that now is not a good time to ask them. But answer this—where in the hell is her husband?"

Celestia squirmed, or tried to, as her belly rolled back and forth. Her stomach was fighting the impending nausea, but she had a horrible feeling it was going to lose.

Viola said, "He left on a holy pilgrimage to Spain."

"What?" Lord Robert bellowed. "He left my 'Tia alone with a group of knights barely old enough to shave? Bess is dead; no one ever found her murderer. Celestia has been accused of witchcraft, and he leaves? Selfish bastard!"

"It seems as if you've found someone to tell you what is happening," Deirdre said dryly.

Her father gave a loud huff. "Forrester. Nice boy. Half in love with our 'Tia, if I don't miss me guess. That is who she should have married!"

"She never wanted to marry at all, remember?" Deirdre put her hand on Celestia's wrist, and the cool press of her mother's fingers was a balm. "We should have moved back to Wales, Robert. What have we done?"

Lord Robert yelled, "If I ever see that low-down knave again, I'll kill him with my bare hands!"

"Lord Robert?"

Celestia quieted for a tiny instant. Was that

Nicholas's voice?

"Lord Robert! When did you arrive?" Nicholas asked.

"You!" her father bellowed.

Helpless, Celestia heard the crunching sound of her father planting his fist in her husband's face.

Nicholas rocked back on his feet, the welcoming smile gone as blood dripped from his nose. "What in God's mercy did you do that for?"

Lord Robert faced him, his fists cocked to hit him again. "I'll tell ye why—did I or did I not warn ye to take good care of my Celestia?"

Nicholas nodded, "Aye."

"Well, she's lying on death's door from being poisoned, and where the devil were you? Gallivanting around the world with a finger bone?"

Nicholas felt the blood drain from more than his nose. The room swayed. "Celestia is hurt?"

"Maybe dying! Are ye deaf?"

Lady Deirdre stood on shaking legs. "This is a sickroom—take your fighting outside, but I'll not have it here, Robert Montehue."

Lady Evianne broke in with a calm voice that reminded him of Celestia soothing her patients. "Lord Nicholas, you can't have gone to Spain and back."

Looking around the small sewing room they'd turned into a sickroom, his gaze found his wife.

She looked dead already, and his stomach hitched.

Nicholas watched as Evianne dropped liquid between Celestia's still lips. Deirdre was radiating fury, Robert was beyond reason, and Viola—she sat in the corner wringing her hands. His eyes went back to Celestia and then he saw no other.

He dropped to his knees and knelt by the bed. "What are you doing to her?" His voice was a mere whisper, but it resonated with anguish. "Why can you not heal her? With the magic in your hands?"

"So you believe, do you?" Evianne looked up after putting the last drop of the belladonna antidote inside Celestia's mouth. "She had a bad fall down the north tower stairs, breaking her arm and her ankle. Grainne and Maude have been feeding her poison from an amanita mushroom. It causes delirium and prostration, resulting in death."

Nicholas, desperate for answers, asked, "She's a healer, why can't she heal herself?"

"Because, you oaf," Deirdre smacked him on the arm, "she loves you, and yet you don't love her. In our family, unrequited love for a healer means that the she loses her powerful gifts. That is why our family has a special marital dispensation."

Nicholas held Celestia's delicate hand in his. "She never said anything. All the time I was talking about what I lost, and yet she never mentioned what she risked by giving her heart to me. She can't die, she can't."

Raising her weary head, Lady Evianne asked the obvious question, "And why is that?"

"I love her." Nicholas bowed his head against the sheet.

"And is that why you came back?"

Nicholas brought Celestia's hand to his lips and kissed each pale knuckle. "I should have ridden faster, hell, I never should have gone. I was selfish, and couldn't think past my own hurt. I cannot lose her now, Lady Evianne, not when I know how much she means to me."

Lady Evianne sighed, then rose to her feet, stretching her sore back along the way. "I would love to hear your story, Nicholas. But I am afraid we don't have time. Deirdre, hand me the bucket. The purging should begin soon."

Nicholas shrugged helplessly. "What would you have me do?"

Evianne grinned, some of her old spark still left. "Hold the bucket, me lord."

At the sound of snickering, Deirdre looked at the doorway and clasped her hand over her mouth. "Ned? Ed? What are you boys doing here? If ye've run away from the baron, you'll ruin your chances for knighthood! Scamps, come here, boys."

She raced forward, enveloping her twins in a hug.

"Your sister did not sacrifice herself in marriage to this," Lord Robert pointed at Nicholas with a grimace, "*imbecile* for you to ruin it all by running away. What were ye thinkin', boys?"

Ned poked his head free from Deirdre's embrace. "We didn't, Father."

Ed's head appeared on the other side. "We swear."

"As soon as ye quit hiding behind your mother's skirts, I'll beat ye for lying."

Nicholas glanced over from where he held onto Celestia's hand. "They aren't lying, Lord Robert. They are to be trained in this keep, under my tutelage, through knighthood."

Lord Robert thundered, "I'll not have it!"

Deirdre smiled delightedly. "Ye'll be with your sister, then. How wonderful."

"Did you forget, Deirdre, that Celestia may be dying?" Lady Evianne scowled, and Nicholas wondered at how they all managed to hear *without* yelling.

Deirdre ran back to the bed, taking her place next to Nicholas.

"Her color is changing," Ela warned. "Grab your bucket!"

The Montehues, and a single Le Blanc knight, spent the night and all the following day crying, praying, and washing pails.

Nicholas was tired, but his body was used to going without sleep. The twins were so exhausted that they'd fallen asleep on the floor of the chamber. He'd sent Viola to bed hours before.

He and the Lady Evianne maintained the vigil, and finally she sat back.

"The fever is gone, she is cool to the touch. The clear mint broth should soothe her stomach. What say you, Nicholas? Are you ready for sleep?"

"I will stay here, if you don't object."

"She is your wife, Nicholas. How could I tell you nay?"

Nicholas chuckled, rubbing the pad of his thumb over Celestia's knuckles. "I've noticed that your family is protective of one another, and a mite bossy and loud if you think you are right. If you felt like forcing me out of this room, you would try." He attempted a smile. "Though I'd not go."

Evianne laughed and Deirdre, whom he'd thought asleep, reached over and patted him on the head.

"Wake up," Deirdre said to Robert, who was snoring in the corner, both boys at his feet. "At least long enough so that ye don't break yer necks on the stairs."

Robert stood, tripping over a twin. "Is she?"

"She lives, and is sleeping peacefully." Nicholas heard the catch in Deirdre's voice and his heart skipped.

Robert turned to his youngest daughter for confirmation. "What color do ye see, Ela?"

Ela smothered a yawn. "Light blue, Father. For Nicholas, too."

He looked at Deirdre. "Is that good?"

"Excellent." She shook Galiana's shoulder. "She is going to be just fine, Gali."

Galiana burst into tears. "It was the comfrey cream, with the merest hint of orange," she sniffed.

The melee died down, and Nicholas found himself alone with his wife. His last sight of her had been at the window, after she'd hit him in the head with his knapsack. Smoothing her hair over the pillow, Nicholas whispered, "I want my warrior back."

He wanted her to stand up to him and fight with him and love him. She looked more fragile than ever, her body wan and fleshless. He traced her eyebrows, wanting to memorize every curve of her face.

"I almost lost you," he told her, as if she didn't know. "Not for so long as I live will I forget how close to the brink of death you tottered. You scared me, Celestia." In truth, there had been a moment when he'd thought she'd left them forever.

He stroked her cheeks, and was pleased with the healthy pink that bloomed beneath his touch. "I am glad that you returned to us; I don't know how I would have borne it if you hadn't."

Bowing his head, he sent his thanks.

"I love you Celestia Montehue. I love you with all of my heart."

He turned from the bed, determined to do what was right by her. He would offer her the choice of an annulment. She had no reason to stay wed, unless she truly loved him. His father had given the Montehue family the land without obligation; he had opted to foster the twins through knighthood. She would not lose her healing gifts, as he loved her dearly. He had removed every threat.

He hoped that he had the strength to endure if she told him good-bye.

Celestia opened her eyes, uncertain as to where she was. She felt disconcerted, separate from herself. Turning her head, she carefully kept her body still and wiggled her toes. They moved. "Nicholas?"

"Nay, daughter. 'Tis just your old father, come all the way from Montehue to save your life."

She giggled. "What are you saying?"

Lord Robert pulled his stool closer to the bed and gently touched her cheek. "I am saying, 'Tia, that it is a beautiful day."

She lifted her hand, which shook with weakness. "Are you crying, Father?"

Lord Robert cleared his throat, clutching her hand between his two large palms. "Pah! Men don't cry, girl—ye know that—damned dusty keep, this is. Henry tells me you've had trouble with the servants. Tell me that you're miserable, and I will take ye home."

Celestia shook her head, confused.

"'Tia! You are finally awake. What took you so long? It has been a day since you began sleeping peaceful. We've all been walking on eggshells, but I was tempted to pinch ye awake."

Ela plopped down on the side of the bed while Celestia tried her hardest to remember what they were all talking about.

Her mother and Gram entered the room next. Deirdre kissed her daughter's forehead and then helped her to sit up. She plumped the pillows behind her, and then did it again.

"What is wrong with all of you? You act like I am dying." Celestia's smile faded as she remembered her father's watery eyes. "How could I be dying?"

"You're not—not anymore. You were poisoned."

"Ela!" Celestia had a horrible memory of burning pain and helplessness.

"It is the truth, ask Mam."

Celestia looked to her mother, who nodded in

confirmation.

She felt sick for all of one heartbeat before exploding, "Will someone kindly tell me what bloody happened?"

Galiana ran to the doorway, her hand over her heart. "I knew you would be better soon, and now you're yelling just like before." She grinned happily. "You've got your temper back. I hate to admit this, 'Tia, but I missed it."

Nicholas turned the corner, Ed and Ned in tow. "Is that her? Is she awake?"

Celestia felt her face flush and she quickly patted her hair as Nicholas came into view. Her father groaned and put his head in his hands.

"Nicholas. You came back from Spain?" The joy was fleeting. "How long have I been, er . . . sick? Years?"

Ed laughed. "Yer funny, 'Tia. Not even a sennight, but it were touch and go for a while."

Ned gave his sister a kiss on the cheek. "Never want to see another puke bucket again. No matter how much I've missed ye."

Celestia's skin burned and she swallowed. Her throat *was* sore.

"The last thing I can remember is Nicholas going on pilgrimage, and fighting with Grainne about opening the north tower. Do you know she wouldn't leave?" She rubbed her throat.

Nicholas stepped farther into the room, and she focused on him. He looked so handsome, so strong, so *hairy*.

"Nicholas? You're growing a beard?"

He grinned and finger combed the black fringe. "I

am a changed man, Celestia."

"So you didn't go all the way to Spain?"

"Nay. What I needed was right here, all along."

"Tell me," she said with a twinkle in her eye.

Nicholas sat down on empty portion of the floor. Montehues were everywhere, and he absorbed their love like water to a starving plant.

"Well, let me see. Petyr caught up with me, as you had sent him to do, and convinced me the baron was the key to the puzzle."

He noticed some of the Montehues' curious looks and explained, "My father never claimed me as his own until I came back from the Crusades, a bitter, broken man." He lifted Celestia's hand and caressed each lovely finger. He kept his tone light, as if telling a humorous story around a campfire. "However, he had sent me on crusade, wearing his colors, to deliver a holy relic to King Richard. The relic, it turned out, was a fake. So the baron had made arrangements for the caravan to be attacked, with no survivors, and no fake relic. He wouldn't be in trouble with the king. But I lived."

Celestia broke in, "Did you tell them about Lady Esmerada's curse?"

Deirdre lifted her brows in amazement. "A curse? Your family really has a curse, too?"

Nicholas said, "Yes, but it is not as powerful as the curse that runs in your family."

"Well, that is fine, then. Who is Lady Esmerelda?"

"Esmerada. She was my mother. The baron had treated her badly, so she cursed him. She lived in the north tower. I think she is the one who hid the relic in the ashlar stone. She must have known the baron wanted it."

Nicholas met Celestia's gaze. "Joseph found the relic; he thought it was a treasure." He pressed her fingers. "Joseph is dead, Celestia. He . . ." Nicholas looked down but would not accept any guilt. "He was a friend to me, at the end."

Evianne sighed. "I have had Geoffrey out looking for Maude and Grainne Kat, but he cannot find them, not even in the village. They would want to know what happened to him."

"Yes. It seems that Grainne Kat has held a grudge against the baron for some time; she even taught her children that he was the devil. Joseph thought he had killed the baron at the end, and he was proud to have done it. But his arrow just nicked the skin of the wily old man's neck."

Celestia gasped. "The baron is dead?"

"Nay! The baron is alive and well. I think he is even going to marry again."

Celestia raised a blond brow. "You gave up vengeance so he could marry?"

"He claims the curse had killed all his other wives and offspring, and now that he has settled with me, the curse should be lifted."

Lord Robert said, "Settled? What does that mean?"

"I will tell you in a moment, if I may."

Celestia clenched her hands into fists. "Grr! I feel that everything has passed me by."

Nicholas kissed her palm. "Nothing has passed you

by, in fact, I have even waited to explore the north tower until you are well."

"You did? Nicholas—but that was your mother's tower. I would understand if you wished to go there alone." She leaned her face closer to Nicholas's.

Ela snorted. "Oh, for heaven's sake, could ye just kiss and have done? I want to know what happened next!"

Celestia blushed as her family laughed.

"Petyr tried to murder the baron and lay the blame on me. Joseph and I burst through his chamber window."

"It was me and Ned's plan, too. Well, mostly Ned's, he worked inside the castle, while I had the pleasure of working with the horses."

"If ye hadn't a been workin' in the stables, then ye'd never have found Lord Nicholas beneath them."

The two proudly pushed each other back and forth until Lord Robert placed a large hand on each shoulder. "Ed here found ye beneath the stables?"

"Aye. He and Joseph helped me escape."

Celestia started to laugh. "You've had all the adventures without me."

Nicholas grinned and cleared his throat. "Well, Petyr and I got into a bit of a . . . skirmish, and I saved the baron's life, and for that he had to grant me a boon."

He reached inside his tunic and pulled out a roll of parchment. He presented it to Lord Robert, bowing from the waist. "I am too comfortable to rise to my feet, my lord."

Lord Robert huffed. "And what is this? Ye already havin' troubles with yer taxes?"

Deirdre rolled her eyes. "Well?"

Lord Robert glanced at Nicholas, then said, "This paper releases us from any obligation to the Baron Peregrine; we will now owe our fealty directly to the king. We own our property, Deirdre." He rolled the paper back up and stared at Nicholas. "Why?"

Celestia looked at her husband with love and pride emanating from her smile. "He is an honorable man, Father. I told you."

Nicholas said, "In thanks for your graciousness when I wed your daughter." He waited for the laughter to die down. "And in part because I know that you all were put into this situation because my father, the Baron Peregrine, is not a fair, nor decent man. I saw a chance to right a wrong, and I took it."

Galiana sighed and fluttered her lashes.

Lord Robert said gruffly, "It will be a fine thing for the twins to be fostered beneath ye, Lord Nicholas."

Celestia clapped her hands together. "Ed and Ned are to stay here at the keep? Oh, Nicholas. I am so happy."

Evianne stood. "I am glad, Celestia, to see you so—but if ye are to stay that way, everybody needs to get out. I'll not have ye relapse! It took all of us to get ye better."

Celestia's eyes pooled. "All of you, yes, thank you so much. But how can I say thank you for saving my life?" She wiped at her face, yet the tears spilled faster than she could catch them. "First you save me, then you'd have me drown in my own tears."

"Say no more, daughter, and you're welcome. But once you are completely better, you might have to pay your brothers and sisters."

"Pay them?" Celestia sent them a confused glance.

"Aye," Deirdre laughed. "'Tis obvious you've never had to clean up after a purging!"

Celestia awoke from a pleasant dream. A dream of a dark-haired lady. She stretched beneath her woolen coverlet, pleased to be alive.

"Lazybones!" Galiana stood at the foot of her bed. "I have a bath ready for *your ladyship*, if you would allow me to attend you?"

Celestia sat up so fast she gave herself a headache. "Galiana, I've missed your teasing. A bath sounds divine." She sniffed. "I don't smell anything."

Gali tossed her a robe. "Upstairs, in the master chamber. Viola has a nice fire going, too."

"I could soak until my toes wrinkle. My head itches. A full week abed is too long."

Soon she was ensconced in warm water up to her nose. "Rose hip?"

Galiana smiled, so beautiful that it brought a smile to Celestia's face, too. "Chamomile and lemon balm. With a pinch of anise for spice."

"Lovely." Celestia curled her toes.

"I am jealous of you, 'Tia."

Celestia, who had been leaning back with her eyes closed, opened her left eye and asked, "Because all of me fits in the bathing tub?"

Gali giggled. "Nay!" She lowered her eyes demurely.

"Nicholas is very handsome. And so generous. Even Father has had to be nice. Mother thinks he can do no wrong, and the boys—well, they follow him around like he was King Richard himself."

Celestia hid her grin in the soap bubbles.

"His hair is so dark, and his shoulders—I do hope that my husband will be as wonderful."

Celestia flicked a bubble at her sister. "Leave my husband be! And tell me, why is it that you have not picked out a man already?"

Averting her head, Galiana ignored the question and asked, "So ye do love him, 'Tia? Then ye won't lose your gifts? I know how important they are to you."

"My healing powers mark me as one of you." Sighing, Celestia slid farther down in the tub. "The legend says that the love must be reciprocated. He has never told me of his feelings, other than that he was afraid to care for me." Her brows drew together. "But I tell you this, Gali—I would give them up for Nicholas, if the choice were mine to make."

Galiana exhaled with a dreamy look on her face. "Of course he loves you—everybody loves you. You are beautiful and kind. And 'tis obvious that Nicholas doesn't mind that you could fit in his pocket."

"Oh!" Celestia squealed and tossed a handful of water at her sister. Ela knocked and joined them. "What are ye doing? Viola and Gram will be very mad if ye get water all over the floor." She stomped over to Celestia and kissed the top of her head. "Light blue. I am so happy that you are feeling better, 'Tia."

Celestia grinned at her youngest sister. "And just when did you get even taller? You'll be the size of Mam, soon."

Ela blushed, disgust evident on her beautiful features. "It seems that I am to be an Amazon, like the rest of the women in our family. I was hoping to be short."

"And why would you want to be short?" Celestia arched her brow in question.

"None of the boys treat me like a girl. I can run faster than they, throw farther, ride better, and," she lowered her voice confidentially, "I am smarter, too."

Celestia and Galiana burst into conspiratorial giggles. Celestia finally realized that Ela did not think this a funny situation at all and gestured to Gali, who drew their youngest sister down on the window seat. "Ela, you are growing up to be a fine young lady. I didn't realize that a woman had to pretend to let the man be more intelligent until I was thirteen."

"But Celestia never had to do that. It isn't fair."

Celestia rolled her eyes. "Yea! But I was *forced* to wed, else I would be a maiden still." The girls laughed; three sisters, three friends.

Chapter TWENTY-ONE

Nicholas paused outside the bedchamber, his mind reeling with what Celestia had just revealed. He'd been drawn by the feminine laughter coming from the bedchamber. How was he to know that he was the butt of such merriment?

He had thought, given the conversation with all of her family yesterday, that she might stay at Falcon Keep because she loved him. After what he had just heard, he had no doubt she would leave.

Closing his eyes, he clenched his jaw tight. Did he dare to offer her the annulment? Or should he hold her captive, and never tell her that he had her freedom in the palm of his hand?

Lord Robert cleared his throat. "Spying on the chicks, were ye?"

Nicholas jumped. "Where the devil did you come from?"

"My chamber." Robert pointed to the room he'd just vacated across the hall.

"Oh."

"Nicholas? Have ye spent much time around the ladies?"

Snorting, Nicholas said, "I was raised in a monastery, what think you? Women, yes; ladies, no."

Lord Robert nodded in comprehension and put his arm around his son-in-law's shoulders. "Ye have much to learn about the magpies, then. Let me share a few vital pieces of information that will help ye stay happily married."

"Sir?"

They walked down the stairs and into the main room. The Montehue women had cleaned and aired out the place, providing a few feminine touches that made a keep a home.

"Ye must always remember that you are king in your own keep. If ye let the wench get the upper hand, ye might never get it back! And when she chatters on and on about her day, ye don't have to really listen, but nod now and again, as if ye've heard every word."

A loud crash sounded behind them, and Deirdre walked out of the downstairs sewing room where Celestia had been staying while ill. She dropped the soap-filled bucket and rag, sending suds all over the floor.

"What else were ye saying, Robert?"

Lord Robert dropped his arm from Nicholas's shoulders and stammered, "Uh, I was simply giving the lad a few helpful hints, so that he can have the happy marriage that you and I share."

Deirdre tapped her foot.

"And I was mentioning that it was most important to listen carefully to whatever Celestia said, to show that he cared."

Deirdre threw the rag at him, hitting him square in the chest. "So you say, my loving husband. How about dumping this bucket of water into the moat for me, then?"

Lord Robert immediately fetched the bucket. "Yes, dear."

When he returned, Nicholas's laughter echoed in the room, but the man himself was gone.

She wanted her husband.

Letting Gali and Ela help her dress meant that she was prepared to be as feminine as she possibly could be. Celestia applied scented powder behind her knees and kept her hair unbound and free. Ela brushed it until it crackled and shone. "Such beautiful hair you have, all long and wavy. I much prefer it to my own mess of curls."

Celestia met her younger sister's eyes in the mirror and remembered when Nicholas had bolstered her own self-confidence. It seemed that most everyone felt they were not perfect.

"You are a lovely young lady, who will most certainly have men tripping over their feet. Your eyes are the color of emeralds; your neck is long and slender. Promise me, Ela, that you will see these things in the future. Your hair is the perfect foil for your skin. Will she not be the loveliest of us all, Gali?"

Galiana wrinkled her nose as she tapped her chin. She walked from one angle to the next, as if undecided. Ela squirmed uncomfortably.

"By heavens, I think ye may be correct. 'Tis a good thing you're so much younger than me, Ela dear. I would hate to have to compete against you for the men in the marriage mart."

Ela blushed and the older girls shared a smile.

Proving she was not just another pretty face, Ela changed the subject in order to escape being the object under discussion. "Why are you spending so much time on your looks this day, 'Tia?"

Gali smirked. "I know. She wants to make sure Nicholas falls in love with her."

Celestia smoothed her hair and refused to answer, lamenting her small bosoms, instead.

"I truly wish that I had more, here, than I do. And spending the last week sick and puking has made them even smaller."

"Stop whining. You look gorgeous." Gali laughed. "And it is long past time for you to go and seduce your husband."

Ela sat back, confused. "You don't know that Nicholas loves you? Your auras spike red whenever you are near each other," she sighed. "It's sort of sweet."

Later, Celestia still wanted her husband, yet he was still nowhere to be found. She'd searched all through the keep. The knights had not seen Nicholas, nor had her family. She eyed the tower. He had said that he would wait for her, but perhaps he had grown too curious. She knew that feeling quite well.

She went down the long, deserted hallway and called into the entrance leading to the tower, "Nicholas?"

Suddenly she knew he had to be there. She ducked through the hole in the wall and faced the stairs. She'd tumbled down them, but it had been Maude who had pulled her. She remembered the way the lock had crumbled to rust beneath her hands, and the odd feeling that she had not been alone.

She drew in a breath for courage, picking up the faint scent of apples, and climbed the circular stairs.

The door was ajar. She pushed inward and gasped.

"Oh, my!" Tapestries hung all around, vibrant and bright. Dust-free furniture gleamed in the sunlight that came through the arrow slits. A large door led to the battlements that circled around the outside of the tower, and it, too, was open. "Nicholas?"

She walked to the center of the room, her feet cushioned by soft furs.

He came in through the door from the battlements, looking wind-tousled from the fresh air.

"Celestia?" He ducked his head, but not before she saw some deep emotion in his gray eyes. "I am sorry, but I found I could not wait after all. The tower seemed to call to me. How are you?"

Waving a hand through the air, she quipped, "A bit out of breath from the climb, my lord." She decided to blame her racing heart on the stairs, rather than the sight of her husband. He looked . . . closed to her. Why?

She affected a trill laugh. "This is a veritable sanctuary,

Nicholas. 'Tis beautiful and so well cared for. It looks as if it were vacated just this morning, and not twenty years ago."

He stepped farther into the room, his steps reluctant. "Aye. I can almost remember my mother here."

"Sit. And tell me everything, Nicholas." She sat on a padded bench. "There is room for you here." She fluttered her lashes and smiled becomingly.

He sat on a three-legged stool instead. "What is there to tell?" He stared at her with pain in his eyes. "Celestia! You do not have to act anymore. I heard what you said to your sisters this morn."

She blushed, thinking of how they had discussed his good looks and noble spirit. She widened her eyes. Had he heard them plan his seduction? Was he ready to say that he loved her, too? "You did?"

"Aye." He sighed, then folded his hands together and met her eyes. "I would offer you an annulment."

"You what?" What happened to poetry and flowers? Love songs? Oh, but the minstrels had it all wrong and she'd made a fool of herself, believing he had come to care for her. "I see." She looked out the door toward the blue sky. How could the sun be shining on a day like today?

"You released my family from any obligation to your father. You saved my brothers from the baron's retribution. And now you want to release me from my vows. I see." She blinked back the tears of hurt; she would not cry! It did not matter that her heart and soul were breaking. She would not lay the pieces at his feet.

"I have the holy relic of Saint James the Apostle. The true relic. I made my father give it to me so that it could be returned to its rightful place."

"Oh, you are so noble, Nicholas . . ." her tone made an art of sarcasm.

His black brows quirked with temper. "What say you? That I am *not* noble?"

She shot to her feet and sank two inches into the plush furs. "Aye, you are noble, you are kind, you are generous, you are handsome. Well, I don't give a fig for all of that!"

Nicholas sat back, stunned by her ire.

"You're still as stupid as a rock!"

He jumped up from the stool. "Stupid? Aye, I suppose I am stupid. I offered you an annulment so that you would have the choice to wed me or nay!" With one large step he had her in his arms. "I retract the offer, Celestia. I cannot let you go."

He kissed her brutally, then stepped back. "I love you, and I thought you loved me, too. But then I heard you tell your sisters that ye would rather be unwed, still."

Celestia licked her bruised lips, drawn to Nicholas's display of passion like a child to a sweet. "You love me, Nicholas?" She threw herself forward and tackled him to the large white fur on the floor. She dropped kisses all over his face and hair and lips, wherever she could reach.

Nicholas wrestled himself on top, pinning her. "You won't leave me?"

"My heart was yours from the moment you walked into Montehue Manor—so belligerent and confused."

"I was bloody well drunk! And I could not believe that they wanted me to wed someone as beautiful and fragile as you . . ."

"I am not fragile, Nicholas." She nipped his lower lip with her teeth.

"True, you are one of the strongest people I've ever known."

She curled her arms around his chest and linked her fingers behind his back so that he was locked to her. "Are you finally at peace with yourself, Nicholas?"

He looked into her eyes and didn't see the separate colors. He saw love shining at him, beckoning him to come closer. "Aye, I have found peace." He leaned down to place a soft kiss on her inviting lips.

She pressed forward, molding her body to his. "I've been a married woman for some time now, Nicholas, and yet I remain a virgin. Is it not a good time to remedy that?"

"I . . ." he paused.

"What is it?" Celestia didn't care for the way he distanced himself from her, so she tugged at his hair and brought his gaze to hers. "Tell me."

"You know that I was captured."

"Yes! So?"

"My body is not a pretty one . . . I have scars all over my back and legs."

"I have seen all of your scars, Nicholas. Do ye really think I care about that?" She scoffed. "Besides, I'm short. I have not the perfect body, either. But would I deny this chance at loving? Scars and—oh! Do you think I will burn you?"

"It wouldn't matter if you did."

Celestia pushed at his solid chest. "I won't. I think

your injured spirit was so much a part of the wounds that they needed to be reopened to finally heal."

Nicholas grabbed her hands and rolled so that she straddled him.

"I agree. Those scars pained me. The memory of being tortured, of being violated, was a sickness inside me that festered. Thanks be to you and your love, I am healed."

She brought his wrists to her lips and kissed the smooth flesh there. "Does this hurt?"

"No."

Celestia could feel the length of him harden beneath her thigh, and her belly warmed. She leaned over to kiss his full lips. "And that?"

"It's heaven, and you are my angel," he whispered against her mouth. His hot breath made her heart skip and her pulse flutter. She pressed her breasts against his chest, her nipples aching.

"I would not hurt you, Nicholas." Celestia could feel the power within her build from her center and spread through her veins. She could heal an entire village, if it was true and he loved her, too.

"I know that. I fear I will somehow hurt you, unintentionally." He squirmed beneath her, and she clenched her thighs around his waist.

"Nicholas, you are noble." She kissed him again, nipping at his earlobe. She could be content to breathe in his unique scent for the rest of her days.

His hips jerked. "'Tia, I would rather not be so noble. I want you to be my wife in truth."

"I thought you would never ask!"

Nicholas groaned with lust at the eager anticipation in his wife's eyes. "I feel like an untried lad."

"Then we can find our way together."

He stood, his hose uncomfortably tight against his throbbing groin. Nicholas's mouth was dry, and his heart thudded against his ribcage. Finally, he could touch all of her. Caress her flesh, taste her skin. Scowling, he reminded himself to go slow, damn it, and not to hurt her.

He shut the door to the tower and turned around, shocked to his toes to see Celestia standing in naught but her chemise and stockings. The cloth was sheer, and the sunlight through the open door showed the curve of leg and hip, the darker skin of her peaked nipples as she smiled shyly in invitation.

With shaking fingers, he removed his tunic, then his linen shirt. She stepped toward him, her hand outstretched. He shivered as she ran her fingers over his bare chest. She walked around him, tracing a path across each scar from the lash of a whip. He bowed his head as she kissed each reminder of his captivity.

"You're shaking, Nicholas. Am I hurting you?"

His voice was hoarse with need as he answered, "Nay."

"I am not burning you?" Her tone was cautious.

"Aye, I am burning, but not in a way that hurts." He turned around and caught her in his arms. "Soon you will be burning in the same manner as I."

He kissed her deeply, and her arms wrapped themselves around his neck. She pressed her breasts into his chest, and he caught her up and placed her on the bed.

He laid her down on the soft, feather-filled comforter and kneeled beside her. He kissed her hair, her forehead, her nose. That stubborn chin. "I love you, 'Tia."

She sat up and trustingly allowed him to remove her chemise. "And I you, Nicholas." She lay back, expecting him to join her on the bed.

Instead he went to her feet and removed her delicate slippers with their happy little bells. He kissed her toes, encased in sheer stockings. He laved his way up the back of her legs and untied the laces at her knees with his teeth. He pulled them down, caressing her calves as he went.

Celestia's face was flushed, her chest heaving. "I am getting most warm, Nicholas . . ."

He grinned, his teeth white in his swarthy face. "I would hope to have you hot." He ran his hands up her thighs and across her midriff. Everywhere he touched with his hands, he placed a kiss.

She shied as he hovered over the nest of blond curls at the apex of her legs. She jumped as he touched her woman's place. "Are you supposed to do that?"

"Aye, Celestia. And this." His fingers parted the folds of her flesh, and his thumb stroked the tight pearl inside.

She moaned. He applied a touch more pressure, the pad of his thumb flicking the bud. Keeping her eyes tightly closed, she clutched at Nicholas's shoulders. He lifted her knees, and replaced his thumb with his tongue.

"Nicholas!" She sat up. "I have never heard of this before." Her eyes were panicked and her skin slick.

"Trust me, 'Tia." He flicked the pearl with his tongue and inserted a single finger inside her, stretching her, preparing her body for his. He moved his finger in sure, rapid motions and felt her body tense as she reached climax.

She screamed her satisfaction. He let her catch her breath as he traced circular patterns over her belly.

"Nicholas? I never thought—" She tried to cover her body, suddenly shy.

"Oh, no, my little angel, we are not through yet."

"Hmmm, there's more . . ."

He gestured toward his erection, evident beneath his tight-fitting hose.

"I didn't realize you were still clothed." She got to her knees. "You distracted me," she accused with a laugh, determined to use the same care on him that he had lavished on her while removing her chemise.

Keeping her eyes averted from his groin, she shyly peeled his leggings from him, revealing muscled thighs and strong calves.

"What's this?"

"Nothing, a slash. Petyr caught me with the tip of his sword."

"But Nicholas, I can heal this." She didn't wait, but tucked her feet beneath her bare bottom and hovered her hands over the gash. Heat spilled readily from her fingertips, and Nicholas groaned in pleasure. She concentrated on knitting the skin, caressing the area with featherlight touches until the flesh was smooth.

Then she moved her hands, still hot and sensitive, up and down the rest of his leg. "My gift is back," she said with amazement, feeling the air crackle with energy.

"Magic—you never lost it, for I loved you always."

"You did?" She looked up from where she'd been massaging his calf, then sat back in surprise as his manhood rose from the triangle of black curls between his thighs.

She swallowed, her breath caught in her throat. "*That* is supposed to fit inside of me?"

Nicholas gave her a masculine look as old as Adam. "Aye, with great pleasure, if done properly."

"All right, Nicholas. Would you have me kiss it?"

Nicholas's smug look left his face. He kissed her on the lips, placing his hips close to hers. "I would not last to take your virginity. Men are not fashioned as women; it takes them some time to climax again."

Her eyes were pools of sensual promise. "But would you not like it?"

His member throbbed against her leg. "Aye. Mayhap too well is what I am trying to say. Can you not feel my desire for you?"

She nodded and reached down between their bodies. She closed her warm hand around his girth, and stroked the length of him. "You make my blood soar like a falcon in flight."

Nicholas's dark gray eyes turned black with passion, and he traced the column of her throat to the point where her pulse beat madly.

She nibbled her lower lip and ran her thumb over the moist tip of his penis. "'Tis like costly velvet." A drop of moisture formed, and her body hummed. "I am getting warm again, Nicholas." She smiled and arched against his leg, his manhood firmly in her hand.

They kissed, their tongues twisting and tasting one another. She couldn't stop touching him. Finally, after all this time, he was hers to love. Celestia pressed her aching breasts into Nicholas, who caressed first one, then the other. He took a nipple between his teeth and tugged, sending a spiral of desire through Celestia's belly.

"They are perfect, 'Tia. Round and firm." He suckled the other breast until she was on fire, throbbing with anticipation. When he flipped her to her back, she eagerly spread her legs to allow Nicholas between them. He positioned his manhood, teasing her opening with the moist tip of his penis. "It may hurt this first time, 'Tia, but only for a moment. You are ready for me, and I for you."

He thrust inside, his mouth capturing her shocked cry. He was sheathed in warmth, and his arms shook with effort to stay still.

He looked down at Celestia's face.

Disappointment warred with her earlier satiation. She said smartly, "I see why you wait to tell a woman that it will hurt, Nicholas. I might not have done it, otherwise." She sniffed, as if he had tricked her on purpose.

He kissed her damp forehead and moved his hips slightly. Her eyes flew open. He rocked his hips, slowly, but with great precision. "Never?"

She moved with him, feeling desire build with each thrust until her entire body was burning with need. She threw back her head, allowing Nicholas access to the sensitive column of her throat; he nibbled and kissed her as she held his hips to her body with her knees. "Nicholas, 'tis hot! Very hot!"

Being the noble man that he was, he pushed forward to put out the flame, sending both of them flying with pleasure to heaven and back.

Chapter TWENTY-TWO

Nicholas held Celestia in his arms, watching her as she dozed. He had never been so content in his life. She opened one eye in a languid manner. "I can feel you stare . . . Are you disappointed, Nicholas?"

He laughed. "I was simply wondering how I could deserve such a treasure." He pinched her bottom.

"Ow! This is how you treat your treasures?"

Nicholas caressed the injured cheek. "I was assuring myself that you were real."

She placed her hand at the juncture of his thighs, her fingers in the ebony curls at the base. His member pulsed against her hand, and she snuggled closer. "Methinks there is at least one part of you that knows this is no dream, my lord."

He pulled her on top of him, content to have her so. For a fleeting instant he recalled Leah, then he firmly, and forever, banished her from his mind. He put his hands on the sides of his beloved wife's face and claimed her soft lips. "You've healed me, 'Tia."

Celestia smiled a mysterious smile and slid atop his seeking manhood. "It certainly feels like magic to me, Nicholas."

It was some time later that the door to the tower flew open with a bang. The tower walls shook, and plaster fell from the ceiling. Nicholas wrapped the linen cover around Celestia and protected her from sight with his body.

Grainne Kat stalked in carrying a short sword in her hands. "Ye've defiled the tower!"

Nicholas scrabbled for his hose, which lay puddled on the floor with his undershirt. He slipped them on, tossing Celestia her tunic.

"What right have you to barge in on my wife and me in my own bloody keep?" His fury was as cold and clipped as his voice, hiding the fear he had for Celestia.

"What right? I have kept this tower sacred for nigh on twenty years! This is the Lady Esmerada's tower, and she detests strangers."

"I am no stranger; I am her son."

"Pah! She didn't want you." Grainne Kat thrust the sword at him. "Why do ye think she sent ye away?"

Nicholas eyed the round tower room, calculating a way out. The wise woman's hatred was cold, and it sapped the warm energy within. Celestia donned her kirtle and slid her hand into his.

"She lies," Celestia said softly, noting the chill of the

room just as a gust of air blew in from the battlements. She rubbed her arms. The chill settled at the nape of her neck.

Nay! Not a time for visions she thought. Stepping closer to Nicholas, she thought to protect him from this madwoman who'd been jealous of Nicholas his entire life.

Suddenly, Celestia was one with the vision. She was not alone in her body or mind. Frightened, she opened her mouth.

"Viperous, vile woman! Get ye gone from here."

Celestia recognized the voice as that of Nicholas's mother.

Nicholas dropped her hand and backed away, staring at her in disbelief. Grainne Kat's wrinkled face paled.

Celestia found her hand being raised, her finger pointed at Grainne. *"Ye've caused enough harm to this family; let them find peace. Yer son is dead, Kat, did ye know?"*

Grainne's sword dropped point down into the floor of the chamber, and she leaned heavily against it. "Joseph?"

"'Twas yer bitterness toward the baron that has caused all of this unhappiness. I had forgiven, Kat, why could ye not?" The voice that came from Celestia's mouth was soft and deep with a Scottish brogue. *"I loved Robbie MacIntosh, 'tis true. Just as you loved his brother. We would have been sisters.* Piuthars."

Grainne's anger flashed from her wrinkled face. "I canna listen to ya! Ye forgot all about Robbie and revenge once ye held yer bairn in yer arms. This was *our* keep! For the clan, and yet you let it lie."

"Yer anger was always dangerous, Kat."

Nicholas's dark gray eyes grew damp and stormy as he

listened to the byplay. He held out his hand to her, well, to his mother, and Celestia let their fingertips touch.

"*Machair?*"

"*Nicholas!*" The voice was filled with love and sorrow, then another wind gust racked the room, knocking against the tapestries along the wall.

Celestia wobbled weakly, bereft of the force inside.

Nicholas enclosed her in his arms, keeping her safe against his hard chest.

Celestia, her voice once again her own, said accusingly to Kat, "You are the Lady Katherine. The friend who took care of the Lady Esmerada as she went mad from grief. The woman who sent Nicholas away."

Celestia's brow furrowed, and she pushed away from Nicholas. Her body shook with indignant anger. "You have lied all along—Lady Esmerada loved her son, I know that as if she were still alive." She placed one hand alongside her head. "I had thought I was dreaming, but Nicholas, your mother came to me when I was so sick from Grainne's poison. She told me—" Celestia stopped, confused. What had the kind woman whispered to her?

She never heard the arrow that almost impaled her. Nicholas knocked her to the ground, furious that his dagger was in his tunic and out of reach.

What kind of knight kept his weapons out of hand?

All three pairs of eyes turned to the wall to see Maude standing before a secret entrance to the chamber. The tapestry that had hidden the door lay at her feet.

"Will ye not die, bitch?" Maude's hair was a rat's nest of

black tangles, leaves and twigs ensnared in the mess.

She aimed the bow with another arrow notched to fly and pointed it at Celestia, who had scrambled to her feet. Nicholas pushed her behind him and faced the new threat. He would protect Celestia with his life, but God, how he hated to feel so powerless.

Maude laughed, the sound as shrill as a broken lute. "Look at ye! Frightened as a doe in the forest." She ground out between giggles, "Nicholas is *mine.* Do ye hear me? I've tried shooting ye, and ye get me instead! I've tried pulling you down the stairs, I've tried poisoning ye, and still ye breathe. Would that I had your magical powers, I would not be rotting away in these damn woods, alone."

Celestia hissed, but Nicholas would not let her step around him.

"I want no other, Maude," Nicholas said firmly. "I would never be yours. My heart belongs to my wife. Put the bow and arrow down, Maude, and we can discuss this rationally."

Celestia snorted.

Maude snickered. "Ye've not had a taste of a real woman, Nicholas." With one hand she tore her dress to reveal her breasts. "I warrant she has none as fine as these, eh?"

Nicholas felt Celestia press her eating dagger into his palm. His fingers clasped around the handle as he said convincingly to Maude, "Well, Maude, my wife has finer. Lay the bow and arrow aside, and let us talk about this further."

Celestia punched him in the back while Grainne Kat yelled, "Nay! Maude, ye daft chick! He'll not marry ye now. Where did I go wrong?" Grainne Kat's voice warbled with grief as she straightened to her full height. "It was all for naught." She held the sword in her hands, the blade steady. "Ye've killed me only son. Ye'll pay, both of ye." She stepped forward as Maude gasped.

"Joe is dead?"

Grainne ignored her daughter, focusing on Celestia and Nicholas. "Who do ye think kept the stories of the curse alive? Who do ye think sent word to the baron of the curse? I did! I tried to keep this heap of stone going, but Esmerada stopped me at every turn. She no longer cared for war! She wanted to raise her son . . . I thought I'd bide me time, for if the bairn was Robbie's, as we thought, I knew Esmerada would change her tune. But once your features became more pronounced, we both knew it was not Robbie's get that she'd nurtured at her breast. Nay!"

Spittle flew from the old woman's mouth. "The child was the spawn of the devil who had killed her love—but would she put the child aside? Nay. She chose to forgive the brat his father, while sending a curse on the baron for not claiming ye."

Grainne's eyes were wild with rage. "What would we have done had the baron chosen to come back here ta live? How could she treat her bonnie Robbie MacIntosh so poorly by loving the brat of her rapist? How could she have forgotten such a massacre? She let Ian die a rebel's death with no help from her, her, her own lover's brother."

She lifted the short, yet deadly, sword. "And my husband. Ian and I had to be secretly handfast, as she would not even allow the MacIntosh clan in Falcon Keep."

Celestia darted from behind her husband. She said with utmost certainty, "You claim the Lady Esmerada was your friend, yet you poisoned her to gain control of the keep. You poisoned her slowly, with your dark herbs and treacherous tongue! It was not the Lady Esmerada who threatened to throw Nicholas from the battlements—it was you."

Grainne's arms faltered. "How could ye know that?"

Celestia shook her head, which was foggy and unclear. "It matters not—what did you hope to gain? You killed your best friend and sent her son away from his home and his mother. You had no claim to this keep. You kept alive the talk of the curse. The haunting of the north tower . . . you scared away the peasants and servants, but why?"

Grainne Kat shrugged, then steadied her arms. "I remained loyal to the Scottish rebels and wore the MacIntosh plaid with pride. I knew that Nicholas would be back someday, and I could again bide me time."

Nicholas pulled Celestia close to him. "Why must we talk with weapons drawn? You have an unfair advantage if we are to work this problem through."

Maude screamed, "I want nothing worked out! *Machair* promised me the keep and you for my husband. Ye were not supposed to come back already married. Was he, Mother?"

Grainne sucked her lower lip; her arms were tiring. "I would have bound ye to Maude, and then Falcon Keep could have been the saving of the rebels. Those who are left."

"Celestia has ruined everything, curse her," Maude

panted, her once pretty eyes now glittering like broken shards of stained glass.

Nicholas stepped forward, the dagger hidden in his palm. "Grainne, I am married to Celestia, and I would not undo the tie. Mayhap there is another way we can help. Let us share some wine, some food."

He could feel Celestia bristling behind him.

Grainne Kat lunged toward him, the sword raised. "Food? Wine? Ye killed me son. Ye must die!"

"I didn't kill him." Nicholas sensed the movement just before she jumped forward; he swerved quickly, taking Celestia with him to the floor. At the same instant Maude let loose a white-feathered arrow.

Grainne screamed.

"Nay! *Machair!*"

Grainne Kat fell to the ground, the arrow quivering from the center of her poisonous heart.

Her wild eyes found Maude's. "Me *dochair*, how could ye?"

Maude dropped to her knees, cradling her mother's head in her lap. "I didna mean it, I did not see you running! I only thought to kill them both. They're rotten, and they've ended it all." Maude sobbed and petted her mother's gray hair.

Celestia calmly stood, her figure wavering with the over-image of a taller, ebony-haired woman. "'*Tis over, Katherine.*"

Grainne's eyes widened, then closed. "Aye, Esmerada, 'tis over."

Maude let loose a bloodcurdling yell and let her

mother's body fall with a thump. She shot to her feet and grabbed Celestia by the hair, murder in her eyes.

Nicholas caught the woman by the shoulders, the small dagger now openly in his hand. He said, "I am so sorry, 'Tia," as he slashed down.

Maude screamed, and Celestia fell to the floor.

Ela clucked over Celestia. "Now, 'Tia, it does not look so bad."

They stood in front of the mirror. Deirdre raised her brows. "Ye could just keep it covered with a veil, and no one would know."

"I hate to wear a veil at all times. And besides, Nicholas would still see."

Galiana nodded her head; her own locks bouncing as she practically swooned. "That is very true. Nicholas saved your life, 'Tia, just like a knight of great chivalry should do."

Celestia's temper flashed. "Aye! But he hacked off my hair to do it! I look ridiculous! I am a shorn sheep, a, a . . ."

Deirdre laughed. "A woman who has realized that she had more vanity than she thought, eh, daughter?"

Blushing, she said, "Nicholas liked my hair."

"I am so glad that this has turned out to be a love match after all." Deirdre hugged her daughter from behind.

Celestia threw her mother's arms off, her chin tilted high. "It will be a love match once his beautiful hair is as lopsided as my own."

Nicholas poked his head in the chamber full of women. "Did I hear you calling for my beautiful head?"

Celestia's brandished the sharp blade in her palm. "Aye! Come sit here, and let me brush your hair."

Galiana squealed, "Nay! Nicholas, she means to shear one side of it."

"Traitor!" Ela threw a pillow at her older sister.

Celestia leaned back with a sigh. "I suppose she is right; you are much too handsome to walk around with uneven locks."

Nicholas chuckled, a sound so full of manly pride it made her knees tremble. He bravely came inside and kissed her cheek. "If saving your life was not proof enough of my love for you, then shear away."

"Honorable brute, can I get no sympathy at all?" She tossed the blade to the vanity table.

Lord Robert knocked on the partially opened door. "Did you start the revels without me, then? I've brought the good Father Michael upstairs with me. I hope ye're all decent." He said loudly to the priest, "Ye never know, with a gaggle of women."

"Enter," Celestia called.

The priest's one eye glittered with joy. "My Lady Celestia, I am so relieved to see ye safe. I have Maude in custody with the nuns. She's confessed to the killing of your good servant, Bess, and shooting Viola, and other things." He shuddered.

"But why?" Celestia asked, her eyes tearing as she remembered her sassy maid.

The priest shifted his feet. "It seems Bess saw her sneaking into the tower and thought to investigate. At the first, Maude insists that it was just an accident, that she did not mean to hit her so hard on the head."

Nicholas scoffed, "I think not—what about the apron tied around the girl's neck? That was no accident; that was deliberate. Poor Bess was an innocent."

Father Michael made the sign of the cross. "Maude says that she could not let Bess live after she had seen the secret entrance into the tower. Bess was unconscious from the blow to the head, but still breathing, so Maude finished her off by strangling her with the apron strings. Then she dragged the body in the moat, and hoped it would sink."

Nicholas shook his head. "The knight's bodies did, and if she had helped Joseph dispose of them, she would have known that."

Galiana blinked rapidly. "Poor Bess!"

Father Michael nodded his head and forced a smile. "The nuns are saying prayers for Bess, that her murdered soul will find the light of heaven. And as for Maude—she is in solitary confinement. Those nuns could give lessons on earthly retribution. If Maude is not sorry now for the sins she has committed, she soon will be."

He said in a loud whisper to Lord Robert, "Now talk about a gaggle of women!"

"Father," Celestia exclaimed. "And have you prayed for Joseph, as well?"

"Yea. He was a simple man, doing as he was taught. I pray that God will forgive his misguided sins."

The good priest shuffled his stance and peered closely at her. "Is something amiss with your hair, my lady?"

Celestia pouted. "Hand me the veil, Mother."

Father Michael puffed with pride and clasped his hands. "On to a happier subject—a ceremony?"

Galiana sighed with delight. "Aye, a renewal of vows in the old apple orchard."

Lord Robert clapped his hand on Nicholas's shoulder. "A true welcome into the family."

Nicholas smiled past the grunt of pain stuck in his throat. "Any more welcomes like that and I won't make it out the door."

Robert flushed.

Ed and Ned raced into the room, their tunics the same ruby red as Nicholas's. "Viola said Sally has everything ready; we have but to show ourselves."

Nicholas gazed at his wife, a vision in ivory and gold. The others around them faded from his mind, and every fiber in his being focused on Celestia. She stood, then walked to him with love shining from her eyes and placed her hand on his arm. He leaned down and captured her lips in a kiss that both promised and demanded.

Ela giggled and Galiana blushed a pretty pink as the older women smiled in remembrance. Lord Robert huffed. "Enough of that! Ye're married, now!"

Deirdre punched her husband in the arm. "And since when has that stopped you from behaving like a man claiming his bride?"

Lord Robert's fair face turned a hot scarlet.

She pursed her lips smugly. "That's right!"

Evianne pulled her granddaughter aside as the boisterous Montehues filed out for the reaffirmation of vows beneath the early summer sun.

"Remember, *cariad*, that *new* love is splendid." She bent down and whispered, "*True* love is uneven hair and onion breath."

Epilogue

Five months later
Santiago de Compostela, Spain

Nicholas, are we there yet?"

He used his knees to turn around on Brenin, the loyal stallion that had been one of many gifts from his wife. "Aye, a bit farther, 'Tia. How are you feeling?"

Her veil billowed in the slight breeze as she shouted, "How do you think I am feeling? My back aches, my hind end is sore, and I am bloody hot!"

She immediately retracted her complaints. "I am sorry, Nicholas. It's not hot. The rain is falling, the wind won't stop howling. I am hot. Burning from the inside out. I am honored to make this pilgrimage with you. All the way to Spain." Her eyes watered and she rubbed her swollen belly. "I didn't know I was pregnant with ten babies when we left! I'm carrying a litter, Nicholas, and you just don't understand."

Nicholas hid his smile as best he could. Ceffyl carried her rider with care, and they had traveled with no hurry. He thought his wife beautiful with her added flesh; she fairly glowed with good health.

He bit his lip and gave her a wink. She was only five months along, yet her frame was so petite that the babe took up most of it.

He cantered back to her and offered her his hand. "I told you that we should have stayed in that pretty village along the coast. We could have made this journey after the babe is born."

She stuck her chin in the air. "Nay. We said that we would make this pilgrimage, and we shall. But I want our child born at Falcon Keep, Nicholas, so no dawdling."

"I could have come alone, Celestia, and you would not be discomfited."

She turned on him, a round and feisty warrior. "You'll not leave me behind! You said you wanted me to make this journey with you. Are you trying to get rid of me, Nicholas?" Her cheeks pinkened. "I am too fat!"

"You are lovely. I am only thinking of you, 'Tia."

She sniffed and studied the landscape, refusing to be mollified.

He chuckled and looked to his men. Forrester doted upon Celestia's every need, even before she thought of it. All doubts as to the knight's loyalty had been put to rest when he'd arrived, with Ed and Ned and Brenin, to help him escape Peregrine Castle without being killed. It seemed the twins had found him in the village stocks, and set him free. Henry, Willy, and Bertram had sworn their fealty, and he knew that any of the four would lay down their lives for his wife.

He was more than content with his lot in life, even if his wife did fluctuate from tears to joy faster than he could keep up.

Nicholas led the way into the village that housed the Cathedral of Santiago. He dismounted before the shrine, bowing his head. He had arrived at the end of this pilgrimage a better man than when he'd planned it so long ago. He helped Celestia down from Ceffyl.

They walked hand in hand through the doors of the cathedral. There, beneath a high altar, lay a marble sarcophagus containing the body of Saint James the Apostle.

They each went to their knees. "I'll need help getting back up again, Nicholas," Celestia said playfully.

"I imagine, 'Tia, that being pregnant is akin to wearing armor."

"If you were to wear it all on your belly, I suppose!"

"We have traveled far to be here," he whispered. "This is truly a holy place."

"Yea. So take your time, husband, in asking for your boon."

He looked at Celestia in surprise. "I have no boon to ask for! I but want to give thanks."

Her heart fluttered. He was such a good man. She bowed her head, sending her gratitude, as well.

Nicholas kissed the velvet box before laying it at the base of the sarcophagus. The sun beat down upon his head through the stained-glass windows, creating a multicolored halo around his body.

Celestia's heart turned. She placed a hand on her stomach. Or was that the babe?

A foot kicked her in the ribs.

Light and warmth suddenly bathed her from the inside out, and she felt both filled and surrounded with love and knowledge. She basked in contentment.

After a time Nicholas nudged his wife, who appeared to be in some sort of a trance. "Celestia? There are others behind us awaiting their turn to kneel."

She allowed him to haul her to her feet. "I am ready, Nicholas."

They walked together out of the cathedral and into the sunshine. "Thank you, Celestia, for coming with me on this journey. I know it has not been one of luxury or comfort."

"Oh, hush, Nicholas!" She rubbed her belly. "James and I are enjoying every minute."

Nicholas stopped. "James?"

She grinned. "Yes. James. A fat and healthy baby boy who will have a wild Scot's heart along with some stubborn English honor. I am most pleased, Nicholas."

Nicholas laughed. "I am delighted that I could accommodate you, my lady."

The smile slipped from her face. "My knees are sore from kneeling so long on the cold floor, and I am hungry. Yes, hungry! I want some fruit—nay—I want bread and gravy." She waddled toward Ceffyl and allowed Forrester to assist her onto the horse.

"Nay, not bread and gravy. Mutton with mint? Beef and lemon? Eels in butter? I vow I am starved, husband."

Nicholas gave a last glance filled with thanks toward the saint who had helped him find his soul.

Saint James the Apostle and *Someone's* sense of humor.

Blessed be.

Don't miss Traci E. Hall's next
Medallion Press novel:

ISBN# 9781933836560
Mass Market Paperback / Paranormal Romance
US $7.95 / CDN $8.95
JUNE 2009

From the author of FIRST, THERE IS A RIVER

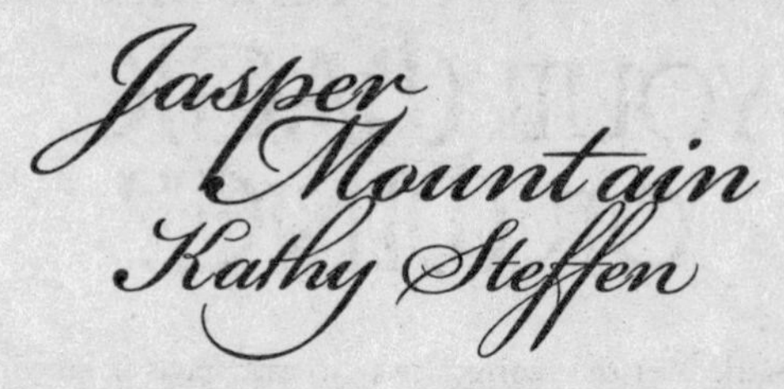

Two lost souls struggle to find their way in the unforgiving West of 1873...

Jack Buchanan, a worker at the Jasper Mining Company, is sure of his place in the outside world, but has lost his faith, hope, and heart to the tragedy of a fire.

Foreign born and raised, Milena Shabanov flees from a home she loves to the strange and barbaric America. A Romani blessed with "the sight," she is content in the company of visions and spirit oracles, but finds herself lost and alone in a brutal mining town with little use for women.

Surrounded by inhumane working conditions at the mine, senseless death, and overwhelming greed, miners begin disappearing and the officers of the mine don't care.

Tempers flare and Jack must decide where he stands: with the officers and mining president—Victor Creely—to whom Jack owes his life, or with the miners, whose lives are worth less to the company than pack animals. Milena, sensing deep despair and death in a mining town infested with restless spirits, searches for answers to the workers' disappearances. But she can't trust anyone, especially not Jack Buchanan, a man haunted by his own past.

ISBN# 9781933836584
Trade Paperback / Historical Fiction
US $15.95 / CDN $17.95
NOVEMBER 2008

ANN MACELA

YOUR MAGIC OR MINE?

A battle over the "correct" way to cast spells is brewing in the magic practitioner community. Theoretical mathematician Marcus Forscher has created an equation, a formula to bring the science of casting into the twenty-first century. Botanist Gloriana Morgan, however, maintains spell casting is an art, as individual as each caster, and warns against throwing out old casting methods and forcing use of the new. A series of heated debates across the country ensues.

Enter the soulmate phenomenon, an ancient compulsion that brings practitioners together and has persuasive techniques and powers—the soulmate imperative—to convince the selected couple they belong together. Marcus and Gloriana, prospective soulmates, want nothing to do with each other, however. To make matters worse, their factions have turned to violence. One adherent in particular, blaming Marcus and Gloriana for the mess, wants to destroy the soulmates.

Something's got to give, or there will be dire consequences. The magic will work for them…or against them. But with two powerful practitioners bent on having their own way, which will it be—Your Magic Or Mine?—and if they don't unite, will either survive?

ISBN# 9781933836324
Mass Market Paperback / Paranormal Romance
US $7.95 / CDN $8.95
OCTOBER 2008

A devil's bargain.

"The photograph must be damning, indisputably so. I mean to see Caledonia Rivers not only ruined but vanquished. Vanquished, St. Claire, I'll settle for nothing less."

Known as The Maid of Mayfair for her unassailable virtue, unwavering resolve, and quiet dignity, suffragette leader, Caledonia ~ Callie — Rivers is the perfect counter for detractors' portrayal of the women as rabble rousers, lunatics, even whores. But a high-ranking enemy within the government will stop at nothing to ensure that the Parliamentary bill to grant the vote to females dies in the Commons — including ruining the reputation of the Movement's chief spokeswoman.

After a streak of disastrous luck at the gaming tables threatens to land him at the bottom of the Thames, photographer Hadrian St. Claire reluctantly agrees to seduce the beautiful suffragist leader and then use his camera to capture her fall from grace. Posing as the photographer commissioned to make her portrait for the upcoming march on Parliament, Hadrian infiltrates Callie's inner circle. But lovely, soft-spoken Callie hardly fits his mental image of a dowdy, man-hating spinster. And as the passion between them flares from spark to full-on flame, Hadrian is the one in danger of being vanquished.

R. GARLAND GRAY

DARKSCAPE

THE REBEL LORD

Lord Lachlan de Douglas, a noble warrior lord, is heir to a Clan of Ancient Earth. Bold, rebellious, possessing strength and passion, he defends his clan from annihilation against a wretched war of masked vengeance and treacherous shadows. Until one day, a sudden horror alters his being, condemning him to a world of private anguish and torment.

Kimberly Kinsale, a diplomat's daughter, is a rare beauty motivated by honesty and integrity. Serving as a lieutenant in an elite combat fighter group aboard a war ship, she governs her life by the intrigue and lies of her commanding officer. A moment of lunacy and folly, a secret revealed, and Kimberly stumbles upon an unspeakable deception.

Now she must decide. Maintain her loyalty, or betray her Clan and ship for a Douglas enemy lord who can prove the truth--never knowing the battle for justice will take her through Lachlan's nightmare, a rage so deep, a suffering grounded in shame and pride, even when peace shines in sight.

For theirs is an unexpected passion, born in the fires of a shared need and desperate struggle. Kimberly must fight the sinister legacy of the matrix robots and trust the handsome enemy lord with her life, her heart, and her very soul. But as time slowly runs out, even an exquisite love may not be enough for salvation.

ISBN# 9781933836485
Mass Market Paperback / Sci-Fi Romance
US $7.95 / CDN $8.95
DECEMBER 2008

about other great titles from

Medallion Press, visit

www.medallionpress.com